CHARLES DICKENS

COMPLETE
WORKS

CENTENNIAL EDITION

Charles Dickens

CHARLES DICKENS

REPRINTED PIECES

THE LAMPLIGHTER
TO BE READ AT DUSK
SUNDAY UNDER THREE HEADS

Introduction by
Michael Foss

Illustrations by
F. Walker

Distributed by
HERON BOOKS

13 002 (030) 34 R2

INTRODUCTION

The articles and stories included in this volume—with the exception of the last three pieces—are all taken from Household Words, *a weekly miscellany 'in the liveliest form', first published in 1850 and continued with success for nine years.* Household Words *satisfied an ambition which Dickens had held for some time. He was no stranger to journalism, and knew that good popular writing was an able prompter towards the social reform he desired. In 1846, he had gladly accepted the editorship of the* Daily News, *but for obscure reasons left after a month. The venture was, he said, 'a brief mistake'. In the late forties, while writing* Dombey and Son, *he had in mind a weekly magazine of his own which he tentatively called* The Cricket, *and which he thought of as 'a kind of* Spectator (*Addison's*)'. *By 1849 he had taken his plans further; 'I think I have', he wrote, 'without a doubt, got the Periodical notion'. The result was the* Household Words *of the next year.*

In a weekly magazine one does not expect to find great themes argued at length. Dickens wrote for the Victorian reader, and very many of his pieces dealt with the local, immediate and temporary problems which are the staple of most popular jour-nalism. But the mention of Addison and the Spectator *shows that Dickens had higher aspirations in mind. He did not wish his magazine to be merely a diary and brief review of the times; he wished also to include imaginative pieces and articles of contemporary criticism. His journal was to be both literate and socially conscious. Also, as so much of Dickens's writing reveals himself, these pieces give many hints at his own expe-rience, and provide many connections with the novels.*

From a writer as great as Dickens one may expect literary art of high quality, even though these pieces were often hasty writings thrown off in the time taken from work on the novels. But again and again one sees glimpses of the conscientious craftsman shaping and forming to a degree not usually required in popular journalism. Examples may be found in The Long Voyage, *with its powerful and sombre opening, ranging ima-ginatively over a wide expanse of history and geography; or in the two short but strongly contrasted fables—*A Child's Dream of a Star, *touching and sentimental, and* Prince Bull, *an amusing and robust condemnation of Red Tape; or again in the witty characterisations and conversation of* Bill-Sticking. *Sometimes the artistic touches are slighter and less obvious. In* A Flight, *Dickens, a railway enthusiast, recounts a train journey from London to Folkestone and laboured to get the rocking, precipitous movement of the train into his prose:*

Flight resumed. Corn-sheaves, hop-gardens, reapers, gleaners, apple-orchards, cherry-orchards. Stations single and double-bar-relled, Ashford.

For all his artistry, Dickens is mainly concerned in these pieces with practical and social matters. The opening volumes of Household Words *held forth at great length on questions of sewage and drainage, until eventually this spartan diet induced a sense of uneasiness in Dickens who, feeling 'a want of some-thing tender', produced* A Child's Dream of a Star. *The author's lasting concern for Public Health can be seen in* Our Vestry. *From the evidence of the novels we know Dickens's concern for the poor, and for children. These interests appear in* The Begging-Letter Writer *and in* A Walk in a Work-house. *In the latter article he made the strong point that the Victorians were often kinder to prisoners than to the poor; he also pointed out the horrid injustice of placing invalids with madmen merely for the sake of administrative convenience. But Dickens, in both these pieces, was sufficiently Victorian so as to suspect indiscriminate charity. He believed that the poor should win their charity by earnestness and hard work. 'Let us give', he wrote in* The Begging-Letter Writer, *'with a high purpose; not to endow the scum of the earth, to its own greater corruption, with the offals of our duty'.*

In politics, Dickens tended towards a liking for authority and centralisation. In articles like A Poor Man's Tale of a Patent, Our Vestry *and* A Monument of French Folly *he praised the administrative efficiency that he thought came from centralisation, and lamented the inconvenience of our local government; in this respect he compared England unfavourably with France. This same admiration for central authority caused him to see the police in very glowing colours; in the 'Detective' stories presented here, he is wholly delighted with their operations. For a man who claimed to have the interests of the poor at heart, this was a strange conclusion; the Victorian policeman was no friend of the poor.*

Among the articles are many which show Dickens's interests and which illuminate his past experience. His passion for railways is well-attested. He composed A Child's Dream *in a railway carriage.* A Flight *has that fine description of a train journey. When he revisited* Our School *he mentioned at once that some of the grounds had been lost to the railway.* A Plated Article *indicates that he was interested, too, in the industrial processes of the Potteries. Some of the pieces look backwards.* Our School *is a description of a return to Wellington House Academy, in Hampstead Road, once run by Mr. Jones, 'the most ignorant man I have ever had the pleasure to know,' and where Dickens, as he told Wilkie Collins, 'distinguished himself like a brick.'* Our English Watering-Place *is Broadstairs which Dickens held in much affection and visited yearly from 1836 to 1851.* Our French Watering-Place *is Boulogne where the author spent a couple of seasons. The Wellington House Academy has obvious affinities with Creakle's school in David Copperfield, and Miss Julia Mills, the heroine of the circulating library in Our English Watering-Place, appears in Copperfield too.*

Of the three articles included in this volume which are not from Household Words, the most interesting is perhaps Sunday under Three Heads. This is an early piece written against the Sunday Observance Bill of 1836. In his article Dickens shows that he is well aware of the hypocritical way in which the English upper classes imposed upon the lower. For all the restrictions suggested by the Bill—on amusement, travel, the opening of shops, etc.—affected only the lower classes. The rich retained their servants and carriages even on Sunday. They had the money and the means to have their meals and their amusements provided as they wished, even on Sunday. Only the poor would suffer.

The pieces collected in this volume cover the full range of Dickens's journalism—stories, reminiscences, descriptions and criticism. The quality and the extent of these pieces remind us what a powerful journalist Dickens was. Great writers are very rarely great journalists. But Dickens's powers of art, allied to terrific energy, great curiosity and strong social conscience, formed that literary rarity—the journalist whose occasional pieces are read with pleasure more than a century after they were written.

Michael Foss

June, 1969.

CONTENTS

REPRINTED PIECES

CONTENTS

LIST OF ILLUSTRATIONS

REPRINTED PIECES

THE LONG VOYAGE

When the wind is blowing and the sleet or rain is driving against the dark windows, I love to sit by the fire, thinking of what I have read in books of voyage and travel. Such books have had a strong fascination for my mind from my earliest childhood; and I wonder it should have come to pass that I never have been round the world, never have been shipwrecked, ice-environed, tomahawked, or eaten.

Sitting on my ruddy hearth in the twilight of New Year's Eve, I find incidents of travel rise around me from all the latitudes and longitudes of the globe. They observe no order or sequence, but appear and vanish as they will—"come like shadows, so depart." Columbus, alone upon the sea with his disaffected crew, looks over the waste of waters from his high station on the poop of his ship, and sees the first uncertain glimmer of the light, "rising and falling with the waves, like a torch in the bark of some fisherman," which is the shining star of a new world. Bruce is caged in Abyssinia, surrounded by the gory horrors which shall often startle him out of his sleep at home when years have passed away. Franklin, come to the end of his unhappy overland journey—would that it had been his last!—lies perishing of hunger with his brave companions: each emaciated figure stretched upon its miserable bed without the power to rise: all, dividing the weary days between their prayers, their remembrances of the dear ones at home, and conversation on the pleasures of eating; the last-named topic being ever present to them, likewise, in their dreams. All the African travellers, wayworn, solitary and sad, submit themselves again to drunken, murderous, man-selling despots, of the lowest order of humanity; and Mungo Park, fainting under a tree and succoured by a woman, gratefully remembers how his Good Samaritan has always come to him in woman's shape, the wide world over.

A shadow on the wall in which my mind's eye can discern some traces of a rocky sea-coast, recalls to me a fearful story of travel derived from that unpromising narrator of such stories, a parliamentary blue-book. A convict is its chief figure, and this man escapes with other prisoners from a penal settlement. It is an island, and they seize a boat, and get to the main land. Their way is by a rugged and precipitous sea-shore, and they have no earthly hope of ultimate escape, for the party of soldiers despatched by an easier course to cut them off, must inevitably arrive at their distant bourne long before them, and retake them if by any hazard they survive the horrors of the way. Famine, as they all must have foreseen, besets them early in their course. Some of the party die and are eaten; some are murdered by the rest and eaten. This one awful creature eats his fill, and sustains his strength, and lives on to be recaptured and taken back. The unrelateable experiences through which he has passed have been so tremendous, that he is not hanged as he might be, but goes back to his old chained-gang work. A little time, and he tempts one other prisoner away, seizes another boat, and flies once more — necessarily in the old hopeless direction, for he can take no other. He is soon cut off, and met by the pursuing party face to face, upon the beach. He is alone. In his former journey

4

he acquired an inappeasable relish for his dreadful food. He urged the new man away, expressly to kill him and eat him. In the pockets on one side of his coarse convict-dress, are portions of the man's body, on which he is regaling ; in the pockets on the other side is an untouched store of salted pork (stolen before he left the island) for which he has no appetite. He is taken back, and he is hanged. But I shall never see that sea-beach on the wall or in the fire, without him, solitary monster, eating as he prowls along, while the sea rages and rises at him.

Captain Bligh (a worse man to be entrusted with arbitrary power there could scarcely be) is handed over the side of the Bounty, and turned adrift on the wide ocean in an open boat, by order of Fletcher Christian, one of his officers, at this very minute. Another flash of my fire, and " Thursday October Christian," five-and-twenty years of age, son of the dead and gone Fletcher by a savage mother, leaps aboard His Majesty's ship Briton, hove-to off Pitcairn's Island ; says his simple grace before eating, in good English ; and knows that a pretty little animal on board is called a dog, because in his childhood he had heard of such strange creatures from his father and the other mutineers, grown grey under the shade of the bread-fruit trees, speaking of their lost country far away.

See the Halsewell, East Indiaman outward bound, driving madly on a January night towards the rocks near Seacombe, on the island of Purbeck ! The captain's two dear daughters are aboard, and five other ladies. The ship has been driving many hours, has seven feet water in her hold, and her main-mast has been cut away. The description of her loss, familiar to me from my early boyhood, seems to be read aloud as she rushes to her destiny.

" About two in the morning of Friday the sixth of January, the ship still driving, and approaching very fast to the shore, Mr. Henry Meriton, the second mate, went again into the cuddy, where the captain then was. Another conversation taking place, Captain Pierce expressed extreme anxiety for the preservation of his beloved daughters, and earnestly asked the officer if he could devise any method of saving them. On his answering with great concern, that he feared it would be impossible, but that their only chance would be to wait for morning, the captain lifted up his hands in silent and distressful ejaculation.

"At this dreadful moment, the ship struck, with such violence as to dash the heads of those standing in the cuddy against the deck above them, and the shock was accompanied by a shriek of horror that burst at one instant from every quarter of the ship.

"Many of the seamen, who had been remarkably inattentive and remiss in their duty during great part of the storm, now poured upon deck, where no exertions of the officers could keep them, while their assistance might have been useful. They had actually skulked in their hammocks, leaving the working of the pumps and other necessary labours to the officers of the ship, and the soldiers, who had made uncommon exertions. Roused by a sense of their danger, the same seamen, at this moment, in frantic exclamations, demanded of heaven and their fellow-sufferers that succour which their own efforts, timely made, might possibly have procured.

"The ship continued to beat on the rocks; and soon bilging, fell with her broadside towards the shore. When she struck, a number of the men climbed up the ensign-staff, under an apprehension of her immediately going to pieces.

"Mr. Meriton, at this crisis, offered to these unhappy beings the best advice which could be given; he recommended that all should come to the side of the ship lying lowest on the rocks, and singly to take the opportunities which might then offer, of escaping to the shore.

"Having thus provided, to the utmost of his power, for the safety of the desponding crew, he returned to the round-house, where, by this time, all the passengers and most of the officers had assembled. The latter were employed in offering consolation to the unfortunate ladies; and, with unparalleled magnanimity, suffering their compassion for the fair and amiable companions of their misfortunes to prevail over the sense of their own danger.

"In this charitable work of comfort, Mr. Meriton now joined, by assurances of his opinion, that the ship would hold together till the morning, when all would be safe. Captain Pierce, observing one of the young gentlemen loud in his exclamations of terror, and frequently cry that the ship was parting, cheerfully bid him be quiet, remarking that though the ship should go to pieces, he would not, but would be safe enough.

"It is difficult to convey a correct idea of the scene of this deplorable catastrophe, without describing the place where it happened. The Haleswell struck on the rocks at a part of the shore where the cliff is of vast height, and rises almost perpendicular from its base. But at this particular spot, the foot of the cliff is excavated into a cavern of ten or twelve yards in depth, and of breadth equal to the length of a large ship. The sides of the cavern are so nearly upright, as to be of extremely difficult access; and the bottom is strewed with sharp and uneven rocks, which seem, by some convulsion of the earth, to have been detached from its roof.

"The ship lay with her broadside opposite to the mouth of this cavern, with her whole length stretched almost from side to side of it. But when she struck, it was too dark for the unfortunate persons on board to discover the real magnitude of the danger, and the extreme horror of such a situation.

"In addition to the company already in the round-house, they had admitted three black women and two soldiers' wives; who, with the husband of one of them, had been allowed to come in, though the seamen, who had tumultuously demanded entrance to get the lights, had been opposed and kept out by

7

Mr. Rogers and Mr. Brimer, the third and fifth mates. The numbers there were, therefore, now increased to near fifty. Captain Pierce sat on a chair, a cot, or some other moveable, with a daughter on each side, whom he alternately pressed to his affectionate breast. The rest of the melancholy assembly were seated on the deck, which was strewed with musical instruments, and the wreck of furniture and other articles.

"Here also Mr. Meriton, after having cut several wax-candles in pieces, and stuck them up in various parts of the round-house, and lighted up all the glass lanthorns he could find, took his seat, intending to wait the approach of dawn; and then assist the partners of his dangers to escape. But, observing that the poor ladies appeared parched and exhausted, he brought a basket of oranges and prevailed on some of them to refresh themselves by sucking a little of the juice. At this time they were all tolerably composed, except Miss Mansel, who was in hysteric fits on the floor of the deck of the round-house.

"But on Mr. Meriton's return to the company, he perceived a considerable alteration in the appearance of the ship; the sides were visibly giving way; the deck seemed to be lifting, and he discovered other strong indications that she could not hold much longer together. On this account, he attempted to go forward to look out, but immediately saw that the ship had separated in the middle, and that the forepart having changed its position, lay rather further out towards the sea. In such an emergency, when the next moment might plunge him into eternity, he determined to seize the present opportunity, and follow the example of the crew and the soldiers, who were now quitting the ship in numbers, and making their way to the shore, though quite ignorant of its nature and description.

"Among other expedients, the ensign-staff had been unshipped, and attempted to be laid between the ship's side and some of the rocks, but without success, for it snapped asunder before it reached them. However, by the light of a lanthorn, which a seaman handed through the skylight of the round-house to the deck, Mr. Meriton discovered a spar which appeared to be laid from the ship's side to the rocks, and on this spar he resolved to attempt his escape.

"Accordingly, lying down upon it, he thrust himself forward; however, he soon found that it had no communication with the rock; he reached the end of it, and then slipped off, receiving a very violent bruise in his fall, and before he could recover his legs, he was washed off by the surge. He now supported himself by swimming, until a returning wave dashed him against the back part of the cavern. Here he laid hold of a small projection in the rock, but was so much benumbed that he was on the point of quitting it, when a seaman, who had already gained a footing, extended his hand, and assisted him until he could secure himself a little on the rock; from which he clambered on a shelf still higher, and out of the reach of the surf.

"Mr. Rogers, the third mate, remained with the captain and the unfortunate ladies and their companions nearly twenty minutes after Mr. Meriton had quitted the ship. Soon after the latter left the round-house, the captain asked what was become of him, to which Mr. Rogers replied, that he was gone on deck to see what could be done. After this, a heavy sea breaking over the ship, the ladies exclaimed, 'Oh, poor Meriton! he is drowned; had he stayed with us he would have been safe!' and they all, particularly Miss Mary Pierce, expressed great concern at the apprehension of his loss.

"The sea was now breaking in at the fore part of the ship, and reached as far as the mainmast. Captain Pierce gave Mr. Rogers a nod, and they took a lamp and went together into the stern-gallery, where, after viewing the rocks for some time, Captain Pierce asked Mr. Rogers if he thought there was any possibility of saving the girls; to which he replied, he feared there was none; for they could only discover the black face of the perpendicular rock, and not the cavern which afforded shelter to those who escaped. They then returned to the round-house, where Mr. Rogers hung up the lamp, and Captain Pierce sat down between his two daughters.

"The sea continuing to break in very fast, Mr. Macmanus, a midshipman, and Mr. Schutz, a passenger, asked Mr. Rogers what they could do to escape. 'Follow me,' he replied, and they all went into the stern-gallery, and from thence to the upper-quarter-gallery on the poop. While there, a very heavy sea fell on board, and the round-house gave way; Mr. Rogers heard the ladies shriek at intervals, as if the water reached them; the noise of the sea at other times drowning their voices.

"Mr. Brimer had followed him to the poop, where they remained together about five minutes, when on the breaking of this heavy sea, they jointly seized a hen-coop. The same wave which proved fatal to some of those below, carried him and his companion to the rock, on which they were violently dashed and miserably bruised.

"Here on the rock were twenty-seven men; but it now being low water, and as they were convinced that on the flowing of the tide all must be washed off, many attempted to get to the back or the sides of the cavern, beyond the reach of the returning sea. Scarcely more than six, besides Mr. Rogers and Mr. Brimer, succeeded.

"Mr. Rogers, on gaining this station, was so nearly exhausted, that had his exertions been protracted only a few minutes longer, he must have sunk under them. He was now prevented from joining Mr. Meriton, by at least twenty men between them, none of whom could move, without the imminent peril of his life.

"They found that a very considerable number of the crew, seamen and soldiers, and some petty officers, were in the same situation as themselves, though many who had reached the rocks below, perished in attempting to ascend. They could yet discern some part of the ship, and in their dreary station solaced themselves with the hopes of its remaining entire until day-break; for, in the midst of their own distress, the sufferings of the females on board affected them with the most poignant anguish; and every sea that broke inspired them with terror for their safety.

"But, alas, their apprehensions were too soon realised! Within a very few minutes of the time that Mr. Rogers gained the rock, an universal shriek, which long vibrated in their ears, in which the voice of female distress was lamentably distinguished, announced the dreadful catastrophe. In a few moments all was hushed, except the roaring of the winds and the dashing of the waves; the wreck was buried in the deep, and not an atom of it was ever afterwards seen."

The most beautiful and affecting incident I know, associated with a shipwreck, succeeds this dismal story for a winter night. The Grosvenor, East Indiaman, homeward bound, goes ashore on the coast of Caffraria. It is resolved that the officers, passengers, and crew, in number one hundred and thirty-five souls, shall endeavour to penetrate on foot, across trackless deserts, infested by wild beasts and cruel savages, to the Dutch settlements at the Cape of Good Hope. With this forlorn object before them, they finally separate into two parties—never more to meet on earth.

There is a solitary child among the passengers—a little boy of seven years old who has no relation there; and when the first party is moving away he cries after some member of it who has been kind to him. The crying of a child might be supposed to be a little thing to men in such great extremity; but it touches them, and he is immediately taken into that detachment.

From which time forth, this child is sublimely made a sacred charge. He is pushed, on a little raft, across broad rivers by the swimming sailors; they carry him by turns through the deep sand and long grass (he patiently walking at all other times); they share with him such putrid fish as they find to eat; they lie down and wait for him when the rough carpenter, who becomes his especial friend, lags behind. Beset by lions and tigers, by savages, by thirst, by hunger, by death in a crowd of ghastly shapes, they never— O Father of all mankind, thy name be blessed for it!—forget this child. The captain stops exhausted, and his faithful coxswain goes back and is seen to sit down by his side, and neither of the two shall be any more beheld until the great last day; but, as the rest go on for their lives, they take the child with them. The carpenter dies of poisonous berries eaten in starvation; and the steward, succeeding to the command of the party, succeeds to the sacred guardianship of the child.

God knows all he does for the poor baby; how he cheerfully carries him in his arms when he himself is weak and ill; how he feeds him when he himself is griped with want; how he folds his ragged jacket round him, lays his little worn face with a woman's tenderness upon his sunburnt breast, soothes him in his sufferings, sings to him as he limps along, unmindful of his own parched and bleeding feet. Divided for a few days from the rest, they dig a grave in the sand and bury their good friend the cooper—these two companions alone in the wilderness—and then the time comes when they both are ill, and beg their wretched partners in despair, reduced and few in number now, to wait by them one day. They wait by them one day, they wait by them two days. On the morning of the third, they move very softly about, in making their preparations for the resumption of their journey; for, the child is sleeping by the fire, and it is agreed with one consent that he shall not be disturbed until the last moment. The moment comes, the fire is dying—and the child is dead.

His faithful friend, the steward, lingers but a little while behind him. His grief is great, he staggers on for a few days, lies down in the desert, and dies. But he shall be

The Long Voyage

re-united in his immortal spirit—who can doubt it!—with the child, where he and the poor carpenter shall be raised up with the words, "Inasmuch as ye have done it unto the least of these, ye have done it unto Me."

As I recall the dispersal and disappearance of nearly all the participators in this once famous shipwreck (a mere handful being recovered at last), and the legends that were long afterwards revived from time to time among the English officers at the Cape, of a white woman with an infant, said to have been seen weeping outside a savage hut far in the interior, who was whisperingly associated with the remembrance of the missing ladies saved from the wrecked vessel, and who was often sought but never found, thoughts of another kind of travel came into my mind.

Thoughts of a voyager unexpectedly summoned from home, who travelled a vast distance, and could never return. Thoughts of this unhappy wayfarer in the depths of his sorrow, in the bitterness of his anguish, in the helplessness of his self-reproach, in the desperation of his desire to set right what he had left wrong, and do what he had left undone.

For, there were many, many things he had neglected. Little matters while he was at home and surrounded by them, but things of mighty moment when he was at an immeasurable distance. There were many many blessings that he had inadequately felt, there were many trivial injuries that he had not forgiven, there was love that he had but poorly returned, there was friendship that he had too lightly prized : there were a million kind words that he might have spoken, a million kind looks that he might have given, uncountable slight easy deeds in which he might have been most truly great and good. O for a day (he would exclaim), for but one day to make amends! But the sun never shone upon that happy day, and out of his remote captivity he never came.

Why does this traveller's fate obscure, on New Year's Eve,

the other histories of travellers with which my mind was
filled but now, and cast a solemn shadow over me! Must I
one day make his journey? Even so. Who shall say, that
I may not then be tortured by such late regrets: that I may
not then look from my exile on my empty place and undone
work? I stand upon a sea-shore, where the waves are years.
They break and fall, and I may little heed them; but, with
every wave the sea is rising, and I know that it will float me
on this traveller's voyage at last.

THE BEGGING-LETTER WRITER

THE amount of money he annually diverts from wholesome and useful purposes in the United Kingdom, would be a set-off against the Window Tax. He is one of the most shameless frauds and impositions of this time. In his idleness, his mendacity, and the immeasurable harm he does to the deserving,—dirtying the stream of true benevolence, and muddling the brains of foolish justices, with inability to distinguish between the base coin of distress, and the true currency we have always among us,—he is more worthy of Norfolk Island than three-fourths of the worst characters who are sent there. Under any rational system, he would have been sent there long ago.

I, the writer of this paper, have been, for some time, a chosen receiver of Begging Letters. For fourteen years, my house has been made as regular a Receiving House for such communications as any one of the great branch Post-Offices is for general correspondence. I ought to know something of the Begging-Letter Writer. He has besieged my door at all hours of the day and night; he has fought my servant; he has lain in ambush for me, going out and coming in; he has followed me out of town into the country; he has appeared at provincial hotels, where I have been staying for only a few hours; he has written to me from immense distances, when I have been out of England. He has fallen sick; he has died and been buried; he has come to life again, and again departed from this transitory scene: he has been his own son, his own mother, his own baby, his idiot brother, his uncle, his aunt, his aged grandfather. He has wanted a greatcoat, to go to India in; a pound to set him up in life for ever; a pair of boots to take him to the coast of China; a hat to get him into a permanent situation under Government. He has frequently been exactly seven-and-sixpence short of independence. He has had such openings at Liverpool—posts of great trust and confidence in merchants' houses, which nothing but seven-and-sixpence was wanting to him to secure—that I wonder he is not Mayor of that flourishing town at the present moment.

The natural phenomena of which he has been the victim, are of a most astounding nature. He has had two children who have never grown up; who have never had anything to cover them at night; who have been continually driving him mad, by asking in vain for food; who have never come out of fevers and measles (which, I suppose, has accounted for his fuming his letters with tobacco smoke, as a disinfectant); who have never changed in the least degree through fourteen long revolving years. As to his wife, what that suffering woman has undergone, nobody knows. She has always been in an interesting situation through the same long period, and has never been confined yet. His devotion to her has been unceasing. He has never cared for himself; *he* could have perished—he would rather, in short—but was it not his Christian duty as a man, a husband, and a father, to write begging letters when he looked at her? (He has usually remarked that he would call in the evening for an answer to this question.)

He has been the sport of the strangest misfortunes. What his brother has done to him would have broken anybody else's heart. His brother went into business with him, and ran away with the money; his brother got him to be security for an immense sum and left him to pay it; his brother would have given him employment to the tune of hundreds a-year if he would have consented to write letters on a Sunday; his brother enunciated principles incompatible with his religious views, and he could not (in consequence) permit his brother to provide for him. His landlord has never shown a spark of human feeling. When he put in that execution I don't know, but he has never taken it out. The broker's man has grown grey in possession. They will have to bury him some day.

He has been attached to every conceivable pursuit. He has been in the army, in the navy, in the church, in the law; connected with the press, the fine arts, public institutions, every description and grade of business. He has been brought up as a gentleman; he has been at every college in Oxford and Cambridge; he can quote Latin in his letters (but generally mis-spells some minor English word); he can tell you what Shakespeare says about begging, better than you know it. It is to be observed, that in the midst of his afflictions he always reads the newspapers; and rounds off his appeal with some allusion, that may be supposed to be in my way, to the popular subject of the hour.

His life presents a series of inconsistencies. Sometimes he has never written such a letter before. He blushes with shame. That is the first time; that shall be the last. Don't answer it, and let it be understood that, then, he will kill himself quietly. Sometimes (and more frequently) he *has* written a few such letters. Then he encloses the answers, with an intimation that they are of inestimable value to him, and a request that they may be carefully returned. He is fond of enclosing something—verses, letters, pawnbrokers' duplicates, anything to necessitate an answer. He is very severe upon "the pampered minion of fortune," who refused him the half-sovereign referred to in the enclosure number two—but he knows me better.

He writes in a variety of styles; sometimes in low spirits; sometimes quite jocosely. When he is in low spirits he writes down-hill and repeats words—these little indications being expressive of the perturbation of his mind. When he is more vivacious, he is frank with me; he is quite the agreeable rattle. I know what human nature is,—who better? Well! He had a little money once, and he ran through it— as many men have done before him. He finds his old friends turn away from him now—many men have done that before him too! Shall he tell me why he writes to me? Because he has no kind of claim upon me. He puts it on that ground plainly; and begs to ask for the loan (as I know human nature) of two sovereigns, to be repaid next Tuesday six weeks, before twelve at noon.

Sometimes, when he is sure that I have found him out, and that there is no chance of money, he writes to inform me that I have got rid of him at last. He has enlisted into the Company's service, and is off directly—but he wants a cheese. He is informed by the serjeant that it is essential to his prospects in the regiment that he should take out a single Gloucester cheese, weighing from twelve to fifteen pounds. Eight or nine shillings would buy it. He does not ask for money, after what has passed; but if he calls at nine to-morrow morning may he hope to find a cheese? And is there anything he can do to show his gratitude in Bengal?

Once he wrote me rather a special letter, proposing relief in kind. He had got into a little trouble by leaving parcels of mud done up in brown paper, at people's houses, on pretence of being a Railway-Porter, in which character he received carriage money. This sportive fancy he expiated in the House of Correction. Not long after his release, and on a Sunday morning, he called with a letter (having first dusted himself all over), in which he gave me to understand that, being resolved to earn an honest livelihood, he had been travelling about the country with a cart of crockery. That he had been doing pretty well until the day before, when his horse had dropped down dead near Chatham, in Kent. That this had reduced him to the unpleasant necessity of getting into the shafts himself, and drawing the cart of crockery to London—a somewhat exhausting pull of thirty miles. That he did not venture to ask again for money; but that if I would have the goodness *to leave him out a donkey*, he would call for the animal before breakfast!

At another time my friend (I am describing actual experiences) introduced himself as a literary gentleman in the last extremity of distress. He had had a play accepted at a certain Theatre—which was really open; its representation was delayed by the indisposition of a leading actor—who was really ill; and he and his were in a state of absolute starvation. If he made his necessities known to the Manager of the Theatre, he put it to me to say what kind of treatment he might expect? Well! we got over that difficulty to our mutual satisfaction. A little while afterwards he was in some other strait. I think Mrs. Southcote, his wife, was in extremity—and we adjusted that point too. A little while afterwards he had taken a new house, and was going headlong to ruin for want of a water-butt. I had my misgivings about the water-butt, and did not reply to that epistle. But a little while afterwards, I had reason to feel penitent for my neglect. He wrote me a few broken-hearted lines, informing me that the dear partner of his sorrows died in his arms last night at nine o'clock!

I despatched a trusty messenger to comfort the bereaved mourner and his poor children; but the messenger went so soon, that the play was not ready to be played out; my friend was not at home, and his wife was in a most delightful state of health. He was taken up by the Mendicity Society (informally it afterwards appeared), and I presented myself at a London Police-Office with my testimony against him. The Magistrate was wonderfully struck by his educational acquirements, deeply impressed by the excellence of his letters, exceedingly sorry to see a man of his attainments there, complimented him highly on his powers of composition, and was quite charmed to have the agreeable duty of discharging him. A collection was made for the "poor fellow," as he was called in the reports, and I left the court with a comfortable sense of being universally regarded as a sort of monster. Next day comes to me a friend of mine, the governor of a large prison. "Why did you ever go to the Police-Office against that man," says he, "without coming to me first? I know all about him and his frauds. He lodged in the house of one of my warders, at the very time when he first wrote to you; and then he was eating spring-lamb at eighteen-pence a pound, and early asparagus at I don't know how much a bundle!" On that very same day, and in that very same hour, my injured gentleman wrote a solemn address to me, demanding to know what compensation I proposed to make him for his having passed the night in a "loathsome dungeon." And next morning an Irish gentleman, a member of the same fraternity, who had read the case, and was very well persuaded I should be chary of going to that Police-Office again, positively refused to leave my door for less than a sovereign, and, resolved to besiege me into compliance, literally "sat down" before it for ten mortal hours. The garrison being well provisioned, I remained within the walls; and he raised the siege at midnight with a prodigious alarum on the bell.

The Begging-Letter Writer often has an extensive circle of acquaintance. Whole pages of the "Court Guide" are ready to be references for him. Noblemen and gentlemen write to say there never was such a man for probity and virtue. They have known him time out of mind, and there is nothing they wouldn't do for him. Somehow, they don't give him that one pound ten he stands in need of; but perhaps it is not enough—they want to do more, and his modesty will not allow it. It is to be remarked of his trade that it is a very fascinating one. He never leaves it; and those who are near to him become smitten with a love of it, too, and sooner or later set up for themselves. He employs a messenger—man, woman, or child. That messenger is certain ultimately to become an independent Begging-Letter Writer. His sons and daughters succeed to his calling, and write begging-letters when he is no more. He throws off the infection of begging-letter writing, like the contagion of disease. What Sydney Smith so happily called "the dangerous luxury of dishonesty" is more tempting, and more catching, it would seem, in this instance than in any other.

He always belongs to a Corresponding-Society of Begging-Letter Writers. Any one who will, may ascertain this fact. Give money to-day in recognition of a begging-letter,—no matter how unlike a common begging-letter,—and for the next fortnight you will have a rush of such communications. Steadily refuse to give; and the begging-letters become Angels' visits, until the Society is from some cause or other in a dull way of business, and may as well try you as anybody else. It is of little use inquiring into the Begging-Letter Writer's circumstances. He may be sometimes accidentally found out, as in the case already mentioned (though that was not the first inquiry made); but apparent misery is always a part of his trade, and real misery very often is, in the intervals of spring-lamb and early asparagus. It is naturally an incident of his dissipated and dishonest life.

That the calling is a successful one, and that large sums of money are gained by it, must be evident to anybody who reads the Police Reports of such cases. But, prosecutions are of rare occurrence, relatively to the extent to which the trade is carried on. The cause of this is to be found (as no one knows better than the Begging-Letter Writer, for it is a part of his speculation) in the aversion people feel to exhibit themselves as having been imposed upon, or as having weakly gratified their consciences with a lazy, flimsy substitute for the noblest of all virtues. There is a man at large, at the moment when this paper is preparing for the press (on the 29th of April, 1850), and never once taken up yet, who, within these twelvemonths, has been probably the most audacious and the most successful swindler that even this

21

trade has ever known. There has been something singularly base in this fellow's proceedings; it has been his business to write to all sorts and conditions of people, in the names of persons of high reputation and unblemished honour, professing to be in distress—the general admiration and respect for whom has ensured a ready and generous reply.

Now, in the hope that the results of the real experience of a real person may do something more to induce reflection on this subject than any abstract treatise—and with a personal knowledge of the extent to which the Begging-Letter Trade has been carried on for some time, and has been for some time constantly increasing—the writer of this paper entreats the attention of his readers to a few concluding words. His experience is a type of the experience of many; some on a smaller, some on an infinitely larger scale. All may judge of the soundness or unsoundness of his conclusions from it.

Long doubtful of the efficacy of such assistance in any case whatever, and able to recall but one, within his whole individual knowledge, in which he had the least after-reason to suppose that any good was done by it, he was led, last autumn, into some serious considerations. The begging-letters flying about by every post, made it perfectly manifest that a set of lazy vagabonds were interposed between the general desire to do something to relieve the sickness and misery under which the poor were suffering, and the suffering poor themselves. That many who sought to do some little to repair the social wrongs, inflicted in the way of preventible sickness and death upon the poor, were strengthening those wrongs, however innocently, by wasting money on pestilent knaves cumbering society. That imagination,—soberly following one of these knaves into his life of punishment in jail, and comparing it with the life of one of these poor in a cholera-stricken alley, or one of the children of one of these poor, soothed in its dying hour by the late lamented Mr. Drouet,—contemplated a grim farce, impossible to be presented very much longer before God or man. That the crowning miracle of all the miracles summed up in the New Testament, after the miracle of the blind seeing, and the lame walking, and the restoration of the dead to life, was the miracle that the poor had the Gospel preached to them. That while the poor were unnaturally and unnecessarily cut off by the thousand, in the prematurity of their age, or in the rottenness of their youth—for of flower or blossom such youth has none—the Gospel was NOT preached to them, saving in hollow and unmeaning voices. That of all wrongs, this was the first mighty wrong the Pestilence warned us to set right. And that no Post-Office Order to any amount, given to a Begging-Letter Writer for the quieting of an uneasy breast, would be presentable on the Last Great Day as any-thing towards it.

The poor never write these letters. Nothing could be more unlike their habits. The writers are public robbers; and we who support them are parties to their depredations. They trade upon every circumstance within their knowledge that affects us, public or private, joyful or sorrowful; they pervert the lessons of our lives; they change what ought to be our strength and virtue into weakness, and encouragement of vice. There is a plain remedy, and it is in our own hands. We must resolve, at any sacrifice of feeling, to be deaf to such appeals, and crush the trade.

There are degrees in murder. Life must be held sacred among us in more ways than one—sacred, not merely from the murderous weapon, or the subtle poison, or the cruel blow, but sacred from preventible diseases, distortions, and pains. That is the first great end we have to set against this miserable imposition. Physical life respected, moral life comes next. What will not content a Begging-Letter Writer for a week, would educate a score of children for a year. Let us give all we can; let us give more than ever. Let us do all we can; let us do more than ever. But let us give, and do, with a high purpose; not to endow the scum of the earth, to its own greater corruption, with the offals of our duty.

A CHILD'S DREAM OF A STAR

THERE was once a child, and he strolled about a good deal, and thought of a number of things. He had a sister, who was a child too, and his constant companion. These two used to wonder all day long. They wondered at the beauty of the flowers; they wondered at the height and blueness of the sky; they wondered at the depth of the bright water; they wondered at the goodness and the power of GOD who made the lovely world.

They used to say to one another, sometimes, Supposing all the children upon earth were to die, would the flowers, and the water, and the sky be sorry? They believed they would be sorry. For, said they, the buds are the children of the flowers, and the little playful streams that gambol down the hill-sides are the children of the water; and the smallest bright specks playing at hide and seek in the sky all night, must surely be the children of the stars; and they would all be grieved to see their playmates, the children of men, no more.

There was one clear shining star that used to come out in the sky before the rest, near the church spire, above the graves. It was larger and more beautiful, they thought, than all the others, and every night they watched for it, standing hand in hand at a window. Whoever saw it first cried out, "I see the star!" And often they cried out both together, knowing so well when it would rise, and where. So they grew to be such friends with it, that, before lying down in their beds, they always looked out once again, to bid it good night; and when they were turning round to sleep, they used to say, "God bless the star!"

But while she was still very young, oh, very, very young, the sister drooped, and came to be so weak that she could no longer stand in the window at night; and then the child looked sadly out by himself, and when he saw the star, turned round and said to the patient pale face on the bed, "I see the star!" and then a smile would come upon the face, and a little weak voice used to say, "God bless my brother and the star!"

And so the time came all too soon! when the child looked out alone, and when there was no face on the bed; and when there was a little grave among the graves, not there before; and when the star made long rays down towards him, as he saw it through his tears.

Now, these rays were so bright, and they seemed to make such a shining way from earth to Heaven, that when the child went to his solitary bed, he dreamed about the star; and dreamed that, lying where he was, he saw a train of people taken up that sparkling road by angels. And the star, opening, showed him a great world of light, where many more such angels waited to receive them.

All these angels, who were waiting, turned their beaming eyes upon the people who were carried up into the star; and some came out from the long rows in which they stood, and fell upon the people's necks, and kissed them tenderly, and went away with them down avenues of light, and were so happy in their company, that lying in his bed he wept for joy.

But, there were many angels who did not go with them, and among them one he knew. The patient face that once had lain upon the bed was glorified and radiant, but his heart found out his sister among all the host.

25

His sister's angel lingered near the entrance of the star, and said to the leader among those who had brought the people thither:

"Is my brother come?"

And he said "No."

She was turning hopefully away, when the child stretched out his arms, and cried, "O, sister, I am here! Take me!" and then she turned her beaming eyes upon him, and it was night; and the star was shining into the room, making long rays down towards him as he saw it through his tears.

From that hour forth, the child looked out upon the star as on the home he was to go to, when his time should come; and he thought that he did not belong to the earth alone, but to the star too, because of his sister's angel gone before.

There was a baby born to be a brother to the child; and while he was so little that he never yet had spoken word, he stretched his tiny form out on his bed, and died.

Again the child dreamed of the open star, and of the company of angels, and the train of people, and the rows of angels with their beaming eyes all turned upon those people's faces.

Said his sister's angel to the leader:

"Is my brother come?"

And he said, "Not that one, but another."

As the child beheld his brother's angel in her arms, he cried, "O, sister, I am here! Take me!" And she turned and smiled upon him, and the star was shining.

He grew to be a young man, and was busy at his books when an old servant came to him and said:

"Thy mother is no more. I bring her blessing on her darling son!"

Again at night he saw the star, and all that former company. Said his sister's angel to the leader:

"Is my brother come?"

And he said, "Thy mother!"

A mighty cry of joy went forth through all the star,

because the mother was re-united to her two children. And he stretched out his arms and cried, "O, mother, sister, and brother, I am here! Take me!" And they answered him, "Not yet," and the star was shining.

He grew to be a man, whose hair was turning grey, and he was sitting in his chair by the fireside, heavy with grief, and with his face bedewed with tears, when the star opened once again.

Said his sister's angel to the leader: "Is my brother come?"

And he said, "Nay, but his maiden daughter."

And the man who had been the child saw his daughter, newly lost to him, a celestial creature among those three, and he said, "My daughter's head is on my sister's bosom, and her arm is around my mother's neck, and at her feet there is the baby of old time, and I can bear the parting from her, GOD be praised!"

And the star was shining.

Thus the child came to be an old man, and his once smooth face was wrinkled, and his steps were slow and feeble, and his back was bent. And one night as he lay upon his bed, his children standing round, he cried, as he had cried so long ago:

"I see the star!"

They whispered one another, "He is dying."

And he said, "I am. My age is falling from me like a garment, and I move towards the star as a child. And O, my Father, now I thank thee that it has so often opened, to receive those dear ones who await me!"

And the star was shining; and it shines upon his grave.

OUR ENGLISH WATERING-PLACE

In the Autumn-time of the year, when the great metropolis is so much hotter, so much noisier, so much more dusty or so much more water-carted, so much more crowded, so much more disturbing and distracting in all respects, than it usually is, a quiet sea-beach becomes indeed a blessed spot. Half awake and half asleep, this idle morning in our sunny window on the edge of a chalk-cliff in the old-fashioned watering-place to which we are a faithful resorter, we feel a lazy inclination to sketch its picture.

The place seems to respond. Sky, sea, beach, and village, lie as still before us as if they were sitting for the picture. It is dead low-water. A ripple plays among the ripening corn upon the cliff, as if it were faintly trying from recollection to imitate the sea; and the world of butterflies hovering over the crop of radish-seed are as restless in their little way as the gulls are in their larger manner when the wind blows. But the ocean lies winking in the sunlight like a drowsy lion —its glassy waters scarcely curve upon the shore—the fishing-boats in the tiny harbour are all stranded in the mud— our two colliers (our watering-place has a maritime trade employing that amount of shipping) have not an inch of water within a quarter of a mile of them, and turn, exhausted, on their sides, like faint fish of an antediluvian species. Rusty cables and chains, ropes and rings, undermost parts of posts and piles and confused timber-defences against the waves, lie strewn about, in a brown litter of tangled sea-weed and fallen cliff which looks as if a family of giants had been making tea here for ages, and had observed an untidy custom of throwing their tea-leaves on the shore.

In truth, our watering-place itself has been left somewhat high and dry by the tide of years. Concerned as we are for its honour, we must reluctantly admit that the time when this pretty little semi-circular sweep of houses, tapering off at the end of the wooden pier into a point in the sea, was a gay place, and when the lighthouse overlooking it shone at daybreak on company dispersing from public balls, is but dimly traditional now. There is a bleak chamber in our watering-place which is yet called the Assembly "Rooms," and understood to be available on hire for balls or concerts ; and, some few seasons since, an ancient little gentleman came down and stayed at the hotel, who said that he had danced there, in bygone ages, with the Honourable Miss Peepy, well known to have been the Beauty of her day and the cruel occasion of innumerable duels. But he was so old and shrivelled, and so very rheumatic in the legs, that it demanded more imagination than our watering-place can usually muster, to believe him ; therefore, except the Master of the " Rooms " (who to this hour wears knee-breeches, and who confirmed the statement with tears in his eyes), nobody did believe in the little lame old gentleman, or even in the Honourable Miss Peepy, long deceased.

As to subscription balls in the Assembly Rooms of our watering-place now, red-hot cannon balls are less improbable. Sometimes, a misguided wanderer of a Ventriloquist, or an Infant Phenomenon, or a Juggler, or somebody with an Orrery that is several stars behind the time, takes the place for a night, and issues bills with the name of his last town lined out, and the name of ours ignominiously written in, but you may be sure this never happens twice to the same unfortunate person. On such occasions the discoloured old

Billiard Table that is seldom played at (unless the ghost of the Honourable Miss Peepy plays at pool with other ghosts) is pushed into a corner, and benches are solemnly constituted into front seats, back seats, and reserved seats—which are much the same after you have paid—and a few dull candles are lighted—wind permitting—and the performer and the scanty audience play out a short match which shall make the other most low-spirited—which is usually a drawn game. After that, the performer instantly departs with maledictory expressions, and is never heard of more.

But the most wonderful feature of our Assembly Rooms, is, that an annual sale of " Fancy and other China," is announced here with mysterious constancy and perseverance. Where the china comes from, where it goes to, why it is annually put up to auction when nobody ever thinks of bidding for it, how it comes to pass that it is always the same china, whether it would not have been cheaper, with the sea at hand, to have thrown it away, say in eighteen hundred and thirty, are standing enigmas. Every year the bills come out, every year the Master of the Rooms gets into a little pulpit on a table, and offers it for sale, every year nobody buys it, every year it is put away somewhere till next year, when it appears again as if the whole thing were a new idea. We have a faint remembrance of an unearthly collection of clocks, purporting to be the work of Parisian and Genevese artists—chiefly bilious-faced clocks, supported on sickly white crutches, with their pendulums dangling like lame legs—to which a similar course of events occurred for several years, until they seemed to lapse away, of mere imbecility.

Attached to our Assembly Rooms is a library. There is a wheel of fortune in it, but it is rusty and dusty, and never turns. A large doll, with moveable eyes, was put up to be raffled for, by five-and-twenty members at two shillings, seven years ago this autumn, and the list is not full yet. We are rather sanguine, now, that the raffle will come off next year.

We think so, because we only want nine members, and should only want eight, but for number two having grown up since her name was entered, and withdrawn it when she was married. Down the street, there is a toy-ship of considerable burden, in the same condition. Two of the boys who were entered for that raffle have gone to India in real ships, since; and one was shot, and died in the arms of his sister's lover, by whom he sent his last words home.

This is the library for the Minerva Press. If you want that kind of reading, come to our watering-place. The leaves of the romances, reduced to a condition very like curl-paper, are thickly studded with notes in pencil: sometimes complimentary, sometimes jocose. Some of these commentators, like commentators in a more extensive way, quarrel with one another. One young gentleman who sarcastically writes "O!!!" after every sentimental passage, is pursued through his literary career by another, who writes "Insulting Beast!" Miss Julia Mills has read the whole collection of these books. She has left marginal notes on the pages, as "Is not this truly touching? J. M." "How thrilling! J. M." "Entranced here by the Magician's potent spell. J. M." She has also italicised her favourite traits in the description of the hero, as "his hair, which was *dark* and *wavy*, clustered in *rich profusion* around a *marble brow*, whose lofty paleness bespoke the intellect within." It reminds her of another hero. She adds, "How like B. L. Can this be mere coincidence? J. M."

You would hardly guess which is the main street of our watering-place, but you may know it by its being always stopped up with donkey-chaises. Whenever you come here, and see harnessed donkeys eating clover out of barrows drawn completely across a narrow thoroughfare, you may be quite sure you are in our High Street. Our Police you may know by his uniform, likewise by his never on any account interfering with anybody—especially the tramps and vagabonds. In our fancy shops we have a capital collection of damaged goods, among which the flies of countless summers "have been roaming." We are great in obsolete seals, and in faded pin-cushions, and in rickety camp-stools, and in exploded cutlery, and in miniature vessels, and in stunted little telescopes, and in objects made of shells that pretend not to be shells. Diminutive spades, barrows, and baskets, are our principal articles of commerce; but even they don't look quite new somehow. They always seem to have been offered and refused somewhere else, before they came down to our watering-place.

Yet, it must not be supposed that our watering-place is an empty place, deserted by all visitors except a few staunch persons of approved fidelity. On the contrary, the chances are that if you came down here in August or September, you wouldn't find a house to lay your head in. As to finding either house or lodging of which you could reduce the terms, you could scarcely engage in a more hopeless pursuit. For all this, you are to observe that every season is the worst season ever known, and that the householding population of our watering-place are ruined regularly every autumn. They are like the farmers, in regard that it is surprising how much ruin they will bear. We have an excellent hotel—capital baths, warm, cold, and shower—first-rate bathing-machines—and as good butchers, bakers, and grocers, as heart could desire. They all do business, it is to be presumed, from motives of philanthropy—but it is quite certain that they are all being ruined. Their interest in strangers, and their politeness under ruin, bespeak their amiable nature. You would say so, if you only saw the baker helping a new comer to find suitable apartments.

So far from being at a discount as to company, we are in fact what would be popularly called rather a nobby place. Some tip-top "Nobbs" come down occasionally—even Dukes and Duchesses. We have known such carriages to blaze among the donkey-chaises, as made beholders wink. Attendant on these equipages come resplendent creatures in plush and powder, who are sure to be stricken disgusted with the indifferent accommodation of our watering-place, and who, of an evening (particularly when it rains), may be seen very much out of drawing, in rooms far too small for their fine figures, looking discontentedly out of little back windows into bye-streets. The lords and ladies get on well enough and quite good-humouredly : but if you want to see the gorgeous phenomena who wait upon them at a perfect non-plus, you should come and look at the resplendent creatures with little back parlours for servants' halls, and turn-up bedsteads to sleep in, at our watering-place. You have no idea how they take it to heart.

We have a pier—a queer old wooden pier, fortunately without the slightest pretensions to architecture, and very picturesque in consequence. Boats are hauled up upon it, ropes are coiled all over it; lobster-pots, nets, masts, oars, spars, sails, ballast, and rickety capstans, make a perfect labyrinth of it. For ever hovering about this pier, with their hands in their pockets, or leaning over the rough bulwark it opposes to the sea, gazing through telescopes which they carry about in the same profound receptacles, are the Boatmen of our watering-place. Looking at them, you would say that surely these must be the laziest boatmen in the world. They lounge about, in obstinate and inflexible pantaloons that are apparently made of wood, the whole season through. Whether talking together about the shipping in the Channel, or gruffly unbending over mugs of beer at the public-house, you would consider them the slowest of men. The chances are a thousand to one that you might stay here for ten seasons, and never see a boatman in a hurry. A certain expression about his loose hands, when they are not in his pockets, as if he were carrying a considerable lump of iron in each, without any inconvenience, suggests strength, but he never seems to use it. He has the appearance of perpetually strolling—running is too inappropriate a word to be thought of—to seed. The only subject on which he seems to feel any approach to enthusiasm, is pitch. He pitches everything he can lay hold of,—the pier, the palings, his boat, his house,—when there is nothing else left he turns to and even pitches his hat, or his rough-weather clothing. Do not judge him by deceitful appearances. These are among the bravest and most skilful mariners that exist. Let a gale arise and swell into a storm, let a sea run that might appal the stoutest heart that ever beat, let the Light-boat on these dangerous sands throw up a rocket in the night, or let them hear through the angry roar the signal-guns of a ship in distress, and these men spring up into activity so dauntless, so valiant, and heroic, that the world cannot surpass it. Cavillers may object that they chiefly live upon the salvage of valuable cargoes. So they do, and God knows it is no great living that they get out of the deadly risks they run. But put that hope of gain aside. Let these rough fellows be asked, in any storm, who volunteers for the life-boat to save some perishing souls, as poor and empty-handed as themselves, whose lives the perfection of human reason does not rate at the value of a farthing each; and that boat will be manned, as surely and as cheerfully, as if a thousand pounds were told down on the weather-beaten pier. For this, and for the recollection of their comrades whom we have known, whom the raging sea has engulfed before their children's eyes in such brave efforts, whom the secret sand has buried, we hold the boatmen of our watering-place in our love and honour, and are tender of the fame they well deserve.

So many children are brought down to our watering-place that, when they are not out of doors, as they usually are in fine weather, it is wonderful where they are put: the whole village seeming much too small to hold them under cover. In the afternoons, you see no end of salt and sandy little boots drying on upper window-sills. At bathing-time in the morning, the little bay re-echoes with every shrill variety of shriek and splash—after which, if the weather be at all fresh, the sands teem with small blue mottled legs. The sands are the children's great resort. They cluster there, like ants: so busy burying their particular friends, and making castles with infinite labour which the next tide overthrows, that it is curious to consider how their play, to the music of the sea, foreshadows the realities of their after lives.

It is curious, too, to observe a natural ease of approach that there seems to be between the children and the boatmen. They mutually make acquaintance, and take individual likings, without any help. You will come upon one of those slow heavy fellows sitting down patiently mending a little ship for a mite of a boy, whom he could crush to death by throwing his lightest pair of trousers on him. You will be sensible of the oddest contrast between the smooth little creature, and the rough man who seems to be carved out of hard-grained wood—between the delicate hand expectantly held out, and the immense thumb and finger that can hardly feel the rigging of thread they mend—between the small voice and the gruff growl—and yet there is a natural propriety in the companionship: always to be noted in confidence between a child and a person who has any merit of reality and genuineness: which is admirably pleasant.

We have a preventive station at our watering-place, and much the same thing may be observed—in a lesser degree, because of their official character—of the coast blockade; a steady, trusty, well-conditioned, well-conducted set of men, with no misgiving about looking you full in the face, and with a quiet thorough-going way of passing along to their duty at night, carrying huge sou'-wester clothing in reserve, that is fraught with all good prepossession. They are handy fellows—neat about their houses—industrious at gardening —would get on with their wives, one thinks, in a desert island—and people it, too, soon.

As to the naval officer of the station, with his hearty fresh face, and his blue eye that has pierced all kinds of weather, it warms our hearts when he comes into church on a Sunday, with that bright mixture of blue coat, buff waistcoat, black neck-kerchief, and gold epaulette, that is associated in the minds of all Englishmen with brave, unpretending, cordial, national service. We like to look at him in his Sunday state; and if we were First Lord (really possessing the indispensable qualification for the office of knowing nothing whatever about the sea), we would give him a ship to-morrow.

We have a church, by-the-by, of course—a hideous temple of flint, like a great petrified haystack. Our chief clerical dignitary, who, to his honour, has done much for education both in time and money, and has established excellent schools, is a sound, shrewd, healthy gentleman, who has got into little occasional difficulties with the neighbouring farmers, but has had a pestilent trick of being right. Under a new regulation, he has yielded the church of our watering-place to another clergyman. Upon the whole we get on in church well. We are a little bilious sometimes, about these days of fraternisation, and about nations arriving at a new and more unprejudiced knowledge of each other (which our Christianity don't quite approve), but it soon goes off, and then we get on very well.

There are two dissenting chapels, besides, in our small watering-place; being in about the proportion of a hundred and twenty guns to a yacht. But the dissension that has torn us lately, has not been a religious one. It has arisen on the novel question of Gas. Our watering-place has been convulsed by the agitation, Gas or No Gas. It was never reasoned why No Gas, but there was a great No Gas party. Broadsides were printed and stuck about—a startling circumstance in our watering-place. The No Gas party rested content with chalking "No Gas!" and "Down with Gas!" and other such angry war-whoops, on the few back gates and scraps of wall which the limits of our watering-place afford; but the Gas party printed and posted bills, wherein they took the high ground of proclaiming against the No Gas party, that it was said Let there be light and there was light; and that not to have light (that is gas-light) in our watering-place, was to contravene the great decree. Whether by these thunderbolts or not, the No Gas party were defeated ; and in this present season we have had our handful of shops illuminated for the first time. Such of the No Gas party, however, as have got shops, remain in opposition and burn tallow—exhibiting in their windows the very picture of the sulkiness that punishes itself, and a new illustration of the old adage about cutting off your nose to be revenged on your face, in cutting off their gas to be revenged on their business.

Other population than we have indicated, our watering-place has none. There are a few old used-up boatmen who creep about in the sunlight with the help of sticks, and there is a poor imbecile shoemaker who wanders his lonely life away among the rocks, as if he were looking for his reason—which he will never find. Sojourners in neighbouring watering-places come occasionally in flys to stare at us, and drive away again as if they thought us very dull ; Italian boys come, Punch comes, the Fantoccini come, the Tumblers come, the Ethiopians come ; Glee-singers come at night, and hum and vibrate (not always melodiously) under our windows. But they all go soon, and leave us to ourselves again. We once had a travelling Circus and Wombwell's Menagerie at the same time. They both know better than ever to try it again ; and the Menagerie had nearly razed us from the face of the earth in getting the elephant away—his caravan was so large, and the watering-place so small. We have a fine sea, wholesome for all people ; profitable for the body, profitable for the mind. The poet's words are sometimes on its awful lips :

> And the stately ships go on
>   To their haven under the hill ;
> But O for the touch of a vanish'd hand,
>   And the sound of a voice that is still !
>
> Break, break, break,
>   At the foot of thy crags, O sea !
> But the tender grace of a day that is dead
>   Will never come back to me.

37

Yet it is not always so, for the speech of the sea is various, and wants not abundant resource of cheerfulness, hope, and lusty encouragement. And since I have been idling at the window here, the tide has risen. The boats are dancing on the bubbling water : the colliers are afloat again ; the white-bordered waves rush in ; the children

> Do chase the ebbing Neptune, and do fly him
> When he comes back ;

the radiant sails are gliding past the shore, and shining on the far horizon ; all the sea is sparkling, heaving, swelling up with life and beauty, this bright morning.

OUR FRENCH WATERING-PLACE

HAVING earned, by many years of fidelity, the right to be sometimes inconstant to our English watering-place, we have dallied for two or three seasons with a French watering-place: once solely known to us as a town with a very long street, beginning with an abattoir and ending with a steam-boat, which it seemed our fate to behold only at daybreak on winter mornings, when (in the days before continental railroads), just sufficiently awake to know that we were most uncomfortably asleep, it was our destiny always to clatter through it, in the coupé of the diligence from Paris, with a sea of mud behind us, and a sea of tumbling waves before. In relation to which latter monster, our mind's eye now recalls a worthy Frenchman in a seal-skin cap with a braided hood over it, once our travelling companion in the coupé aforesaid, who, waking up with a pale and crumpled visage, and looking ruefully out at the grim row of breakers enjoying themselves fanatically on an instrument of torture called "the Bar," inquired of us whether we were ever sick at sea? Both to prepare his mind for the abject creature we were presently to become, and also to afford him consolation, we replied, "Sir, your servant is always sick when it is possible to be so." He returned, altogether uncheered by the bright example, "Ah, Heaven, but I am always sick, even when it is *im*possible to be so."

OUR FRENCH WATERING-PLACE

The means of communication between the French capital and our French watering-place are wholly changed since those days; but, the Channel remains unbridged as yet, and the old floundering and knocking about go on there. It must be confessed that saving in reasonable (and therefore rare) sea-weather, the act of arrival at our French watering-place from England is difficult to be achieved with dignity. Several little circumstances combine to render the visitor an object of humiliation. In the first place, the steamer no sooner touches the port, than all the passengers fall into captivity: being boarded by an overpowering force of Custom-house officers, and marched into a gloomy dungeon. In the second place, the road to this dungeon is fenced off with ropes breast-high, and outside those ropes all the English in the place who have lately been sea-sick and are now well, assemble in their best clothes to enjoy the degradation of their dilapidated fellow-creatures. "Oh, my gracious! how ill this one has been!" "Here's a damp one coming next!" "*Here's* a pale one!" "Oh! Ain't he green in the face, this next one!" Even we ourself (not deficient in natural dignity) have a lively remembrance of staggering up this detested lane one September day in a gale of wind, when we were received like an irresistible comic actor, with a burst of laughter and applause, occasioned by the extreme imbecility of our legs.

We were coming to the third place. In the third place, the captives, being shut up in the gloomy dungeon, are strained, two or three at a time, into an inner cell, to be examined as to passports; and across the doorway of communication, stands a military creature making a bar of his arm. Two ideas are generally present to the British mind during these ceremonies; first, that it is necessary to make for the cell with violent struggles, as if it were a life-boat and the dungeon a ship going down; secondly, that the military creature's arm is a national affront, which the government at home ought instantly to "take up." The

British mind and body becoming heated by these fantasies, delirious answers are made to inquiries, and extravagant actions performed. Thus, Johnson persists in giving Johnson as his baptismal name, and substituting for his ancestral designation the national " Dam ! " Neither can he by any means be brought to recognise the distinction between a portmanteau-key and a passport, but will obstinately persevere in tendering the one when asked for the other. This brings him to the fourth place, in a state of mere idiotcy ; and when he is, in the fourth place, cast out at a little door into a howling wilderness of touters, he becomes a lunatic with wild eyes and floating hair until rescued and soothed. If friendless and unrescued, he is generally put into a railway omnibus and taken to Paris.

But, our French watering-place, when it is once got into, is a very enjoyable place. It has a varied and beautiful country around it, and many characteristic and agreeable things within it. To be sure, it might have fewer bad smells and less decaying refuse, and it might be better drained, and much cleaner in many parts, and therefore infinitely more healthy. Still, it is a bright, airy, pleasant, cheerful town ; and if you were to walk down either of its three well-paved main streets, towards five o'clock in the afternoon, when delicate odours of cookery fill the air, and its hotel windows (it is full of hotels) give glimpses of long tables set out for dinner, and made to look sumptuous by the aid of napkins folded fan-wise, you would rightly judge it to be an uncommonly good town to eat and drink in.

We have an old walled town, rich in cool public wells of water, on the top of a hill within and above the present business-town ; and if it were some hundreds of miles further from England, instead of being, on a clear day, within sight of the grass growing in the crevices of the chalk-cliffs of Dover, you would long ago have been bored to death about that town. It is more picturesque and quaint than half the innocent places which tourists, following their leader like

sheep, have made impostors of. To say nothing of its houses
with grave courtyards, its queer by-corners, and its many-
windowed streets white and quiet in the sunlight, there is an
ancient belfry in it that would have been in all the Annuals
and Albums, going and gone, these hundred years, if it had
but been more expensive to get at. Happily it has escaped
so well, being only in our French watering-place, that you
may like it of your own accord in a natural manner, without
being required to go into convulsions about it. We regard
it as one of the later blessings of our life, that BILKINS, the
only authority on Taste, never took any notice that we can
find out, of our French watering-place. Bilkins never wrote
about it, never pointed out anything to be seen in it, never
measured anything in it, always left it alone. For which
relief, Heaven bless the town and the memory of the immortal Bilkins likewise!

There is a charming walk, arched and shaded by trees, on
the old walls that form the four sides of this High Town,
whence you get glimpses of the streets below, and changing
views of the other town and of the river, and of the hills and
of the sea. It is made more agreeable and peculiar by some
of the solemn houses that are rooted in the deep streets
below, bursting into a fresher existence a-top, and having
doors and windows, and even gardens, on these ramparts. A
child going in at the courtyard gate of one of these houses,
climbing up the many stairs, and coming out at the fourth-
floor window, might conceive himself another Jack, alighting
on enchanted ground from another bean-stalk. It is a place
wonderfully populous in children; English children, with
governesses reading novels as they walk down the shady lanes
of trees, or nursemaids interchanging gossip on the seats;
French children with their smiling bonnes in snow-white caps,
and themselves—if little boys—in straw head-gear like bee-
hives, work-baskets and church hassocks. Three years ago,
there were three weazen old men, one bearing a frayed red
ribbon in his threadbare button-hole, always to be found

walking together among these children, before dinner-time. If they walked for an appetite, they doubtless lived en pension —were contracted for—otherwise their poverty would have made it a rash action. They were stooping, blear-eyed, dull old men, slip-shod and shabby, in long-skirted short-waisted coats and meagre trousers, and yet with a ghost of gentility hovering in their company. They spoke little to each other, and looked as if they might have been politically discontented if they had had vitality enough. Once, we overheard red-ribbon feebly complain to the other two that somebody, or something, was "a Robber;" and then they all three set their mouths so that they would have ground their teeth if they had had any. The ensuing winter gathered red-ribbon unto the great company of faded ribbons, and next year the remaining two were there—getting themselves entangled with hoops and dolls—familiar mysteries to the children—probably in the eyes of most of them, harmless creatures who had never been like children, and whom children could never be like. Another winter came, and another old man went, and so, this present year, the last of the triumvirate, left off walking —it was no good, now—and sat by himself on a little solitary bench, with the hoops and the dolls as lively as ever all about him.

In the Place d'Armes of this town, a little decayed market is held, which seems to slip through the old gateway, like water, and go rippling down the hill, to mingle with the murmuring market in the lower town, and get lost in its movement and bustle. It is very agreeable on an idle summer morning to pursue this market-stream from the hill-top. It begins, dozingly and dully, with a few sacks of corn; starts into a surprising collection of boots and shoes; goes brawling down the hill in a diversified channel of old cordage, old iron, old crockery, old clothes, civil and military, old rags, new cotton goods, flaming prints of saints, little looking-glasses, and incalculable lengths of tape; dives into a back-way, keeping out of sight for a little while, as streams will, or only sparkling for a moment in the shape of a market drinking-shop; and suddenly reappears behind the great church, shooting itself into a bright confusion of white-capped women and blue-bloused men, poultry, vegetables, fruits, flowers, pots, pans, praying-chairs, soldiers, country butter, umbrellas and other sun-shades, girl-porters waiting to be hired with baskets at their backs, and one weazen little old man in a cocked hat, wearing a cuirass of drinking-glasses and carrying on his shoulder a crimson temple fluttering with flags, like a glorified pavior's rammer without the handle, who rings a little bell in all parts of the scene, and cries his cooling drink Hola, Hola, Ho-o-o! in a shrill cracked voice that somehow makes itself heard, above all the chaffering and vending hum. Early in the afternoon, the whole course of the stream is dry. The praying-chairs are put back in the church, the umbrellas are folded up, the unsold goods are carried away, the stalls and stands disappear, the square is swept, the hackney coaches lounge there to be hired, and on all the country roads (if you walk about, as much as we do) you will see the peasant women, always neatly and comfortably dressed, riding home, with the pleasantest saddle-furniture of clean milk-pails, bright butter-kegs, and the like, on the jolliest little donkeys in the world.

We have another market in our French watering-place— that is to say, a few wooden hutches in the open street, down by the Port—devoted to fish. Our fishing-boats are famous everywhere; and our fishing people, though they love lively colours, and taste is neutral (see Bilkins), are among the most picturesque people we ever encountered. They have not only a quarter of their own in the town itself, but they occupy whole villages of their own on the neighbouring cliffs. Their churches and chapels are their own; they consort with one another, they intermarry among themselves, their customs are their own, and their costume is their own and never changes. As soon as one of their boys can walk, he is provided with a long bright red nightcap; and one of their men

would as soon think of going afloat without his head, as
without that indispensable appendage to it. Then, they
wear the noblest boots, with the hugest tops—flapping and
bulging over anyhow; above which, they encase themselves
in such wonderful overalls and petticoat trousers, made to
all appearance of tarry old sails, so additionally stiffened with
pitch and salt, that the wearers have a walk of their own,
and go straddling and swinging about among the boats and
barrels and nets and rigging, a sight to see. Then, their
younger women, by dint of going down to the sea barefoot,
to fling their baskets into the boats as they come in with
the tide, and bespeak the first fruits of the haul with pro-
pitiatory promises to love and marry that dear fisherman who
shall fill that basket like an Angel, have the finest legs ever
carved by Nature in the brightest mahogany, and they walk
like Juno. Their eyes, too, are so lustrous that their long
gold ear-rings turn dull beside those brilliant neighbours;
and when they are dressed, what with these beauties, and
their fine fresh faces, and their many petticoats—striped
petticoats, red petticoats, blue petticoats, always clean and
smart, and never too long—and their home-made stockings,
mulberry-coloured, blue, brown, purple, lilac—which the
older women, taking care of the Dutch-looking children, sit
in all sorts of places knitting, knitting, knitting from morning to night—and what with their little saucy bright blue
jackets, knitted too, and fitting close to their handsome
figures; and what with the natural grace with which they
wear the commonest cap, or fold the commonest handkerchief round their luxuriant hair—we say, in a word and out
of breath, that taking all these premises into our consideration, it has never been a matter of the least surprise to us
that we have never once met, in the cornfields, on the dusty
roads, by the breezy windmills, on the plots of short sweet
grass overhanging the sea—anywhere—a young fisherman
and fisherwoman of our French watering-place together, but
the arm of that fisherman has invariably been, as a matter of

45

course and without any absurd attempt to disguise so plain a necessity, round the neck or waist of that fisherwoman. And we have had no doubt whatever, standing looking at their uphill streets, house rising above house, and terrace above terrace, and bright garments here and there lying sunning on rough stone parapets, that the pleasant mist on all such objects, caused by their being seen through the brown nets hung across on poles to dry, is, in the eyes of every true young fisherman, a mist of love and beauty, setting off the goddess of his heart.

Moreover it is to be observed that these are an industrious people, and a domestic people, and an honest people. And though we are aware that at the bidding of Bilkins it is our duty to fall down and worship the Neapolitans, we make bold very much to prefer the fishing people of our French watering-place—especially since our last visit to Naples within these twelvemonths, when we found only four conditions of men remaining in the whole city: to wit, lazzaroni, priests, spies, and soldiers, and all of them beggars; the paternal government having banished all its subjects except the rascals.

But we can never henceforth separate our French watering-place from our own landlord of two summers, M. Loyal Devasseur, citizen and town-councillor. Permit us to have the pleasure of presenting M. Loyal Devasseur.

His own family name is simply Loyal; but, as he is married, and as in that part of France a husband always adds to his own name the family name of his wife, he writes himself Loyal Devasseur. He owns a compact little estate of some twenty or thirty acres on a lofty hill-side, and on it he has built two country houses, which he lets furnished. They are by many degrees the best houses that are so let near our French watering-place; we have had the honour of living in both, and can testify. The entrance-hall of the first we inhabited was ornamented with a plan of the estate, representing it as about twice the size of Ireland; insomuch that when we were yet new to the property (M. Loyal always speaks of it as "La propriété") we went three miles straight on end in search of the bridge of Austerlitz—which we afterwards found to be immediately outside the window. The Château of the Old Guard, in another part of the grounds, and, according to the plan, about two leagues from the little dining-room, we sought in vain for a week, until, happening one evening to sit upon a bench in the forest (forest in the plan), a few yards from the house-door, we observed at our feet, in the ignominious circumstances of being upside down and greenly rotten, the Old Guard himself: that is to say, the painted effigy of a member of that distinguished corps, seven feet high, and in the act of carrying arms, who had had the misfortune to be blown down in the previous winter. It will be perceived that M. Loyal is a staunch admirer of the great Napoleon. He is an old soldier himself—captain of the National Guard, with a handsome gold vase on his chimney-piece, presented to him by his company—and his respect for the memory of the illustrious general is enthusiastic. Medallions of him, portraits of him, busts of him, pictures of him, are thickly sprinkled all over the property. During the first month of our occupation, it was our affliction to be constantly knocking down Napoleon: if we touched a shelf in a dark corner, he toppled over with a crash; and every door we opened, shook him to the soul. Yet M. Loyal is not a man of mere castles in the air, or, as he would say, in Spain. He has a specially practical, contriving, clever, skilful eye and hand. His houses are delightful. He unites French elegance and English comfort, in a happy manner quite his own. He has an extraordinary genius for making tasteful little bedrooms in angles of his roofs, which an Englishman would as soon think of turning to any account as he would think of cultivating the Desert. We have ourself reposed deliciously in an elegant chamber of M. Loyal's construction, with our head as nearly in the kitchen chimney-pot as we can conceive it likely for the head of any

47

gentleman, not by profession a Sweep, to be. And, into whatsoever strange nook M. Loyal's genius penetrates, it, in that nook, infallibly constructs a cupboard and a row of pegs. In either of our houses, we could have put away the knapsacks and hung up the hats of the whole regiment of Guides.

Aforetime, M. Loyal was a tradesman in the town. You can transact business with no present tradesman in the town, and give your card " chez M. Loyal," but a brighter face shines upon you directly. We doubt if there is, ever was, or ever will be, a man so universally pleasant in the minds of people as M. Loyal is in the minds of the citizens of our French watering-place. They rub their hands and laugh when they speak of him. Ah, but he is such a good child, such a brave boy, such a generous spirit, that Monsieur Loyal! It is the honest truth. M. Loyal's nature is the nature of a gentleman. He cultivates his ground with his own hands (assisted by one little labourer, who falls into a fit now and then); and he digs and delves from morn to eve in prodigious perspirations—" works always," as he says—but, cover him with dust, mud, weeds, water, any stains you will, you never can cover the gentleman in M. Loyal. A portly, upright, broad-shouldered, brown-faced man, whose soldierly bearing gives him the appearance of being taller than he is, look into the bright eye of M. Loyal, standing before you in his working-blouse and cap, not particularly well shaved, and, it may be, very earthy, and you shall discern in M. Loyal a gentleman whose true politeness is ingrain, and confirmation of whose word by his bond you would blush to think of. Not without reason is M. Loyal when he tells that story, in his own vivacious way, of his travelling to Fulham, near London, to buy all these hundreds and hundreds of trees you now see upon the Property, then a bare, bleak hill; and of his sojourning in Fulham three months; and of his jovial evenings with the market-gardeners; and of the crowning banquet before his departure, when the market-gardeners rose as one man, clinked their glasses all together (as the custom at Fulham is), and cried, "Vive Loyal!"

M. Loyal has an agreeable wife, but no family; and he loves to drill the children of his tenants, or run races with them, or do anything with them, or for them, that is good-natured. He is of a highly convivial temperament, and his hospitality is unbounded. Billet a soldier on him, and he is delighted. Five-and-thirty soldiers had M. Loyal billeted on him this present summer, and they all got fat and red-faced in two days. It became a legend among the troops that whosoever got billeted on M. Loyal rolled in clover; and so it fell out that the fortunate man who drew the billet "M. Loyal Devasseur" always leaped into the air, though in heavy marching order. M. Loyal cannot bear to admit anything that might seem by any implication to disparage the military profession. We hinted to him once, that we were conscious of a remote doubt arising in our mind, whether a sou a day for pocket-money, tobacco, stockings, drink, washing, and social pleasures in general, left a very large margin for a soldier's enjoyment. Pardon! said Monsieur Loyal, rather wincing. It was not a fortune, but—à la bonne heure—it was better than it used to be! What, we asked him on another occasion, were all those neighbouring peasants, each living with his family in one room, and each having a soldier (perhaps two) billeted on him every other night, required to provide for those soldiers? "Faith!" said M. Loyal, reluctantly; "a bed, monsieur, and fire to cook with, and a candle. And they share their supper with those soldiers. It is not possible that they could eat alone."—"And what allowance do they get for this?" said we. Monsieur Loyal drew himself up taller, took a step back, laid his hand upon his breast, and said, with majesty, as speaking for himself and all France, "Monsieur, it is a contribution to the State!"

It is never going to rain, according to M. Loyal. When it is impossible to deny that it is now raining in torrents, he says it will be fine—charming—magnificent—to-morrow. It is never hot on the Property, he contends. Likewise it is never cold. The flowers, he says, come out, delighting to grow there; it is like Paradise this morning; it is like the Garden of Eden. He is a little fanciful in his language: smilingly observing of Madame Loyal, when she is absent at vespers, that she is "gone to her salvation"—allée à son salut. He has a great enjoyment of tobacco, but nothing would induce him to continue smoking face to face with a lady. His short black pipe immediately goes into his breast pocket, scorches his blouse, and nearly sets him on fire. In the Town Council and on occasions of ceremony, he appears in a full suit of black, with a waistcoat of magnificent breadth across the chest, and a shirt-collar of fabulous proportions. Good M. Loyal! Under blouse or waistcoat, he carries one of the gentlest hearts that beat in a nation teeming with gentle people. He has had losses, and has been at his best under them. Not only the loss of his way by night in the Fulham times—when a bad subject of an Englishman, under pretence of seeing him home, took him into all the night public-houses, drank "arfanarf" in every one at his expense, and finally fled, leaving him shipwrecked at Cleefeeway, which we apprehend to be Ratcliffe Highway—but heavier losses than that. Long ago a family of children and a mother were left in one of his houses without money, a whole year. M. Loyal —anything but as rich as we wish he had been—had not the heart to say "you must go;" so they stayed on and stayed on, and paying-tenants who would have come in couldn't come in, and at last they managed to get helped home across the water; and M. Loyal kissed the whole group, and said, "Adieu, my poor infants!" and sat down in their deserted salon and smoked his pipe of peace.—"The rent, M. Loyal?" "Eh! well! The rent!" M. Loyal shakes his head. "Le bon Dieu," says M. Loyal presently, "will recompense me," and he laughs and smokes his pipe of peace. May he smoke it on the Property, and not be recompensed, these fifty years!

There are public amusements in our French watering-place, or it would not be French. They are very popular, and very cheap. The sea-bathing—which may rank as the most favoured daylight entertainment, inasmuch as the French visitors bathe all day long, and seldom appear to think of remaining less than an hour at a time in the water—is astoundingly cheap. Omnibuses convey you, if you please, from a convenient part of the town to the beach and back again; you have a clean and comfortable bathing-machine, dress, linen, and all appliances; and the charge for the whole is half-a-franc, or fivepence. On the pier, there is usually a guitar, which seems presumptuously enough to set its tinkling against the deep hoarseness of the sea, and there is always some boy or woman who sings, without any voice, little songs without any tune: the strain we have most frequently heard being an appeal to "the sportsman" not to bag that choicest of game, the swallow. For bathing purposes, we have also a subscription establishment with an esplanade, where people lounge about with telescopes, and seem to get a good deal of weariness for their money; and we have also an association of individual machine proprietors combined against this formidable rival. M. Féroce, our own particular friend in the bathing line, is one of these. How he ever came by his name we cannot imagine. He is as gentle and polite a man as M. Loyal Devasseur himself; immensely stout withal; and of a beaming aspect. M. Féroce has saved so many people from drowning, and has been decorated with so many medals in consequence, that his stoutness seems a special dispensation of Providence to enable him to wear them; if his girth were the girth of an ordinary man, he could never hang them on, all at once. It is only on very great occasions that M. Féroce displays his shining honours. At other times they lie by, with rolls of manuscript testifying to the causes of their presentation, in a huge glass case in the red-sofa'd salon of his private residence on the beach, where M. Féroce also keeps his family pictures, his portraits of himself as he appears both in bathing life and in private life, his little boats that rock by clockwork, and his other ornamental possessions.

Then, we have a commodious and gay Theatre—or had, for it is burned down now—where the opera was always preceded by a vaudeville, in which (as usual) everybody, down to the little old man with the large hat and the little cane and tassel, who always played either my Uncle or my Papa, suddenly broke out of the dialogue into the mildest vocal snatches, to the great perplexity of unaccustomed strangers from Great Britain, who never could make out when they were singing and when they were talking—and indeed it was pretty much the same. But, the caterers in the way of entertainment to whom we are most beholden, are the Society of Welldoing, who are active all the summer, and give the proceeds of their good works to the poor. Some of the most agreeable fêtes they contrive, are announced as " Dedicated to the children ; " and the taste with which they turn a small public enclosure into an elegant garden beautifully illuminated ; and the thorough-going heartiness and energy with which they personally direct the childish pleasures ; are supremely delightful. For fivepence a head, we have on these occasions donkey races with English " Jokeis," and other rustic sports ; lotteries for toys ; roundabouts, dancing on the grass to the music of an admirable band, fire-balloons and fireworks. Further, almost every week all through the summer—never mind, now, on what day of the week—there is a fête in some adjoining village (called in that part of the country a Ducasse), where the people—really *the people*—dance on the green turf in the open air, round a little orchestra, that seems itself to dance, there is such an airy motion of flags and streamers all about it. And we do not suppose that between the Torrid Zone and the North Pole there are to be found male dancers with such astonishingly loose legs, furnished with so many joints in wrong places, utterly unknown to Professor Owen, as those who here disport themselves. Sometimes, the fête appertains to a particular trade; you will see among the cheerful young women at the joint Ducasse of the milliners and tailors, a wholesome knowledge of the art of making common and cheap things uncommon and pretty, by good sense and good taste, that is a practical lesson to any rank of society in a whole island we could mention. The oddest feature of these agreeable scenes is the everlasting Round-about (we preserve an English word wherever we can, as we are writing the English language), on the wooden horses of which machine grown-up people of all ages are wound round and round with the utmost solemnity, while the proprietor's wife grinds an organ, capable of only one tune, in the centre.

As to the boarding-houses of our French watering-place, they are Legion, and would require a distinct treatise. It is not without a sentiment of national pride that we believe them to contain more bores from the shores of Albion than all the clubs in London. As you walk timidly in their neighbourhood, the very neckcloths and hats of your elderly compatriots cry to you from the stones of the streets, "We are Bores—avoid us!" We have never overheard at street corners such lunatic scraps of political and social discussion as among these dear countrymen of ours. They believe everything that is impossible and nothing that is true. They carry rumours, and ask questions, and make corrections and improvements on one another, staggering to the human intellect. And they are for ever rushing into the English library, propounding such incomprehensible paradoxes to the fair mistress of that establishment, that we beg to recommend her to her Majesty's gracious consideration as a fit object for a pension.

The English form a considerable part of the population of our French watering-place, and are deservedly addressed and respected in many ways. Some of the surface-addresses to them are odd enough, as when a laundress puts a placard outside her house announcing her possession of that curious British instrument, a "Mingle;" or when a tavern-keeper provides accommodation for the celebrated English game of " Nokemdon." But, to us, it is not the least pleasant feature of our French watering-place that a long and constant fusion of the two great nations there, has taught each to like the other, and to learn from the other, and to rise superior to the absurd prejudices that have lingered among the weak and ignorant in both countries equally.

Drumming and trumpeting of course go on for ever in our French watering-place. Flag-flying is at a premium, too; but, we cheerfully avow that we consider a flag a very pretty object, and that we take such outward signs of innocent liveliness to our heart of hearts. The people, in the town and in the country, are a busy people who work hard; they are sober, temperate, good-humoured, light-hearted, and generally remarkable for their engaging manners. Few just men, not immoderately bilious, could see them in their recreations without very much respecting the character that is so easily, so harmlessly, and so simply, pleased.

BILL-STICKING

If I had an enemy whom I hated—which Heaven forbid! —and if I knew of something which sat heavy on his conscience, I think I would introduce that something into a Posting-Bill, and place a large impression in the hands of an active sticker. I can scarcely imagine a more terrible revenge. I should haunt him, by this means, night and day. I do not mean to say that I would publish his secret, in red letters two feet high, for all the town to read: I would darkly refer to it. It should be between him, and me, and the Posting-Bill. Say, for example, that, at a certain period of his life, my enemy had surreptitiously possessed himself of a key. I would then embark my capital in the lock business, and conduct that business on the advertising principle. In all my placards and advertisements, I would throw up the line SECRET KEYS. Thus, if my enemy passed an uninhabited house, he would see his conscience glaring down on him from the parapets, and peeping up at him from the cellars. If he took a dead wall in his walk, it would be alive with reproaches. If he sought refuge in an omnibus, the panels thereof would become Belshazzar's palace to him. If he took boat, in a wild endeavour to escape, he would see the fatal words lurking under the arches of the bridges over the Thames. If he walked the streets with downcast eyes, he would recoil from the very stones of the pavement, made eloquent by lamp-black lithograph. If he drove or rode, his way would be blocked up by enormous vans, each proclaiming the same words over and over again from its whole extent of surface. Until, having gradually grown thinner and paler, and having at last totally rejected food, he would miserably perish, and I should be revenged. This conclusion I should, no doubt, celebrate by laughing a hoarse laugh in three syllables, and folding my arms tight upon my chest agreeably to most of the examples of glutted animosity that I have had an opportunity of observing in connexion with the Drama—which, by-the-by, as involving a good deal of noise, appears to me to be occasionally confounded with the Drummer.

The foregoing reflections presented themselves to my mind, the other day, as I contemplated (being newly come to London from the East Riding of Yorkshire, on a house-hunting expedition for next May), an old warehouse which rotting paste and rotting paper had brought down to the condition of an old cheese. It would have been impossible to say, on the most conscientious survey, how much of its front was brick and mortar, and how much decaying and decayed plaster. It was so thickly encrusted with fragments of bills, that no ship's keel after a long voyage could be half so foul. All traces of the broken windows were billed out, the doors were billed across, the water-spout was billed over. The building was shored up to prevent its tumbling into the street; and the very beams erected against it were less wood than paste and paper, they had been so continually posted and reposted. The forlorn dregs of old posters so encumbered this wreck, that there was no hold for new posters, and the stickers had abandoned the place in despair, except one enterprising man who had hoisted the last masquerade to a clear spot near the level of the stack of chimneys where it waved and drooped like a shattered flag. Below the rusty cellar-grating, crumpled remnants of old bills torn down, rotted away in wasting heaps of fallen leaves. Here and there, some of the thick rind of the house had peeled off in strips, and fluttered heavily down, littering the street; but, still, below these rents and gashes, layers of decomposing posters showed themselves, as if they were interminable. I thought the building could never even be pulled down, but in one adhesive heap of rottenness and poster. As to getting in—I don't believe that if the Sleeping Beauty and her Court had been so billed up, the young Prince could have done it.

Knowing all the posters that were yet legible, intimately, and pondering on their ubiquitous nature, I was led into the reflections with which I began this paper, by considering what an awful thing it would be, ever to have wronged—say M. JULLIEN for example—and to have his avenging name in characters of fire incessantly before my eyes. Or to have injured MADAME TUSSAUD, and undergo a similar retribution. Has any man a self-reproachful thought associated with pills, or ointment? What an avenging spirit to that man is PROFESSOR HOLLOWAY! Have I sinned in oil? CABBURN pursues me. Have I a dark remembrance associated with any gentlemanly garments, bespoke or ready made? MOSES and SON are on my track. Did I ever aim a blow at a defenceless fellow-creature's head? That head eternally being measured for a wig, or that worse head which was bald before it used the balsam, and hirsute afterwards—enforcing the benevolent moral, " Better to be bald as a Dutch cheese than come to this,"—undoes me. Have I no sore places in my mind which MECHI touches—which NICOLL probes—which no registered article whatever lacerates? Does no discordant note within me thrill responsive to mysterious watchwords, as " Revalenta Arabica," or " Number One St. Paul's Churchyard "? Then may I enjoy life, and be happy.

Lifting up my eyes, as I was musing to this effect, I beheld advancing towards me (I was then on Cornhill, near to the Royal Exchange), a solemn procession of three advertising vans, of first-class dimensions, each drawn by a very little horse. As the cavalcade approached, I was at a loss to reconcile the careless deportment of the drivers of these vehicles, with the terrific announcements they conducted through the city, which being a summary of the contents of a Sunday newspaper, were of the most thrilling kind. Robbery, fire, murder, and the ruin of the United Kingdom —each discharged in a line by itself, like a separate broadside of red-hot shot—were among the least of the warnings addressed to an unthinking people. Yet, the Ministers of Fate who drove the awful cars, leaned forward with their arms upon their knees in a state of extreme lassitude, for want of any subject of interest. The first man, whose hair I might naturally have expected to see standing on end, scratched his head—one of the smoothest I ever beheld— with profound indifference. The second whistled. The third yawned.

Pausing to dwell upon this apathy, it appeared to me, as the fatal cars came by me, that I descried in the second car, through the portal in which the charioteer was seated, a figure stretched upon the floor. At the same time, I thought I smelt tobacco. The latter impression passed quickly from me; the former remained. Curious to know whether this prostrate figure was the one impressible man of the whole capital who had been stricken insensible by the terrors revealed to him, and whose form had been placed in the car by the charioteer, from motives of humanity, I followed the procession. It turned into Leadenhall-market, and halted at a public-house. Each driver dismounted. I then distinctly heard, proceeding from the second car, where I had dimly seen the prostrate form, the words:

"And a pipe!"

The driver entering the public-house with his fellows, apparently for purposes of refreshment, I could not refrain from mounting on the shaft of the second vehicle, and looking in at the portal. I then beheld, reclining on his back upon the floor, on a kind of mattress or divan, a little man in a shooting-coat. The exclamation "Dear me" which irresistibly escaped my lips caused him to sit upright, and survey me. I found him to be a good-looking little man of about fifty, with a shining face, a tight head, a bright eye, a moist wink, a quick speech, and a ready air. He had something of a sporting way with him.

He looked at me, and I looked at him, until the driver displaced me by handing in a pint of beer, a pipe, and what I understand is called "a screw" of tobacco—an object which has the appearance of a curl-paper taken off the barmaid's head, with the curl in it.

"I beg your pardon," said I, when the removed person of the driver again admitted of my presenting my face at the portal. "But—excuse my curiosity, which I inherit from my mother—do you live here?"

"That's good, too!" returned the little man, composedly laying aside a pipe he had smoked out, and filling the pipe just brought to him.

"Oh, you *don't* live here then?" said I.

He shook his head, as he calmly lighted his pipe by means of a German tinder-box, and replied, "This is my carriage. When things are flat, I take a ride sometimes, and enjoy myself. I am the inventor of these wans."

His pipe was now alight. He drank his beer all at once, and he smoked and he smiled at me.

"It was a great idea!" said I.

"Not so bad," returned the little man, with the modesty of merit.

"Might I be permitted to inscribe your name upon the tablets of my memory?" I asked.

"There's not much odds in the name," returned the little man, "—no name particular—I am the King of the Bill-Stickers."

"Good gracious!" said I.

The monarch informed me, with a smile, that he had never been crowned or installed with any public ceremonies, but, that he was peaceably acknowledged as King of the Bill-Stickers in right of being the oldest and most respected member of "the old school of bill-sticking." He likewise gave me to understand that there was a Lord Mayor of the Bill-Stickers, whose genius was chiefly exercised within the limits of the city. He made some allusion, also, to an inferior potentate, called "Turkey-legs;" but I did not understand that this gentleman was invested with much power. I rather inferred that he derived his title from some peculiarity of gait, and that it was of an honorary character.

"My father," pursued the King of the Bill-Stickers, "was Engineer, Beadle, and Bill-Sticker to the parish of St. Andrew's, Holborn, in the year one thousand seven hundred and eighty. My father stuck bills at the time of the riots of London."

"You must be acquainted with the whole subject of bill-sticking, from that time to the present!" said I.

"Pretty well so," was the answer.

"Excuse me," said I; "but I am a sort of collector——"

"Not Income-tax?" cried His Majesty, hastily removing his pipe from his lips.

"No, no," said I.

"Water-rate?" said His Majesty.

"No, no," I returned.

"Gas? Assessed? Sewers?" said His Majesty.

"You misunderstand me," I replied, soothingly. "Not that sort of collector at all: a collector of facts."

"Oh, if it's only facts," cried the King of the Bill-Stickers, recovering his good-humour, and banishing the great mistrust that had suddenly fallen upon him, "come in and welcome! If it had been income, or winders, I think I should have pitched you out of the wan, upon my soul!"

Readily complying with the invitation, I squeezed myself in at the small aperture. His Majesty, graciously handing me a little three-legged stool on which I took my seat in a corner, inquired if I smoked.

"I do;—that is, I can," I answered.

"Pipe and a screw!" said His Majesty to the attendant charioteer. "Do you prefer a dry smoke, or do you moisten it?"

As unmitigated tobacco produces most disturbing effects upon my system (indeed, if I had perfect moral courage, I doubt if I should smoke at all, under any circumstances), I advocated moisture, and begged the Sovereign of the Bill-Stickers to name his usual liquor, and to concede to me the privilege of paying for it. After some delicate reluctance on his part, we were provided, through the instrumentality of the attendant charioteer, with a can of cold rum-and-water, flavoured with sugar and lemon. We were also furnished with a tumbler, and I was provided with a pipe. His Majesty, then observing that we might combine business with conversation, gave the word for the car to proceed; and, to my great delight, we jogged away at a foot pace.

I say to my great delight, because I am very fond of novelty, and it was a new sensation to be jolting through the tumult of the city in that secluded Temple, partly open to the sky, surrounded by the roar without, and seeing nothing but the clouds. Occasionally, blows from whips fell heavily on the Temple's walls, when by stopping up the road longer than usual, we irritated carters and coachmen to madness; but they fell harmless upon us within and disturbed not the serenity of our peaceful retreat. As I looked upward, I felt, I should imagine, like the Astronomer Royal. I was enchanted by the contrast between the freezing nature of our external mission on the blood of the populace, and the perfect composure reigning within those sacred precincts: where His Majesty, reclining easily on his left arm, smoked his pipe and drank his rum-and-water from his own side of the tumbler, which stood impartially between us. As I looked down from the clouds and caught his royal eye, he understood my reflections. "I have an idea," he observed, with an upward glance, "of training scarlet runners across in the season,—making a arbour of it,—and sometimes taking tea in the same, according to the song."

I nodded approval.

" And here you repose and think ? " said I.

" And think," said he, " of posters—walls—and hoardings."

We were both silent, contemplating the vastness of the subject. I remembered a surprising fancy of dear THOMAS HOOD'S, and wondered whether this monarch ever sighed to repair to the great wall of China, and stick bills all over it.

"And so," said he, rousing himself, " it's facts as you collect ? "

"Facts," said I.

" The facts of bill-sticking," pursued His Majesty, in a benignant manner, "as known to myself, air as following. When my father was Engineer, Beadle, and Bill-Sticker to the parish of St. Andrew's, Holborn, he employed women to post bills for him. He employed women to post bills at the time of the riots of London. He died at the age of seventy-five year, and was buried by the murdered Eliza Grimwood, over in the Waterloo Road."

As this was somewhat in the nature of a royal speech, I listened with deference and silently. His Majesty, taking a scroll from his pocket, proceeded, with great distinctness, to pour out the following flood of information:—

" ' The bills being at that period mostly proclamations and declarations, and which were only a demy size, the manner of posting the bills (as they did not use brushes) was by means of a piece of wood which they called a "dabber." Thus things continued till such time as the State Lottery was passed, and then the printers began to print larger bills, and men were employed instead of women, as the State Lottery Commissioners then began to send men all over England to post bills, and would keep them out for six or eight months at a time, and they were called by the London bill-stickers ' trampers,' their wages at the time being ten shillings per day, besides expenses. They used sometimes to be stationed in large towns for five or six months together, distributing the schemes to all the houses in the town. And then there were more caricature wood-block engravings for posting-bills than there are at the present time, the principal printers, at that time, of posting-bills being Messrs. Evans and Ruffy, of Budge Row; Thoroughgood and Whiting, of the present day; and Messrs. Gye and Balne, Gracechurch Street, City. The largest bills printed at that period were a two-sheet double crown; and when they commenced printing four-sheet bills, two bill-stickers would work together. They had no settled wages per week, but had a fixed price for their work, and the London bill-stickers, during a lottery week, have been known to earn, each, eight or nine pounds per week, till the day of drawing; likewise the men who carried boards in the street used to have one pound per week, and the bill-stickers at that time would not allow any one to wilfully cover or destroy their bills, as they had a society amongst themselves, and very frequently dined together at some public-house where they used to go of an evening to have their work delivered out untoe 'em.'"

All this His Majesty delivered in a gallant manner; posting it, as it were, before me, in a great proclamation. I took advantage of the pause he now made, to inquire what a "two-sheet double crown" might express?

"A two-sheet double crown," replied the King, "is a bill thirty-nine inches wide by thirty inches high."

"Is it possible," said I, my mind reverting to the gigantic admonitions we were then displaying to the multitude— which were as infants to some of the posting-bills on the rotten old warehouse—"that some few years ago the largest bill was no larger than that?"

"The fact," returned the King, "is undoubtedly so." Here he instantly rushed again into the scroll.

"'Since the abolishing of the State Lottery all that good feeling has gone, and nothing but jealousy exists, through the rivalry of each other. Several bill-sticking companies have started, but have failed. The first party that started a company was twelve year ago; but what was left of the old school and their dependants joined together and opposed them. And for some time we were quiet again, till a printer of Hatton Garden formed a company by hiring the sides of houses; but he was not supported by the public, and he left his wooden frames fixed up for rent. The last company that started, took advantage of the New Police Act, and hired of Messrs. Grissell and Peto the hoarding of Trafalgar Square, and established a bill-sticking office in Cursitor Street, Chancery Lane, and engaged some of the new bill-stickers to do their work, and for a time got the half of all our work, and with such spirit did they carry on their opposition towards us, that they used to give us in charge before the magistrate, and get us fined; but they found it so expensive, that they could not keep it up, for they were always employing a lot of ruffians from the Seven Dials to come and fight us; and on one occasion the old bill-stickers went to Trafalgar Square to attempt to post bills, when they were given in custody by the watchman in their employ, and fined at Queen Square five pounds, as they would not allow any of us to speak in the office; but when they were gone, we had an interview with the magistrate, who mitigated the fine to fifteen shillings. During the time the men were waiting for the fine, this company started off to a public-house that we were in the habit of using, and waited for us coming back, where a fighting scene took place that beggars description. Shortly after this, the principal one day came and shook hands with us, and acknowledged that he had broken up the company, and that he himself had lost five hundred pound in trying to overthrow us. We then took possession of the hoarding in Trafalgar Square; but Messrs. Grissell and Peto would not allow us to post our bills on the said hoarding without paying them—and from first to last we paid upwards of two hundred pounds for that hoarding, and likewise the hoarding of the Reform Club-house, Pall Mall.'"

NO STRANGER TO BLACK EYES

His Majesty, being now completely out of breath, laid down his scroll (which he appeared to have finished), puffed at his pipe, and took some rum-and-water. I embraced the opportunity of asking how many divisions the art and mystery of bill-sticking comprised? He replied, three—auctioneers' bill-sticking, theatrical bill-sticking, general bill-sticking.

"The auctioneers' porters," said the King, "who do their bill-sticking, are mostly respectable and intelligent, and generally well paid for their work, whether in town or country. The price paid by the principal auctioneers for country work is nine shillings per day; that is, seven shillings for day's work, one shilling for lodging, and one for paste. Town work is five shillings a day, including paste."

"Town work must be rather hot work," said I, "if there be many of those fighting scenes that beggar description, among the bill-stickers?"

"Well," replied the King, "I an't a stranger, I assure you, to black eyes; a bill-sticker ought to know how to handle his fists a bit. As to that row I have mentioned, that grew out of competition, conducted in an uncompromising spirit. Besides a man in a horse-and-shay continually following us about, the company had a watchman on duty, night and day, to prevent us sticking bills upon the hoarding in Trafalgar Square. We went there, early one morning, to stick bills and to black-wash their bills if we were interfered with. We *were* interfered with, and I gave the word for laying on the wash. It *was* laid on—pretty brisk—and we were all taken to Queen Square: but they couldn't fine *me*. *I* knew that," —with a bright smile—"I'd only give directions—I was only the General."

Charmed with this monarch's affability, I inquired if he had ever hired a hoarding himself.

"Hired a large one," he replied, "opposite the Lyceum Theatre, when the buildings was there. Paid thirty pound for it; let out places on it, and called it 'The External Paper-Hanging Station.' But it didn't answer. Ah!" said

His Majesty thoughtfully, as he filled the glass, "Bill-stickers have a deal to contend with. The bill-sticking clause was got into the Police Act by a member of Parliament that employed me at his election. The clause is pretty stiff respecting where bills go; but *he* didn't mind where *his* bills went. It was all right enough, so long as they was *his* bills!"

Fearful that I observed a shadow of misanthropy on the King's cheerful face, I asked whose ingenious invention that was, which I greatly admired, of sticking bills under the arches of the bridges.

"Mine!" said His Majesty. "I was the first that ever stuck a bill under a bridge! Imitators soon rose up, of course.—When don't they? But they stuck 'em at low-water, and the tide came and swept the bills clean away. *I* knew that!" The King laughed.

"What may be the name of that instrument, like an immense fishing-rod," I inquired, "with which bills are posted on high places?"

"The joints," returned His Majesty. "Now, we use the joints where formerly we used ladders—as they do still in country places. Once, when Madame" (Vestris, understood) "was playing in Liverpool, another bill-sticker and me were at it together on the wall outside the Clarence Dock—me with the joints—him on a ladder. Lord! I had my bill up, right over his head, yards above him, ladder and all, while he was crawling to his work. The people going in and out of the docks, stood and laughed!—It's about thirty years since the joints come in."

"Are there any bill-stickers who can't read?" I took the liberty of inquiring.

"Some," said the King. "But they know which is the right side up'ards of their work. They keep it as it's given out to 'em. I have seen a bill or so stuck wrong side up'ards. But it's very rare."

Our discourse sustained some interruption at this point,

by the procession of cars occasioning a stoppage of about three-quarters of a mile in length, as nearly as I could judge. His Majesty, however, entreating me not to be discomposed by the contingent uproar, smoked with great placidity, and surveyed the firmament.

When we were again in motion, I begged to be informed what was the largest poster His Majesty had ever seen. The King replied, " A thirty-six sheet poster." I gathered, also, that there were about a hundred and fifty bill-stickers in London, and that His Majesty considered an average hand equal to the posting of one hundred bills (single sheets) in a day. The King was of opinion, that, although posters had much increased in size, they had not increased in number; as the abolition of the State Lotteries had occasioned a great falling off, especially in the country. Over and above which change, I bethought myself that the custom of advertising in newspapers had greatly increased. The completion of many London improvements, as Trafalgar Square (I particularly observed the singularity of His Majesty's calling *that* an improvement), the Royal Exchange, &c., had of late years reduced the number of advantageous posting-places. Bill-Stickers at present rather confine themselves to districts, than to particular descriptions of work. One man would strike over Whitechapel, another would take round Houndsditch, Shoreditch, and the City Road; one (the King said) would stick to the Surrey side; another would make a beat of the West-end.

His Majesty remarked, with some approach to severity, on the neglect of delicacy and taste, gradually introduced into the trade by the new school: a profligate and inferior race of impostors who took jobs at almost any price, to the detriment of the old school, and the confusion of their own misguided employers. He considered that the trade was overdone with competition, and observed speaking of his subjects, "There are too many of 'em." He believed, still, that things were a little better than they had been ; adducing, as a proof, the fact that particular posting places were now reserved, by common consent, for particular posters; those places, however, must be regularly occupied by those posters, or, they lapsed and fell into other hands. It was of no use giving a man a Drury Lane bill this week and not next. Where was it to go? He was of opinion that going to the expense of putting up your own board on which your sticker could display your own bills, was the only complete way of posting yourself at the present time; but, even to effect this, on payment of a shilling a week to the keepers of steamboat piers and other such places, you must be able, besides, to give orders for theatres and public exhibitions, or you would be sure to be cut out by somebody. His Majesty regarded the passion for orders, as one of the most unappeasable appetites of human nature. If there were a building, or if there were repairs, going on, anywhere, you could generally stand something and make it right with the foreman of the works; but, orders would be expected from you, and the man who could give the most orders was the man who would come off best. There was this other objectionable point, in orders, that workmen sold them for drink, and often sold them to persons who were likewise troubled with the weakness of thirst: which led (His Majesty said) to the presentation of your orders at Theatre doors, by individuals who were "too shakery" to derive intellectual profit from the entertainments, and who brought a scandal on you. Finally, His Majesty said that you could hardly put too little in a poster; what you wanted, was, two or three good catch-lines for the eye to rest on—then, leave it alone—and there you were!

These are the minutes of my conversation with His Majesty, as I noted them down shortly afterwards. I am not aware that I have been betrayed into any alteration or suppression. The manner of the King was frank in the extreme; and he seemed to me to avoid, at once that slight tendency to repetition which may have been observed in the conversation of His Majesty King George the Third, and that slight under-current of egotism which the curious observer may perhaps detect in the conversation of Napoleon Bonaparte.

I must do the King the justice to say that it was I, and not he, who closed the dialogue. At this juncture, I became the subject of a remarkable optical delusion; the legs of my stool appeared to me to double up; the car to spin round and round with great violence; and a mist to arise between myself and His Majesty. In addition to these sensations, I felt extremely unwell. I refer these unpleasant effects, either to the paste with which the posters were affixed to the van: which may have contained some small portion of arsenic; or, to the printer's ink, which may have contained some equally deleterious ingredient. Of this, I cannot be sure. I am only sure that I was not affected, either by the smoke, or the rum-and-water. I was assisted out of the vehicle, in a state of mind which I have only experienced in two other places —I allude to the Pier at Dover, and to the corresponding portion of the town of Calais—and sat upon a door-step until I recovered. The procession had then disappeared. I have since looked anxiously for the King in several other cars, but I have not yet had the happiness of seeing His Majesty.

"BIRTHS. MRS. MEEK, OF A SON"

My name is Meek. I am, in fact, Mr. Meek. That son is mine and Mrs. Meek's. When I saw the announcement in the Times, I dropped the paper. I had put it in, myself, and paid for it, but it looked so noble that it overpowered me.

As soon as I could compose my feelings, I took the paper up to Mrs. Meek's bedside. "Maria Jane," said I (I allude to Mrs. Meek), "you are now a public character." We read the review of our child, several times, with feelings of the strongest emotion; and I sent the boy who cleans the boots and shoes, to the office for fifteen copies. No reduction was made on taking that quantity.

It is scarcely necessary for me to say, that our child had been expected. In fact, it had been expected, with comparative confidence, for some months. Mrs. Meek's mother, who resides with us—of the name of Bigby—had made every preparation for its admission to our circle.

I hope and believe I am a quiet man. I will go farther. I *know* I am a quiet man. My constitution is tremulous, my voice was never loud, and, in point of stature, I have been from infancy, small. I have the greatest respect for Maria Jane's Mama. She is a most remarkable woman. I honour Maria Jane's Mama. In my opinion she would storm a town, single-handed, with a hearth-broom, and carry it. I have never known her to yield any point whatever, to mortal man. She is calculated to terrify the stoutest heart.

MRS. PRODGIT AND MARIA JANE'S MAMA

Still—but I will not anticipate.

The first intimation I had, of any preparations being in progress, on the part of Maria Jane's Mama, was one afternoon, several months ago. I came home earlier than usual from the office, and, proceeding into the dining-room, found an obstruction behind the door, which prevented it from opening freely. It was an obstruction of a soft nature. On looking in, I found it to be a female.

The female in question stood in the corner behind the door, consuming Sherry Wine. From the nutty smell of that beverage pervading the apartment, I have no doubt she was consuming a second glassful. She wore a black bonnet of large dimensions, and was copious in figure. The expression of her countenance was severe and discontented. The words to which she gave utterance on seeing me, were these, " Oh, git along with you, Sir, if *you* please; me and Mrs. Bigby don't want no male parties here!"

That female was Mrs. Prodgit.

I immediately withdrew, of course. I was rather hurt, but I made no remark. Whether it was that I showed a lowness of spirits after dinner, in consequence of feeling that I seemed to intrude, I cannot say. But, Maria Jane's Mama said to me on her retiring for the night: in a low distinct voice, and with a look of reproach that completely subdued me: " George Meek, Mrs. Prodgit is your wife's nurse!"

I bear no ill-will towards Mrs. Prodgit. Is it likely that I, writing this with tears in my eyes, should be capable of deliberate animosity towards a female, so essential to the welfare of Maria Jane? I am willing to admit that Fate may have been to blame, and not Mrs. Prodgit; but, it is undeniably true, that the latter female brought desolation and devastation into my lowly dwelling.

We were happy after her first appearance; we were sometimes exceedingly so. But, whenever the parlour door was opened, and " Mrs. Prodgit!" announced (and she was very

71

often announced), misery ensued. I could not bear Mrs.
Prodgit's look. I felt that I was far from wanted, and had
no business to exist in Mrs. Prodgit's presence. Between
Maria Jane's Mama, and Mrs. Prodgit, there was a dreadful,
secret, understanding—a dark mystery and conspiracy, pointing me out as a being to be shunned. I appeared to have
done something that was evil. Whenever Mrs. Prodgit
called, after dinner, I retired to my dressing-room—where
the temperature is very low indeed, in the wintry time of
the year—and sat looking at my frosty breath as it rose
before me, and at my rack of boots ; a serviceable article of
furniture, but never, in my opinion, an exhilarating object.
The length of the councils that were held with Mrs. Prodgit,
under these circumstances, I will not attempt to describe.
I will merely remark, that Mrs. Prodgit always consumed
Sherry Wine while the deliberations were in progress ; that
they always ended in Maria Jane's being in wretched spirits
on the sofa ; and that Maria Jane's Mama always received
me, when I was recalled, with a look of desolate triumph that
too plainly said, " *Now*, George Meek ! You see my child,
Maria Jane, a ruin, and I hope you are satisfied ! '

I pass, generally, over the period that intervened between
the day when Mrs. Prodgit entered her protest against male
parties, and the ever-memorable midnight when I brought
her to my unobtrusive home in a cab, with an extremely
large box on the roof, and a bundle, a bandbox, and a
basket, between the driver's legs. I have no objection to
Mrs. Prodgit (aided and abetted by Mrs. Bigby, who I never
can forget is the parent of Maria Jane) taking entire possession of my unassuming establishment. In the recesses of my
own breast, the thought may linger that a man in possession
cannot be so dreadful as a woman, and that woman Mrs.
Prodgit ; but, I ought to bear a good deal, and I hope I can,
and do. Huffing and snubbing, prey upon my feelings ; but,
I can bear them without complaint. They may tell in the
long run ; I may be hustled about, from post to pillar,

beyond my strength; nevertheless, I wish to avoid giving rise to words in the family.

The voice of Nature, however, cries aloud in behalf of Augustus George, my infant son. It is for him that I wish to utter a few plaintive household words. I am not at all angry; I am mild—but miserable.

I wish to know why, when my child, Augustus George, was expected in our circle, a provision of pins was made, as if the little stranger were a criminal who was to be put to the torture immediately on his arrival, instead of a holy babe? I wish to know why haste was made to stick those pins all over his innocent form, in every direction? I wish to be informed why light and air are excluded from Augustus George, like poisons? Why, I ask, is my unoffending infant so hedged into a basket-bedstead, with dimity and calico, with miniature sheets and blankets, that I can only hear him snuffle (and no wonder!) deep down under the pink hood of a little bathing-machine, and can never peruse even so much of his lineaments as his nose.

Was I expected to be the father of a French Roll, that the brushes of All Nations were laid in, to rasp Augustus George? Am I to be told that his sensitive skin was ever intended by Nature to have rashes brought out upon it, by the premature and incessant use of those formidable little instruments?

Is my son a Nutmeg, that he is to be grated on the stiff edges of sharp frills? Am I the parent of a Muslin boy, that his yielding surface is to be crimped and small plaited? Or is my child composed of Paper or of Linen, that impressions of the finer getting-up art, practised by the laundress, are to be printed off, all over his soft arms and legs, as I constantly observe them? The starch enters his soul; who can wonder that he cries?

Was Augustus George intended to have limbs, or to be born a Torso? I presume that limbs were the intention, as they are the usual practice. Then, why are my poor child's limbs fettered and tied up? Am I to be told that there is any analogy between Augustus George Meek and Jack Sheppard?

Analyse Castor Oil at any Institution of Chemistry that may be agreed upon, and inform me what resemblance, in taste, it bears to that natural provision which it is at once the pride and duty of Maria Jane to administer to Augustus George! Yet, I charge Mrs. Prodgit (aided and abetted by Mrs. Bigby) with systematically forcing Castor Oil on my innocent son, from the first hour of his birth. When that medicine, in its efficient action, causes internal disturbance to Augustus George, I charge Mrs. Prodgit (aided and abetted by Mrs. Bigby) with insanely and inconsistently administering opium to allay the storm she has raised! What is the meaning of this?

If the days of Egyptian Mummies are past, how dare Mrs. Prodgit require, for the use of my son, an amount of flannel and linen that would carpet my humble roof? Do I wonder that she requires it? No! This morning, within an hour, I beheld this agonising sight. I beheld my son—Augustus George—in Mrs. Prodgit's hands, and on Mrs. Prodgit's knee, being dressed. He was at the moment, comparatively speaking, in a state of nature; having nothing on, but an extremely short shirt, remarkably disproportionate to the length of his usual outer garments. Trailing from Mrs. Prodgit's lap, on the floor, was a long narrow roller or bandage—I should say of several yards in extent. In this, I saw Mrs. Prodgit tightly roll the body of my unoffending infant, turning him over and over, now presenting his unconscious face upwards, now the back of his bald head, until the unnatural feat was accomplished, and the bandage secured by a pin, which I have every reason to believe entered the body of my only child. In this tourniquet, he passes the present phase of his existence. Can I know it, and smile!

I fear I have been betrayed into expressing myself warmly, but I feel deeply. Not for myself; for Augustus George. I

74

dare not interfere. Will any one ? Will any publication ?
Any doctor ? Any parent ? Any body ? I do not complain that Mrs. Prodgit (aided and abetted by Mrs. Bigby)
entirely alienates Maria Jane's affections from me, and interposes an impassable barrier between us. I do not complain
of being made of no account. I do not want to be of any
account. But, Augustus George is a production of Nature
(I cannot think otherwise), and I claim that he should be
treated with some remote reference to Nature. In my opinion,
Mrs. Prodgit is, from first to last, a convention and a superstition. Are all the faculty afraid of Mrs. Prodgit ? If not,
why don't they take her in hand and improve her ?

P.S. Maria Jane's Mama boasts of her own knowledge
of the subject, and says she brought up seven children
besides Maria Jane. But how do *I* know that she might
not have brought them up much better ? Maria Jane herself
is far from strong, and is subject to headaches, and nervous
indigestion. Besides which, I learn from the statistical tables
that one child in five dies within the first year of its life ;
and one child in three, within the fifth. That don't look
as if we could never improve in these particulars, I think !

P.P.S. Augustus George is in convulsions.

LYING AWAKE

"My uncle lay with his eyes half closed, and his nightcap drawn almost down to his nose. His fancy was already wandering, and began to mingle up the present scene with the crater of Vesuvius, the French Opera, the Coliseum at Rome, Dolly's Chop-house in London, and all the farrago of noted places with which the brain of a traveller is crammed; in a word, he was just falling asleep."

Thus, that delightful writer, WASHINGTON IRVING, in his Tales of a Traveller. But, it happened to me the other night to be lying: not with my eyes half closed, but with my eyes wide open; not with my nightcap drawn almost down to my nose, for on sanitary principles I never wear a nightcap: but with my hair pitchforked and touzled all over the pillow; not just falling asleep by any means, but glaringly, persistently, and obstinately, broad awake. Perhaps, with no scientific intention or invention, I was illustrating the theory of the Duality of the Brain; perhaps one part of my brain, being wakeful, sat up to watch the other part which was sleepy. Be that as it may, something in me was as desirous to go to sleep as it possibly could be, but something else in me *would not* go to sleep, and was as obstinate as George the Third.

Thinking of George the Third—for I devote this paper to my train of thoughts as I lay awake: most people lying

awake sometimes, and having some interest in the subject—
put me in mind of BENJAMIN FRANKLIN, and so Benjamin
Franklin's paper on the art of procuring pleasant dreams,
which would seem necessarily to include the art of going to
sleep, came into my head. Now, as I often used to read
that paper when I was a very small boy, and as I recollect
everything I read then as perfectly as I forget everything
I read now, I quoted "Get out of bed, beat up and turn
your pillow, shake the bed-clothes well with at least twenty
shakes, then throw the bed open and leave it to cool; in
the meanwhile, continuing undrest, walk about your chamber.
When you begin to feel the cold air unpleasant, then return
to your bed, and you will soon fall asleep, and your sleep
will be sweet and pleasant." Not a bit of it! I performed
the whole ceremony, and if it were possible for me to be
more saucer-eyed than I was before, that was the only result
that came of it.

Except Niagara. The two quotations from Washington
Irving and Benjamin Franklin may have put it in my head
by an American association of ideas; but there I was, and
the Horse-shoe Fall was thundering and tumbling in my
eyes and ears, and the very rainbows that I left upon the
spray when I really did last look upon it, were beautiful to
see. The night-light being quite as plain, however, and
sleep seeming to be many thousand miles further off than
Niagara, I made up my mind to think a little about Sleep;
which I no sooner did than I whirled off in spite of myself
to Drury Lane Theatre, and there saw a great actor and
dear friend of mine (whom I had been thinking of in the
day) playing Macbeth, and heard him apostrophising "the
death of each day's life," as I have heard him many a time,
in the days that are gone.

But, Sleep. I *will* think about Sleep. I am determined
to think (this is the way I went on) about Sleep. I must
hold the word Sleep, tight and fast, or I shall be off at
a tangent in half a second. I feel myself unaccountably

straying, already, into Clare Market. Sleep. It would be curious, as illustrating the equality of sleep, to inquire how many of its phenomena are common to all classes, to all degrees of wealth and poverty, to every grade of education and ignorance. Here, for example, is her Majesty Queen Victoria in her palace, this present blessed night, and here is Winking Charley, a sturdy vagrant, in one of her Majesty's jails. Her Majesty has fallen, many thousands of times, from that same Tower, which *I* claim a right to tumble off now and then. So has Winking Charley. Her Majesty in her sleep has opened or prorogued Parliament, or has held a Drawing Room, attired in some very scanty dress, the deficiencies and improprieties of which have caused her great uneasiness. I, in my degree, have suffered unspeakable agitation of mind from taking the chair at a public dinner at the London Tavern in my night-clothes, which not all the courtesy of my kind friend and host Mr. BATHE could persuade me were quite adapted to the occasion. Winking Charley has been repeatedly tried in a worse condition. Her Majesty is no stranger to a vault or firmament, of a sort of floorcloth, with an indistinct pattern distantly resembling eyes, which occasionally obtrudes itself on her repose. Neither am I. Neither is Winking Charley. It is quite common to all three of us to skim along with airy strides a little above the ground; also to hold, with the deepest interest, dialogues with various people, all represented by ourselves; and to be at our wit's end to know what they are going to tell us; and to be indescribably astonished by the secrets they disclose. It is probable that we have all three committed murders and hidden bodies. It is pretty certain that we have all desperately wanted to cry out, and have had no voice; that we have all gone to the play and not been able to get in; that we have all dreamed much more of our youth than of our later lives; that—I have lost it! The thread's broken.

And up I go. I, lying here with the night-light before me, up I go, for no reason on earth that I can find out, and drawn by no links that are visible to me, up the Great Saint Bernard! I have lived in Switzerland, and rambled among the mountains; but, why I should go there now, and why up the Great Saint Bernard in preference to any other mountain, I have no idea. As I lie here broad awake, and with every sense so sharpened that I can distinctly hear distant noises inaudible to me at another time, I make that journey, as I really did, on the same summer day, with the same happy party—ah! two since dead, I grieve to think —and there is the same track, with the same black wooden arms to point the way, and there are the same storm-refuges here and there; and there is the same snow falling at the top, and there are the same frosty mists, and there is the same intensely cold convent with its ménagerie smell, and the same breed of dogs fast dying out, and the same breed of jolly young monks whom I mourn to know as humbugs, and the same convent parlour with its piano and the sitting round the fire, and the same supper, and the same lone night in a cell, and the same bright fresh morning when going out into the highly rarefied air was like a plunge into an icy bath. Now, see here what comes along; and why does this thing stalk into my mind on the top of a Swiss mountain!

It is a figure that I once saw, just after dark, chalked upon a door in a little back lane near a country church— my first church. How young a child I may have been at the time I don't know, but it horrified me so intensely—in connexion with the churchyard, I suppose, for it smokes a pipe, and has a big hat with each of its ears sticking out in a horizontal line under the brim, and is not in itself more oppressive than a mouth from ear to ear, a pair of goggle eyes, and hands like two bunches of carrots, five in each, can make it—that it is still vaguely alarming to me to recall (as I have often done before, lying awake) the running home, the looking behind, the horror, of its following me; though whether disconnected from the door, or door and all, I can't say, and perhaps never could. It lays a disagreeable train.

LYING AWAKE

I must resolve to think of something on the voluntary principle.

The balloon ascents of this last season. They will do to think about, while I lie awake, as well as anything else. I must hold them tight though, for I feel them sliding away, and in their stead are the Mannings, husband and wife, hanging on the top of Horsemonger Lane Jail. In connexion with which dismal spectacle, I recall this curious fantasy of the mind. That, having beheld that execution, and having left those two forms dangling on the top of the entrance gateway—the man's, a limp, loose suit of clothes as if the man had gone out of them; the woman's, a fine shape, so elaborately corseted and artfully dressed, that it was quite unchanged in its trim appearance as it slowly swung from side to side—I never could, by my uttermost efforts, for some weeks, present the outside of that prison to myself (which the terrible impression I had received continually obliged me to do) without presenting it with the two figures still hanging in the morning air. Until, strolling past the gloomy place one night, when the street was deserted and quiet, and actually seeing that the bodies were not there, my fancy was persuaded, as it were, to take them down and bury them within the precincts of the jail, where they have lain ever since.

The balloon ascents of last season. Let me reckon them up. There were the horse, the bull, the parachute, and the tumbler hanging on—chiefly by his toes, I believe—below the car. Very wrong, indeed, and decidedly to be stopped. But, in connexion with these and similar dangerous exhibitions, it strikes me that that portion of the public whom they entertain, is unjustly reproached. Their pleasure is in the difficulty overcome. They are a public of great faith, and are quite confident that the gentleman will not fall off the horse, or the lady off the bull or out of the parachute, and that the tumbler has a firm hold with his toes. They do not go to see the adventurer vanquished, but triumphant.

A DISAGREEABLE INTRUSION

There is no parallel in public combats between men and beasts, because nobody can answer for the particular beast —unless it were always the same beast, in which case it would be a mere stage-show, which the same public would go in the same state of mind to see, entirely believing in the brute being beforehand safely subdued by the man. That they are not accustomed to calculate hazards and dangers with any nicety, we may know from their rash exposure of themselves in overcrowded steamboats, and unsafe conveyances and places of all kinds. And I cannot help thinking that instead of railing, and attributing savage motives to a people naturally well disposed and humane, it is better to teach them, and lead them argumentatively and reasonably—for they are very reasonable, if you will discuss a matter with them—to more considerate and wise conclusions.

This is a disagreeable intrusion! Here is a man with his throat cut, dashing towards me as I lie awake! A recollection of an old story of a kinsman of mine, who, going home one foggy winter night to Hampstead, when London was much smaller and the road lonesome, suddenly encountered such a figure rushing past him, and presently two keepers from a madhouse in pursuit. A very unpleasant creature indeed, to come into my mind unbidden, as I lie awake.

—The balloon ascents of last season. I must return to the balloons. Why did the bleeding man start out of them? Never mind; if I inquire, he will be back again. The balloons. This particular public have inherently a great pleasure in the contemplation of physical difficulties overcome; mainly, as I take it, because the lives of a large majority of them are exceedingly monotonous and real, and further, are a struggle against continual difficulties, and further still, because anything in the form of accidental injury, or any kind of illness or disability is so very serious in their own sphere. I will explain this seeming paradox of mine. Take the case of a Christmas Pantomime. Surely nobody supposes that the young mother in the pit who falls into fits of

81

laughter when the baby is boiled or sat upon, would be at all diverted by such an occurrence off the stage. Nor is the decent workman in the gallery, who is transported beyond the ignorant present by the delight with which he sees a stout gentleman pushed out of a two pair of stairs window, to be slandered by the suspicion that he would be in the least entertained by such a spectacle in any street in London, Paris, or New York. It always appears to me that the secret of this enjoyment lies in the temporary superiority to the common hazards and mischances of life; in seeing casualties, attended when they really occur with bodily and mental suffering, tears, and poverty, happen through a very rough sort of poetry without the least harm being done to any one—the pretence of distress in a pantomime being so broadly humorous as to be no pretence at all. Much as in the comic fiction I can understand the mother with a very vulnerable baby at home, greatly relishing the invulnerable baby on the stage, so in the Cremorne reality I can understand the mason who is always liable to fall off a scaffold in his working jacket and to be carried to the hospital, having an infinite admiration of the radiant personage in spangles who goes into the clouds upon a bull, or upside down, and who, he takes it for granted—not reflecting upon the thing —has, by uncommon skill and dexterity, conquered such mischances as those to which he and his acquaintance are continually exposed.

I wish the Morgue in Paris would not come here as I lie awake, with its ghastly beds, and the swollen saturated clothes hanging up, and the water dripping, dripping all day long, upon that other swollen saturated something in the corner, like a heap of crushed over-ripe figs that I have seen in Italy! And this detestable Morgue comes back again at the head of a procession of forgotten ghost stories. This will never do. I must think of something else as I lie awake; or, like that sagacious animal in the United States who recognised the colonel who was such a dead shot,

A BETTER SYSTEM OF PUNISHMENT

I am a gone 'Coon. What shall I think of? The late brutal assaults. Very good subject. The late brutal assaults.

(Though whether, supposing I should see, here before me as I lie awake, the awful phantom described in one of those ghost stories, who, with a head-dress of shroud, was always seen looking in through a certain glass door at a certain dead hour—whether, in such a case it would be the least consolation to me to know on philosophical grounds that it was merely my imagination, is a question I can't help asking myself by the way.)

The late brutal assaults. I strongly question the expediency of advocating the revival of whipping for those crimes. It is a natural and generous impulse to be indignant at the perpetration of inconceivable brutality, but I doubt the whipping panacea gravely. Not in the least regard or pity for the criminal, whom I hold in far lower estimation than a mad wolf, but in consideration for the general tone and feeling, which is very much improved since the whipping times. It is bad for a people to be familiarised with such punishments. When the whip went out of Bridewell, and ceased to be flourished at the cart's tail and at the whipping-post, it began to fade out of madhouses, and workhouses, and schools and families, and to give place to a better system everywhere, than cruel driving. It would be hasty, because a few brutes may be inadequately punished, to revive, in any aspect, what, in so many aspects, society is hardly yet happily rid of. The whip is a very contagious kind of thing, and difficult to confine within one set of bounds. Utterly abolish punishment by fine—a barbarous device, quite as much out of date as wager by battle, but particularly connected in the vulgar mind with this class of offence—at least quadruple the term of imprisonment for aggravated assaults—and above all let us, in such cases, have no Pet Prisoning, vain glorifying, strong soup, and roasted meats, but hard work, and one unchanging and uncompromising dietary of bread and water, well or ill; and we shall do much better than by going down into the dark to grope for the whip among the rusty fragments of the rack, and the branding iron, and the chains and gibbet from the public roads, and the weights that pressed men to death in the cells of Newgate.

I had proceeded thus far, when I found I had been lying awake so long that the very dead began to wake too, and to crowd into my thoughts most sorrowfully. Therefore, I resolved to lie awake no more, but to get up and go out for a night walk—which resolution was an acceptable relief to me, as I dare say it may prove now to a great many more.

THE GHOST OF ART

I AM a bachelor, residing in rather a dreary set of chambers in the Temple. They are situated in a square court of high houses, which would be a complete well, but for the want of water and the absence of a bucket. I live at the top of the house, among the tiles and sparrows. Like the little man in the nursery-story, I live by myself, and all the bread and cheese I get—which is not much—I put upon a shelf. I need scarcely add, perhaps, that I am in love, and that the father of my charming Julia objects to our union.

I mention these little particulars as I might deliver a letter of introduction. The reader is now acquainted with me, and perhaps will condescend to listen to my narrative.

I am naturally of a dreamy turn of mind; and my abundant leisure—for I am called to the Bar—coupled with much lonely listening to the twittering of sparrows, and the pattering of rain, has encouraged that disposition. In my "top set" I hear the wind howl on a winter night, when the man on the ground floor believes it is perfectly still weather. The dim lamps with which our Honourable Society (supposed to be as yet unconscious of the new discovery called Gas) make the horrors of the staircase visible, deepen the gloom which generally settles on my soul when I go home at night.

I am in the Law, but not of it. I can't exactly make out what it means. I sit in Westminster Hall sometimes (in character) from ten to four; and when I go out of Court, I don't know whether I am standing on my wig or my boots.

It appears to me (I mention this in confidence) as if there were too much talk and too much law—as if some grains of truth were started overboard into a tempestuous sea of chaff.

All this may make me mystical. Still, I am confident that what I am going to describe myself as having seen and heard, I actually did see and hear.

It is necessary that I should observe that I have a great delight in pictures. I am no painter myself, but I have studied pictures and written about them. I have seen all the most famous pictures in the world; my education and reading have been sufficiently general to possess me before-hand with a knowledge of most of the subjects to which a Painter is likely to have recourse; and, although I might be in some doubt as to the rightful fashion of the scabbard of King Lear's sword, for instance, I think I should know King Lear tolerably well, if I happened to meet with him.

I go to all the Modern Exhibitions every season, and of course I revere the Royal Academy. I stand by its forty Academical articles almost as firmly as I stand by the thirty-nine Articles of the Church of England. I am convinced that in neither case could there be, by any rightful possibility, one article more or less.

It is now exactly three years—three years ago, this very month—since I went from Westminster to the Temple, one Thursday afternoon, in a cheap steamboat. The sky was black, when I imprudently walked on board. It began to thunder and lighten immediately afterwards, and the rain poured down in torrents. The deck seeming to smoke with the wet, I went below; but so many passengers were there, smoking too, that I came up again, and buttoning my pea-coat, and standing in the shadow of the paddle-box, stood as upright as I could, and made the best of it.

It was at this moment that I first beheld the terrible Being, who is the subject of my present recollections.

A TERRIBLE BEING

Standing against the funnel, apparently with the intention of drying himself by the heat as fast as he got wet, was a shabby man in threadbare black, and with his hands in his pockets, who fascinated me from the memorable instant when I caught his eye.

Where had I caught that eye before? Who was he? Why did I connect him, all at once, with the Vicar of Wakefield, Alfred the Great, Gil Blas, Charles the Second, Joseph and his Brethren, the Fairy Queen, Tom Jones, the Decameron of Boccaccio, Tam O'Shanter, the Marriage of the Doge of Venice with the Adriatic, and the Great Plague of London? Why, when he bent one leg, and placed one hand upon the back of the seat near him, did my mind associate him wildly with the words, "Number one hundred and forty-two, Portrait of a gentleman?" Could it be that I was going mad?

I looked at him again, and now I could have taken my affidavit that he belonged to the Vicar of Wakefield's family. Whether he was the Vicar, or Moses, or Mr. Burchill, or the Squire, or a conglomeration of all four, I knew not; but I was impelled to seize him by the throat, and charge him with being, in some fell way, connected with the Primrose blood. He looked up at the rain, and then—oh Heaven!— he became Saint John. He folded his arms, resigning himself to the weather, and I was frantically inclined to address him as the Spectator, and firmly demand to know what he had done with Sir Roger de Coverley.

The frightful suspicion that I was becoming deranged, returned upon me with redoubled force. Meantime, this awful stranger, inexplicably linked to my distress, stood drying himself at the funnel; and ever, as the steam rose from his clothes, diffusing a mist around him, I saw through the ghostly medium all the people I have mentioned, and a score more, sacred and profane.

I am conscious of a dreadful inclination that stole upon me, as it thundered and lightened, to grapple with this man, or demon, and plunge him over the side. But, I constrained myself—I know not how—to speak to him, and in a pause of the storm, I crossed the deck, and said:

"What are you?"

He replied, hoarsely, "A Model."

"A what?" said I.

"A Model," he replied. "I sets to the profession for a bob a-hour." (All through this narrative I give his own words, which are indelibly imprinted on my memory.)

The relief which this disclosure gave me, the exquisite delight of the restoration of my confidence in my own sanity, I cannot describe. I should have fallen on his neck, but for the consciousness of being observed by the man at the wheel.

"You then," said I, shaking him so warmly by the hand, that I wrung the rain out of his coat-cuff, "are the gentleman whom I have so frequently contemplated, in connection with a high-backed chair with a red cushion, and a table with twisted legs."

"I am that Model," he rejoined moodily, "and I wish I was anything else."

"Say not so," I returned. "I have seen you in the society of many beautiful young women;" as in truth I had, and always (I now remember) in the act of making the most of his legs.

"No doubt," said he. "And you've seen me along with warses of flowers, and any number of table-kivers, and antique cabinets, and warious gammon."

"Sir?" said I.

"And warious gammon," he repeated, in a louder voice. "You might have seen me in armour, too, if you had looked sharp. Blessed if I ha'n't stood in half the suits of armour as ever came out of Pratt's shop: and sat, for weeks together, a-eating nothing, out of half the gold and silver dishes as has ever been lent for the purpose out of Storrses, and Mortimerses, or Garrardses, and Davenportseseses,"

Excited, as it appeared, by a sense of injury, I thought he would never have found an end for the last word. But, at length it rolled sullenly away with the thunder.

"Pardon me," said I, "you are a well-favoured, well-made man, and yet—forgive me—I find, on examining my mind, that I associate you with—that my recollection indistinctly makes you, in short—excuse me—a kind of powerful monster."

"It would be a wonder if it didn't," he said. "Do you know what my points are?"

"No," said I.

"My throat and my legs," said he. "When I don't set for a head, I mostly sets for a throat and a pair of legs. Now, granted you was a painter, and was to work at my throat for a week together, I suppose you'd see a lot of lumps and bumps there, that would never be there at all, if you looked at me, complete, instead of only my throat. Wouldn't you?"

"Probably," said I, surveying him.

"Why, it stands to reason," said the Model. "Work another week at my legs, and it'll be the same thing. You'll make 'em out as knotty and as knobby, at last, as if they was the trunks of two old trees. Then, take and stick my legs and throat on to another man's body, and you'll make a reg'lar monster. And that's the way the public gets their reg'lar monsters, every first Monday in May, when the Royal Academy Exhibition opens."

"You are a critic," said I, with an air of deference.

"I'm in an uncommon ill humour, if that's it," rejoined the Model, with great indignation. "As if it warn't bad enough for a bob a-hour, for a man to be mixing himself up with that there jolly old furniter that one 'ud think the public know'd the wery nails in by this time—or to be putting on greasy old 'ats and cloaks, and playing tambourines in the Bay o' Naples, with Wesuvius a smokin' according to pattern in the background, and the wines a bearing wonderful in the middle distance—or to be unpolitely kicking up his legs among a lot o' gals, with no reason whatever in his mind but to show 'em—as if this warn't bad enough, I'm to go and be thrown out of employment too!"

"Surely no!" said I.

"Surely yes," said the indignant Model. "BUT I'LL GROW ONE."

The gloomy and threatening manner in which he muttered the last words, can never be effaced from my remembrance. My blood ran cold.

I asked of myself, what was it that this desperate Being was resolved to grow. My breast made no response.

I ventured to implore him to explain his meaning. With a scornful laugh, he uttered this dark prophecy:

"I'LL GROW ONE. AND, MARK MY WORDS, IT SHALL HAUNT YOU!"

We parted in the storm, after I had forced half-a-crown on his acceptance, with a trembling hand. I conclude that something supernatural happened to the steamboat, as it bore his reeking figure down the river; but it never got into the papers.

Two years elapsed, during which I followed my profession without any vicissitudes; never holding so much as a motion, of course. At the expiration of that period, I found myself making my way home to the Temple, one night, in precisely such another storm of thunder and lightning as that by which I had been overtaken on board the steamboat—except that this storm, bursting over the town at midnight, was rendered much more awful by the darkness and the hour.

As I turned into my court, I really thought a thunderbolt would fall, and plough the pavement up. Every brick and stone in the place seemed to have an echo of its own for the thunder. The waterspouts were overcharged, and the rain came tearing down from the house-tops as if they had been mountain-tops.

Mrs. Parkins, my laundress—wife of Parkins the porter, then newly dead of a dropsy—had particular instructions to place a bedroom candle and a match under the staircase lamp on my landing, in order that I might light my candle there, whenever I came home. Mrs. Parkins invariably disregarding all instructions, they were never there. Thus it happened that on this occasion I groped my way into my sitting-room to find the candle, and came out to light it.

What were my emotions when, underneath the staircase lamp, shining with wet as if he had never been dry since our last meeting, stood the mysterious Being whom I had encountered on the steamboat in a thunderstorm, two years before! His prediction rushed upon my mind, and I turned faint.

"I said I'd do it," he observed, in a hollow voice, "and I have done it. May I come in?"

"Misguided creature, what have you done?" I returned.

"I'll let you know," was his reply, "if you'll let me in."

Could it be murder that he had done? And had he been so successful that he wanted to do it again, at my expense?

I hesitated.

"May I come in?" said he.

I inclined my head, with as much presence of mind as I could command, and he followed me into my chambers. There, I saw that the lower part of his face was tied up, in what is commonly called a Belcher handkerchief. He slowly removed this bandage, and exposed to view a long dark beard, curling over his upper lip, twisting about the corners of his mouth, and hanging down upon his breast.

"What is this?" I exclaimed involuntarily, "and what have you become?"

"I am the Ghost of Art!" said he.

The effect of these words, slowly uttered in the thunderstorm at midnight, was appalling in the last degree. More dead than alive, I surveyed him in silence.

"The German taste came up," said he, "and threw me out of bread. I am ready for the taste now."

He made his beard a little jagged with his hands, folded his arms, and said,

"Severity!"

I shuddered. It was so severe.

He made his beard flowing on his breast, and, leaning both hands on the staff of a carpet-broom which Mrs. Parkins had left among my books, said:

"Benevolence."

I stood transfixed. The change of sentiment was entirely in the beard. The man might have left his face alone, or had no face. The beard did everything.

He lay down, on his back, on my table, and with that action of his head threw up his beard at the chin.

"That's death!" said he.

He got off my table and, looking up at the ceiling, cocked his beard a little awry; at the same time making it stick out before him.

"Adoration, or a vow of vengeance," he observed.

He turned his profile to me, making his upper lip very bulky with the upper part of his beard.

"Romantic character," said he.

He looked sideways out of his beard, as if it were an ivy-bush. "Jealousy," said he. He gave it an ingenious twist in the air, and informed me that he was carousing. He made it shaggy with his fingers—and it was Despair; lank—and it was avarice: tossed it all kinds of ways—and it was rage. The beard did everything.

"I am the Ghost of Art," said he. "Two bob a-day now, and more when it's longer! Hair's the true expression. There is no other. I SAID I'D GROW IT, AND I'VE GROWN IT, AND IT SHALL HAUNT YOU!"

He may have tumbled down-stairs in the dark, but he never walked down or ran down. I looked over the banisters, and I was alone with the thunder.

Need I add more of my terrific fate? IT HAS haunted me ever since. It glares upon me from the walls of the Royal

Academy, (except when MACLISE subdues it to his genius,) it fills my soul with terror at the British Institution, it lures young artists on to their destruction. Go where I will, the Ghost of Art, eternally working the passions in hair, and expressing everything by beard, pursues me. The prediction is accomplished, and the victim has no rest.

OUT OF TOWN

Sitting, on a bright September morning, among my books and papers at my open window on the cliff overhanging the sea-beach, I have the sky and ocean framed before me like a beautiful picture. A beautiful picture, but with such movement in it, such changes of light upon the sails of ships and wake of steamboats, such dazzling gleams of silver far out at sea, such fresh touches on the crisp wave-tops as they break and roll towards me—a picture with such music in the billowy rush upon the shingle, the blowing of morning wind through the corn-sheaves where the farmers' waggons are busy, the singing of the larks, and the distant voices of children at play—such charms of sight and sound as all the Galleries on earth can but poorly suggest.

So dreamy is the murmur of the sea below my window, that I may have been here, for anything I know, one hundred years. Not that I have grown old, for, daily on the neighbouring downs and grassy hill-sides, I find that I can still in reason walk any distance, jump over anything, and climb up anywhere; but, that the sound of the ocean seems to have become so customary to my musings, and other realities seem so to have gone aboard ship and floated away over the horizon, that, for aught I will undertake to the contrary, I am the enchanted son of the King my father, shut up in a tower on the sea-shore, for protection against an old she-goblin who insisted on being my godmother, and who foresaw

at the font—wonderful creature!—that I should get into a
scrape before I was twenty-one. I remember to have been in
a City (my Royal parent's dominions, I suppose), and apparently not long ago either, that was in the dreariest condition. The principal inhabitants had all been changed into
old newspapers, and in that form were preserving their
window-blinds from dust, and wrapping all their smaller
household gods in curl-papers. I walked through gloomy
streets where every house was shut up and newspapered, and
where my solitary footsteps echoed on the deserted pavements.
In the public rides there were no carriages, no horses, no
animated existence, but a few sleepy policemen, and a few
adventurous boys taking advantage of the devastation to
swarm up the lamp-posts. In the Westward streets there was
no traffic; in the Westward shops, no business. The water-
patterns which the 'Prentices had trickled out on the pavements
early in the morning, remained uneffaced by human feet.
At the corners of mews, Cochin-China fowls stalked gaunt
and savage; nobody being left in the deserted city (as it
appeared to me), to feed them. Public Houses, where
splendid footmen swinging their legs over gorgeous hammer-
cloths beside wigged coachmen were wont to regale, were
silent, and the unused pewter pots shone, too bright for
business, on the shelves. I beheld a Punch's Show leaning
against a wall near Park Lane, as if it had fainted. It was
deserted, and there were none to heed its desolation. In
Belgrave Square I met the last man—an ostler—sitting on a
post in a ragged red waistcoat, eating straw, and mildewing
away.

If I recollect the name of the little town, on whose shore
this sea is murmuring—but I am not just now, as I have
premised, to be relied upon for anything—it is Pavilionstone.
Within a quarter of a century, it was a little fishing town,
and they do say, that the time was, when it was a little
smuggling town. I have heard that it was rather famous in
the hollands and brandy way, and that coevally with that

reputation the lamplighter's was considered a bad life at the Assurance Offices. It was observed that if he were not particular about lighting up, he lived in peace; but that, if he made the best of the oil-lamps in the steep and narrow streets, he usually fell over the cliff at an early age. Now, gas and electricity run to the very water's edge, and the South-Eastern Railway Company screech at us in the dead of night.

But, the old little fishing and smuggling town remains, and is so tempting a place for the latter purpose, that I think of going out some night next week, in a fur cap and a pair of petticoat trousers, and running an empty tub, as a kind of archæological pursuit. Let nobody with corns come to Pavilionstone, for there are breakneck flights of ragged steps, connecting the principal streets by back-ways, which will cripple that visitor in half an hour. These are the ways by which, when I run that tub, I shall escape. I shall make a Thermopylæ of the corner of one of them, defend it with my cutlass against the coast-guard until my brave companions have sheered off, then dive into the darkness, and regain my Susan's arms. In connection with these breakneck steps I observe some wooden cottages, with tumble-down out-houses, and back-yards three feet square, adorned with garlands of dried fish, in one of which (though the General Board of Health might object) my Susan dwells.

The South-Eastern Company have brought Pavilionstone into such vogue, with their tidal trains and splendid steam-packets, that a new Pavilionstone is rising up. I am, myself, of New Pavilionstone. We are a little mortary and limey at present, but we are getting on capitally. Indeed, we were getting on so fast, at one time, that we rather overdid it, and built a street of shops, the business of which may be expected to arrive in about ten years. We are sensibly laid out in general; and with a little care and pains (by no means wanting, so far), shall become a very pretty place. We ought to be, for our situation is delightful, our air is delicious, and our breezy hills and downs, carpeted with wild thyme, and decorated with millions of wild flowers, are, on the faith of a pedestrian, perfect. In New Pavilionstone we are a little too much addicted to small windows with more bricks in them than glass, and we are not over-fanciful in the way of decorative architecture, and we get unexpected sea-views through cracks in the street doors; on the whole, however, we are very snug and comfortable, and well accommodated. But the Home Secretary (if there be such an officer) cannot too soon shut up the burial-ground of the old parish church. It is in the midst of us, and Pavilionstone will get no good of it, if it be too long left alone.

The lion of Pavilionstone is its Great Hotel. A dozen years ago, going over to Paris by South-Eastern Tidal Steamer, you used to be dropped upon the platform of the main line Pavilionstone Station (not a junction then), at eleven o'clock on a dark winter's night, in a roaring wind; and in the howling wilderness outside the station, was a short omnibus which brought you up by the forehead the instant you got in at the door; and nobody cared about you, and you were alone in the world. You bumped over infinite chalk, until you were turned out at a strange building which had just left off being a barn without having quite begun to be a house, where nobody expected your coming, or knew what to do with you when you were come, and where you were usually blown about, until you happened to be blown against the cold beef, and finally into bed. At five in the morning you were blown out of bed, and after a dreary breakfast, with crumpled company, in the midst of confusion, were hustled on board a steamboat and lay wretched on deck until you saw France lunging and surging at you with great vehemence over the bowsprit.

Now, you come down to Pavilionstone in a free and easy manner, an irresponsible agent, made over in trust to the South-Eastern Company, until you get out of the railway-carriage at high-water mark. If you are crossing by the

boat at once, you have nothing to do but walk on board
and be happy there if you can—I can't. If you are going
to our Great Pavilionstone Hotel, the sprightliest porters
under the sun, whose cheerful looks are a pleasant welcome,
shoulder your luggage, drive it off in vans, bowl it away in
trucks, and enjoy themselves in playing athletic games with
it. If you are for public life at our great Pavilionstone
Hotel, you walk into that establishment as if it were your
club; and find ready for you, your news-room, dining-room,
smoking-room, billiard-room, music-room, public breakfast,
public dinner twice a-day (one plain, one gorgeous), hot
baths and cold baths. If you want to be bored, there are
plenty of bores always ready for you, and from Saturday to
Monday in particular, you can be bored (if you like it)
through and through. Should you want to be private at our
Great Pavilionstone Hotel, say but the word, look at the
list of charges, choose your floor, name your figure—there
you are, established in your castle, by the day, week, month,
or year, innocent of all comers or goers, unless you have my
fancy for walking early in the morning down the groves of
boots and shoes, which so regularly flourish at all the chamber-
doors before breakfast, that it seems to me as if nobody ever
got up or took them in. Are you going across the Alps,
and would you like to air your Italian at our Great Pavilionstone Hotel? Talk to the Manager—always conversational,
accomplished, and polite. Do you want to be aided, abetted,
comforted, or advised, at our Great Pavilionstone Hotel? Send
for the good landlord, and he is your friend. Should you,
or any one belonging to you, ever be taken ill at our Great
Pavilionstone Hotel, you will not soon forget him or his kind
wife. And when you pay your bill at our Great Pavilionstone Hotel, you will not be put out of humour by anything
you find in it.

A thoroughly good inn, in the days of coaching and posting, was a noble place. But no such inn would have been
equal to the reception of four or five hundred people, all of

them wet through, and half of them dead sick, every day in the year. This is where we shine, in our Pavilionstone Hotel. Again—who, coming and going, pitching and tossing, boating and training, hurrying in, and flying out, could ever have calculated the fees to be paid at an old-fashioned house? In our Pavilionstone Hotel vocabulary, there is no such word as fee. Everything is done for you; every service is provided at a fixed and reasonable charge; all the prices are hung up in all the rooms; and you can make out your own bill beforehand, as well as the book-keeper.

In the case of your being a pictorial artist, desirous of studying at small expense the physiognomies and beards of different nations, come, on receipt of this, to Pavilionstone. You shall find all the nations of the earth, and all the styles of shaving and not shaving, hair cutting and hair letting alone, for ever flowing through our hotel. Couriers you shall see by hundreds; fat leathern bags for five-franc pieces, closing with violent snaps, like discharges of fire-arms, by thousands; more luggage in a morning than, fifty years ago, all Europe saw in a week. Looking at trains, steamboats, sick travellers, and luggage, is our great Pavilionstone recreation. We are not strong in other public amusements. We have a Literary and Scientific Institution, and we have a Working Men's Institution—may it hold many gipsy holidays in summer fields, with the kettle boiling, the band of music playing, and the people dancing; and may I be on the hillside, looking on with pleasure at a wholesome sight too rare in England!—and we have two or three churches, and more chapels than I have yet added up. But public amusements are scarce with us. If a poor theatrical manager comes with his company to give us, in a loft, Mary Bax, or the Murder on the Sand Hills, we don't care much for him—starve him out, in fact. We take more kindly to wax-work, especially if it moves; in which case it keeps much clearer of the second commandment than when it is still. Cooke's Circus (Mr. Cooke is my friend, and always leaves a good name behind him) gives us only a night in passing through. Nor does the travelling menagerie think us worth a longer visit. It gave us a look-in the other day, bringing with it the residentiary van with the stained glass windows, which Her Majesty kept ready-made at Windsor Castle, until she found a suitable opportunity of submitting it for the proprietor's acceptance. I brought away five wonderments from this exhibition. I have wondered ever since, Whether the beasts ever do get used to those small places of confinement; Whether the monkeys have that very horrible flavour in their free state; Whether wild animals have a natural ear for time and tune, and therefore every four-footed creature began to howl in despair when the band began to play; What the giraffe does with his neck when his cart is shut up; and, Whether the elephant feels ashamed of himself when he is brought out of his den to stand on his head in the presence of the whole Collection.

We are a tidal harbour at Pavilionstone, as indeed I have implied already in my mention of tidal trains. At low water, we are a heap of mud, with an empty channel in it where a couple of men in big boots always shovel and scoop: with what exact object, I am unable to say. At that time, all the stranded fishing-boats turn over on their sides, as if they were dead marine monsters; the colliers and other shipping stick disconsolate in the mud; the steamers look as if their white chimneys would never smoke more, and their red paddles never turn again; the green sea-slime and weed upon the rough stones at the entrance, seem records of obsolete high tides never more to flow; the flagstaff-halyards droop; the very little wooden lighthouse shrinks in the idle glare of the sun. And here I may observe of the very little wooden lighthouse, that when it is lighted at night,—red and green,—it looks so like a medical man's, that several distracted husbands have at various times been found, on occasions of premature domestic anxiety, going round and round it, trying to find the Nightbell.

But, the moment the tide begins to make, the Pavilion-stone Harbour begins to revive. It feels the breeze of the rising water before the water comes, and begins to flutter and stir. When the little shallow waves creep in, barely overlapping one another, the vanes at the mastheads wake, and become agitated. As the tide rises, the fishing-boats get into good spirits and dance, the flagstaff hoists a bright red flag, the steamboat smokes, cranes creak, horses and carriages dangle in the air, stray passengers and luggage appear. Now, the shipping is afloat, and comes up buoy-antly, to look at the wharf. Now, the carts that have come down for coals, load away as hard as they can load. Now, the steamer smokes immensely, and occasionally blows at the paddle-boxes like a vaporous whale—greatly disturbing nervous loungers. Now, both the tide and the breeze have risen, and you are holding your hat on (if you want to see how the ladies hold *their* hats on, with a stay, passing over the broad brim and down the nose, come to Pavilionstone). Now, everything in the harbour splashes, dashes, and bobs. Now, the Down Tidal Train is telegraphed, and you know (without knowing how you know), that two hundred and eighty-seven people are coming. Now, the fishing-boats that have been out, sail in at the top of the tide. Now, the bell goes, and the locomotive hisses and shrieks, and the train comes gliding in, and the two hundred and eighty-seven come scuffling out. Now, there is not only a tide of water, but a tide of people, and a tide of luggage—all tumbling and flowing and bouncing about together. Now, after infinite bustle, the steamer steams out, and we (on the Pier) are all delighted when she rolls as if she would roll her funnel out, and are all disappointed when she don't. Now, the other steamer is coming in, and the Custom House prepares, and the wharf-labourers assemble, and the hawsers are made ready, and the Hotel Porters come rattling down with van and truck, eager to begin more Olympic games with more luggage. And this is the way in which we go on, down at

Pavilionstone, every tide. And, if you want to live a life of luggage, or to see it lived, or to breathe sweet air which will send you to sleep at a moment's notice at any period of the day or night, or to disport yourself upon or in the sea, or to scamper about Kent, or to come out of town for the enjoyment of all or any of these pleasures, come to Pavilionstone.

OUT OF THE SEASON

It fell to my lot, this last bleak Spring, to find myself in a watering-place out of the Season. A vicious north-east squall blew me into it from foreign parts, and I tarried in it alone for three days, resolved to be exceedingly busy.

On the first day, I began business by looking for two hours at the sea, and staring the Foreign Militia out of countenance. Having disposed of these important engagements, I sat down at one of the two windows of my room, intent on doing something desperate in the way of literary composition, and writing a chapter of unheard-of excellence—with which the present essay has no connexion.

It is a remarkable quality in a wa ering-place out of the season, that everything in it, will and must be looked at. I had no previous suspicion of this fatal truth; but, the moment I sat down to write, I began to perceive it. I had scarcely fallen into my most promising attitude, and dipped my pen in the ink, when I found the clock upon the pier—a red-faced clock with a white rim—importuning me in a highly vexatious manner to consult my watch, and see how I was off for Greenwich time. Having no intention of making a voyage or taking an observation, I had not the least need of Greenwich time, and could have put up with watering-place time as a sufficiently accurate article. The pier-clock, however, persisting, I felt it necessary to lay down my pen, compare my watch with him, and fall into a grave solicitude about half-seconds. I had taken up my pen again, and was about to commence that valuable chapter, when a Custom-house cutter under the window requested that I would hold a naval review of her, immediately.

It was impossible, under the circumstances, for any mental resolution, merely human, to dismiss the Custom-house cutter, because the shadow of her topmast fell upon my paper, and the vane played on the masterly blank chapter. I was therefore under the necessity of going to the other window ; sitting astride of the chair there, like Napoleon bivouacking in the print ; and inspecting the cutter as she lay, all that day, in the way of my chapter, O! She was rigged to carry a quantity of canvas, but her hull was so very small that four giants aboard of her (three men and a boy) who were vigilantly scraping at her, all together, inspired me with a terror lest they should scrape her away. A fifth giant, who appeared to consider himself "below"—as indeed he was, from the waist downwards—meditated, in such close proximity with the little gusty chimney-pipe, that he seemed to be smoking it. Several boys looked on from the wharf, and, when the gigantic attention appeared to be fully occupied, one or other of these would furtively swing himself in mid-air over the Custom-house cutter, by means of a line pendant from her rigging, like a young spirit of the storm. Presently, a sixth hand brought down two little water-casks ; presently afterwards, a truck came, and delivered a hamper. I was now under an obligation to consider that the cutter was going on a cruise, and to wonder where she was going, and when she was going, and why she was going, and at what date she might be expected back, and who commanded her ? With these pressing questions I was fully occupied when the Packet, making ready to go across, and blowing off her spare steam, roared, " Look at me ! "

It became a positive duty to look at the Packet preparing to go across ; aboard of which, the people newly come down by the railroad were hurrying in a great fluster. The crew had got their tarry overalls on—and one knew what *that* meant—not to mention the white basins, ranged in neat little piles of a dozen each, behind the door of the after-cabin. One lady as I looked, one resigning and far-seeing woman, took her basin from the store of crockery, as she might have taken a refreshment-ticket, laid herself down on deck with that utensil at her ear, muffled her feet in one shawl, solemnly covered her countenance after the antique manner with another, and on the completion of these preparations appeared by the strength of her volition to become insensible. The mail-bags (O that I myself had the sea-legs of a mail-bag!) were tumbled aboard; the Packet left off roaring, warped out, and made at the white line upon the bar. One dip, one roll, one break of the sea over her bows, and Moore's Almanack or the sage Raphael could not have told me more of the state of things aboard, than I knew.

The famous chapter was all but begun now, and would have been quite begun, but for the wind. It was blowing stiffly from the east, and it rumbled in the chimney and shook the house. That was not much; but, looking out into the wind's grey eye for inspiration, I laid down my pen again to make the remark to myself, how emphatically everything by the sea declares that it has a great concern in the state of the wind. The trees blown all one way; the defences of the harbour reared highest and strongest against the raging point; the shingle flung up on the beach from the same direction; the number of arrows pointed at the common enemy; the sea tumbling in and rushing towards them as if it were inflamed by the sight. This put it in my head that I really ought to go out and take a walk in the wind; so, I gave up the magnificent chapter for that day, entirely persuading myself that I was under a moral obligation to have a blow.

I had a good one, and that on the high road—the very high

road—on the top of the cliffs, where I met the stage-coach with all the outsides holding their hats on and themselves too, and overtook a flock of sheep with the wool about their necks blown into such great ruffs that they looked like fleecy owls. The wind played upon the lighthouse as if it were a great whistle, the spray was driven over the sea in a cloud of haze, the ships rolled and pitched heavily, and at intervals long slants and flaws of light made mountain-steeps of communication between the ocean and the sky. A walk of ten miles brought me to a seaside town without a cliff, which, like the town I had come from, was out of the season too. Half of the houses were shut up; half of the other half were to let; the town might have done as much business as it was doing then, if it had been at the bottom of the sea. Nobody seemed to flourish save the attorney; his clerk's pen was going in the bow-window of his wooden house; his brass door-plate alone was free from salt, and had been polished up that morning. On the beach, among the rough luggers and capstans, groups of storm-beaten boatmen, like a sort of marine monsters, watched under the lee of those objects, or stood leaning forward against the wind, looking out through battered spy-glasses. The parlour bell in the Admiral Benbow had grown so flat with being out of the season, that neither could I hear it ring when I pulled the handle for lunch, nor could the young woman in black stockings and strong shoes, who acted as waiter out of the season, until it had been tinkled three times.

Admiral Benbow's cheese was out of the season, but his home-made bread was good, and his beer was perfect. Deluded by some earlier spring day which had been warm and sunny, the Admiral had cleared the firing out of his parlour stove, and had put some flower-pots in—which was amiable and hopeful in the Admiral, but not judicious: the room being, at that present visiting, transcendantly cold. I therefore took the liberty of peeping out across a little stone passage into the Admiral's kitchen, and, seeing a high settle with its back towards me drawn out in front of the Admiral's kitchen fire, I strolled in, bread and cheese in hand, munching and looking about. One landsman and two boatmen were seated on the settle, smoking pipes and drinking beer out of thick pint crockery mugs—mugs peculiar to such places, with parti-coloured rings round them, and ornaments between the rings like frayed-out roots. The landsman was relating his experience, as yet only three nights old, of a fearful running-down case in the Channel, and therein presented to my imagination a sound of music that it will not soon forget.

"At that identical moment of time," said he (he was a prosy man by nature, who rose with his subject), "the night being light and calm, but with a grey mist upon the water that didn't seem to spread for more than two or three mile, I was walking up and down the wooden causeway next the pier, off where it happened, along with a friend of mine, which his name is Mr. Clocker. Mr. Clocker is a grocer over yonder." (From the direction in which he pointed the bowl of his pipe, I might have judged Mr. Clocker to be a merman, established in the grocery trade in five-and-twenty fathoms of water.) "We were smoking our pipes, and walking up and down the causeway, talking of one thing and talking of another. We were quite alone there, except that a few hovellers" (the Kentish name for 'long-shore boatmen like his companions) "were hanging about their lugs, waiting while the tide made, as hovellers will." (One of the two boatmen, thoughtfully regarding me, shut up one eye; this I understood to mean: first, that he took me into the conversation: secondly, that he confirmed the proposition: thirdly, that he announced himself as a hoveller.) "All of a sudden Mr. Clocker and me stood rooted to the spot, by hearing a sound come through the stillness, right over the sea, *like a great sorrowful flute or Æolian harp*. We didn't in the least know what it was, and judge of our surprise when we saw the hovellers, to a man, leap into the boats and tear about to hoist sail and get off, as if they had every one of em gone, in a moment, raving mad! But *they* knew it was the cry of distress from the sinking emigrant ship."

When I got back to my watering-place out of the season, and had done my twenty miles in good style, I found that the celebrated Black Mesmerist intended favouring the public that evening in the Hall of the Muses, which he had engaged for the purpose. After a good dinner, seated by the fire in an easy chair, I began to waver in a design I had formed of waiting on the Black Mesmerist, and to incline towards the expediency of remaining where I was. Indeed a point of gallantry was involved in my doing so, inasmuch as I had not left France alone, but had come from the prisons of St. Pélagie with my distinguished and unfortunate friend Madame Roland (in two volumes which I bought for two francs each, at the book-stall in the Place de la Concorde, Paris, at the corner of the Rue Royale). Deciding to pass the evening tête-à-tête with Madame Roland, I derived, as I always do, great pleasure from that spiritual woman's society, and the charms of her brave soul and engaging conversation. I must confess that if she had only some more faults, only a few more passionate failings of any kind, I might love her better; but I am content to believe that the deficiency is in me, and not in her. We spent some sadly interesting hours together on this occasion, and she told me again of her cruel discharge from the Abbaye, and of her being re-arrested before her free feet had sprung lightly up half-a-dozen steps of her own staircase, and carried off to the prison which she only left for the guillotine.

Madame Roland and I took leave of one another before midnight, and I went to bed full of vast intentions for next day, in connexion with the unparalleled chapter. To hear the foreign mail-steamers coming in at dawn of day, and to know that I was not aboard or obliged to get up, was very comfortable; so, I rose for the chapter in great force.

I had advanced so far as to sit down at my window again

on my second morning, and to write the first half-line of the chapter and strike it out, not liking it, when my conscience reproached me with not having surveyed the watering-place out of the season, after all, yesterday, but with having gone straight out of it at the rate of four miles and a half an hour. Obviously the best amends that I could make for this remissness was to go and look at it without another moment's delay. So—altogether as a matter of duty—I gave up the magnificent chapter for another day, and sauntered out with my hands in my pockets.

All the houses and lodgings ever let to visitors, were to let that morning. It seemed to have snowed bills with To Let upon them. This put me upon thinking what the owners of all those apartments did, out of the season; how they employed their time, and occupied their minds. They could not be always going to the Methodist chapels, of which I passed one every other minute. They must have some other recreation. Whether they pretended to take one another's lodgings, and opened one another's tea-caddies in fun? Whether they cut slices off their own beef and mutton, and made believe that it belonged to somebody else? Whether they played little dramas of life, as children do, and said, "I ought to come and look at your apartments, and you ought to ask two guineas a-week too much, and then I ought to say I must have the rest of the day to think of it, and then you ought to say that another lady and gentleman with no children in family had made an offer very close to your own terms, and you had passed your word to give them a positive answer in half an hour, and indeed were just going to take the bill down when you heard the knock, and then I ought to take them, you know?" Twenty such speculations engaged my thoughts. Then, after passing, still clinging to the walls, defaced rags of the bills of last year's Circus, I came to a back field near a timber-yard where the Circus itself had been, and where there was yet a sort of monkish tonsure on the grass, indicating the spot where the young lady had gone round upon her pet steed Firefly in her daring flight. Turning into the town again, I came among the shops, and they were emphatically out of the season. The chemist had no boxes of ginger-beer powders, no beautifying sea-side soaps and washes, no attractive scents; nothing but his great goggle-eyed red bottles, looking as if the winds of winter and the drift of the salt-sea had inflamed them. The grocers' hot pickles, Harvey's Sauce, Doctor Kitchener's Zest, Anchovy Paste, Dundee Marmalade, and the whole stock of luxurious helps to appetite, were hybernating somewhere underground. The china-shop had no trifles from anywhere. The Bazaar had given in altogether, and presented a notice on the shutters that this establishment would re-open at Whitsuntide, and that the proprietor in the meantime might be heard of at Wild Lodge, East Cliff. At the Sea-bathing Establishment, a row of neat little wooden houses seven or eight feet high, I *saw* the proprietor in bed in the shower-bath. As to the bathing-machines, they were (how they got there, is not for me to say) at the top of a hill at least a mile and a half off. The library, which I had never seen otherwise than wide open, was tight shut; and two peevish bald old gentlemen seemed to be hermetically sealed up inside, eternally reading the paper. That wonderful mystery, the music-shop, carried it off as usual (except that it had more cabinet pianos in stock), as if season or no season were all one to it. It made the same prodigious display of bright brazen wind-instruments, horribly twisted, worth, as I should conceive, some thousands of pounds, and which it is utterly impossible that anybody in any season can ever play or want to play. It had five triangles in the window, six pairs of castanets, and three harps; likewise every polka with a coloured frontispiece that ever was published; from the original one where a smooth male and female Pole of high rank are coming at the observer with their arms a-kimbo, to the Ratcatcher's Daughter. Astonishing establishment, amazing enigma! Three other shops were pretty much out of the season, what they were used to be in it. First, the shop where they sell the sailors' watches, which had still the old collection of enormous timekeepers, apparently designed to break a fall from the masthead : with places to wind them up, like fire-plugs. Secondly, the shop where they sell the sailors' clothing, which displayed the old sou'-westers, and the old oily suits, and the old pea-jackets, and the old one sea-chest, with its handles like a pair of rope ear-rings. Thirdly, the unchangeable shop for the sale of literature that has been left behind. Here, Dr. Faustus was still going down to very red and yellow perdition, under the superintendence of three green personages of a scaly humour, with excrescential serpents growing out of their blade-bones. Here, the Golden Dreamer, and the Norwood Fortune Teller, were still on sale at sixpence each, with instructions for making the dumb cake, and reading destinies in tea-cups, and with a picture of a young woman with a high waist lying on a sofa in an attitude so uncomfortable as almost to account for her dreaming at one and the same time of a conflagration, a shipwreck, an earthquake, a skeleton, a church-porch, lightning, funerals performed, and a young man in a bright blue coat and canary pantaloons. Here, were Little Warblers and Fairburn's Comic Songsters. Here, too, were ballads on the old ballad paper and in the old confusion of types ; with an old man in a cocked hat, and an arm-chair, for the illustration to Will Watch the bold Smuggler ; and the Friar of Orders Grey, represented by a little girl in a hoop, with a ship in the distance. All these as of yore, when they were infinite delights to me !

It took me so long fully to relish these many enjoyments, that I had not more than an hour before bedtime to devote to Madame Roland. We got on admirably together on the subject of her convent education, and I rose next morning with the full conviction that the day for the great chapter was at last arrived.

It had fallen calm, however, in the night, and as I sat at

breakfast I blushed to remember that I had not yet been on the Downs. I a walker, and not yet on the Downs! Really, on so quiet and bright a morning this must be set right. As an essential part of the Whole Duty of Man, therefore, I left the chapter to itself—for the present—and went on the Downs. They were wonderfully green and beautiful, and gave me a good deal to do. When I had done with the free air and the view, I had to go down into the valley and look after the hops (which I know nothing about), and to be equally solicitous as to the cherry orchards. Then I took it on myself to cross-examine a tramping family in black (mother alleged, I have no doubt by herself in person, to have died last week), and to accompany eighteenpence which produced a great effect, with moral admonitions which produced none at all. Finally, it was late in the afternoon before I got back to the unprecedented chapter, and then I determined that it was out of the season, as the place was, and put it away.

I went at night to the benefit of Mrs. B. Wedgington at the Theatre, who had placarded the town with the admonition, "DON'T FORGET IT!" I made the house, according to my calculation, four and ninepence to begin with, and it may have warmed up, in the course of the evening, to half a sovereign. There was nothing to offend any one,—the good Mr. Baines of Leeds excepted. Mrs. B. Wedgington sang to a grand piano. Mr. B. Wedgington did the like, and also took off his coat, tucked up his trousers, and danced in clogs. Master B. Wedgington, aged ten months, was nursed by a shivering young person in the boxes, and the eye of Mrs. B. Wedgington wandered that way more than once. Peace be with all the Wedgingtons from A. to Z. May they find themselves in the Season somewhere!

A POOR MAN'S TALE OF A PATENT

I AM not used to writing for print. What working-man, that never labours less (some Mondays, and Christmas Time and Easter Time excepted) than twelve or fourteen hours a day, is? But I have been asked to put down, plain, what I have got to say; and so I take pen-and-ink, and do it to the best of my power, hoping defects will find excuse.

I was born nigh London, but have worked in a shop at Birmingham (what you would call Manufactories, we call Shops), almost ever since I was out of my time. I served my apprenticeship at Deptford, nigh where I was born, and I am a smith by trade. My name is John. I have been called "Old John" ever since I was nineteen year of age, on account of not having much hair. I am fifty-six year of age at the present time, and I don't find myself with more hair, nor yet with less, to signify, than at nineteen year of age aforesaid.

I have been married five and thirty year, come next April. I was married on All Fools' Day. Let them laugh that win. I won a good wife that day, and it was as sensible a day to me as ever I had.

We have had a matter of ten children, six whereof are living. My eldest son is engineer in the Italian steam-packet "Mezzo Giorno, plying between Marseilles and Naples, and calling at Genoa, Leghorn, and Civita Vecchia." He

113

was a good workman. He invented a many useful little things that brought him in—nothing. I have two sons doing well at Sydney, New South Wales—single, when last heard from. One of my sons (James) went wild and for a soldier, where he was shot in India, living six weeks in hospital with a musket-ball lodged in his shoulder-blade, which he wrote with his own hand. He was the best looking. One of my two daughters (Mary) is comfortable in her circumstances, but water on the chest. The other (Charlotte), her husband run away from her in the basest manner, and she and her three children live with us. The youngest, six year old, has a turn for mechanics.

I am not a Chartist, and I never was. I don't mean to say but what I see a good many public points to complain of, still I don't think that's the way to set them right. If I did think so, I should be a Chartist. But I don't think so, and I am not a Chartist. I read the paper, and hear discussion, at what we call " a parlour," in Birmingham, and I know many good men and workmen who are Chartists. Note. Not Physical force.

It won't be took as boastful in me, if I make the remark (for I can't put down what I have got to say, without putting that down before going any further), that I have always been of an ingenious turn. I once got twenty pound by a screw, and it's in use now. I have been twenty year, off and on, completing an Invention and perfecting it. I perfected of it, last Christmas Eve at ten o'clock at night. Me and my wife stood and let some tears fall over the Model, when it was done and I brought her in to take a look at it.

A friend of mine, by the name of William Butcher, is a Chartist. Moderate. He is a good speaker. He is very animated. I have often heard him deliver that what is, at every turn, in the way of us working-men, is, that too many places have been made, in the course of time, to provide for people that never ought to have been provided for ; and that we have to obey forms and to pay fees to support those

A Poor Man's Tale of a Patent

places when we shouldn't ought. "True," (delivers William Butcher), "all the public has to do this, but it falls heaviest on the working-man, because he has least to spare; and likewise because impediments shouldn't be put in his way, when he wants redress of wrong or furtherance of right." Note. I have wrote down those words from William Butcher's own mouth. W. B. delivering them fresh for the aforesaid purpose.

Now, to my Model again. There it was, perfected of, on Christmas Eve, gone nigh a year, at ten o'clock at night. All the money I could spare I had laid out upon the Model; and when times was bad, or my daughter Charlotte's children sickly, or both, it had stood still, months at a spell. I had pulled it to pieces, and made it over again with improvements, I don't know how often. There it stood, at last, a perfected Model as aforesaid.

William Butcher and me had a long talk, Christmas Day, respecting of the Model. William is very sensible. But sometimes cranky. William said, "What will you do with it, John?" I said, "Patent it." William said, "How patent it, John?" I said, "By taking out a Patent." William then delivered that the law of Patent was a cruel wrong. William said, "John, if you make your invention public, before you get a Patent, any one may rob you of the fruits of your hard work. You are put in a cleft stick, John. Either you must drive a bargain very much against yourself, by getting a party to come forward beforehand with the great expenses of the Patent; or, you must be put about, from post to pillar, among so many parties, trying to make a better bargain for yourself, and showing your invention, that your invention will be took from you over your head." I said, "William Butcher, are you cranky? You are sometimes cranky." William said, "No, John, I tell you the truth;" which he then delivered more at length. I said to W. B. I would Patent the invention myself.

My wife's brother, George Bury of West Bromwich (his

wife unfortunately took to drinking, made away with every-thing, and seventeen times committed to Birmingham Jail before happy release in every point of view), left my wife, his sister, when he died, a legacy of one hundred and twenty-eight pound ten, Bank of England Stocks. Me and my wife never broke into that money yet. Note. We might come to be old and past our work. We now agreed to Patent the invention. We said we would make a hole in it—I mean in the aforesaid money—and Patent the invention. William Butcher wrote me a letter to Thomas Joy, in London. T. J. is a carpenter, six foot four in height, and plays quoits well. He lives in Chelsea, London, by the church. I got leave from the shop, to be took on again when I come back. I am a good workman. Not a Teetotaller; but never drunk. When the Christmas holidays were over, I went up to London by the Parliamentary Train, and hired a lodging for a week with Thomas Joy. He is married. He has one son gone to sea.

Thomas Joy delivered (from a book he had) that the first step to be took, in Patenting the invention, was to prepare a petition unto Queen Victoria. William Butcher had delivered similar, and drawn it up. Note. William is a ready writer. A declaration before a Master in Chancery was to be added to it. That, we likewise drew up. After a deal of trouble I found out a Master, in Southampton Buildings, Chancery Lane, nigh Temple Bar, where I made the declaration, and paid eighteen-pence. I was told to take the declaration and petition to the Home Office, in Whitehall, where I left it to be signed by the Home Secretary (after I had found the office out), and where I paid two pound, two, and sixpence. In six days he signed it, and I was told to take it to the Attorney-General's chambers, and leave it there for a report. I did so, and paid four pound, four. Note. Nobody all through, ever thankful for their money, but all uncivil.

My lodging at Thomas Joy's was now hired for another week, whereof five days were gone. The Attorney-General made what they called a Report-of-course (my invention being, as William Butcher had delivered before starting, unopposed), and I was sent back with it to the Home Office. They made a Copy of it, which was called a Warrant. For this warrant, I paid seven pound, thirteen, and six. It was sent to the Queen, to sign. The Queen sent it back, signed. The Home Secretary signed it again. The gentleman throwed it at me when I called, and said, "Now take it to the Patent Office in Lincoln's Inn." I was then in my third week at Thomas Joy's living very sparing, on account of fees. I found myself losing heart.

At the Patent Office in Lincoln's Inn, they made "a draft of the Queen's bill," of my invention, and a "docket of the bill." I paid five pound, ten, and six, for this. They "engrossed two copies of the bill; one for the Signet Office, and one for the Privy-Seal Office." I paid one pound, seven, and six, for this. Stamp duty over and above, three pound. The Engrossing Clerk of the same office engrossed the Queen's bill for signature. I paid him one pound, one. Stamp-duty, again, one pound, ten. I was next to take the Queen's bill to the Attorney-General again, and get it signed again. I took it, and paid five pound more. I fetched it away, and took it to the Home Secretary again. He sent it to the Queen again. She signed it again. I paid seven pound, thirteen, and six, more, for this. I had been over a month at Thomas Joy's. I was quite wore out, patience and pocket.

Thomas Joy delivered all this, as it went on, to William Butcher. William Butcher delivered it again to three Birmingham Parlours, from which it got to all the other Parlours, and was took, as I have been told since, right through all the shops in the North of England. Note. William Butcher delivered, at his Parlour, in a speech, that it was a Patent way of making Chartists.

But I hadn't nigh done yet. The Queen's bill was to be took to the Signet Office in Somerset House, Strand—where the stamp shop is. The Clerk of the Signet made "a Signet bill for the Lord Keeper of the Privy Seal." I paid him four pound, seven. The Clerk of the Lord Keeper of the Privy Seal made "a Privy-Seal bill for the Lord Chancellor." I paid him, four pound, two. The Privy-Seal bill was handed over to the Clerk of the Patents, who engrossed the aforesaid. I paid him five pound, seventeen, and eight; at the same time, I paid Stamp-duty for the Patent, in one lump, thirty pound. I next paid for "boxes for the Patent," nine and sixpence. Note. Thomas Joy would have made the same at a profit for eighteen-pence. I next paid "fees to the Deputy, the Lord Chancellor's Purse-bearer," two pound, two. I next paid "fees to the Clerk of the Hanaper," seven pound, thirteen. I next paid "fees to the Deputy Clerk of the Hanaper," ten shillings. I next paid, to the Lord Chancellor again, one pound, eleven, and six. Last of all, I paid "fees to the Deputy Sealer, and Deputy Chaff-wax," ten shillings and sixpence. I had lodged at Thomas Joy's over six weeks, and the unopposed Patent for my invention, for England only, had cost me ninety-six pound, seven, and eightpence. If I had taken it out for the United Kingdom, it would have cost me more than three hundred pound.

Now, teaching had not come up but very limited when I was young. So much the worse for me you'll say. I say the same. William Butcher is twenty year younger than me. He knows a hundred year more. If William Butcher had wanted to Patent an invention, he might have been sharper than myself when hustled backwards and forwards among all those offices, though I doubt if so patient. Note. William being sometimes cranky, and consider porters, messengers, and clerks.

Thereby I say nothing of my being tired of my life, while I was Patenting my invention. But I put this: Is it reasonable to make a man feel as if, in inventing an ingenious improvement meant to do good, he had done something wrong? How else can a man feel, when he is met by such difficulties at every turn? All inventors taking out a Patent MUST feel so. And look at the expense. How hard on me, and how hard on the country if there's any merit in me (and my invention is took up now, I am thankful to say, and doing well), to put me to all that expense before I can move a finger! Make the addition yourself, and it'll come to ninety-six pound, seven, and eightpence. No more, and no less.

What can I say against William Butcher, about places? Look at the Home Secretary, the Attorney-General, the Patent Office, the Engrossing Clerk, the Lord Chancellor, the Privy Seal, the Clerk of the Patents, the Lord Chancellor's Purse-bearer, the Clerk of the Hanaper, the Deputy Clerk of the Hanaper, the Deputy Sealer, and the Deputy Chaff-wax. No man in England could get a Patent for an Indian-rubber band, or an iron-hoop, without feeing all of them. Some of them, over and over again. I went through thirty-five stages. I began with the Queen upon the Throne. I ended with the Deputy Chaff-wax. Note. I should like to see the Deputy Chaff-wax. Is it a man, or what is it?

What I had to tell, I have told. I have wrote it down. I hope it's plain. Not so much in the handwriting (though nothing to boast of there), as in the sense of it. I will now conclude with Thomas Joy. Thomas said to me, when we parted, "John, if the laws of this country were as honest as they ought to be, you would have come to London— registered an exact description and drawing of your invention —paid half-a-crown or so for doing of it—and therein and thereby have got your Patent."

My opinion is the same as Thomas Joy. Further. In William Butcher's delivering "that the whole gang of Hanapers and Chaff-waxes must be done away with, and that England has been chaffed and waxed sufficient," I agree.

THE NOBLE SAVAGE

To come to the point at once, I beg to say that I have not the least belief in the Noble Savage. I consider him a prodigious nuisance, and an enormous superstition. His calling rum fire-water, and me a pale face, wholly fail to reconcile me to him. I don't care what he calls me. I call him a savage, and I call a savage a something highly desirable to be civilised off the face of the earth. I think a mere gent (which I take to be the lowest form of civilisation) better than a howling, whistling, clucking, stamping, jumping, tearing savage. It is all one to me, whether he sticks a fish-bone through his visage, or bits of trees through the lobes of his ears, or bird's feathers in his head; whether he flattens his hair between two boards, or spreads his nose over the breadth of his face, or drags his lower lip down by great weights, or blackens his teeth, or knocks them out, or paints one cheek red and the other blue, or tattoos himself, or oils himself, or rubs his body with fat, or crimps it with knives. Yielding to whichsoever of these agreeable eccentricities, he is a savage—cruel, false, thievish, murderous; addicted more or less to grease, entrails, and beastly customs; a wild animal with the questionable gift of boasting; a conceited, tiresome, bloodthirsty, monotonous humbug.

Yet it is extraordinary to observe how some people will talk about him, as they talk about the good old times; how they will regret his disappearance, in the course of this world's development, from such and such lands where his absence is a blessed relief and an indispensable preparation for the sowing of the very first seeds of any influence that can exalt humanity; how, even with the evidence of himself before them, they will either be determined to believe, or will suffer themselves to be persuaded into believing, that he is something which their five senses tell them he is not.

There was Mr. Catlin, some few years ago, with his Ojibbeway Indians. Mr. Catlin was an energetic, earnest man, who had lived among more tribes of Indians than I need reckon up here, and who had written a picturesque and glowing book about them. With his party of Indians squatting and spitting on the table before him, or dancing their miserable jigs after their own dreary manner, he called, in all good faith, upon his civilised audience to take notice of their symmetry and grace, their perfect limbs, and the exquisite expression of their pantomime; and his civilised audience, in all good faith, complied and admired. Whereas, as mere animals, they were wretched creatures, very low in the scale and very poorly formed; and as men and women possessing any power of truthful dramatic expression by means of action, they were no better than the chorus at an Italian Opera in England—and would have been worse if such a thing were possible.

Mine are no new views of the noble savage. The greatest writers on natural history found him out long ago. BUFFON knew what he was, and showed why he is the sulky tyrant that he is to his women, and how it happens (Heaven be praised!) that his race is spare in numbers. For evidence of the quality of his moral nature, pass himself for a moment and refer to his "faithful dog." Has he ever improved a dog, or attached a dog, since his nobility first ran wild in woods, and was brought down (at a very long shot) by POPE? Or does the animal that is the friend of man, always degenerate in his low society?

THE NOBLE SAVAGE

It is not the miserable nature of the noble savage that is the new thing; it is the whimpering over him with maudlin admiration, and the affecting to regret him, and the drawing of any comparison of advantage between the blemishes of civilisation and the tenor of his swinish life. There may have been a change now and then in those diseased absurdities, but there is none in him.

Think of the Bushmen. Think of the two men and the two women who have been exhibited about England for some years. Are the majority of persons—who remember the horrid little leader of that party in his festering bundle of hides, with his filth and his antipathy to water, and his straddled legs, and his odious eyes shaded by his brutal hand, and his cry of " Qu-u-u-u-aaa ! " (Bosjesman for something desperately insulting I have no doubt)—conscious of an affectionate yearning towards that noble savage, or is it idiosyncratic in me to abhor, detest, abominate, and abjure him ? I have no reserve on this subject, and will frankly state that, setting aside that stage of the entertainment when he counterfeited the death of some creature he had shot, by laying his head on his hand and shaking his left leg—at which time I think it would have been justifiable homicide to slay him—I have never seen that group sleeping, smoking, and expectorating round their brazier, but I have sincerely desired that something might happen to the charcoal smouldering therein, which would cause the immediate suffocation of the whole of the noble strangers.

There is at present a party of Zulu Kaffirs exhibiting at the St. George's Gallery, Hyde Park Corner, London. These noble savages are represented in a most agreeable manner; they are seen in an elegant theatre, fitted with appropriate scenery of great beauty, and they are described in a very sensible and unpretending lecture, delivered with a modesty which is quite a pattern to all similar exponents. Though extremely ugly, they are much better shaped than such of their predecessors as I have referred to; and they are rather picturesque to the eye, though far from odoriferous to the nose. What a visitor left to his own interpretings and imaginings might suppose these noblemen to be about, when they give vent to that pantomimic expression which is quite settled to be the natural gift of the noble savage, I cannot possibly conceive; for it is so much too luminous for my personal civilisation that it conveys no idea to my mind beyond a general stamping, ramping, and raving, remarkable (as everything in savage life is) for its dire uniformity. But let us—with the interpreter's assistance, of which I for one stand so much in need—see what the noble savage does in Zulu Kaffirland.

The noble savage sets a king to reign over him, to whom he submits his life and limbs without a murmur or question, and whose whole life is passed chin deep in a lake of blood; but who, after killing incessantly, is in his turn killed by his relations and friends, the moment a grey hair appears on his head. All the noble savage's wars with his fellow-savages (and he takes no pleasure in anything else) are wars of extermination—which is the best thing I know of him, and the most comfortable to my mind when I look at him. He has no moral feelings of any kind, sort, or description; and his "mission" may be summed up as simply diabolical.

The ceremonies with which he faintly diversifies his life are, of course, of a kindred nature. If he wants a wife he appears before the kennel of the gentleman whom he has selected for his father-in-law, attended by a party of male friends of a very strong flavour, who screech and whistle and stamp an offer of so many cows for the young lady's hand. The chosen father-in-law—also supported by a high-flavoured party of male friends—screeches, whistles, and yells (being seated on the ground, he can't stamp) that there never was such a daughter in the market as his daughter, and that he must have six more cows. The son-in-law and his select circle of backers, screech, whistle, stamp, and yell in reply, that they will give three more cows. The father-in-law (an old deluder, overpaid at the beginning) accepts four, and rises to bind the bargain. The whole party, the young lady included, then falling into epileptic convulsions, and screeching, whistling, stamping, and yelling together—and nobody taking any notice of the young lady (whose charms are not to be thought of without a shudder)—the noble savage is considered married, and his friends make demoniacal leaps at him by way of congratulation.

When the noble savage finds himself a little unwell, and mentions the circumstance to his friends, it is immediately perceived that he is under the influence of witchcraft. A learned personage, called an Imyanger or Witch Doctor, is immediately sent for to Nooker the Umtargartie, or smell out the witch. The male inhabitants of the kraal being seated on the ground, the learned doctor, got up like a grizzly bear, appears, and administers a dance of a most terrific nature, during the exhibition of which remedy he incessantly gnashes his teeth, and howls :—" I am the original physician to Nooker the Umtargartie. Yow yow yow! No connexion with any other establishment. Till till till! All other Umtargarties are feigned Umtargarties, Boroo Boroo! but I perceive here a genuine and real Umtargartie, Hoosh Hoosh Hoosh! in whose blood I, the original Imyanger and Nookerer, Blizzerum Boo! will wash these bear's claws of mine. O yow yow yow!" All this time the learned physician is looking out among the attentive faces for some unfortunate man who owes him a cow, or who has given him any small offence, or against whom, without offence, he has conceived a spite. Him he never fails to Nooker as the Umtargartie, and he is instantly killed. In the absence of such an individual, the usual practice is to Nooker the quietest and most gentlemanly person in company. But the nookering is invariably followed on the spot by the butchering.

Some of the noble savages in whom Mr. Catlin was so strongly interested, and the diminution of whose numbers, by rum and small-pox, greatly affected him, had a custom not unlike this, though much more appalling and disgusting in its odious details.

The women being at work in the fields, hoeing the Indian corn, and the noble savage being asleep in the shade, the chief has sometimes the condescension to come forth, and lighten the labour by looking at it. On these occasions, he seats himself in his own savage chair, and is attended by his shield-bearer: who holds over his head a shield of cowhide—in shape like an immense mussel shell—fearfully and wonderfully, after the manner of a theatrical supernumerary. But lest the great man should forget his greatness in the contemplation of the humble works of agriculture, there suddenly rushes in a poet, retained for the purpose, called a Praiser. This literary gentleman wears a leopard's head over his own, and a dress of tigers' tails; he has the appearance of having come express on his hind legs from the Zoological Gardens; and he incontinently strikes up the chief's praises, plunging and tearing all the while. There is a frantic wickedness in this brute's manner of worrying the air, and gnashing out, "O what a delightful chief he is! O what a delicious quantity of blood he sheds! O how majestically he laps it up! O how charmingly cruel he is! O how he tears the flesh of his enemies and crunches the bones! O how like the tiger and the leopard and the wolf and the bear he is! O, row row row row, how fond I am of him!" which might tempt the Society of Friends to charge at a hand-gallop into the Swartz-Kop location and exterminate the whole kraal.

When war is afoot among the noble savages—which is always—the chief holds a council to ascertain whether it is the opinion of his brothers and friends in general that the enemy shall be exterminated. On this occasion, after the performance of an Umsebeuza, or war song,—which is exactly like all the other songs,—the chief makes a speech to his brothers and friends, arranged in single file. No particular order is observed during the delivery of this address, but every gentleman who finds himself excited by the subject, instead of crying "Hear, hear!" as is the custom with us, darts from the rank and tramples out the life, or crushes the skull, or mashes the face, or scoops out the eyes, or breaks the limbs, or performs a whirlwind of atrocities on the body, of an imaginary enemy. Several gentlemen becoming thus excited at once, and pounding away without the least regard to the orator, that illustrious person is rather in the position of an orator in an Irish House of Commons. But, several of these scenes of savage life bear a strong generic resemblance to an Irish election, and I think would be extremely well received and understood at Cork.

In all these ceremonies the noble savage holds forth to the utmost possible extent about himself; from which (to turn him to some civilised account) we may learn, I think, that as egotism is one of the most offensive and contemptible littlenesses a civilised man can exhibit, so it is really incompatible with the interchange of ideas; inasmuch as if we all talked about ourselves we should soon have no listeners, and must be all yelling and screeching at once on our own separate accounts: making society hideous. It is my opinion that if we retained in us anything of the noble savage, we could not get rid of it too soon. But the fact is clearly otherwise. Upon the wife and dowry question, substituting coin for cows, we have assuredly nothing of the Zulu Kaffir left. The endurance of despotism is one great distinguishing mark of a savage always. The improving world has quite got the better of that too. In like manner, Paris is a civilised city, and the Théâtre Français a highly civilised theatre; and we shall never hear, and never have heard in these later days (of course) of the Praiser *there*. No, no, civilised poets have better work to do. As to Nookering Umtargarties, there are no pretended Umtargarties in Europe, and no European powers to Nooker them; that would be mere spydom, subordination, small malice, superstition, and false pretence. And as to private Umtargarties, are we not in the year eighteen hundred and fifty-three, with spirits rapping at our doors?

ONE USEFUL LESSON

To conclude as I began. My position is, that if we have anything to learn from the Noble Savage, it is what to avoid. His virtues are a fable; his happiness is a delusion; his nobility, nonsense. We have no greater justification for being cruel to the miserable object, than for being cruel to a WILLIAM SHAKESPEARE or an ISAAC NEWTON; but he passes away before an immeasurably better and higher power than ever ran wild in any earthly woods, and the world will be all the better when his place knows him no more.

A FLIGHT

WHEN Don Diego de—I forget his name—the inventor of the last new Flying Machines, price so many francs for ladies, so many more for gentlemen—when Don Diego, by permission of Deputy Chaff-wax and his noble band, shall have taken out a Patent for the Queen's dominions, and shall have opened a commodious Warehouse in an airy situation.; and when all persons of any gentility will keep at least a pair of wings, and be seen skimming about in every direction; I shall take a flight to Paris (as I soar round the world) in a cheap and independent manner. At present, my reliance is on the South-Eastern Railway Company, in whose Express Train here I sit, at eight of the clock on a very hot morning, under the very hot roof of the Terminus at London Bridge, in danger of being "forced" like a cucumber or a melon, or a pine-apple. And talking of pine-apples, I suppose there never were so many pine-apples in a Train as there appear to be in this Train.

Whew! The hot-house air is faint with pine-apples. Every French citizen or citizeness is carrying pine-apples home. The compact little Enchantress in the corner of my carriage (French actress, to whom I yielded up my heart under the auspices of that brave child, "MEAT-CHELL," at the St. James's Theatre the night before last) has a pine-apple in her lap. Compact Enchantress's friend, confidante, mother, mystery, Heaven knows what, has two pine-apples in her lap, and a bundle of them under the seat. Tobacco-smoky Frenchman in Algerine wrapper, with peaked hood behind, who might be Abd-el-Kader dyed rifle-green, and who seems to be dressed entirely in dirt and braid, carries pine-apples in a covered basket. Tall, grave, melancholy Frenchman, with black Vandyke beard, and hair close-cropped, with expansive chest to waistcoat, and compressive waist to coat: saturnine as to his pantaloons, calm as to his feminine boots, precious as to his jewellery, smooth and white as to his linen: dark-eyed, high-foreheaded, hawk-nosed—got up, one thinks, like Lucifer or Mephistopheles, or Zamiel, transformed into a highly genteel Parisian—has the green end of a pine-apple sticking out of his neat valise.

Whew! If I were to be kept here long, under this forcing-frame, I wonder what would become of me—whether I should be forced into a giant, or should sprout or blow into some other phenomenon! Compact Enchantress is not ruffled by the heat—she is always composed, always compact. O look at her little ribbons, frills, and edges, at her shawl, at her gloves, at her hair, at her bracelets, at her bonnet, at everything about her! How is it accomplished? What does she do to be so neat? How is it that every trifle she wears belongs to her, and cannot choose but be a part of her? And even Mystery, look at *her*! A model. Mystery is not young, not pretty, though still of an average candle-light passability; but she does such miracles in her own behalf, that, one of these days, when she dies, they'll be amazed to find an old woman in her bed, distantly like her. She was an actress once, I shouldn't wonder, and had a Mystery attendant on herself. Perhaps, Compact Enchantress will live to be a Mystery, and to wait with a shawl at the side-scenes, and to sit opposite to Mademoiselle in railway carriages, and smile and talk subserviently, as Mystery does now. That's hard to believe!

Two Englishmen, and now our carriage is full. First

Englishman, in the monied interest—flushed, highly respectable—Stock Exchange, perhaps—City, certainly. Faculties of second Englishman entirely absorbed in hurry. Plunges into the carriage, blind. Calls out of window concerning his luggage, deaf. Suffocates himself under pillows of greatcoats, for no reason, and in a demented manner. Will receive no assurance from any porter whatsoever. Is stout and hot, and wipes his head, and makes himself hotter by breathing so hard. Is totally incredulous respecting assurance of Collected Guard, that "there's no hurry." No hurry! And a flight to Paris in eleven hours!

It is all one to me in this drowsy corner, hurry or no hurry. Until Don Diego shall send home my wings, my flight is with the South-Eastern Company. I can fly with the South-Eastern, more lazily, at all events, than in the upper air. I have but to sit here thinking as idly as I please, and be whisked away. I am not accountable to anybody for the idleness of my thoughts in such an idle summer flight; my flight is provided for by the South-Eastern and is no business of mine.

The bell! With all my heart. It does not require *me* to do so much as even to flap my wings. Something snorts for me, something shrieks for me, something proclaims to everything else that it had better keep out of my way,—and away I go.

Ah! The fresh air is pleasant after the forcing-frame, though it does blow over these interminable streets, and scatter the smoke of this vast wilderness of chimneys. Here we are—no, I mean there we were, for it has darted far into the rear—in Bermondsey where the tanners live. Flash! The distant shipping in the Thames is gone. Whirr! The little streets of new brick and red tile, with here and there a flagstaff growing like a tall weed out of the scarlet beans, and, everywhere, plenty of open sewer and ditch for the promotion of the public health, have been fired off in a volley. Whizz! Dust-heaps, market-gardens, and waste grounds.

Rattle! New Cross Station. Shock! There we were at Croydon. Bur-r-r-r! The tunnel.

I wonder why it is that when I shut my eyes in a tunnel I begin to feel as if I were going at an Express pace the other way. I am clearly going back to London now. Compact Enchantress must have forgotten something, and reversed the engine. No! After long darkness, pale fitful streaks of light appear. I am still flying on for Folkestone. The streaks grow stronger—become continuous—become the ghost of day—become the living day—became I mean—the tunnel is miles and miles away, and here I fly through sunlight, all among the harvest and the Kentish hops.

There is a dreamy pleasure in this flying. I wonder where it was, and when it was, that we exploded, blew into space somehow, a Parliamentary Train, with a crowd of heads and faces looking at us out of cages, and some hats waving. Monied Interest says it was at Reigate Station. Expounds to Mystery how Reigate Station is so many miles from London, which Mystery again develops to Compact Enchantress. There might be neither a Reigate nor a London for me, as I fly away among the Kentish hops and harvest. What do *I* care?

Bang! We have let another Station off, and fly away regardless. Everything is flying. The hop-gardens turn gracefully towards me, presenting regular avenues of hops in rapid flight, then whirl away. So do the pools and rushes, haystacks, sheep, clover in full bloom delicious to the sight and smell, corn-sheaves, cherry-orchards, apple-orchards, reapers, gleaners, hedges, gates, fields that taper off into little angular corners, cottages, gardens, now and then a church. Bang, bang! A double-barrelled Station! Now a wood, now a bridge, now a landscape, now a cutting, now a— Bang! a single-barrelled Station—there was a cricket-match somewhere with two white tents, and then four flying cows, then turnips— now the wires of the electric telegraph are all alive, and spin, and blurr their edges, and go up and down, and make the intervals between each other most irregular : contracting and expanding in the strangest manner. Now we slacken. With a screwing, and a grinding, and a smell of water thrown on ashes, now we stop !

Demented Traveller, who has been for two or three minutes watchful, clutches his great-coats, plunges at the door, rattles it, cries "Hi !" eager to embark on board of impossible packets, far inland. Collected Guard appears. "Are you for Tunbridge, sir ? " "Tunbridge ? No. Paris." "Plenty of time, sir. No hurry. Five minutes here, sir, for refreshment." I am so blest (anticipating Zamiel, by half a second) as to procure a glass of water for Compact Enchantress.

Who would suppose we had been flying at such a rate, and shall take wing again directly ? Refreshment-room full, platform full, porter with watering-pot deliberately cooling a hot wheel, another porter with equal deliberation helping the rest of the wheels bountifully to ice cream. Monied Interest and I re-entering the carriage first, and being there alone, he intimates to me that the French are "no go" as a Nation. I ask why ? He says, that Reign of Terror of theirs was quite enough. I ventured to inquire whether he remembers anything that preceded said Reign of Terror ? He says not particularly. "Because," I remark, " the harvest that is reaped, has sometimes been sown." Monied Interest repeats, as quite enough for him, that the French are revolutionary, —" and always at it."

Bell. Compact Enchantress, helped in by Zamiel (whom the stars confound !), gives us her charming little side-box look, and smites me to the core. Mystery eating sponge-cake. Pine-apple atmosphere faintly tinged with suspicions of sherry. Demented Traveller flits past the carriage, looking for it. Is blind with agitation, and can't see it. Seems singled out by Destiny to be the only unhappy creature in the flight, who has any cause to hurry himself. Is nearly left behind. Is seized by Collected Guard after the Train is in motion, and bundled in. Still, has lingering suspicions that there must be a boat in the neighbourhood, and *will* look wildly out of window for it.

Flight resumed. Corn - sheaves, hop - gardens, reapers, gleaners, apple-orchards, cherry-orchards, Stations single and double-barrelled, Ashford. Compact Enchantress (constantly talking to Mystery, in an exquisite manner) gives a little scream; a sound that seems to come from high up in her precious little head; from behind her bright little eyebrows. "Great Heaven, my pine-apple! My Angel! It is lost!" Mystery is desolated. A search made. It is not lost. Zamiel finds it. I curse him (flying) in the Persian manner. May his face be turned upside down, and jackasses sit upon his uncle's grave!

Now fresher air, now glimpses of unenclosed Down-land with flapping crows flying over it whom we soon outfly, now the Sea, now Folkestone at a quarter after ten. "Tickets ready, gentlemen!" Demented dashes at the door. "For Paris, sir? No hurry."

Not the least. We are dropped slowly down to the Port, and sidle to and fro (the whole Train) before the insensible Royal George Hotel, for some ten minutes. The Royal George takes no more heed of us than its namesake under water at Spithead, or under earth at Windsor, does. The Royal George's dog lies winking and blinking at us, without taking the trouble to sit up; and the Royal George's "wedding party" at the open window (who seem, I must say, rather tired of bliss) don't bestow a solitary glance upon us, flying thus to Paris in eleven hours. The first gentleman in Folkestone is evidently used up, on this subject.

Meanwhile, Demented chafes. Conceives that every man's hand is against him, and exerting itself to prevent his getting to Paris. Refuses consolation. Rattles door. Sees smoke on the horizon, and "knows" it's the boat gone without him. Monied Interest resentfully explains that *he* is going to Paris too. Demented signifies that if Monied Interest chooses to be left behind, *he* don't.

A FLIGHT

"Refreshments in the Waiting-Room, ladies and gentlemen. No hurry, ladies and gentlemen, for Paris. No hurry whatever!"

Twenty minutes' pause, by Folkestone clock, for looking at Enchantress while she eats a sandwich, and at Mystery while she eats of everything there that is eatable, from porkpie, sausage, jam, and gooseberries, to lumps of sugar. All this time, there is a very waterfall of luggage, with a spray of dust, tumbling slantwise from the pier into the steamboat. All this time, Demented (who has no business with it) watches it with starting eyes, fiercely requiring to be shown *his* luggage. When it at last concludes the cataract, he rushes hotly to refresh—is shouted after, pursued, jostled, brought back, pitched into the departing steamer upside down, and caught by mariners disgracefully.

A lovely harvest-day, a cloudless sky, a tranquil sea. The piston-rods of the engines so regularly coming up from below, to look (as well they may) at the bright weather, and so regularly almost knocking their iron heads against the cross beam of the skylight, and never doing it! Another Parisian actress is on board, attended by another Mystery. Compact Enchantress greets her sister artist—Oh, the Compact One's pretty teeth!—and Mystery greets Mystery. *My* Mystery soon ceases to be conversational—is taken poorly, in a word, having lunched too miscellaneously—and goes below. The remaining Mystery then smiles upon the sister artists (who, I am afraid, wouldn't greatly mind stabbing each other), and is upon the whole ravished.

And now I find that all the French people on board begin to grow, and all the English people to shrink. The French are nearing home, and shaking off a disadvantage, whereas we are shaking it on. Zamiel is the same man, and Abd-el-Kader is the same man, but each seems to come into possession of an indescribable confidence that departs from us—from Monied Interest, for instance, and from me. Just what they gain, we lose. Certain British "Gents" about the steersman, intellectually nurtured at home on parody of everything and truth of nothing, become subdued, and in a manner forlorn; and when the steersman tells them (not exultingly) how he has "been upon this station now eight year, and never see the old town of Bullum yet," one of them, with an imbecile reliance on a reed, asks him what he considers to be the best hotel in Paris?

Now, I tread upon French ground, and am greeted by the three charming words, Liberty, Equality, Fraternity, painted up (in letters a little too thin for their height) on the Custom-house wall—also by the sight of large cocked hats, without which demonstrative head-gear nothing of a public nature can be done upon this soil. All the rabid Hotel population of Boulogne howl and shriek outside a distant barrier, frantic to get at us. Demented, by some unlucky means peculiar to himself, is delivered over to their fury, and is presently seen struggling in a whirlpool of Touters—is somehow understood to be going to Paris—is, with infinite noise, rescued by two cocked hats, and brought into Custom-house bondage with the rest of us.

Here, I resign the active duties of life to an eager being, of preternatural sharpness, with a shelving forehead and a shabby snuff-coloured coat, who (from the wharf) brought me down with his eye before the boat came into port. He darts upon my luggage, on the floor where all the luggage is strewn like a wreck at the bottom of the great deep; gets it proclaimed and weighed as the property of "Monsieur a traveller unknown;" pays certain francs for it, to a certain functionary behind a Pigeon Hole, like a pay-box at a Theatre (the arrangements in general are on a wholesale scale, half military and half theatrical); and I suppose I shall find it when I come to Paris—he says I shall. I know nothing about it, except that I pay him his small fee, and pocket the ticket he gives me, and sit upon a counter, involved in the general distraction.

Railway station. "Lunch or dinner, ladies and gentlemen.

Plenty of time for Paris. Plenty of time!" Large hall, long counter, long strips of dining-table, bottles of wine, plates of meat, roast chickens, little loaves of bread, basins of soup, little caraffes of brandy, cakes, and fruit. Comfortably restored from these resources, I begin to fly again.

I saw Zamiel (before I took wing) presented to Compact Enchantress and Sister Artist, by an officer in uniform, with a waist like a wasp's, and pantaloons like two balloons. They all got into the next carriage together, accompanied by the two Mysteries. They laughed. I am alone in the carriage (for I don't consider Demented anybody) and alone in the world.

Fields, windmills, low grounds, pollard-trees, windmills, fields, fortifications, Abbeville, soldiering and drumming. I wonder where England is, and when I was there last—about two years ago, I should say. Flying in and out among these trenches and batteries, skimming the clattering drawbridges, looking down into the stagnant ditches, I become a prisoner of state, escaping. I am confined with a comrade in a fortress. Our room is in an upper story. We have tried to get up the chimney, but there's an iron grating across it, imbedded in the masonry. After months of labour, we have worked the grating loose with the poker, and can lift it up. We have also made a hook, and twisted our rugs and blankets into ropes. Our plan is, to go up the chimney, hook our ropes to the top, descend hand over hand upon the roof of the guard-house far below, shake the hook loose, watch the opportunity of the sentinel's pacing away, hook again, drop into the ditch, swim across it, creep into the shelter of the wood. The time is come—a wild and stormy night. We are up the chimney, we are on the guard-house roof, we are swimming in the murky ditch, when lo! "Qui v'là?" a bugle, the alarm, a crash! What is it? Death? No, Amiens.

More fortifications, more soldiering and drumming, more basins of soup, more little loaves of bread, more bottles of wine, more caraffes of brandy, more time for refreshment.

A RAPID REVIEW

Everything good, and everything ready. Bright, unsubstantial-looking, scenic sort of station. People waiting. Houses, uniforms, beards, moustaches, some sabots, plenty of neat women, and a few old-visaged children. Unless it be a delusion born of my giddy flight, the grown-up people and the children seem to change places in France. In general, the boys and girls are little old men and women, and the men and women lively boys and girls.

Bugle, shriek, flight resumed. Monied Interest has come into my carriage. Says the manner of refreshing is "not bad," but considers it French. Admits great dexterity and politeness in the attendants. Thinks a decimal currency may have something to do with their despatch in settling accounts, and don't know but what it's sensible and convenient. Adds, however, as a general protest, that they're a revolutionary people—and always at it.

Ramparts, canals, cathedral, river, soldiering and drumming, open country, river, earthenware manufactures, Creil. Again ten minutes. Not even Demented in a hurry. Station, a drawing-room with a verandah: like a planter's house. Monied Interest considers it a band-box, and not made to last. Little round tables in it, at one of which the Sister Artists and attendant Mysteries are established with Wasp and Zamiel, as if they were going to stay a week.

Anon, with no more trouble than before, I am flying again, and lazily wondering as I fly. What has the South-Eastern done with all the horrible little villages we used to pass through, in the *Diligence*? What have they done with all the summer dust, with all the winter mud, with all the dreary avenues of little trees, with all the ramshackle postyards, with all the beggars (who used to turn out at night with bits of lighted candle, to look in at the coach windows), with all the long-tailed horses who were always biting one another, with all the big postilions in jack-boots—with all the mouldy cafés that we used to stop at, where a long mildewed table-cloth, set forth with jovial bottles of vinegar and oil, and with a Siamese arrangement of pepper and salt, was never wanting? Where are the grass-grown little towns, the wonderful little market-places all unconscious of markets, the shops that nobody kept, the streets that nobody trod, the churches that nobody went to, the bells that nobody rang, the tumble-down old buildings plastered with many-coloured bills that nobody read? Where are the two-and-twenty weary hours of long, long day and night journey, sure to be either insupportably hot or insupportably cold? Where are the pains in my bones, where are the fidgets in my legs, where is the Frenchman with the nightcap who never *would* have the little coupé-window down, and who always fell upon me when he went to sleep, and always slept all night snoring onions?

A voice breaks in with "Paris! Here we are!"

I have overflown myself, perhaps, but I can't believe it. I feel as if I were enchanted or bewitched. It is barely eight o'clock yet—it is nothing like half-past—when I have had my luggage examined at that briskest of Custom-houses attached to the station, and am rattling over the pavement in a hackney-cabriolet.

Surely, not the pavement of Paris? Yes, I think it is, too. I don't know any other place where there are all these high houses, all these haggard-looking wine shops, all these billiard tables, all these stocking-makers with flat red or yellow legs of wood for signboard, all these fuel shops with stacks of billets painted outside, and real billets sawing in the gutter, all these dirty corners of streets, all these cabinet pictures over dark doorways representing discreet matrons nursing babies. And yet this morning—I'll think of it in a warm-bath.

Very like a small room that I remember in the Chinese baths upon the Boulevard, certainly; and, though I see it through the steam, I think that I might swear to that peculiar hot-linen basket, like a large wicker hour-glass. When can it have been that I left home? When was it that I paid "through to Paris" at London Bridge, and discharged myself of all responsibility, except the preservation of a voucher ruled into three divisions, of which the first was snipped off at Folkestone, the second aboard the boat, and the third taken at my journey's end? It seems to have been ages ago. Calculation is useless. I will go out for a walk.

The crowds in the streets, the lights in the shops and balconies, the elegance, variety, and beauty of their decorations, the number of the theatres, the brilliant cafés with their windows thrown up high and their vivacious groups at little tables on the pavement, the light and glitter of the houses turned as it were inside out, soon convince me that it is no dream; that I am in Paris, howsoever I got here. I stroll down to the sparkling Palais Royal, up the Rue de Rivoli, to the Place Vendôme. As I glance into a print-shop window, Monied Interest, my late travelling companion, comes upon me, laughing with the highest relish of disdain. " Here's a people!" he says, pointing to Napoleon in the window and Napoleon on the column. " Only one idea all over Paris! A monomania!" Humph! I THINK I have seen Napoleon's match? There WAS a statue, when I came away, at Hyde Park Corner, and another in the City, and a print or two in the shops.

I walk up to the Barrière de l'Etoile, sufficiently dazed by my flight to have a pleasant doubt of the reality of everything about me; of the lively crowd, the overhanging trees, the performing dogs, the hobby-horses, the beautiful perspectives of shining lamps: the hundred and one enclosures, where the singing is, in gleaming orchestras of azure and gold, and where a star-eyed Houri comes round with a box for voluntary offerings. So, I pass to my hotel, enchanted; sup, enchanted; go to bed, enchanted; pushing back this morning (if it really were this morning) into the remoteness of time, blessing the South-Eastern Company for realising the Arabian Nights in these prose days, murmuring, as I wing my idle flight into the land of dreams, "No hurry, ladies and gentlemen, going to Paris in eleven hours. It is so well done, that there really is no hurry!"

THE DETECTIVE POLICE

WE are not by any means devout believers in the old Bow Street Police. To say the truth, we think there was a vast amount of humbug about those worthies. Apart from many of them being men of very indifferent character, and far too much in the habit of consorting with thieves and the like, they never lost a public occasion of jobbing and trading in mystery and making the most of themselves. Continually puffed besides by incompetent magistrates anxious to conceal their own deficiencies, and hand-in-glove with the penny-a-liners of that time, they became a sort of superstition. Although as a Preventive Police they were utterly ineffective, and as a Detective Police were very loose and uncertain in their operations, they remain with some people a superstition to the present day.

On the other hand, the Detective Force organised since the establishment of the existing Police, is so well chosen and trained, proceeds so systematically and quietly, does its business in such a workmanlike manner, and is always so calmly and steadily engaged in the service of the public, that the public really do not know enough of it, to know a tithe of its usefulness. Impressed with this conviction, and interested in the men themselves, we represented to the authorities at Scotland Yard, that we should be glad, if there were no official objection, to have some talk with the

140

INSPECTORS WIELD AND STALKER

Detectives. A most obliging and ready permission being given, a certain evening was appointed with a certain Inspector for a social conference between ourselves and the Detectives, at The Household Words Office in Wellington Street, Strand, London. In consequence of which appointment the party "came off," which we are about to describe. And we beg to repeat that, avoiding such topics as it might for obvious reasons be injurious to the public, or disagreeable to respectable individuals, to touch upon in print, our description is as exact as we can make it.

The reader will have the goodness to imagine the Sanctum Sanctorum of Household Words. Anything that best suits the reader's fancy, will best represent that magnificent chamber. We merely stipulate for a round table in the middle, with some glasses and cigars arranged upon it; and the editorial sofa elegantly hemmed in between that stately piece of furniture and the wall.

It is a sultry evening at dusk. The stones of Wellington Street are hot and gritty, and the watermen and hackney-coachmen at the Theatre opposite, are much flushed and aggravated. Carriages are constantly setting down the people who have come to Fairy-Land; and there is a mighty shouting and bellowing every now and then, deafening us for the moment, through the open windows.

Just at dusk, Inspectors Wield and Stalker are announced; but we do not undertake to warrant the orthography of any of the names here mentioned. Inspector Wield presents Inspector Stalker. Inspector Wield is a middle-aged man of a portly presence, with a large, moist, knowing eye, a husky voice, and a habit of emphasising his conversation by the aid of a corpulent fore-finger, which is constantly in juxta-position with his eyes or nose. Inspector Stalker is a shrewd, hard-headed Scotchman—in appearance not at all unlike a very acute, thoroughly-trained schoolmaster, from the Normal Establishment at Glasgow. Inspector Wield one might have known, perhaps, for what he is—Inspector Stalker, never.

THE DETECTIVE POLICE

The ceremonies of reception over, Inspectors Wield and Stalker observe that they have brought some sergeants with them. The sergeants are presented—five in number, Sergeant Dornton, Sergeant Witchem, Sergeant Mith, Sergeant Fendall, and Sergeant Straw. We have the whole Detective Force from Scotland Yard, with one exception. They sit down in a semi-circle (the two Inspectors at the two ends) at a little distance from the round table, facing the editorial sofa. Every man of them, in a glance, immediately takes an inventory of the furniture and an accurate sketch of the editorial presence. The Editor feels that any gentleman in company could take him up, if need should be, without the smallest hesitation, twenty years hence.

The whole party are in plain clothes. Sergeant Dornton about fifty years of age, with a ruddy face and a high sunburnt forehead, has the air of one who has been a Sergeant in the army—he might have sat to Wilkie for the Soldier in the Reading of the Will. He is famous for steadily pursuing the inductive process, and, from small beginnings, working on from clue to clue until he bags his man. Sergeant Witchem, shorter and thicker-set, and marked with the small-pox, has something of a reserved and thoughtful air, as if he were engaged in deep arithmetical calculations. He is renowned for his acquaintance with the swell mob. Sergeant Mith, a smooth-faced man with a fresh bright complexion, and a strange air of simplicity, is a dab at housebreakers. Sergeant Fendall, a light-haired, well-spoken, polite person, is a prodigious hand at pursuing private inquiries of a delicate nature. Straw, a little wiry Sergeant of meek demeanour and strong sense, would knock at a door and ask a series of questions in any mild character you choose to prescribe to him, from a charity-boy upwards, and seem as innocent as an infant. They are, one and all, respectable-looking men; of perfectly good deportment and unusual intelligence; with nothing lounging or slinking in their manners; with an air of keen observation and quick perception when addressed; and generally presenting in their faces, traces more or less marked of habitually leading lives of strong mental excitement. They have all good eyes; and they all can, and they all do, look full at whomsoever they speak to.

We light the cigars, and hand round the glasses (which are very temperately used indeed), and the conversation begins by a modest amateur reference on the Editorial part to the swell mob. Inspector Wield immediately removes his cigar from his lips, waves his right hand, and says, "Regarding the swell mob, sir, I can't do better than call upon Sergeant Witchem. Because the reason why? I'll tell you. Sergeant Witchem is better acquainted with the swell mob than any officer in London."

Our heart leaping up when we beheld this rainbow in the sky, we turn to Sergeant Witchem, who very concisely, and in well-chosen language, goes into the subject forthwith. Meantime, the whole of his brother officers are closely interested in attending to what he says, and observing its effect. Presently they begin to strike in, one or two together, when an opportunity offers, and the conversation becomes general. But these brother officers only come in to the assistance of each other—not to the contradiction—and a more amicable brotherhood there could not be. From the swell mob, we diverge to the kindred topics of cracksmen, fences, public-house dancers, area-sneaks, designing young people who go out "gonophing," and other "schools." It is observable throughout these revelations, that Inspector Stalker, the Scotchman, is always exact and statistical, and that when any question of figures arises, everybody as by one consent pauses, and looks to him.

When we have exhausted the various schools of Art— during which discussion the whole body have remained profoundly attentive, except when some unusual noise at the Theatre over the way has induced some gentleman to glance inquiringly towards the window in that direction, behind his next neighbour's back—we burrow for information on such points as the following. Whether there really are any highway robberies in London, or whether some circumstances not convenient to be mentioned by the aggrieved party, usually precede the robberies complained of, under that head, which quite change their character? Certainly the latter, almost always. Whether in the case of robberies in houses, where servants are necessarily exposed to doubt, innocence under suspicion ever becomes so like guilt in appearance, that a good officer need be cautious how he judges it? Undoubtedly. Nothing is so common or deceptive as such appearances at first. Whether in a place of public amusement, a thief knows an officer, and an officer knows a thief—supposing them, beforehand, strangers to each other—because each recognises in the other, under all disguise, an inattention to what is going on, and a purpose that is not the purpose of being entertained? Yes. That's the way exactly. Whether it is reasonable or ridiculous to trust to the alleged experiences of thieves as narrated by themselves, in prisons, or penitentiaries, or anywhere? In general, nothing more absurd. Lying is their habit and their trade; and they would rather lie—even if they hadn't an interest in it, and didn't want to make themselves agreeable—than tell the truth.

From these topics, we glide into a review of the most celebrated and horrible of the great crimes that have been committed within the last fifteen or twenty years. The men engaged in the discovery of almost all of them, and in the pursuit or apprehension of the murderers, are here, down to the very last instance. One of our guests gave chase to and boarded the emigrant ship, in which the murderess last hanged in London was supposed to have embarked. We learn from him that his errand was not announced to the passengers, who may have no idea of it to this hour. That he went below, with the captain, lamp in hand—it being dark, and the whole steerage abed and sea-sick—and engaged the Mrs. Manning who *was* on board, in a conversation about her luggage, until she was, with no small pains, induced to raise her head, and turn her face towards the light. Satisfied that she was not the object of his search, he quietly re-embarked in the Government steamer alongside, and steamed home again with the intelligence.

When we have exhausted these subjects, too, which occupy a considerable time in the discussion, two or three leave their chairs, whisper Sergeant Witchem, and resume their seats. Sergeant Witchem, leaning forward a little, and placing a hand on each of his legs, then modestly speaks as follows:

"My brother-officers wish me to relate a little account of my taking Tally-ho Thompson. A man oughtn't to tell what he has done himself; but still, as nobody was with me, and, consequently, as nobody but myself can tell it, I'll do it in the best way I can, if it should meet your approval."

We assure Sergeant Witchem that he will oblige us very much, and we all compose ourselves to listen with great interest and attention.

"Tally-ho Thompson," says Sergeant Witchem, after merely wetting his lips with his brandy-and-water, "Tally-ho Thompson was a famous horse-stealer, couper, and magsman. Thompson, in conjunction with a pal that occasionally worked with him, gammoned a countryman out of a good round sum of money, under pretence of getting him a situation— the regular old dodge—and was afterwards in the 'Hue and Cry' for a horse—a horse that he stole, down in Hertfordshire. I had to look after Thompson, and I applied myself, of course, in the first instance, to discovering where he was. Now, Thompson's wife lived, along with a little daughter, at Chelsea. Knowing that Thompson was somewhere in the country, I watched the house—especially at post-time in the morning—thinking Thompson was pretty likely to write to her. Sure enough, one morning the postman comes up, and delivers a letter at Mrs. Thompson's door. Little girl opens the door, and takes it in. We're not always sure of postmen, though the people at the post-offices are always very obliging. A postman may help us, or he may not,—just as it happens. However, I go across the road, and I say to the postman, after he has left the letter, 'Good morning! how are you?' 'How are *you*?' says he. 'You've just delivered a letter for Mrs. Thompson.' 'Yes, I have.' 'You didn't happen to remark what the post-mark was, perhaps?' 'No,' says he, 'I didn't.' 'Come,' says I, 'I'll be plain with you. I'm in a small way of business, and I have given Thompson credit, and I can't afford to lose what he owes me. I know he's got money, and I know he's in the country, and if you could tell me what the post-mark was, I should be very much obliged to you, and you'd do a service to a tradesman in a small way of business that can't afford a loss.' 'Well,' he said, 'I do assure you that I did not observe what the post-mark was; all I know is, that there was money in the letter—I should say a sovereign.' This was enough for me, because of course I knew that Thompson having sent his wife money, it was probable she'd write to Thompson, by return of post, to acknowledge the receipt. So I said 'Thankee' to the postman, and I kept on the watch. In the afternoon I saw the little girl come out. Of course I followed her. She went into a stationer's shop, and I needn't say to you that I looked in at the window. She bought some writing-paper and envelopes, and a pen. I think to myself, 'That'll do!'—watch her home again—and don't go away, you may be sure, knowing that Mrs. Thompson was writing her letter to Tally-ho, and that the letter would be posted presently. In about an hour or so, out came the little girl again, with the letter in her hand. I went up, and said something to the child, whatever it might have been; but I couldn't see the direction of the letter, because she held it with the seal upwards. However, I observed that on the back of the letter there was what we call a kiss—a drop of wax by the side of the seal—and again, you understand, that was enough for me. I saw her post the letter, waited till she was gone, then went into the shop, and asked to see the Master. When he came out, I told him, 'Now, I'm an Officer in the Detective Force; there's a letter with a kiss been posted here just now, for a man that I'm in search of; and what I have to ask of you, is, that you will let me look at the direction of that letter.' He was very civil—took a lot of letters from the box in the window—shook 'em out on the counter with the faces downwards—and there among 'em was the identical letter with the kiss. It was directed, Mr. Thomas Pigeon, Post Office, B——, to be left 'till called for. Down I went to B—— (a hundred and twenty miles or so) that night. Early next morning I went to the Post Office; saw the gentleman in charge of that department; told him who I was; and that my object was to see, and track, the party that should come for the letter for Mr. Thomas Pigeon. He was very polite, and said, 'You shall have every assistance we can give you; you can wait inside the office; and we'll take care to let you know when anybody comes for the letter.' Well, I waited there three days, and began to think that nobody ever *would* come. At last the clerk whispered to me, 'Here! Detective! Somebody's come for the letter!' 'Keep him a minute,' said I, and I ran round to the outside of the office. There I saw a young chap with the appearance of an Ostler, holding a horse by the bridle—stretching the bridle across the pavement, while he waited at the Post Office Window for the letter. I began to pat the horse, and that; and I said to the boy, 'Why, this is Mr. Jones's Mare!' 'No. It an't.' 'No?' said I. 'She's very like Mr. Jones's Mare!' 'She an't Mr. Jones's Mare, anyhow,' says he. 'It's Mr. So and So's, of the Warwick Arms.' And up he jumped, and off he went—letter and all. I got a cab, followed on the box, and was so quick after him that I came into the stable-yard of the Warwick Arms, by one gate, just as he came in by another. I went into the bar, where there was a young woman serving, and called for a glass of brandy-and-water. He came in directly, and handed her the letter. She casually looked at it, without saying anything, and stuck it up behind the glass over the chimney-piece. What was to be done next?

"I turned it over in my mind while I drank my brandy-and-water (looking pretty sharp at the letter the while), but I couldn't see my way out of it at all. I tried to get lodgings in the house, but there had been a horse-fair, or something of that sort, and it' was full. I was obliged to put up somewhere else, but I came backwards and forwards to the bar for a couple of days, and there was the letter always behind the glass. At last I thought I'd write a letter to Mr. Pigeon myself, and see what that would do. So I wrote one, and posted it, but I purposely addressed it, Mr. John Pigeon, instead of Mr. Thomas Pigeon, to see what *that* would do. In the morning (a very wet morning it was) I watched the postman down the street, and cut into the bar, just before he reached the Warwick Arms. In he came presently with my letter. 'Is there a Mr. John Pigeon staying here?' 'No!—stop a bit though,' says the barmaid; and she took down the letter behind the glass. 'No,' says she, 'it's Thomas, and *he* is not staying here. Would you do me a favour, and post this for me, as it is so wet?' The postman said Yes; she folded it in another envelope, directed it, and gave it him. He put it in his hat, and away he went.

"I had no difficulty in finding out the direction of that letter. It was addressed Mr. Thomas Pigeon, Post Office, R——, Northamptonshire, to be left till called for. Off I started directly for R——; I said the same at the Post Office there, as I had said at B——; and again I waited three days before anybody came. At last another chap on horseback came. 'Any letters for Mr. Thomas Pigeon?' 'Where do you come from?' 'New Inn, near R——.' He got the letter, and away *he* went at a canter.

"I made my inquiries about the New Inn, near R——, and hearing it was a solitary sort of house, a little in the horse line, about a couple of miles from the station, I thought

I'd go and have a look at it. I found it what it had been described, and sauntered in, to look about me. The landlady was in the bar, and I was trying to get into conversation with her; asked her how business was, and spoke about the wet weather, and so on; when I saw, through an open door, three men sitting by the fire in a sort of parlour, or kitchen; and one of those men, according to the description I had of him, was Tally-ho Thompson!

"I went and sat down among 'em, and tried to make things agreeable; but they were very shy—wouldn't talk at all—looked at me, and at one another, in a way quite the reverse of sociable. I reckoned 'em up, and finding that they were all three bigger men than me, and considering that their looks were ugly—that it was a lonely place—railroad station two miles off—and night coming on—thought I couldn't do better than have a drop of brandy-and-water to keep my courage up. So I called for my brandy-and-water; and as I was sitting drinking it by the fire, Thompson got up and went out.

"Now the difficulty of it was, that I wasn't sure it *was* Thompson, because I had never set eyes on him before; and what I had wanted was to be quite certain of him. However, there was nothing for it now, but to follow, and put a bold face upon it. I found him talking, outside in the yard, with the landlady. It turned out afterwards that he was wanted by a Northampton officer for something else, and that, knowing that officer to be pock-marked (as I am myself), he mistook me for him. As I have observed, I found him talking to the landlady, outside. I put my hand upon his shoulder—this way—and said, 'Tally-ho Thompson, it's no use. I know you. I'm an officer from London, and I take you into custody for felony!' 'That be d—d!' says Tally-ho Thompson.

"We went back into the house, and the two friends began to cut up rough, and their looks didn't please me at all, I assure you. 'Let the man go. What are you going to do with him?' 'I'll tell you what I'm going to do with him. I'm going to take him to London to-night, as sure as I'm alive. I'm not alone here, whatever you may think. You mind your own business, and keep yourselves to yourselves. It'll be better for you, for I know you both very well.' I'd never seen or heard of 'em in all my life, but my bouncing cowed 'em a bit, and they kept off, while Thompson was making ready to go. I thought to myself, however, that they might be coming after me on the dark road, to rescue Thompson; so I said to the landlady, 'What men have you got in the house, Missis?' 'We haven't got no men here,' she says, sulkily. 'You have got an ostler, I suppose?' 'Yes, we've got an ostler.' 'Let me see him.' Presently he came, and a shaggy-headed young fellow he was. 'Now attend to me, young man,' says I; 'I'm a Detective Officer from London. This man's name is Thompson. I have taken him into custody for felony. I am going to take him to the railroad station. I call upon you in the Queen's name to assist me; and mind you, my friend, you'll get yourself into more trouble than you know of, if you don't!' You never saw a person open his eyes so wide. 'Now, Thompson, come along!' says I. But when I took out the handcuffs, Thompson cries, 'No! None of that! I won't stand *them!* I'll go along with you quiet, but I won't bear none of that!' 'Tally-ho Thompson,' I said, 'I'm willing to behave as a man to you, if you are willing to behave as a man to me. Give me your word that you'll come peaceably along, and I don't want to handcuff you.' 'I will,' says Thompson, 'but I'll have a glass of brandy first.' 'I don't care if I've another,' said I. 'We'll have two more, Missis,' said the friends, 'and con-found you, Constable, you'll give your man a drop, won't you?' I was agreeable to that, so we had it all round, and then my man and I took Tally-ho Thompson safe to the railroad, and I carried him to London that night. He was afterwards acquitted, on account of a defect in the evidence; and I understand he always praises me up to the skies, and says I'm one of the best of men."

This story coming to a termination amidst general applause, Inspector Wield, after a little grave smoking, fixes his eye on his host, and thus delivers himself:

"It wasn't a bad plant that of mine, on Fikey, the man accused of forging the Sou'-Western Railway debentures— it was only t'other day—because the reason why? I'll tell you.

"I had information that Fikey and his brother kept a factory over yonder there,"—indicating any region on the Surrey side of the river—"where he bought second-hand carriages; so after I'd tried in vain to get hold of him by other means, I wrote him a letter in an assumed name, saying that I'd got a horse and shay to dispose of, and would drive down next day that he might view the lot, and make an offer—very reasonable it was, I said—a reg'lar bargain. Straw and me then went off to a friend of mine that's in the livery and job business, and hired a turn-out for the day, a precious smart turn-out it was—quite a slap-up thing! Down we drove, accordingly, with a friend (who's not in the Force himself); and leaving my friend in the shay near a public-house, to take care of the horse, we went to the factory, which was some little way off. In the factory, there was a number of strong fellows at work, and after reckoning 'em up, it was clear to me that it wouldn't do to try it on there. They were too many for us. We must get our man out of doors. 'Mr. Fikey at home?' 'No, he ain't.' 'Expected home soon?' 'Why, no, not soon.' 'Ah! Is his brother here?' '*I*'m his brother.' 'Oh! well, this is an ill-conwenience, this is. I wrote him a letter yesterday, saying I'd got a little turn-out to dispose of, and I've took the trouble to bring the turn-out down a' purpose, and now he ain't in the way.' 'No, he ain't in the way. You couldn't make it convenient to call again, could you?' 'Why, no, I couldn't. I want to sell; that's the fact; and I can't put it off. Could you find him anywheres?' At first he said No, he couldn't, and then he wasn't sure about it, and then he'd go and try. So at last he went up-stairs, where there was a sort of loft, and presently down comes my man himself in his shirt-sleeves.

"'Well,' he says, 'this seems to be rayther a pressing matter of yours.' 'Yes,' I says, 'it *is* rayther a pressing matter, and you'll find it a bargain—dirt cheap.' 'I ain't in partickler want of a bargain just now,' he says, 'but where is it?' 'Why,' I says, 'the turn-out's just outside. Come and look at it.' He hasn't any suspicions, and away we go. And the first thing that happens is, that the horse runs away with my friend (who knows no more of driving than a child) when he takes a little trot along the road to show his paces. You never saw such a game in your life!

"When the bolt is over, and the turn-out has come to a standstill again, Fikey walks round and round it as grave as a judge—me too. 'There, sir!' I says. 'There's a neat thing!' 'It ain't a bad style of thing,' he says. 'I believe you,' says I. 'And there's a horse!'—for I saw him looking at it. 'Rising eight!' I says, rubbing his fore-legs. (Bless you, there ain't a man in the world knows less of horses than I do, but I'd heard my friend at the Livery Stables say he was eight year old, so I says, as knowing as possible, 'Rising eight.') 'Rising eight, is he?' says he. 'Rising eight,' says I. 'Well,' he says, 'what do you want for it?' 'Why, the first and last figure for the whole concern is five-and-twenty pound!' 'That's very cheap!' he says, looking at me. 'Ain't it?' I says. 'I told you it was a bargain! Now, without any higgling and haggling about it, what I want is to sell, and that's my price. Further, I'll make it easy to you, and take half the money down, and you can do a bit of stiff* for the balance.' 'Well,' he says again, 'that's very cheap.' 'I believe you,' says I; 'get in and try it, and you'll buy it. Come! take a trial!'

"Ecod, he gets in, and we get in, and we drive along the

* Give a bill.

road, to show him to one of the railway clerks that was hid in the public-house window to identify him. But the clerk was bothered, and didn't know whether it was him, or wasn't— because the reason why? I'll tell you,—on account of his having shaved his whiskers. 'It's a clever little horse,' he says, 'and trots well; and the shay runs light.' 'Not a doubt about it,' I says. 'And now, Mr. Fikey, I may as well make it all right, without wasting any more of your time. The fact is, I'm Inspector Wield, and you're my prisoner.' 'You don't mean that?' he says. 'I do, indeed.' 'Then burn my body,' says Fikey, 'if this ain't *too* bad!'

"Perhaps you never saw a man so knocked over with surprise. 'I hope you'll let me have my coat?' he says. 'By all means.' 'Well, then, let's drive to the factory.' 'Why, not exactly that, I think,' said I; 'I've been there, once before, to-day. Suppose we send for it.' He saw it was no go, so he sent for it, and put it on, and we drove him up to London, comfortable."

This reminiscence is in the height of its success, when a general proposal is made to the fresh-complexioned, smooth-faced officer, with the strange air of simplicity, to tell the "Butcher's Story."

The fresh-complexioned, smooth-faced officer, with the strange air of simplicity, began with a rustic smile, and in a soft, wheedling tone of voice, to relate the Butcher's Story, thus:

"It's just about six years ago, now, since information was given at Scotland Yard of there being extensive robberies of lawns and silks going on, at some wholesale houses in the City. Directions were given for the business being looked into; and Straw, and Fendall, and me, we were all in it."

"When you received your instructions," said we, "you went away, and held a sort of Cabinet Council together!"

The smooth-faced officer coaxingly replied, "Ye-es. Just so. We turned it over among ourselves a good deal. It appeared, when we went into it, that the goods were sold by the receivers extraordinarily cheap—much cheaper than they could have been if they had been honestly come by. The receivers were in the trade, and kept capital shops—establishments of the first respectability—one of 'em at the West End, one down in Westminster. After a lot of watching and inquiry, and this and that among ourselves, we found that the job was managed, and the purchases of the stolen goods made, at a little public-house near Smithfield, down by Saint Bartholomew's; where the Warehouse Porters, who were the thieves, took 'em for that purpose, don't you see? and made appointments to meet the people that went between themselves and the receivers. This public-house was principally used by journeymen butchers from the country, out of place, and in want of situations; so, what did we do, but—ha, ha, ha!—we agreed that I should be dressed up like a butcher myself, and go and live there!"

Never, surely, was a faculty of observation better brought to bear upon a purpose, than that which picked out this officer for the part. Nothing in all creation could have suited him better. Even while he spoke, he became a greasy, sleepy, shy, good-natured, chuckle-headed, unsuspicious, and confiding young butcher. His very hair seemed to have suet in it, as he made it smooth upon his head, and his fresh complexion to be lubricated by large quantities of animal food.

"—So I—ha, ha, ha!" (always with the confiding snigger of the foolish young butcher) "so I dressed myself in the regular way, made up a little bundle of clothes, and went to the public-house, and asked if I could have a lodging there? They says, 'yes, you can have a lodging here,' and I got a bedroom, and settled myself down in the tap. There was a number of people about the place, and coming backwards and forwards to the house; and first one says, and then another says, 'Are you from the country, young man?' 'Yes,' I says, 'I am. I'm come out of Northamptonshire, and I'm quite lonely here, for I don't know London

at all, and it's such a mighty big town.' 'It *is* a big town,'
they says. 'Oh, it's a *very* big town!' I says. 'Really and
truly I never was in such a town. It quite confuses of me!'
—and all that, you know.

"When some of the Journeymen Butchers that used the
house, found that I wanted a place, they says, 'Oh, we'll get
you a place!' And they actually took me to a sight of
places, in Newgate Market, Newport Market, Clare, Carnaby
—I don't know where all. But the wages was—ha, ha, ha!—
was not sufficient, and I never could suit myself, don't you
see? Some of the queer frequenters of the house were a
little suspicious of me at first, and I was obliged to be very
cautious indeed how I communicated with Straw or Fendall.
Sometimes, when I went out, pretending to stop and look
into the shop windows, and just casting my eye round, I
used to see some of 'em following me; but, being perhaps
better accustomed than they thought for, to that sort of
thing, I used to lead 'em on as far as I thought necessary
or convenient—sometimes a long way—and then turn sharp
round, and meet 'em, and say, 'Oh, dear, how glad I am to
come upon you so fortunate! This London's such a place,
I'm blowed if I ain't lost again!' And then we'd go back
all together, to the public-house, and—ha, ha, ha! and
smoke our pipes, don't you see?

"They were very attentive to me, I am sure. It was a
common thing, while I was living there, for some of 'em to
take me out, and show me London. They showed me the
Prisons—showed me Newgate—and when they showed me
Newgate, I stops at the place where the Porters pitch their
loads, and says, 'Oh dear, is this where they hang the men?
Oh Lor!' 'That!' they says, 'what a simple cove he is!
That ain't it!' And then, they pointed out which *was* it,
and I says 'Lor!' and they says, 'Now you'll know it agen,
won't you?' And I said I thought I should if I tried hard
—and I assure you I kept a sharp look out for the City
Police when we were out in this way, for if any of 'em had

happened to know me, and had spoke to me, it would have been all up in a minute. However, by good luck such a thing never happened, and all went on quiet: though the difficulties I had in communicating with my brother officers were quite extraordinary.

"The stolen goods that were brought to the public-house by the Warehouse Porters, were always disposed of in a back parlour. For a long time, I never could get into this parlour, or see what was done there. As I sat smoking my pipe, like an innocent young chap, by the tap-room fire, I'd hear some of the parties to the robbery, as they came in and out, say softly to the landlord, 'Who's that? What does *he* do here?' 'Bless your soul,' says the landlord, 'he's only a'—ha, ha, ha! —'he's only a green young fellow from the country, as is looking for a butcher's sitivation. Don't mind *him!*' So, in course of time, they were so convinced of my being green, and got to be so accustomed to me, that I was as free of the parlour as any of 'em, and I have seen as much as Seventy Pounds' Worth of fine lawn sold there, in one night, that was stolen from a warehouse in Friday Street. After the sale the buyers always stood treat—hot supper, or dinner, or what not—and they'd say on those occasions, 'Come on, Butcher! Put your best leg foremost, young 'un, and walk into it!' Which I used to do—and hear, at table, all manner of particulars that it was very important for us Detectives to know.

"This went on for ten weeks. I lived in the public-house all the time, and never was out of the Butcher's dress—except in bed. At last, when I had followed seven of the thieves, and set 'em to rights—that's an expression of ours, don't you see, by which I mean to say that I traced 'em, and found out where the robberies were done, and all about 'em—Straw, and Fendall, and I, gave one another the office, and at a time agreed upon, a descent was made upon the public-house, and the apprehensions effected. One of the first things the officers did, was to collar me—for the parties to the robbery weren't to suppose yet, that I was anything but a Butcher—on which the landlord cries out, 'Don't take *him*,' he says, 'whatever you do! He's only a poor young chap from the country, and butter wouldn't melt in his mouth!' However, they—ha, ha, ha!—they took me, and pretended to search my bedroom, where nothing was found but an old fiddle belonging to the landlord, that had got there somehow or another. But, it entirely changed the landlord's opinion, for when it was produced, he says, 'My fiddle! The Butcher's a pur-loiner! I give him into custody for the robbery of a musical instrument!'

"The man that had stolen the goods in Friday Street was not taken yet. He had told me, in confidence, that he had his suspicions there was something wrong (on account of the City Police having captured one of the party), and that he was going to make himself scarce. I asked him, 'Where do you mean to go, Mr. Shepherdson?' 'Why, Butcher,' says he, 'the Setting Moon, in the Commercial Road, is a snug house, and I shall hang out there for a time. I shall call myself Simpson, which appears to me to be a modest sort of a name. Perhaps you'll give us a look in, Butcher?' 'Well,' says I, 'I think I *will* give you a call'—which I fully intended, don't you see, because, of course, he was to be taken! I went over to the Setting Moon next day, with a brother officer, and asked at the bar for Simpson. They pointed out his room, up-stairs. As we were going up, he looks down over the banisters, and calls out, 'Halloa, Butcher! is that you?' 'Yes, it's me. How do find your-self?' 'Bobbish,' he says; 'but who's that with you?' 'It's only a young man, that's a friend of mine,' I says. 'Come along, then,' says he; 'any friend of the Butcher's is as welcome as the Butcher!' So, I made my friend acquainted with him, and we took him into custody.

"You have no idea, sir, what a sight it was, in Court, when they first knew that I wasn't a Butcher, after all! I wasn't produced at the first examination, when there was a remand; but I was at the second. And when I stepped into the box, in full police uniform, and the whole party saw how they had been done, actually a groan of horror and dismay proceeded from 'em in the dock!

"At the Old Bailey, when their trials came on, Mr. Clarkson was engaged for the defence, and he *couldn't* make out how it was, about the Butcher. He thought, all along, it was a real Butcher. When the counsel for the prosecution said, 'I will now call before you, gentlemen, the Police-officer,' meaning myself, Mr. Clarkson says, 'Why Police-officer? Why more Police-officers? I don't want Police. We have had a great deal too much of the Police. I want the Butcher!' However, sir, he had the Butcher and the Police-officer, both in one. Out of seven prisoners committed for trial, five were found guilty, and some of 'em were transported. The respectable firm at the West End got a term of imprisonment; and that's the Butcher's Story!"

The story done, the chuckle-headed Butcher again resolved himself into the smooth-faced Detective. But, he was so extremely tickled by their having taken him about, when he was that Dragon in disguise, to show him London, that he could not help reverting to that point in his narrative; and gently repeating with the Butcher snigger, "'Oh, dear,' I says, 'is that where they hang the men? Oh, Lor!' '*That!*' says they. 'What a simple cove he is!'"

It being now late, and the party very modest in their fear of being too diffuse, there were some tokens of separation; when Sergeant Dornton, the soldierly-looking man, said, looking round him with a smile:

"Before we break up, sir, perhaps you might have some amusement in hearing of the Adventures of a Carpet Bag. They are very short; and, I think, curious."

We welcomed the Carpet Bag, as cordially as Mr. Shepherdson welcomed the false Butcher at the Setting Moon. Sergeant Dornton proceeded.

"In 1847, I was despatched to Chatham, in search of one

Mesheck, a Jew. He had been carrying on, pretty heavily, in the bill-stealing way, getting acceptances from young men of good connexions (in the army chiefly), on pretence of discount, and bolting with the same.

" Mesheck was off, before I got to Chatham. All I could learn about him was, that he had gone, probably to London, and had with him—a Carpet Bag.

" I came back to town, by the last train from Blackwall, and made inquiries concerning a Jew passenger with—a Carpet Bag.

" The office was shut up, it being the last train. There were only two or three porters left. Looking after a Jew with a Carpet Bag, on the Blackwall Railway, which was then the high road to a great Military Depôt, was worse than looking after a needle in a hayrick. But it happened that one of these porters had carried, for a certain Jew, to a certain public-house, a certain—Carpet Bag.

" I went to the public-house, but the Jew had only left his luggage there for a few hours, and had called for it in a cab, and taken it away. I put such questions there, and to the porter, as I thought prudent, and got at this description of—the Carpet Bag.

" It was a bag which had, on one side of it, worked in worsted, a green parrot on a stand. A green parrot on a stand was the means by which to identify that—Carpet Bag.

" I traced Mesheck, by means of this green parrot on a stand, to Cheltenham, to Birmingham, to Liverpool, to the Atlantic Ocean. At Liverpool he was too many for me. He had gone to the United States, and I gave up all thoughts of Mesheck, and likewise of his—Carpet Bag.

" Many months afterwards—near a year afterwards—there was a bank in Ireland robbed of seven thousand pounds, by a person of the name of Doctor Dundey, who escaped to America ; from which country some of the stolen notes came home. He was supposed to have bought a farm in New Jersey. Under proper management, that estate could be seized and sold, for the benefit of the parties he had defrauded. I was sent off to America for this purpose.

"I landed at Boston. I went on to New York. I found that he had lately changed New York paper-money for New Jersey paper-money, and had banked cash in New Brunswick. To take this Doctor Dundey, it was necessary to entrap him into the State of New York, which required a deal of artifice and trouble. At one time, he couldn't be drawn into an appointment. At another time, he appointed to come to meet me, and a New York officer, on a pretext I made; and then his children had the measles. At last he came, per steamboat, and I took him, and lodged him in a New York prison called the Tombs; which I dare say you know, sir?"

Editorial acknowledgment to that effect.

"I went to the Tombs, on the morning after his capture, to attend the examination before the magistrate. I was passing through the magistrate's private room, when, happening to look round me to take notice of the place, as we generally have a habit of doing, I clapped my eyes, in one corner, on a—Carpet Bag.

"What did I see upon that Carpet Bag, if you'll believe me, but a green parrot on a stand, as large as life!

"'That Carpet Bag, with the representation of a green parrot on a stand,' said I, 'belongs to an English Jew, name Aaron Mesheck, and to no other man, alive or dead!'

"I give you my word the New York Police Officers were doubled up with surprise.

"'How did you ever come to know that?' said they.

"'I think I ought to know that green parrot by this time,' said I; 'for I have had as pretty a dance after that bird, at home, as ever I had, in all my life!'"

"And was it Mesheck's?" we submissively inquired.

"Was it, sir? Of course it was! He was in custody for another offence, in that very identical Tombs, at that very identical time. And, more than that! Some memoranda, relating to the fraud for which I had vainly endeavoured to take him, were found to be, at that moment, lying in that very same individual—Carpet Bag ! "

Such are the curious coincidences and such is the peculiar ability, always sharpening and being improved by practice, and always adapting itself to every variety of circumstances, and opposing itself to every new device that perverted ingenuity can invent, for which this important social branch of the public service is remarkable ! For ever on the watch, with their wits stretched to the utmost, these officers have, from day to day and year to year, to set themselves against every novelty of trickery and dexterity that the combined imaginations of all the lawless rascals in England can devise, and to keep pace with every such invention that comes out. In the Courts of Justice, the materials of thousands of such stories as we have narrated—often elevated into the marvellous and romantic, by the circumstances of the case—are dryly compressed into the set phrase, " in consequence of information I received, I did so and so." Suspicion was to be directed, by careful inference and deduction, upon the right person ; the right person was to be taken, wherever he had gone, or whatever he was doing to avoid detection : he is taken ; there he is at the bar ; that is enough. From information I, the officer, received, I did it ; and, according to the custom in these cases, I say no more.

These games of chess, played with live pieces, are played before small audiences, and are chronicled nowhere. The interest of the game supports the player. Its results are enough for Justice. To compare great things with small, suppose LEVERRIER or ADAMS informing the public that from information he had received he had discovered a new planet ; or COLUMBUS informing the public of his day that from information he had received he had discovered a new continent ; so the Detectives inform it that they have discovered a new fraud or an old offender, and the process is unknown.

Thus, at midnight, closed the proceedings of our curious and interesting party. But one other circumstance finally wound up the evening, after our Detective guests had left us. One of the sharpest among them, and the officer best acquainted with the Swell Mob, had his pocket picked, going home!

THREE "DETECTIVE" ANECDOTES

I.—THE PAIR OF GLOVES

"It's a singler story, sir," said Inspector Wield, of the Detective Police, who, in company with Sergeants Dornton and Mith, paid us another twilight visit, one July evening; "and I've been thinking you might like to know it.

"It's concerning the murder of the young woman, Eliza Grimwood, some years ago, over in the Waterloo Road. She was commonly called The Countess, because of her handsome appearance and her proud way of carrying of herself; and when I saw the poor Countess (I had known her well to speak to), lying dead, with her throat cut, on the floor of her bedroom, you'll believe me that a variety of reflections calculated to make a man rather low in his spirits, came into my head.

"That's neither here nor there. I went to the house the morning after the murder, and examined the body, and made a general observation of the bedroom where it was. Turning down the pillow of the bed with my hand, I found, underneath it, a pair of gloves. A pair of gentleman's dress gloves, very dirty; and inside the lining, the letters Tr, and a cross.

"Well, sir, I took them gloves away, and I showed 'em to the magistrate, over at Union Hall, before whom the case was. He says, 'Wield,' he says, 'there's no doubt this is a discovery that may lead to something very important; and what you have got to do, Wield, is, to find out the owner of these gloves.'

"I was of the same opinion, of course, and I went at it immediately. I looked at the gloves pretty narrowly, and it was my opinion that they had been cleaned. There was a smell of sulphur and rosin about 'em, you know, which cleaned gloves usually have, more or less. I took 'em over to a friend of mine at Kennington, who was in that line, and I put it to him. 'What do you say now? Have these gloves been cleaned?' 'These gloves have been cleaned,' says he. 'Have you any idea who cleaned them?' says I. 'Not at all,' says he; 'I've a very distinct idea who *didn't* clean 'em, and that's myself. But I'll tell you what, Wield, there ain't above eight or nine reg'lar glove-cleaners in London,'—there were not, at that time, it seems—'and I think I can give you their addresses, and you may find out, by that means, who did clean 'em.' Accordingly, he gave me the directions, and I went here, and I went there, and I looked up this man, and I looked up that man; but, though they all agreed that the gloves had been cleaned, I couldn't find the man, woman, or child, that had cleaned that aforesaid pair of gloves.

"What with this person not being at home, and that person being expected home in the afternoon, and so forth, the inquiry took me three days. On the evening of the third day, coming over Waterloo Bridge from the Surrey side of the river, quite beat, and very much vexed and disappointed, I thought I'd have a shilling's worth of entertainment at the Lyceum Theatre to freshen myself up. So I went into the Pit, at half-price, and I sat myself down next to a very quiet, modest sort of young man. Seeing I was a stranger (which I thought it just as well to appear to be) he told me the names of the actors on the stage, and we got into conversation. When the play was over, we came out together, and I said, 'We've been very companionable and agreeable, and perhaps you wouldn't object to a drain?' 'Well, you're very good,' says he; 'I *shouldn't* object to a drain.' Accordingly, we went to a public-house, near the Theatre, sat ourselves down in a quiet room up-stairs on the first floor, and called for a pint of half-and-half, apiece, and a pipe.

"Well, sir, we put our pipes aboard, and we drank our half-and-half, and sat a-talking, very sociably, when the young man says, 'You must excuse me stopping very long,' he says, 'because I'm forced to go home in good time. I must be at work all night.' 'At work all night?' says I. 'You ain't a baker?' 'No,' he says, laughing, 'I ain't a baker.' 'I thought not,' says I, 'you haven't the looks of a baker.' 'No,' says he, 'I'm a glove-cleaner.'

"I never was more astonished in my life, than when I heard them words come out of his lips. 'You're a glove-cleaner, are you?' says I. 'Yes,' he says, 'I am.' 'Then, perhaps,' says I, taking the gloves out of my pocket, 'you can tell me who cleaned this pair of gloves? It's a rum story,' I says. 'I was dining over at Lambeth, the other day, at a free-and-easy—quite promiscuous—with a public company —when some gentleman, he left these gloves behind him! Another gentleman and me, you see, we laid a wager of a sovereign, that I wouldn't find out who they belonged to. I've spent as much as seven shillings already, in trying to discover ; but, if you could help me, I'd stand another seven and welcome. 'You see there's TR and a cross, inside.' '*I* see,' he says. 'Bless you, *I* know these gloves very well! I've seen dozens of pairs belonging to the same party.' 'No?' says I. 'Yes,' says he. 'Then you know who cleaned 'em?' says I. 'Rather so,' says he. 'My father cleaned 'em.'

"'Where does your father live?' says I. 'Just round the corner,' says the young man, 'near Exeter Street, here. He'll tell you who they belong to, directly.' 'Would you come round with me now?' says I. 'Certainly,' says he, 'but you needn't tell my father that you found me at the play, you know, because he mightn't like it.' 'All right!' We went round to the place, and there we found an old man in a white apron, with two or three daughters, all rubbing and cleaning away at lots of gloves, in a front parlour. 'Oh, Father!'

says the young man, 'here's a person been and made a bet about the ownership of a pair of gloves, and I've told him you can settle it.' 'Good evening, sir,' says I to the old gentleman. 'Here's the gloves your son speaks of. Letters TR, you see, and a cross.' 'Oh yes,' he says, 'I know these gloves very well; I've cleaned dozens of pairs of 'em. They belong to Mr. Trinkle, the great upholsterer in Cheapside.' 'Did you get 'em from Mr. Trinkle, direct,' says I, 'if you'll excuse my asking the question?' 'No,' says he; 'Mr. Trinkle always sends 'em to Mr. Phibbs's, the haberdasher's, opposite his shop, and the haberdasher sends 'em to me.' 'Perhaps *you* wouldn't object to a drain?' says I. 'Not in the least!' says he. So I took the old gentleman out, and had a little more talk with him and his son, over a glass, and we parted ex-cellent friends.

"This was late on a Saturday night. First thing on the Monday morning, I went to the haberdasher's shop, opposite Mr. Trinkle's, the great upholsterer's in Cheapside. 'Mr. Phibbs in the way?' 'My name is Phibbs.' 'Oh! I believe you sent this pair of gloves to be cleaned?' 'Yes, I did, for young Mr. Trinkle over the way. There he is in the shop!' 'Oh! that's him in the shop, is it? Him in the green coat?' 'The same individual.' 'Well, Mr. Phibbs, this is an unpleasant affair; but the fact is, I am Inspector Wield of the Detective Police, and I found these gloves under the pillow of the young woman that was murdered the other day, over in the Waterloo Road?' 'Good Heaven!' says he. 'He's a most respectable young man, and if his father was to hear of it, it would be the ruin of him!' 'I'm very sorry for it,' says I, 'but I must take him into custody.' 'Good Heaven!' says Mr. Phibbs, again; 'can nothing be done!' 'Nothing,' says I. 'Will you allow me to call him over here,' says he, 'that his father may not see it done?' 'I don't object to that,' says I; 'but unfortunately, Mr. Phibbs, I can't allow of any communication between you. If any was attempted, I should have to interfere directly.

166

Perhaps you'll beckon him over here?' Mr. Phibbs went to the door and beckoned, and the young fellow came across the street directly; a smart, brisk young fellow.

"'Good morning, sir,' says I. 'Good morning, sir,' says he. 'Would you allow me to inquire, sir,' says I, 'if you ever had any acquaintance with a party of the name of Grimwood?' 'Grimwood! Grimwood!' says he. 'No!' 'You know the Waterloo Road?' 'Oh! of course I know the Waterloo Road!' 'Happen to have heard of a young woman being murdered there?' 'Yes, I read it in the paper, and very sorry I was to read it.' 'Here's a pair of gloves belonging to you, that I found under her pillow the morning afterwards!'

"He was in a dreadful state, sir; a dreadful state! 'Mr. Wield,' he says, 'upon my solemn oath I never was there. I never so much as saw her, to my knowledge, in my life!' 'I am very sorry,' says I. 'To tell you the truth; I don't think you *are* the murderer, but I must take you to Union Hall in a cab. However, I think it's a case of that sort, that, at present, at all events, the magistrate will hear it in private.'

"A private examination took place, and then it came out that this young man was acquainted with a cousin of the unfortunate Eliza Grimwood, and that, calling to see this cousin a day or two before the murder, he left these gloves upon the table. Who should come in, shortly afterwards, but Eliza Grimwood! 'Whose gloves are these?' she says, taking 'em up. 'Those are Mr. Trinkle's gloves,' says her cousin. 'Oh!' says she, 'they are very dirty, and of no use to him, I am sure. I shall take 'em away for my girl to clean the stoves with.' And she put 'em in her pocket. The girl had used 'em to clean the stoves, and, I have no doubt, had left 'em lying on the bedroom mantelpiece, or on the drawers, or somewhere; and her mistress, looking round to see that the room was tidy, had caught 'em up and put 'em under the pillow where I found 'em.

"That's the story, sir."

II.—THE ARTFUL TOUCH

"One of the most *beautiful* things that ever was done, perhaps," said Inspector Wield, emphasising the adjective, as preparing us to expect dexterity or ingenuity rather than strong interest, "was a move of Sergeant Witchem's. It was a lovely idea!

"Witchem and me were down at Epsom one Derby Day, waiting at the station for the Swell Mob. As I mentioned, when we were talking about these things before, we are ready at the station when there's races, or an Agricultural Show, or a Chancellor sworn in for an university, or Jenny Lind, or anything of that sort; and as the Swell Mob come down, we send 'em back again by the next train. But some of the Swell Mob, on the occasion of this Derby that I refer to, so far kidded us as to hire a horse and shay; start away from London by Whitechapel, and miles round; come into Epsom from the opposite direction; and go to work, right and left, on the course, while we were waiting for 'em at the Rail. That, however, ain't the point of what I'm going to tell you.

"While Witchem and me were waiting at the station, there comes up one Mr. Tatt; a gentleman formerly in the public line, quite an amateur Detective in his way, and very much respected. 'Halloa, Charley Wield,' he says. 'What are you doing here? On the look out for some of your old friends?' 'Yes, the old move, Mr. Tatt.' 'Come along,' he says, 'you and Witchem, and have a glass of sherry.' 'We can't stir from the place,' says I, 'till the next train comes in; but after that, we will with pleasure.' Mr. Tatt waits, and the train comes in, and then Witchem and me go off with him to the Hotel. Mr. Tatt he's got up quite regardless of expense, for the occasion; and in his shirt-front there's a beautiful diamond prop, cost him fifteen or twenty pound—a very handsome pin indeed. We drink our sherry at the bar, and have had our three or four glasses, when Witchem cries suddenly, 'Look out, Mr. Wield! stand fast!' and a dash is made into the place by the Swell Mob—four of 'em—that have come down as I tell you, and in a moment Mr. Tatt's prop is gone! Witchem, he cuts 'em off at the door, I lay about me as hard as I can, Mr. Tatt shows fight like a good 'un, and there we are, all down together, heads and heels, knocking about on the floor of the bar—perhaps you never see such a scene of confusion! However, we stick to our men (Mr. Tatt being as good as any officer), and we take 'em all, and carry 'em off to the station. The station's full of people, who have been took on the course; and it's a precious piece of work to get 'em secured. However, we do it at last, and we search 'em; but nothing's found upon 'em, and they're locked up; and a pretty state of heat we are in by that time, I assure you!

"I was very blank over it, myself, to think that the prop had been passed away; and I said to Witchem, when we had set 'em to rights, and were cooling ourselves along with Mr. Tatt, 'we don't take much by *this* move, anyway, for nothing's found upon 'em, and it's only the braggadocia,* after all.' 'What do you mean, Mr. Wield?' says Witchem. 'Here's the diamond pin!' and in the palm of his hand there it was, safe and sound! 'Why, in the name of wonder,' says me and Mr. Tatt, in astonishment, 'how did you come by that?' 'I'll tell you how I come by it,' says he. 'I saw which of 'em took it; and when we were all down on the floor together, knocking about, I just gave him a little touch on the back of his hand, as I knew his pal would; and he thought it was his pal; and gave it me!' It was beautiful, beau-ti-ful!

"Even that was hardly the best of the case, for that chap was tried at the Quarter Sessions at Guildford. You know what Quarter Sessions are, sir. Well, if you'll believe me, while them slow justices were looking over the Acts of

* Three months' imprisonment as reputed thieves.

Parliament, to see what they could do to him, I'm blowed if he didn't cut out of the dock before their faces! He cut out of the dock, sir, then and there; swam across a river; and got up into a tree to dry himself. In the tree he was took —an old woman having seen him climb up—and Witchem's artful touch transported him!"

III.—THE SOFA

"What young men will do, sometimes, to ruin themselves and break their friends' hearts," said Sergeant Dornton, "it's surprising! I had a case at Saint Blank's Hospital which was of this sort. A bad case, indeed, with a bad end!

"The Secretary, and the House-Surgeon, and the Treasurer, of Saint Blank's Hospital, came to Scotland Yard to give information of numerous robberies having been committed on the students. The students could leave nothing in the pockets of their great-coats, while the great-coats were hanging at the hospital, but it was almost certain to be stolen. Property of various descriptions was constantly being lost; and the gentlemen were naturally uneasy about it, and anxious, for the credit of the institution, that the thief or thieves should be discovered. The case was entrusted to me, and I went to the hospital.

"'Now, gentlemen,' said I, after we had talked it over; 'I understand this property is usually lost from one room.'

"Yes, they said. It was.

"'I should wish, if you please,' said I, 'to see the room.'

"It was a good-sized bare room down-stairs, with a few tables and forms in it, and a row of pegs, all round, for hats and coats.

"'Next, gentlemen,' said I, 'do you suspect anybody?'

"Yes, they said. They did suspect somebody. They were sorry to say, they suspected one of the porters.

"'I should like,' said I, 'to have that man pointed out to me, and to have a little time to look after him.'

170

The Sofa

UNDER THE SOFA

"He was pointed out, and I looked after him, and then I went back to the hospital, and said, 'Now, gentlemen, it's not the porter. He's, unfortunately for himself, a little too fond of drink, but he's nothing worse. My suspicion is, that these robberies are committed by one of the students; and if you'll put me a sofa into that room where the pegs are —as there's no closet—I think I shall be able to detect the thief. I wish the sofa, if you please, to be covered with chintz, or something of that sort, so that I may lie on my chest, underneath it, without being seen.'

"The sofa was provided, and next day at eleven o'clock, before any of the students came, I went there, with those gentlemen, to get underneath it. It turned out to be one of those old-fashioned sofas with a great cross-beam at the bottom, that would have broken my back in no time if I could ever have got below it. We had quite a job to break all this away in the time; however, I fell to work, and they fell to work, and we broke it out, and made a clear place for me. I got under the sofa, lay down on my chest, took out my knife, and made a convenient hole in the chintz to look through. It was then settled between me and the gentlemen that when the students were all up in the wards, one of the gentlemen should come in, and hang up a great-coat on one of the pegs. And that that great-coat should have, in one of the pockets, a pocket-book containing marked money.

"After I had been there some time, the students began to drop into the room, by ones, and twos, and threes, and to talk about all sorts of things, little thinking there was anybody under the sofa—and then to go up-stairs. At last there came in one who remained until he was alone in the room by himself. A tallish, good-looking young man of one or two and twenty, with a light whisker. He went to a particular hat-peg, took off a good hat that was hanging there, tried it on, hung his own hat in its place, and hung that hat on another peg, nearly opposite to me. I then felt quite certain that he was the thief, and would come back by-and-by.

"When they were all up-stairs, the gentleman came in with the great-coat. I showed him where to hang it, so that I might have a good view of it; and he went away; and I lay under the sofa on my chest, for a couple of hours or so, waiting.

"At last, the same young man came down. He walked across the room, whistling—stopped and listened—took another walk and whistled—stopped again, and listened—then began to go regularly round the pegs, feeling in the pockets of all the coats. When he came to THE great-coat, and felt the pocket-book, he was so eager and so hurried that he broke the strap in tearing it open. As he began to put the money in his pocket, I crawled out from under the sofa, and his eyes met mine.

"My face, as you may perceive, is brown now, but it was pale at that time, my health not being good; and looked as long as a horse's. Besides which, there was a great draught of air from the door, underneath the sofa, and I had tied a handkerchief round my head; so what I looked like, altogether, I don't know. He turned blue—literally blue—when he saw me crawling out, and I couldn't feel surprised at it.

"'I am an officer of the Detective Police,' said I, 'and have been lying here, since you first came in this morning. I regret, for the sake of yourself and your friends, that you should have done what you have; but this case is complete. You have the pocket-book in your hand and the money upon you; and I must take you into custody!

"It was impossible to make out any case in his behalf, and on his trial he pleaded guilty. How or when he got the means I don't know; but while he was awaiting his sentence, he poisoned himself in Newgate."

We inquired of this officer, on the conclusion of the foregoing anecdote, whether the time appeared long, or short, when he lay in that constrained position under the sofa?

THE TIME SEEMED SHORT

."Why, you see, sir," he replied, "if he hadn't come in, the first time, and I had not been quite sure he was the thief, and would return, the time would have seemed long. But, as it was, I being dead certain of my man, the time seemed pretty short."

ON DUTY WITH INSPECTOR FIELD

How goes the night? Saint Giles's clock is striking nine. The weather is dull and wet, and the long lines of street lamps are blurred, as if we saw them through tears. A damp wind blows and rakes the pieman's fire out, when he opens the door of his little furnace, carrying away an eddy of sparks.

Saint Giles's clock strikes nine. We are punctual. Where is Inspector Field? Assistant Commissioner of Police is already here, enwrapped in oil-skin cloak, and standing in the shadow of Saint Giles's steeple. Detective Sergeant, weary of speaking French all day to foreigners unpacking at the Great Exhibition, is already here. Where is Inspector Field?

Inspector Field is, to-night, the guardian genius of the British Museum. He is bringing his shrewd eye to bear on every corner of its solitary galleries, before he reports "all right." Suspicious of the Elgin marbles, and not to be done by cat-faced Egyptian giants with their hands upon their knees, Inspector Field, sagacious, vigilant, lamp in hand, throwing monstrous shadows on the walls and ceilings, passes through the spacious rooms. If a mummy trembled in an atom of its dusty covering, Inspector Field would say, "Come out of that, Tom Green. I know you!" If the smallest "Gonoph" about town were crouching at the bottom of a

174

classic bath, Inspector Field would nose him with a finer scent than the ogre's, when adventurous Jack lay trembling in his kitchen copper. But all is quiet, and Inspector Field goes warily on, making little outward show of attending to anything in particular, just recognising the Ichthyosaurus as a familiar acquaintance, and wondering, perhaps, how the detectives did it in the days before the Flood.

Will Inspector Field be long about this work? He may be half-an-hour longer. He sends his compliments by Police Constable, and proposes that we meet at St. Giles's Station House, across the road. Good. It were as well to stand by the fire, there, as in the shadow of Saint Giles's steeple.

Anything doing here to-night? Not much. We are very quiet. A lost boy, extremely calm and small, sitting by the fire, whom we now confide to a constable to take home, for the child says that if you show him Newgate Street, he can show you where he lives—a raving drunken woman in the cells, who has screeched her voice away, and has hardly power enough left to declare, even with the passionate help of her feet and arms, that she is the daughter of a British officer, and, strike her blind and dead, but she'll write a letter to the Queen! but who is soothed with a drink of water—in another cell, a quiet woman with a child at her breast, for begging— in another, her husband in a smock-frock, with a basket of watercresses—in another, a pickpocket—in another, a meek tremulous old pauper man who has been out for a holiday "and has took but a little drop, but it has overcome him after so many months in the house"—and that's all as yet. Presently, a sensation at the Station House door. Mr. Field, gentlemen!

Inspector Field comes in, wiping his forehead, for he is of a burly figure, and has come fast from the ores and metals of the deep mines of the earth, and from the Parrot Gods of the South Sea Islands, and from the birds and beetles of the tropics, and from the Arts of Greece and Rome, and from the Sculptures of Nineveh, and from the traces of an elder world, when these were not. Is Rogers ready? Rogers is ready, strapped and great-coated, with a flaming eye in the middle of his waist, like a deformed Cyclops. Lead on, Rogers, to Rats' Castle!

How many people may there be in London, who, if we had brought them deviously and blindfold, to this street, fifty paces from the Station House, and within call of Saint Giles's church, would know it for a not remote part of the city in which their lives are passed? How many, who amidst this compound of sickening smells, these heaps of filth, these tumbling houses, with all their vile contents, animate, and inanimate, slimily overflowing into the black road, would believe that they breathe *this* air? How much Red Tape may there be, that could look round on the faces which now hem us in—for our appearance here has caused a rush from all points to a common centre—the lowering foreheads, the sallow cheeks, the brutal eyes, the matted hair, the infected, vermin-haunted heaps of rags—and say, "I have thought of this. I have not dismissed the thing. I have neither blustered it away, nor frozen it away, nor tied it up and put it away, nor smoothly said pooh, pooh! to it when it has been shown to me?"

This is not what Rogers wants to know, however. What Rogers wants to know, is, whether you *will* clear the way here, some of you, or whether you won't; because if you don't do it right on end, he'll lock you up! "What! *You* are there, are you, Bob Miles? You haven't had enough of it yet, haven't you? You want three months more, do you? Come away from that gentleman! What are you creeping round there for?"

"What am I a doing, thinn, Mr. Rogers?" says Bob Miles, appearing, villainous, at the end of a lane of light, made by the lantern.

"I'll let you know pretty quick, if you don't hook it. WILL you hook it?"

A sycophantic murmur rises from the crowd. "Hook it,

Bob, when Mr. Rogers and Mr. Field tells you! Why don't you hook it, when you are told to?"

The most importunate of the voices strikes familiarly on Mr. Rogers's ear. He suddenly turns his lantern on the owner.

"What! *You* are there, are you, Mister Click? You hook it too—come!"

"What for?" says Mr. Click, discomfited.

"You hook it, will you!" says Mr. Rogers with stern emphasis.

Both Click and Miles *do* "hook it," without another word, or, in plainer English, sneak away.

"Close up there, my men!" says Inspector Field to two constables on duty who have followed. "Keep together, gentlemen; we are going down here. Heads!"

Saint Giles's church strikes half-past ten. We stoop low, and creep down a precipitous flight of steps into a dark close cellar. There is a fire. There is a long deal table. There are benches. The cellar is full of company, chiefly very young men in various conditions of dirt and raggedness. Some are eating supper. There are no girls or women present. Welcome to Rats' Castle, gentlemen, and to this company of noted thieves!

"Well, my lads! How are you, my lads? What have you been doing to-day? Here's some company come to see you, my lads! *There's* a plate of beefsteak, sir, for the supper of a fine young man! And there's a mouth for a steak, sir! Why, I should be too proud of such a mouth as that, if I had it myself! Stand up and show it, sir! Take off your cap. There's a fine young man for a nice little party, sir! An't he?"

Inspector Field is the bustling speaker. Inspector Field's eye is the roving eye that searches every corner of the cellar as he talks. Inspector Field's hand is the well-known hand that has collared half the people here, and motioned their brothers, sisters, fathers, mothers, male and female friends, inexorably to New South Wales. Yet Inspector Field stands in this den, the Sultan of the place. Every thief here cowers before him, like a schoolboy before his schoolmaster. All watch him, all answer when addressed, all laugh at his jokes, all seek to propitiate him. This cellar company alone—to say nothing of the crowd surrounding the entrance from the street above, and making the steps shine with eyes—is strong enough to murder us all, and willing enough to do it; but, let Inspector Field have a mind to pick out one thief here, and take him; let him produce that ghostly truncheon from his pocket, and say, with his business-air, "My lad, I want you!" and all Rats' Castle shall be stricken with paralysis, and not a finger move against him, as he fits the handcuffs on!

Where's the Earl of Warwick?—Here he is, Mr. Field! Here's the Earl of Warwick, Mr. Field!—O there you are, my Lord. Come for'ard. There's a chest, sir, not to have a clean shirt on. An't it? Take your hat off, my Lord. Why, I should be ashamed if I was you—and an Earl, too—to show myself to a gentleman with my hat on!—The Earl of Warwick laughs and uncovers. All the company laugh. One pickpocket, especially, laughs with great enthusiasm. O what a jolly game it is, when Mr. Field comes down—and don't want nobody!

So, *you* are here, too, are you, you tall, grey, soldierly-looking, grave man, standing by the fire?—Yes, sir. Good evening, Mr. Field!—Let us see. You lived servant to a nobleman once?—Yes, Mr. Field.—And what is it you do now; I forget?—Well, Mr. Field, I job about as well as I can. I left my employment on account of delicate health. The family is still kind to me. Mr. Wix of Piccadilly is also very kind to me when I am hard up. Likewise Mr. Nix of Oxford Street. I get a trifle from them occasionally, and rub on as well as I can, Mr. Field. Mr. Field's eye rolls enjoyingly, for this man is a notorious begging-letter writer. —Good night, my lads! — Good night, Mr. Field, and thank'ee, sir!

AMONG THE TRAMPS

Clear the street here, half a thousand of you! Cut it, Mrs. Stalker—none of that—we don't want you! Rogers of the flaming eye, lead on to the tramps' lodging-house!

A dream of baleful faces attends to the door. Now, stand back all of you! In the rear Detective Sergeant plants himself, composedly whistling, with his strong right arm across the narrow passage. Mrs. Stalker, I am something'd that need not be written here, if you won't get yourself into trouble, in about half a minute, if I see that face of yours again!

Saint Giles's church clock, striking eleven, hums through our hand from the dilapidated door of a dark outhouse as we open it, and are stricken back by the pestilent breath that issues from within. Rogers to the front with the light, and let us look!

Ten, twenty, thirty—who can count them! Men, women, children, for the most part naked, heaped upon the floor like maggots in a cheese! Ho! In that dark corner yonder! Does anybody lie there? Me sir, Irish me, a widder, with six children. And yonder? Me sir, Irish me, with me wife and eight poor babes. And to the left there? Me sir, Irish me, along with two more Irish boys as is me friends. And to the right there? Me sir and the Murphy fam'ly, numbering five blessed souls. And what's this, coiling, now, about my foot? Another Irish me, pitifully in want of shaving, whom I have awakened from sleep—and across my other foot lies his wife—and by the shoes of Inspector Field lie their three eldest—and their three youngest are at present squeezed between the open door and the wall. And why is there no one on that little mat before the sullen fire? Because O'Donovan, with his wife and daughter, is not come in from selling Lucifers! Nor on the bit of sacking in the nearest corner? Bad luck! Because that Irish family is late to-night, a-cadging in the streets!

They are all awake now, the children excepted, and most of them sit up, to stare. Wheresoever Mr. Rogers turns the flaming eye, there is a spectral figure rising, unshrouded, from a grave of rags. Who is the landlord here?—I am, Mr. Field! says a bundle of ribs and parchment against the wall, scratching itself.—Will you spend this money fairly, in the morning, to buy coffee for 'em all?—Yes, sir, I will!— O he'll do it, sir, he'll do it fair. He's honest! cry the spectres. And with thanks and Good Night sink into their graves again.

Thus, we make our New Oxford Streets, and our other new streets, never heeding, never asking, where the wretches whom we clear out, crowd. With such scenes at our doors, with all the plagues of Egypt tied up with bits of cobweb in kennels so near our homes, we timorously make our Nuisance Bills and Boards of Health, nonentities, and think to keep away the Wolves of Crime and Filth, by our electioneering ducking to little vestrymen and our gentlemanly handling of Red Tape!

Intelligence of the coffee-money has got abroad. The yard is full, and Rogers of the flaming eye is beleaguered with entreaties to show other Lodging Houses. Mine next! Mine! Mine! Rogers, military, obdurate, stiff-necked, immovable, replies not, but leads away; all falling back before him. Inspector Field follows. Detective Sergeant, with his barrier of arm across the little passage, deliberately waits to close the procession. He sees behind him, without any effort, and exceedingly disturbs one individual far in the rear by coolly calling out, "It won't do, Mr. Michael! Don't try it!"

After council holden in the street, we enter other lodging-houses, public-houses, many lairs and holes; all noisome and offensive; none so filthy and so crowded as where Irish are. In one, The Ethiopian party are expected home presently —were in Oxford Street when last heard of—shall be fetched, for our delight, within ten minutes. In another, one of the two or three Professors who draw Napoleon Buonaparte and a couple of mackerel, on the pavement, and then let the work of art out to a speculator, is refreshing after his labours.

THE OLD MINT

In another, the vested interest of the profitable nuisance
has been in one family for a hundred years, and the landlord
drives in comfortably from the country to his snug little
stew in town. In all, Inspector Field is received with warmth.
Coiners and smashers droop before him; pickpockets defer
to him; the gentle sex (not very gentle here) smile upon him.
Half-drunken hags check themselves in the midst of pots of
beer, or pints of gin, to drink to Mr. Field, and pressingly
to ask the honour of his finishing the draught. One beldame
in rusty black has such admiration for him, that she runs a
whole street's length to shake him by the hand; tumbling
into a heap of mud by the way, and still pressing her attentions when her very form has ceased to be distinguishable
through it. Before the power of the law, the power of
superior sense—for common thieves are fools beside these
men—and the power of a perfect mastery of their character,
the garrison of Rats' Castle and the adjacent Fortresses make
but a skulking show indeed when reviewed by Inspector Field.

Saint Giles's clock says it will be midnight in half-an-hour,
and Inspector Field says we must hurry to the Old Mint in
the Borough. The cab-driver is low-spirited, and has a solemn
sense of his responsibility. Now, what's your fare, my lad?
—O *you* know, Inspector Field, what's the good of asking *me!*

Say, Parker, strapped and great-coated, and waiting in dim
Borough doorway by appointment, to replace the trusty
Rogers whom we left deep in Saint Giles's, are you ready?
Ready, Inspector Field, and at a motion of my wrist behold
my flaming eye.

This narrow street, sir, is the chief part of the Old Mint,
full of low lodging-houses, as you see by the transparent
canvas-lamps and blinds, announcing beds for travellers!
But it is greatly changed, friend Field, from my former
knowledge of it; it is infinitely quieter and more subdued
than when I was here last, some seven years ago? O yes!
Inspector Haynes, a first-rate man, is on this station now
and plays the Devil with them!

Well, my lads! How are you to-night, my lads? Playing cards here, eh? Who wins?—Why, Mr. Field, I, the sulky gentleman with the damp flat side-curls, rubbing my bleared eye with the end of my neckerchief which is like a dirty eel-skin, am losing just at present, but I suppose I must take my pipe out of my mouth, and be submissive to *you*—I hope I see you well, Mr. Field?—Aye, all right, my lad. Deputy, who have you got up-stairs? Be pleased to show the rooms!

Why Deputy, Inspector Field can't say. He only knows that the man who takes care of the beds and lodgers is always called so. Steady, O Deputy, with the flaring candle in the blacking-bottle, for this is a slushy back-yard, and the wooden staircase outside the house creaks and has holes in it.

Again, in these confined intolerable rooms, burrowed out like the holes of rats or the nests of insect-vermin, but fuller of intolerable smells, are crowds of sleepers, each on his foul truckle-bed coiled up beneath a rug. Halloa here! Come! Let us see you! Show your face! Pilot Parker goes from bed to bed and turns their slumbering heads towards us, as a salesman might turn sheep. Some wake up with an execration and a threat.—What! who spoke? O! If it's the accursed glaring eye that fixes me, go where I will, I am helpless. Here! I sit up to be looked at. Is it me you want? Not you, lie down again! and I lie down, with a woful growl.

Wherever the turning lane of light becomes stationary for a moment, some sleeper appears at the end of it, submits himself to be scrutinised, and fades away into the darkness.

There should be strange dreams here, Deputy. They sleep sound enough, says Deputy, taking the candle out of the blacking-bottle, snuffing it with his fingers, throwing the snuff into the bottle, and corking it up with the candle; that's all *I* know. What is the inscription, Deputy, on all the discoloured sheets? A precaution against loss of linen. Deputy turns down the rug of an unoccupied bed and discloses it. Stop Thief!

THE OLD FARM HOUSE

To lie at night, wrapped in the legend of my slinking life; to take the cry that pursues me, waking, to my breast in sleep; to have it staring at me, and clamouring for me, as soon as consciousness returns; to have it for my first-foot on New-Year's day, my Valentine, my Birthday salute, my Christmas greeting, my parting with the old year. STOP THIEF!

And to know that I *must* be stopped, come what will. To know that I am no match for this individual energy and keenness, or this organised and steady system! Come across the street, here, and, entering by a little shop and yard, examine these intricate passages and doors, contrived for escape, flapping and counter-flapping, like the lids of the conjurer's boxes. But what avail they? Who gets in by a nod, and shows their secret working to us? Inspector Field.

Don't forget the old Farm House, Parker! Parker is not the man to forget it. We are going there, now. It is the old Manor-House of these parts, and stood in the country once. Then, perhaps, there was something, which was not the beastly street, to see from the shattered low fronts of the overhanging wooden houses we are passing under—shut up now, pasted over with bills about the literature and drama of the Mint, and mouldering away. This long paved yard was a paddock or a garden once, or a court in front of the Farm House. Perchance, with a dovecot in the centre, and fowls pecking about—with fair elm trees, then, where discoloured chimney-stacks and gables are now—noisy, then, with rooks which have yielded to a different sort of rookery. It's likelier than not, Inspector Field thinks, as we turn into the common kitchen, which is in the yard, and many paces from the house.

Well, my lads and lasses, how are you all? Where's Blackey, who has stood near London Bridge these five-and-twenty years, with a painted skin to represent disease?— Here he is, Mr. Field!—How are you, Blackey?—Jolly, sa!

Not playing the fiddle to-night, Blackey?—Not a night, sa!
A sharp, smiling youth, the wit of the kitchen, interposes.
He an't musical to-night, sir. I've been giving him a moral
lecture; I've been a talking to him about his latter end, you
see. A good many of these are my pupils, sir. This here
young man (smoothing down the hair of one near him,
reading a Sunday paper) is a pupil of mine. I'm a teaching
of him to read, sir. He's a promising cove, sir. He's a
smith, he is, and gets his living by the sweat of the brow,
sir. So do I, myself, sir. This young woman is my sister,
Mr. Field. *She's* getting on very well too. I've a deal of
trouble with 'em, sir, but I'm richly rewarded, now I see
'em all a doing so well, and growing up so creditable.
That's a great comfort, that is, an't it, sir?—In the midst
of the kitchen (the whole kitchen is in ecstasies with this
impromptu " chaff") sits a young, modest, gentle-looking
creature, with a beautiful child in her lap. She seems to
belong to the company, but is so strangely unlike it. She
has such a pretty, quiet face and voice, and is so proud to
hear the child admired—thinks you would hardly believe
that he is only nine months old! Is she as bad as the rest,
I wonder? Inspectorial experience does not engender a belief
contrariwise, but prompts the answer, Not a ha'porth of
difference!

There is a piano going in the old Farm House as we
approach. It stops. Landlady appears. Has no objections,
Mr. Field, to gentlemen being brought, but wishes it were
at earlier hours, the lodgers complaining of ill-conwenience.
Inspector Field is polite and soothing—knows his woman
and the sex. Deputy (a girl in this case) shows the way up
a heavy, broad old staircase, kept very clean, into clean rooms
where many sleepers are, and where painted panels of an
older time look strangely on the truckle beds. The sight
of whitewash and the smell of soap—two things we seem by
this time to have parted from in infancy—make the old Farm
House a phenomenon, and connect themselves with the so

curiously misplaced picture of the pretty mother and child long after we have left it,—long after we have left, besides, the neighbouring nook with something of a rustic flavour in it yet, where once, beneath a low wooden colonnade still standing as of yore, the eminent Jack Sheppard condescended to regale himself, and where, now, two old bachelor brothers in broad hats (who are whispered in the Mint to have made a compact long ago that if either should ever marry, he must forfeit his share of the joint property) still keep a sequestered tavern, and sit o' nights smoking pipes in the bar, among ancient bottles and glasses, as our eyes behold them.

How goes the night now? Saint George of Southwark answers with twelve blows upon his bell. Parker, good night, for Williams is already waiting over in the region of Ratcliffe Highway, to show the houses where the sailors dance.

I should like to know where Inspector Field was born. In Ratcliffe Highway, I would have answered with confidence, but for his being equally at home wherever we go. *He* does not trouble his head as I do, about the river at night. *He* does not care for its creeping, black and silent, on our right there, rushing through sluice-gates, lapping at piles and posts and iron rings, hiding strange things in its mud, running away with suicides and accidentally drowned bodies faster than midnight funeral should, and acquiring such various experience between its cradle and its grave. It has no mystery for *him*. Is there not the Thames Police!

Accordingly, Williams leads the way. We are a little late, for some of the houses are already closing. No matter. You show us plenty. All the landlords know Inspector Field. All pass him, freely and good-humouredly, wheresoever he wants to go. So thoroughly are all these houses open to him and our local guide, that, granting that sailors must be entertained in their own way—as I suppose they must, and have a right to be—I hardly know how such places could be better regulated. Not that I call the company very select, or the dancing very graceful—even so graceful as that of the German

Sugar Bakers, whose assembly, by the Minories, we stopped to visit—but there is watchful maintenance of order in every house, and swift expulsion where need is. Even in the midst of drunkenness, both of the lethargic kind and the lively, there is sharp landlord supervision, and pockets are in less peril than out of doors. These houses show, singularly, how much of the picturesque and romantic there truly is in the sailor, requiring to be especially addressed. All the songs (sung in a hailstorm of halfpence, which are pitched at the singer without the least tenderness for the time or tune—mostly from great rolls of copper carried for the purpose—and which he occasionally dodges like shot as they fly near his head) are of the sentimental sea sort. All the rooms are decorated with nautical subjects. Wrecks, engagements, ships on fire, ships passing lighthouses on iron-bound coasts, ships blowing up, ships going down, ships running ashore, men lying out upon the main-yard in a gale of wind, sailors and ships in every variety of peril, constitute the illustrations of fact. Nothing can be done in the fanciful way, without a thumping boy upon a scaly dolphin.

How goes the night now? Past one. Black and Green are waiting in Whitechapel to unveil the mysteries of Wentworth Street. Williams, the best of friends must part. Adieu!

Are not Black and Green ready at the appointed place? O yes! They glide out of shadow as we stop. Imperturbable Black opens the cab-door; Imperturbable Green takes a mental note of the driver. Both Green and Black then open each his flaming eye, and marshal us the way that we are going.

The lodging-house we want is hidden in a maze of streets and courts. It is fast shut. We knock at the door, and stand hushed looking up for a light at one or other of the begrimed old lattice windows in its ugly front, when another constable comes up—supposes that we want " to see the school." Detective Sergeant meanwhile has got over a rail, opened a gate, dropped down an area, overcome some other little obstacles, and tapped at a window. Now returns. The landlord will send a deputy immediately.

Deputy is heard to stumble out of bed. Deputy lights a candle, draws back a bolt or two, and appears at the door. Deputy is a shivering shirt and trousers by no means clean, a yawning face, a shock head much confused externally and internally. We want to look for some one. You may go up with the light, and take 'em all, if you like, says Deputy, resigning it, and sitting down upon a bench in the kitchen with his ten fingers sleepily twisting in his hair.

Halloa here! Now then! Show yourselves. That'll do. It's not you. Don't disturb yourself any more! So on, through a labyrinth of airless rooms, each man responding, like a wild beast, to the keeper who has tamed him, and who goes into his cage. What, you haven't found him, then? says Deputy, when we came down. A woman mysteriously sitting up all night in the dark by the smouldering ashes of the kitchen fire, says it's only tramps and cadgers here; it's gonophs over the way. A man mysteriously walking about the kitchen all night in the dark, bids her hold her tongue. We come out. Deputy fastens the door and goes to bed again.

Black and Green, you know Bark, lodging-house keeper and receiver of stolen goods?—O yes, Inspector Field.— Go to Bark's next.

Bark sleeps in an inner wooden hutch, near his street door. As we parley on the step with Bark's Deputy, Bark growls in his bed. We enter, and Bark flies out of bed. Bark is a red villain and a wrathful, with a sanguine throat that looks very much as if it were expressly made for hanging, as he stretches it out, in pale defiance, over the half-door of his hutch. Bark's parts of speech are of an awful sort— principally adjectives. I won't, says Bark, have no adjective police and adjective strangers in my adjective premises! I won't, by adjective and substantive! Give me my trousers, and I'll send the whole adjective police to adjective and substantive! Give me, says Bark, my adjective trousers! I'll put an adjective knife in the whole bileing of 'em. I'll punch their adjective heads. I'll rip up their adjective substantives. Give me my adjective trousers! says Bark, and I'll spile the bileing of 'em!

Now, Bark, what's the use of this? Here's Black and Green, Detective Sergeant, and Inspector Field. You know we will come in.—I know you won't! says Bark. Somebody give me my adjective trousers! Bark's trousers seem difficult to find. He calls for them as Hercules might for his club. Give me my adjective trousers! says Bark, and I'll spile the bileing of 'em.

Inspector Field holds that it's all one whether Bark likes the visit or don't like it. He, Inspector Field, is an Inspector of the Detective Police, Detective Sergeant *is* Detective Sergeant, Black and Green are constables in uniform. Don't you be a fool, Bark, or you know it will be the worse for you.—I don't care, says Bark. Give me my adjective trousers!

At two o'clock in the morning, we descend into Bark's low kitchen, leaving Bark to foam at the mouth above, and Imperturbable Black and Green to look at him. Bark's kitchen is crammed full of thieves, holding a *conversazione* there by lamp-light. It is by far the most dangerous assembly we have seen yet. Stimulated by the ravings of Bark, above, their looks are sullen, but not a man speaks. We ascend again. Bark has got his trousers, and is in a state of madness in the passage with his back against a door that shuts off the upper staircase. We observe, in other respects, a ferocious individuality in Bark. Instead of "Stop Thief!" on his linen, he prints "Stolen from Bark's!"

Now, Bark, we are going up-stairs!—No, you ain't!—You refuse admission to the Police, do you, Bark?—Yes, I do! I refuse it to all the adjective police, and to all the adjective substantives. If the adjective coves in the kitchen was men, they'd come up now, and do for you! Shut me that there door! says Bark, and suddenly we are enclosed in the passage. They'd come up and do for you! cries Bark, and waits. Not a sound in the kitchen! They'd come up and do for you! cries Bark again, and waits. Not a sound in the kitchen! We are shut up, half-a-dozen of us, in Bark's house in the innermost recesses of the worst part of London, in the dead of the night—the house is crammed with notorious robbers and ruffians—and not a man stirs. No, Bark. They know the weight of the law, and they know Inspector Field and Co. too well.

We leave bully Bark to subside at leisure out of his passion and his trousers, and, I dare say, to be inconveniently reminded of this little brush before long. Black and Green do ordinary duty here, and look serious.

As to White, who waits on Holborn Hill to show the courts that are eaten out of Rotten Gray's Inn Lane, where other lodging-houses are, and where (in one blind alley) the Thieves' Kitchen and Seminary for the teaching of the art to children is, the night has so worn away, being now

almost at odds with morning, which is which,

that they are quiet, and no light shines through the chinks in the shutters. As undistinctive Death will come here, one day, sleep comes now. The wicked cease from troubling sometimes, even in this life.

DOWN WITH THE TIDE

A VERY dark night it was, and bitter cold; the east wind blowing bleak, and bringing with it stinging particles from marsh, and moor, and fen—from the Great Desert and Old Egypt, may be. Some of the component parts of the sharp-edged vapour that came flying up the Thames at London might be mummy-dust, dry atoms from the Temple at Jerusalem, camels' foot-prints, crocodiles' hatching-places, loosened grains of expression from the visages of blunt-nosed sphynxes, waifs and strays from caravans of turbaned merchants, vegetation from jungles, frozen snow from the Himalayas. O! It was very, very dark upon the Thames, and it was bitter, bitter cold.

"And yet," said the voice within the great pea-coat at my side, "you'll have seen a good many rivers too, I dare say?"

"Truly," said I, "when I come to think of it, not a few. From the Niagara, downward to the mountain rivers of Italy, which are like the national spirit—very tame, or chafing suddenly and bursting bounds, only to dwindle away again. The Moselle, and the Rhine, and the Rhone; and the Seine, and the Saone; and the St. Lawrence, Mississippi, and Ohio; and the Tiber, the Po, and the Arno; and the——"

Peacoat coughing as if he had had enough of that, I said no more. I could have carried the catalogue on to a teasing length, though, if I had been in the cruel mind.

"And after all," said he, "this looks so dismal?"

WATCHING THE WATER-RATS

"So awful," I returned, "at night. The Seine at Paris is very gloomy too, at such a time, and is probably the scene of far more crime and greater wickedness; but this river looks so broad and vast, so murky and silent, seems such an image of death in the midst of the great city's life, that—— "

That Peacoat coughed again. He *could not* stand my holding forth.

We were in a four-oared Thames Police Galley, lying on our oars in the deep shadow of Southwark Bridge—under the corner arch on the Surrey side—having come down with the tide from Vauxhall. We were fain to hold on pretty tight, though close in shore, for the river was swollen and the tide running down very strong. We were watching certain water-rats of human growth, and lay in the deep shade as quiet as mice; our light hidden and our scraps of conversation carried on in whispers. Above us, the massive iron girders of the arch were faintly visible, and below us its ponderous shadow seemed to sink down to the bottom of the stream.

We had been lying here some half an hour. With our backs to the wind, it is true; but the wind being in a determined temper blew straight through us, and would not take the trouble to go round. I would have boarded a fireship to get into action, and mildly suggested as much to my friend Pea.

"No doubt," says he as patiently as possible; "but shore-going tactics wouldn't do with us. River-thieves can always get rid of stolen property in a moment by dropping it overboard. We want to take them *with* the property, so we lurk about and come out upon 'em sharp. If they see us or hear us, over it goes."

Pea's wisdom being indisputable, there was nothing for it but to sit there and be blown through, for another half-hour. The water-rats thinking it wise to abscond at the end of that time without commission of felony, we shot out, disappointed, with the tide.

"Grim they look, don't they?" said Pea, seeing me glance over my shoulder at the lights upon the bridge, and downward at their long crooked reflections in the river.

"Very," said I, "and make one think with a shudder of Suicides. What a night for a dreadful leap from that parapet!"

"Aye, but Waterloo's the favourite bridge for making holes in the water from," returned Pea. "By the bye—avast pulling, lads!—would you like to speak to Waterloo on the subject?"

My face confessing a surprised desire to have some friendly conversation with Waterloo Bridge, and my friend Pea being the most obliging of men, we put about, pulled out of the force of the stream, and in place of going at great speed with the tide, began to strive against it, close in shore again. Every colour but black seemed to have departed from the world. The air was black, the water was black, the barges and hulks were black, the piles were black, the buildings were black, the shadows were only a deeper shade of black upon a black ground. Here and there, a coal fire in an iron cresset blazed upon a wharf; but, one knew that it too had been black a little while ago, and would be black again soon. Uncomfortable rushes of water suggestive of gurgling and drowning, ghostly rattlings of iron chains, dismal clankings of discordant engines, formed the music that accompanied the dip of our oars and their rattling in the rowlocks. Even the noises had a black sound to me—as the trumpet sounded red to the blind man.

Our dexterous boat's crew made nothing of the tide, and pulled us gallantly up to Waterloo Bridge. Here Pea and I disembarked, passed under the black stone archway, and climbed the steep stone steps. Within a few feet of their summit, Pea presented me to Waterloo (or an eminent toll-taker representing that structure), muffled up to the eyes in a thick shawl, and amply great-coated and fur-capped.

Waterloo received us with cordiality, and observed of the

night that it was "a Searcher." He had been originally called the Strand Bridge, he informed us, but had received his present name at the suggestion of the proprietors, when Parliament had resolved to vote three hundred thousand pound for the erection of a monument in honour of the victory. Parliament took the hint (said Waterloo, with the least flavour of misanthropy) and saved the money. Of course the late Duke of Wellington was the first passenger, and of course he paid his penny, and of course a noble lord preserved it evermore. The treadle and index at the toll-house (a most ingenious contrivance for rendering fraud impossible), were invented by Mr. Lethbridge, then property-man at Drury Lane Theatre.

Was it suicide, we wanted to know about? said Waterloo. Ha! Well, he had seen a good deal of that work, he did assure us. He had prevented some. Why, one day a woman, poorish looking, came in between the hatch, slapped down a penny, and wanted to go on without the change! Waterloo suspected this, and says to his mate, "give an eye to the gate," and bolted after her. She had got to the third seat between the piers, and was on the parapet just a going over, when he caught her and gave her in charge. At the police office next morning, she said it was along of trouble and a bad husband.

"Likely enough," observed Waterloo to Pea and myself, as he adjusted his chin in his shawl. "There's a deal of trouble about, you see—and bad husbands too!"

Another time, a young woman at twelve o'clock in the open day, got through, darted along; and, before Waterloo could come near her, jumped upon the parapet, and shot herself over sideways. Alarm given, watermen put off, lucky escape.—Clothes buoyed her up.

"This is where it is," said Waterloo. "If people jump off straight forwards from the middle of the parapet of the bays of the bridge, they are seldom killed by drowning, but are smashed, poor things; that's what *they* are; they dash themselves upon the buttress of the bridge. But you jump off," said Waterloo to me, putting his forefinger in a button-hole of my great-coat; "you jump off from the side of the bay, and you'll tumble, true, into the stream under the arch. What you have got to do, is to mind how you jump in! There was poor Tom Steele from Dublin. Didn't dive! Bless you, didn't dive at all! Fell down so flat into the water, that he broke his breast-bone, and lived two days!"

I asked Waterloo if there were a favourite side of his bridge for this dreadful purpose? He reflected, and thought yes, there was. He should say the Surrey side.

Three decent-looking men went through one day, soberly and quietly, and went on abreast for about a dozen yards: when the middle one, he sung out, all of a sudden, "Here goes, Jack!" and was over in a minute.

Body found? Well. Waterloo didn't rightly recollect about that. They were compositors, *they* were.

He considered it astonishing how quick people were! Why, there was a cab came up one Boxing-night, with a young woman in it, who looked, according to Waterloo's opinion of her, a little the worse for liquor; very handsome she was too—very handsome. She stopped the cab at the gate, and said she'd pay the cabman then, which she did, though there was a little hankering about the fare, because at first she didn't seem quite to know where she wanted to be drove to. However, she paid the man, and the toll too, and looking Waterloo in the face (he thought she knew him, don't you see!) said, "I'll finish it somehow!" Well, the cab went off, leaving Waterloo a little doubtful in his mind, and while it was going on at full speed the young woman jumped out, never fell, hardly staggered, ran along the bridge pavement a little way, passing several people, and jumped over from the second opening. At the inquest it was giv' in evidence that she had been quarrelling at the Hero of Waterloo, and it was brought in jealousy. (One of the results of Waterloo's experience was, that there was a deal of jealousy about.)

THE TOLL-TAKER'S EXPERIENCE

"Do we ever get madmen?" said Waterloo, in answer to an inquiry of mine. "Well, we *do* get madmen. Yes, we have had one or two; escaped from 'Sylums, I suppose. One hadn't a halfpenny; and because I wouldn't let him through, he went back a little way, stooped down, took a run, and butted at the hatch like a ram. He smashed his hat rarely, but his head didn't seem no worse—in my opinion on account of his being wrong in it afore. Sometimes people haven't got a halfpenny. If they are really tired and poor we give 'em one and let 'em through. Other people will leave things—pocket-handkerchiefs mostly. I *have* taken cravats and gloves, pocket-knives, tooth-picks, studs, shirt-pins, rings (generally from young gents, early in the morning), but handkerchiefs is the general thing."

"Regular customers?" said Waterloo. "Lord, yes! We have regular customers. One, such a worn-out, used-up old file as you can scarcely picter, comes from the Surrey side as regular as ten o'clock at night comes; and goes over, *I* think, to some flash house on the Middlesex side. He comes back, he does, as reg'lar as the clock strikes three in the morning, and then can hardly drag one of his old legs after the other. He always turns down the water-stairs, comes up again, and then goes on down the Waterloo Road. He always does the same thing, and never varies a minute. Does it every night—even Sundays."

I asked Waterloo if he had given his mind to the possibility of this particular customer going down the water-stairs at three o'clock some morning, and never coming up again? He didn't think *that* of him, he replied. In fact, it was Waterloo's opinion, founded on his observation of that file, that he know'd a trick worth two of it.

"There's another queer old customer," said Waterloo, "comes over, as punctual as the almanack, at eleven o'clock on the sixth of January, at eleven o'clock on the fifth of April, at eleven o'clock on the sixth of July, at eleven o'clock on the tenth of October. Drives a shaggy little, rough pony, in a sort of a rattle-trap arm-chair sort of a thing. White hair he has, and white whiskers, and muffles himself up with all manner of shawls. He comes back again the same afternoon, and we never see more of him for three months. He is a captain in the navy—retired—wery old—wery odd—and served with Lord Nelson. He is particular about drawing his pension at Somerset House afore the clock strikes twelve every quarter. I *have* heerd say that he thinks it wouldn't be according to the Act of Parliament, if he didn't draw it afore twelve."

Having related these anecdotes in a natural manner, which was the best warranty in the world for their genuine nature, our friend Waterloo was sinking deep into his shawl again, as having exhausted his communicative powers and taken in enough east wind, when my other friend Pea in a moment brought him to the surface by asking whether he had not been occasionally the subject of assault and battery in the execution of his duty? Waterloo recovering his spirits, instantly dashed into a new branch of his subject. We learnt how "both these teeth"—here he pointed to the places where two front teeth were not—were knocked out by an ugly customer who one night made a dash at him (Waterloo) while his (the ugly customer's) pal and coadjutor made a dash at the toll-taking apron where the money-pockets were; how Waterloo, letting the teeth go (to Blazes, he observed indefinitely), grappled with the apron-seizer, permitting the ugly one to run away; and how he saved the bank, and captured his man, and consigned him to fine and imprisonment. Also how, on another night, "a Cove" laid hold of Waterloo, then presiding at the horse-gate of his bridge, and threw him unceremoniously over his knee, having first cut his head open with his whip. How Waterloo "got right," and started after the Cove all down the Waterloo Road, through Stamford Street, and round to the foot of Blackfriars Bridge, where the Cove "cut into" a public-house. How Waterloo cut in too; but how an aider and abettor of the Cove's, who happened to be taking a promiscuous drain at the bar, stopped Waterloo; and the Cove cut out again, ran across the road down Holland Street, and where not, and into a beer-shop. How Waterloo breaking away from his detainer was close upon the Cove's heels, attended by no end of people, who, seeing him running with the blood streaming down his face, thought something worse was "up," and roared Fire! and Murder! on the hopeful chance of the matter in hand being one or both. How the Cove was ignominiously taken, in a shed where he had run to hide, and how at the Police Court they at first wanted to make a sessions job of it; but eventually Waterloo was allowed to be "spoke to," and the Cove made it square with Waterloo by paying his doctor's bill (W. was laid up for a week) and giving him "Three, ten." Likewise we learnt what we had faintly suspected before, that your sporting amateur on the Derby day, albeit a captain, can be—"if he be," as Captain Bobadil observes, "so generously minded"—anything but a man of honour and a gentleman; not sufficiently gratifying his nice sense of humour by the witty scattering of flour and rotten eggs on obtuse civilians, but requiring the further excitement of "bilking the toll," and "pitching into" Waterloo, and "cutting him about the head with his whip;" finally being, when called upon to answer for the assault, what Waterloo described as "Minus," or, as I humbly conceived it, not to be found. Likewise did Waterloo inform us, in reply to my inquiries, admiringly and deferentially preferred through my friend Pea, that the takings at the Bridge had more than doubled in amount, since the reduction of the toll one half. And being asked if the aforesaid takings included much bad money, Waterloo responded, with a look far deeper than the deepest part of the river, he should think not!—and so retired into his shawl for the rest of the night.

Then did Pea and I once more embark in our four-oared galley, and glide swiftly down the river with the tide. And while the shrewd East rasped and notched us, as with jagged razors, did my friend Pea impart to me confidences of interest relating to the Thames Police; we, between whiles, finding "duty boats" hanging in dark corners under banks, like weeds —our own was a "supervision boat"—and they, as they reported "all right!" flashing their hidden light on us, and we flashing ours on them. These duty boats had one sitter in each: an Inspector: and were rowed "Ran-dan," which— for the information of those who never graduated, as I was once proud to do, under a fireman-waterman and winner of Kean's Prize Wherry: who, in the course of his tuition, took hundreds of gallons of rum and egg (at my expense) at the various houses of note above and below bridge; not by any means because he liked it, but to cure a weakness in his liver, for which the faculty had particularly recommended it —may be explained as rowed by three men, two pulling an oar each, and one a pair of sculls.

Thus, floating down our black highway, sullenly frowned upon by the knitted brows of Blackfriars, Southwark, and London, each in his lowering turn, I was shown by my friend Pea that there are, in the Thames Police Force, whose district extends from Battersea to Barking Creek, ninety-eight men, eight duty boats, and two supervision boats; and that these go about so silently, and lie in wait in such dark places, and so seem to be nowhere, and so may be anywhere, that they have gradually become a police of prevention, keeping the river almost clear of any great crimes, even while the increased vigilance on shore has made it much harder than of yore to live by "thieving" in the streets. And as to the various kinds of water-thieves, said my friend Pea, there were the Tier-rangers, who silently dropped alongside the tiers of shipping in the Pool, by night, and who, going to the companion-head, listened for two snores—snore number one, the skipper's; snore number two, the mate's—mates and skippers always snoring great guns, and being dead sure to be hard at it if they had turned in and were asleep. Hearing the double fire, down went the Rangers into the skippers' cabins;

groped for the skippers' inexpressibles, which it was the custom of those gentlemen to shake off, watch, money, braces, boots, and all together, on the floor; and therewith made off as silently as might be. Then there were the Lumpers, or labourers employed to unload vessels. They wore loose canvas jackets with a broad hem in the bottom, turned inside, so as to form a large circular pocket in which they could conceal, like clowns in pantomimes, packages of surprising sizes. A great deal of property was stolen in this manner (Pea confided to me) from steamers; first, because steamers carry a larger number of small packages than other ships; next, because of the extreme rapidity with which they are obliged to be unladen for their return voyages. The Lumpers dispose of their booty easily to marine store dealers, and the only remedy to be suggested is that marine store shops should be licensed, and thus brought under the eye of the police as rigidly as public-houses. Lumpers also smuggle goods ashore for the crews of vessels. The smuggling of tobacco is so considerable, that it is well worth the while of the sellers of smuggled tobacco to use hydraulic presses, to squeeze a single pound into a package small enough to be contained in an ordinary pocket. Next, said my friend Pea, there were the Truckers—less thieves than smugglers, whose business it was to land more considerable parcels of goods than the Lumpers could manage. They sometimes sold articles of grocery and so forth, to the crews, in order to cloak their real calling, and get aboard without suspicion. Many of them had boats of their own, and made money. Besides these, there were the Dredgermen, who, under pretence of dredging up coals and such like from the bottom of the river, hung about barges and other undecked craft, and when they saw an opportunity, threw any property they could lay their hands on overboard: in order slyly to dredge it up when the vessel was gone. Sometimes, they dexterously used their dredges to whip away anything that might lie within reach. Some of them were mighty neat at this, and the accomplishment was called dry dredging. Then, there was a vast deal of property, such as copper nails, sheathing, hardwood, &c., habitually brought away by shipwrights and other workmen from their employers' yards, and disposed of to marine store dealers, many of whom escaped detection through hard swearing, and their extraordinary artful ways of accounting for the possession of stolen property. Likewise, there were special-pleading practitioners, for whom barges "drifted away of their own selves"—they having no hand in it, except first cutting them loose, and afterwards plundering them—innocents, meaning no harm, who had the misfortune to observe those foundlings wandering about the Thames.

We were now going in and out, with little noise and great nicety, among the tiers of shipping, whose many hulls, lying close together, rose out of the water like black streets. Here and there, a Scotch, an Irish, or a foreign steamer, getting up her steam as the tide made, looked, with her great chimney and high sides, like a quiet factory among the common buildings. Now, the streets opened into clearer spaces, now contracted into alleys; but the tiers were so like houses, in the dark, that I could almost have believed myself in the narrower bye-ways of Venice. Everything was wonderfully still; for, it wanted full three hours of flood, and nothing seemed awake but a dog here and there.

So we took no Tier-rangers captive, nor any Lumpers, nor Truckers, nor Dredgermen, nor other evil-disposed person or persons; but went ashore at Wapping, where the old Thames Police office is now a station-house, and where the old Court, with its cabin windows looking on the river, is a quaint charge room: with nothing worse in it usually than a stuffed cat in a glass case, and a portrait, pleasant to behold, of a rare old Thames Police officer, Mr. Superintendent Evans, now succeeded by his son. We looked over the charge books, admirably kept, and found the prevention so good that there were not five hundred entries (including drunken and disorderly) in a whole year. Then, we looked into the store-room; where there was an oakum smell, and a nautical seasoning of dreadnought clothing, rope yarn, boat-hooks, sculls and oars, spare stretchers, rudders, pistols, cutlasses, and the like. Then, into the cell, aired high up in the wooden wall through an opening like a kitchen plate-rack: wherein there was a drunken man, not at all warm, and very wishful to know if it were morning yet. Then, into a better sort of watch and ward room, where there was a squadron of stone bottles drawn up, ready to be filled with hot water and applied to any unfortunate creature who might be brought in apparently drowned. Finally, we shook hands with our worthy friend Pea, and ran all the way to Tower Hill, under strong Police suspicion occasionally. before we got warm.

A WALK IN A WORKHOUSE

On a certain Sunday, I formed one of the congregation assembled in the chapel of a large metropolitan Workhouse. With the exception of the clergyman and clerk, and a very few officials, there were none but paupers present. The children sat in the galleries; the women in the body of the chapel, and in one of the side aisles; the men in the remaining aisle. The service was decorously performed, though the sermon might have been much better adapted to the comprehension and to the circumstances of the hearers. The usual supplications were offered, with more than the usual significancy in such a place, for the fatherless children and widows, for all sick persons and young children, for all that were desolate and oppressed, for the comforting and helping of the weak-hearted, for the raising-up of them that had fallen; for all that were in danger, necessity, and tribulation. The prayers of the congregation were desired "for several persons in the various wards dangerously ill;" and others who were recovering returned their thanks to Heaven.

Among this congregation, were some evil-looking young women, and beetle-browed young men; but not many— perhaps that kind of characters kept away. Generally, the faces (those of the children excepted) were depressed and subdued, and wanted colour. Aged people were there, in every variety. Mumbling, blear-eyed, spectacled, stupid, deaf,

A LITTLE WORLD OF POVERTY

lame; vacantly winking in the gleams of sun that now and then crept in through the open doors, from the paved yard; shading their listening ears, or blinking eyes, with their withered hands; poring over their books, leering at nothing, going to sleep, crouching and drooping in corners. There were weird old women, all skeleton within, all bonnet and cloak without, continually wiping their eyes with dirty dusters of pocket-handkerchiefs; and there were ugly old crones, both male and female, with a ghastly kind of contentment upon them which was not at all comforting to see. Upon the whole, it was the dragon, Pauperism, in a very weak and impotent condition; toothless, fangless, drawing his breath heavily enough, and hardly worth chaining up.

When the service was over, I walked with the humane and conscientious gentleman whose duty it was to take that walk, that Sunday morning, through the little world of poverty enclosed within the workhouse walls. It was inhabited by a population of some fifteen hundred or two thousand paupers, ranging from the infant newly born or not yet come into the pauper world, to the old man dying on his bed.

In a room opening from a squalid yard, where a number of listless women were lounging to and fro, trying to get warm in the ineffectual sunshine of the tardy May morning—in the "Itch Ward," not to compromise the truth—a woman such as HOGARTH has often drawn, was hurriedly getting on her gown before a dusty fire. She was the nurse, or wardswoman, of that insalubrious department—herself a pauper—flabby, raw-boned, untidy—unpromising and coarse of aspect as need be. But, on being spoken to about the patients whom she had in charge, she turned round, with her shabby gown half on, half off, and fell a crying with all her might. Not for show, not querulously, not in any mawkish sentiment, but in the deep grief and affliction of her heart; turning away her dishevelled head: sobbing most bitterly, wringing her hands, and letting fall abundance of great tears, that choked her utterance. What was the matter with the nurse of the itch-ward? Oh, "the dropped child" was dead! Oh, the child that was found in the street, and she had brought up ever since, had died an hour ago, and see where the little creature lay, beneath this cloth! The dear, the pretty dear!

The dropped child seemed too small and poor a thing for Death to be in earnest with, but Death had taken it; and already its diminutive form was neatly washed, composed, and stretched as if in sleep upon a box. I thought I heard a voice from Heaven saying, It shall be well for thee, O nurse of the itch-ward, when some less gentle pauper does those offices to thy cold form, that such as the dropped child are the angels who behold my Father's face!

In another room, were several ugly old women crouching, witch-like, round a hearth, and chattering and nodding, after the manner of the monkeys. "All well here? And enough to eat?" A general chattering and chuckling; at last an answer from a volunteer. "Oh yes, gentleman! Bless you, gentleman! Lord bless the Parish of St. So-and-So! It feed the hungry, sir, and give drink to the thusty, and it warm them which is cold, so it do, and good luck to the parish of St. So-and-So, and thankee, gentleman!" Elsewhere, a party of pauper nurses were at dinner. "How do *you* get on?" "Oh pretty well, sir! We works hard, and we lives hard—like the sodgers!"

In another room, a kind of purgatory or place of transition, six or eight noisy madwomen were gathered together, under the superintendence of one sane attendant. Among them was a girl of two or three and twenty, very prettily dressed, of most respectable appearance and good manners, who had been brought in from the house where she had lived as domestic servant (having, I suppose, no friends), on account of being subject to epileptic fits, and requiring to be removed under the influence of a very bad one. She was by no means of the same stuff, or the same breeding, or the same experience, or in the same state of mind, as those by whom she was surrounded; and she pathetically complained that the daily association and the nightly noise made her worse, and was driving her mad—which was perfectly evident. The case was noted for inquiry and redress, but she said she had already been there for some weeks.

If this girl had stolen her mistress's watch, I do not hesitate to say she would have been infinitely better off. We have come to this absurd, this dangerous, this monstrous pass, that the dishonest felon is, in respect of cleanliness, order, diet, and accommodation, better provided for, and taken care of, than the honest pauper.

And this conveys no special imputation on the workhouse of the parish of St. So-and-So, where, on the contrary, I saw many things to commend. It was very agreeable, recollecting that most infamous and atrocious enormity committed at Tooting—an enormity which, a hundred years hence, will still be vividly remembered in the bye-ways of English life, and which has done more to engender a gloomy discontent and suspicion among many thousands of the people than all the Chartist leaders could have done in all their lives—to find the pauper children in this workhouse looking robust and well, and apparently the objects of very great care. In the Infant School—a large, light, airy room at the top of the building—the little creatures, being at dinner, and eating their potatoes heartily, were not cowed by the presence of strange visitors, but stretched out their small hands to be shaken, with a very pleasant confidence. And it was comfortable to see two mangy pauper rocking-horses rampant in a corner. In the girls' school, where the dinner was also in progress, everything bore a cheerful and healthy aspect. The meal was over, in the boys' school, by the time of our arrival there, and the room was not yet quite re-arranged; but the boys were roaming unrestrained about a large and airy yard, as any other schoolboys might have done. Some of them had been drawing large ships upon the schoolroom wall; and if they had a mast with shrouds and stays set up for practice (as they have in the Middlesex House of Correction), it would be so much the better. At present, if a boy should feel a strong impulse upon him to learn the art of going aloft, he could only gratify it, I presume, as the men and women paupers gratify their aspirations after better board and lodging, by smashing as many workhouse windows as possible, and being promoted to prison.

In one place, the Newgate of the Workhouse, a company of boys and youths were locked up in a yard alone; their day-room being a kind of kennel where the casual poor used formerly to be littered down at night. Divers of them had been there some long time. "Are they never going away?" was the natural inquiry. "Most of them are crippled, in some form or other," said the Wardsman, "and not fit for anything." They slunk about, like dispirited wolves or hyænas; and made a pounce at their food when it was served out, much as those animals do. The big-headed idiot shuffling his feet along the pavement, in the sunlight outside, was a more agreeable object everyway.

Groves of babies in arms; groves of mothers and other sick women in bed; groves of lunatics; jungles of men in stone-paved down-stairs day-rooms, waiting for their dinners; longer and longer groves of old people, in up-stairs Infirmary wards, wearing out life, God knows how—this was the scenery through which the walk lay, for two hours. In some of these latter chambers, there were pictures stuck against the wall, and a neat display of crockery and pewter on a kind of side-board; now and then it was a treat to see a plant or two; in almost every ward there was a cat.

In all of these Long Walks of aged and infirm, some old people were bedridden, and had been for a long time; some were sitting on their beds half-naked; some dying in their beds; some out of bed, and sitting at a table near the fire. A sullen or lethargic indifference to what was asked, a blunted sensibility to everything but warmth and food, a moody absence of complaint as being of no use, a dogged silence and resentful desire to be left alone again, I thought were generally apparent. On our walking into the midst of one of these dreary perspectives of old men, nearly the following little dialogue took place, the nurse not being immediately at hand:

" All well here ? "

No answer. An old man in a Scotch cap sitting among others on a form at the table, eating out of a tin porringer, pushes back his cap a little to look at us, claps it down on his forehead again with the palm of his hand, and goes on eating.

" All well here ? " (repeated).

No answer. Another old man sitting on his bed, paralytically peeling a boiled potato, lifts his head and stares.

" Enough to eat ? "

No answer. Another old man, in bed, turns himself and coughs.

" How are *you* to-day ? " To the last old man.

That old man says nothing; but another old man, a tall old man of very good address, speaking with perfect correctness, comes forward from somewhere, and volunteers an answer. The reply almost always proceeds from a volunteer, and not from the person looked at or spoken to.

" We are very old, sir," in a mild, distinct voice. " We can't expect to be well, most of us."

" Are you comfortable ? "

" I have no complaint to make, sir." With a half shake of his head, a half shrug of his shoulders, and a kind of apologetic smile.

" Enough to eat ? "

" Why, sir, I have but a poor appetite," with the same air as before; "and yet I get through my allowance very easily."

" But," showing a porringer with a Sunday dinner in it; " here is a portion of mutton, and three potatoes. You can't starve on that ? "

" Oh dear no, sir," with the same apologetic air. " Not starve."

" What do you want ? "

" We have very little bread, sir. It's an exceedingly small quantity of bread."

The nurse, who is now rubbing her hands at the questioner's elbow, interferes with, ' It ain't much raly, sir. You see they've only six ounces a day, and when they've took their breakfast, there *can* only be a little left for night, sir."

Another old man, hitherto invisible, rises out of his bed-clothes, as out of a grave, and looks on.

" You have tea at night ? " The questioner is still addressing the well-spoken old man.

" Yes, sir, we have tea at night."

" And you save what bread you can from the morning, to eat with it ? "

" Yes, sir—if we can save any."

" And you want more to eat with it ? "

" Yes, sir." With a very anxious face.

The questioner, in the kindness of his heart, appears a little discomposed, and changes the subject.

" What has become of the old man who used to lie in that bed in the corner ? "

The nurse don't remember what old man is referred to. There has been such a many old men. The well-spoken old man is doubtful. The spectral old man who has come to life in bed, says, " Billy Stevens." Another old man who has previously had his head in the fireplace, pipes out,

" Charley Walters."

Something like a feeble interest is awakened. I suppose Charley Walters had conversation in him.

" He's dead," says the piping old man.

Another old man, with one eye screwed up, hastily displaces the piping old man, and says :

" Yes ! Charley Walters died in that bed, and—and—— "

" Billy Stevens," persists the spectral old man.

" No, no ! and Johnny Rogers died in that bed, and—and

—they're both on 'em dead—and Sam'l Bowyer;" this seems very extraordinary to him; "he went out!"

With this he subsides, and all the old men (having had quite enough of it) subside, and the spectral old man goes into his grave again, and takes the shade of Billy Stevens with him.

As we turn to go out at the door, another previously invisible old man, a hoarse old man in a flannel gown, is standing there, as if he had just come up through the floor.

"I beg your pardon, sir, could I take the liberty of saying a word?"

"Yes; what is it?"

"I am greatly better in my health, sir; but what I want, to get me quite round," with his hand on his throat, "is a little fresh air, sir. It has always done my complaint so much good, sir. The regular leave for going out, comes round so seldom, that if the gentlemen, next Friday, would give me leave to go out walking, now and then—for only an hour or so, sir!—— "

Who could wonder, looking through those weary vistas of bed and infirmity, that it should do him good to meet with some other scenes, and assure himself that there was something else on earth? Who could help wondering why the old men lived on as they did; what grasp they had on life; what crumbs of interest or occupation they could pick up from its bare board; whether Charley Walters had ever described to them the days when he kept company with some old pauper woman in the bud, or Billy Stevens ever told them of the time when he was a dweller in the far-off foreign land called Home!

The morsel of burnt child, lying in another room, so patiently, in bed, wrapped in lint, and looking steadfastly at us with his bright quiet eyes when we spoke to him kindly, looked as if the knowledge of these things, and of all the tender things there are to think about, might have been in his mind—as if he thought, with us, that there was a fellow-feeling in the pauper nurses which appeared to make them more kind to their charges than the race of common nurses in the hospitals—as if he mused upon the Future of some older children lying around him in the same place, and thought it best, perhaps, all things considered, that he should die—as if he knew, without fear, of those many coffins, made and unmade, piled up in the store below—and of his unknown friend, "the dropped child," calm upon the box-lid covered with a cloth. But there was something wistful and appealing, too, in his tiny face, as if, in the midst of all the hard necessities and incongruities he pondered on, he pleaded, in behalf of the helpless and the aged poor, for a little more liberty—and a little more bread.

PRINCE BULL. A FAIRY TALE

ONCE upon a time, and of course it was in the Golden Age, and I hope you may know when that was, for I am sure I don't, though I have tried hard to find out, there lived in a rich and fertile country, a powerful Prince whose name was BULL. He had gone through a great deal of fighting, in his time, about all sorts of things, including nothing; but, had gradually settled down to be a steady, peaceable, good-natured, corpulent, rather sleepy Prince.

This Puissant Prince was married to a lovely Princess whose name was Fair Freedom. She had brought him a large fortune, and had borne him an immense number of children, and had set them to spinning, and farming, and engineering, and soldiering, and sailoring, and doctoring, and lawyering, and preaching, and all kinds of trades. The coffers of Prince Bull were full of treasure, his cellars were crammed with delicious wines from all parts of the world, the richest gold and silver plate that ever was seen adorned his sideboards, his sons were strong, his daughters were handsome, and in short you might have supposed that if there ever lived upon earth a fortunate and happy Prince, the name of that Prince, take him for all in all, was assuredly Prince Bull.

But, appearances, as we all know, are not always to be trusted—far from it; and if they had led you to this conclusion respecting Prince Bull, they would have led you wrong as they often have led me.

PRINCE BULL. A FAIRY TALE

For, this good Prince had two sharp thorns in his pillow, two hard knobs in his crown, two heavy loads on his mind, two unbridled nightmares in his sleep, two rocks ahead in his course. He could not by any means get servants to suit him, and he had a tyrannical old godmother, whose name was Tape.

She was a Fairy, this Tape, and was a bright red all over. She was disgustingly prim and formal, and could never bend herself a hair's breadth this way or that way, out of her naturally crooked shape. But, she was very potent in her wicked art. She could stop the fastest thing in the world, change the strongest thing into the weakest, and the most useful into the most useless. To do this she had only to put her cold hand upon it, and repeat her own name, Tape. Then it withered away.

At the Court of Prince Bull—at least I don't mean literally at his court, because he was a very genteel Prince, and readily yielded to his godmother when she always reserved that for his hereditary Lords and Ladies—in the dominions of Prince Bull, among the great mass of the community who were called in the language of that polite country the Mobs and the Snobs, were a number of very ingenious men, who were always busy with some invention or other, for promoting the prosperity of the Prince's subjects, and augmenting the Prince's power. But, whenever they submitted their models for the Prince's approval, his godmother stepped forward, laid her hand upon them, and said "Tape." Hence it came to pass, that when any particularly good discovery was made, the discoverer usually carried it off to some other Prince, in foreign parts, who had no old godmother who said Tape. This was not on the whole an advantageous state of things for Prince Bull, to the best of my understanding.

The worst of it was, that Prince Bull had in course of years lapsed into such a state of subjection to this unlucky godmother, that he never made any serious effort to rid himself of her tyranny. I have said this was the worst of it, but there I was wrong, because there is a worse consequence still, behind. The Prince's numerous family became so downright sick and tired of Tape, that when they should have helped the Prince out of the difficulties into which that evil creature led him, they fell into a dangerous habit of moodily keeping away from him in an impassive and indifferent manner, as though they had quite forgotten that no harm could happen to the Prince their father, without its inevitably affecting themselves.

Such was the aspect of affairs at the court of Prince Bull, when this great Prince found it necessary to go to war with Prince Bear. He had been for some time very doubtful of his servants, who, besides being indolent and addicted to enriching their families at his expense, domineered over him dreadfully ; threatening to discharge themselves if they were found the least fault with, pretending that they had done a wonderful amount of work when they had done nothing, making the most unmeaning speeches that ever were heard in the Prince's name, and uniformly showing themselves to be very inefficient indeed. Though, that some of them had excellent characters from previous situations is not to be denied. Well ; Prince Bull called his servants together, and said to them one and all, " Send out my army against Prince Bear. Clothe it, arm it, feed it, provide it with all necessaries and contingencies, and I will pay the piper ! Do your duty by my brave troops," said the Prince, " and do it well, and I will pour my treasure out like water, to defray the cost. Who ever heard ME complain of money well laid out ! " Which indeed he had reason for saying, inasmuch as he was well known to be a truly generous and munificent Prince.

When the servants heard those words, they sent out the army against Prince Bear, and they set the army tailors to work, and the army provision merchants, and the makers of guns both great and small, and the gunpowder makers, and the makers of ball, shell, and shot ; and they bought up all manner of stores and ships, without troubling their heads

about the price, and appeared to be so busy that the good
Prince rubbed his hands, and (using a favourite expression
of his), said, "It's all right!" But, while they were thus
employed, the Prince's godmother, who was a great favourite
with those servants, looked in upon them continually all day
long, and whenever she popped in her head at the door said,
"How do you do, my children? What are you doing here?"
"Official business, godmother." "Oho!" says this wicked
Fairy. "—Tape!" And then the business all went wrong,
whatever it was, and the servants' heads became so addled
and muddled that they thought they were doing wonders.

Now, this was very bad conduct on the part of the vicious
old nuisance, and she ought to have been strangled, even if
she had stopped here; but, she didn't stop here, as you shall
learn. For, a number of the Prince's subjects, being very
fond of the Prince's army who were the bravest of men,
assembled together and provided all manner of eatables and
drinkables, and books to read, and clothes to wear, and
tobacco to smoke, and candles to burn, and nailed them up
in great packing-cases, and put them aboard a great many
ships, to be carried out to that brave army in the cold and
inclement country where they were fighting Prince Bear.
Then, up comes this wicked Fairy as the ships were weighing
anchor, and says, "How do you do, my children? What are
you doing here?"—"We are going with all these comforts
to the army, godmother."—"Oho!" says she. "A pleasant
voyage, my darlings.—Tape!" And from that time forth,
those enchanted ships went sailing, against wind and tide and
rhyme and reason, round and round the world, and whenever
they touched at any port were ordered off immediately, and
could never deliver their cargoes anywhere.

This, again, was very bad conduct on the part of the
vicious old nuisance, and she ought to have been strangled
for it if she had done nothing worse; but, she did something
worse still, as you shall learn. For, she got astride of an
official broomstick, and muttered as a spell these two sentences,

" On Her Majesty's service," and " I have the honour to be, sir, your most obedient servant," and presently alighted in the cold and inclement country where the army of Prince Bull were encamped to fight the army of Prince Bear. On the sea-shore of that country, she found piled together, a number of houses for the army to live in, and a quantity of provisions for the army to live upon, and a quantity of clothes for the army to wear: while, sitting in the mud gazing at them, were a group of officers as red to look at as the wicked old woman herself. So, she said to one of them, " Who are you, my darling, and how do you do ? "—" I am the Quarter-master General's Department, godmother, and I am pretty well." Then she said to another, " Who are *you*, my darling, and how do *you* do ? "—" I am the Commissariat Department, godmother, and *I* am pretty well." Then she said to another, " Who are *you*, my darling, and how do *you* do ? "—" I am the Head of the Medical Department, godmother, and I am pretty well." Then, she said to some gentlemen scented with lavender, who kept themselves at a great distance from the rest, " And who are *you*, my pretty pets, and how do *you* do ? " And they answered, " We-aw-are-the-aw-Staff-aw-Department, godmother, and we are very well indeed."—" I am delighted to see you all, my beauties," says this wicked old Fairy, " —Tape ! " Upon that, the houses, clothes, and provisions, all mouldered away ; and the soldiers who were sound, fell sick ; and the soldiers who were sick, died miserably : and the noble army of Prince Bull perished.

When the dismal news of his great loss was carried to the Prince, he suspected his godmother very much indeed ; but, he knew that his servants must have kept company with the malicious beldame, and must have given way to her, and therefore he resolved to turn those servants out of their places. So, he called to him a Roebuck who had the gift of speech, and he said, " Good Roebuck, tell them they must go." So, the good Roebuck delivered his message, so like a man that you might have supposed him to be nothing but a man, and they were turned out—but, not without warning, for that they had had a long time.

And now comes the most extraordinary part of the history of this Prince. When he had turned out those servants, of course he wanted others. What was his astonishment to find that in all his dominions, which contained no less than twenty-seven millions of people, there were not above five-and-twenty servants altogether! They were so lofty about it, too, that instead of discussing whether they should hire themselves as servants to Prince Bull, they turned things topsy-turvy, and considered whether as a favour they should hire Prince Bull to be their master! While they were arguing this point among themselves quite at their leisure, the wicked old red Fairy was incessantly going up and down, knocking at the doors of twelve of the oldest of the five-and-twenty, who were the oldest inhabitants in all that country, and whose united ages amounted to one thousand, saying, "Will *you* hire Prince Bull for your master?—Will *you* hire Prince Bull for your master?" To which one answered, "I will if next door will;" and another, "I won't if over the way does;" and another, "I can't if he, she, or they, might, could, would, or should." And all this time Prince Bull's affairs were going to rack and ruin.

At last, Prince Bull in the height of his perplexity assumed a thoughtful face, as if he were struck by an entirely new idea. The wicked old Fairy, seeing this, was at his elbow directly, and said, "How do you do, my Prince, and what are you thinking of?"—"I am thinking, godmother," says he, "that among all the seven-and-twenty millions of my subjects who have never been in service, there are men of intellect and business who have made me very famous both among my friends and enemies."—"Aye, truly?" says the Fairy.—"Aye, truly," says the Prince.—"And what then?" says the Fairy.—"Why, then," says he, "since the regular old class of servants do so ill, are so hard to get, and carry it with so high a hand, perhaps I might try to make good servants of some of these." The words had no sooner passed his lips than she returned, chuckling, "You think so, do you? Indeed, my Prince?—Tape!" Thereupon he directly forgot what he was thinking of, and cried out lamentably to the old servants, "O, do come and hire your poor old master! Pray do! On any terms!"

And this, for the present, finishes the story of Prince Bull. I wish I could wind it up by saying that he lived happy ever afterwards, but I cannot in my conscience do so; for, with Tape at his elbow, and his estranged children fatally repelled by her from coming near him, I do not, to tell you the plain truth, believe in the possibility of such an end to it.

A PLATED ARTICLE

Putting up for the night in one of the chiefest towns of
Staffordshire, I find it to be by no means a lively town. In
fact, it is as dull and dead a town as any one could desire not
to see. It seems as if its whole population might be im-
prisoned in its Railway Station. The Refreshment Room at
that Station is a vortex of dissipation compared with the
extinct town-inn, the Dodo, in the dull High Street.

Why High Street? Why not rather Low Street, Flat
Street, Low-Spirited Street, Used-up Street? Where are the
people who belong to the High Street? Can they all be
dispersed over the face of the country, seeking the unfortunate Strolling Manager who decamped from the mouldy little
Theatre last week, in the beginning of his season (as his
play-bills testify), repentantly resolved to bring him back,
and feed him, and be entertained? Or, can they all be
gathered to their fathers in the two old churchyards near to
the High Street—retirement into which churchyards appears
to be a mere ceremony, there is so very little life outside their
confines, and such small discernible difference between being
buried alive in the town, and buried dead in the town tombs?
Over the way, opposite to the staring blank bow windows of
the Dodo, are a little ironmonger's shop, a little tailor's shop
(with a picture of the Fashions in the small window and a
bandy-legged baby on the pavement staring at it)—a watch-

maker's shop, where all the clocks and watches must be stopped, I am sure, for they could never have the courage to go, with the town in general, and the Dodo in particular, looking at them.   Shade of Miss Linwood, erst of Leicester Square, London, thou art welcome here, and thy retreat is fitly chosen!   I myself was one of the last visitors to that awful storehouse of thy life's work, where an anchorite old man and woman took my shilling with a solemn wonder, and conducting me to a gloomy sepulchre of needlework dropping to pieces with dust and age and shrouded in twilight at high noon, left me there, chilled, frightened, and alone.   And now, in ghostly letters on all the dead walls of this dead town, I read thy honoured name, and find that thy Last Supper, worked in Berlin Wool, invites inspection as a powerful excitement!

Where are the people who are bidden with so much cry to this feast of little wool?   Where are they?   Who are they? They are not the bandy-legged baby studying the fashions in the tailor's window.   They are not the two earthy plough-men lounging outside the saddler's shop, in the stiff square where the Town Hall stands, like a brick and mortar private on parade.   They are not the landlady of the Dodo in the empty bar, whose eye had trouble in it and no welcome, when I asked for dinner.   They are not the turnkeys of the Town Jail, looking out of the gateway in their uniforms, as if they had locked up all the balance (as my American friends would say) of the inhabitants, and could now rest a little.   They are not the two dusty millers in the white mill down by the river, where the great water-wheel goes heavily round and round, like the monotonous days and nights in this forgotten place.   Then who are they, for there is no one else?   No; this deponent maketh oath and saith that there is no one else, save and except the waiter at the Dodo, now laying the cloth.   I have paced the streets, and stared at the houses, and am come back to the blank bow window of the Dodo; and the town clocks strike seven, and the reluctant echoes seem to cry, "Don't wake us!" and the bandy-legged baby has gone home to bed.

If the Dodo were only a gregarious bird—if he had only some confused idea of making a comfortable nest—I could hope to get through the hours between this and bed-time, without being consumed by devouring melancholy. But, the Dodo's habits are all wrong. It provides me with a trackless desert of sitting-room, with a chair for every day in the year, a table for every month, and a waste of sideboard where a lonely China vase pines in a corner for its mate long departed, and will never make a match with the candlestick in the opposite corner if it live till Doomsday. The Dodo has nothing in the larder. Even now, I behold the Boots returning with my sole in a piece of paper; and with that portion of my dinner, the Boots, perceiving me at the blank bow window, slaps his leg as he comes across the road, pretending it is something else. The Dodo excludes the outer air. When I mount up to my bedroom, a smell of closeness and flue gets lazily up my nose like sleepy snuff. The loose little bits of carpet writhe under my tread, and take wormy shapes. I don't know the ridiculous man in the looking-glass, beyond having met him once or twice in a dish-cover—and I can never shave *him* to-morrow morning! The Dodo is narrow-minded as to towels; expects me to wash on a free-mason's apron without the trimming: when I asked for soap, gives me a stony-hearted something white, with no more lather in it than the Elgin marbles. The Dodo has seen better days, and possesses interminable stables at the back—silent, grass-grown, broken-windowed, horseless.

This mournful bird can fry a sole, however, which is much. Can cook a steak, too, which is more. I wonder where it gets its Sherry? If I were to send my pint of wine to some famous chemist to be analysed, what would it turn out to be made of? It tastes of pepper, sugar, bitter-almonds, vinegar, warm knives, any flat drinks, and a little brandy. Would it unman a Spanish exile by reminding him of his native land at all? I think not. If there really be any townspeople out of the churchyards, and if a caravan of them ever do dine, with a bottle of wine per man, in this desert of the Dodo, it must make good for the doctor next day!

Where was the waiter born? How did he come here? Has he any hope of getting away from here? Does he ever receive a letter, or take a ride upon the railway, or see anything but the Dodo? Perhaps he has seen the Berlin Wool. He appears to have a silent sorrow on him, and it may be that. He clears the table; draws the dingy curtains of the great bow window, which so unwillingly consent to meet, that they must be pinned together; leaves me by the fire with my pint decanter, and a little thin funnel-shaped wine-glass, and a plate of pale biscuits—in themselves engendering desperation.

No book, no newspaper! I left the Arabian Nights in the railway carriage, and have nothing to read but Bradshaw, and "that way madness lies." Remembering what prisoners and shipwrecked mariners have done to exercise their minds in solitude, I repeat the multiplication table, the pence table, and the shilling table: which are all the tables I happen to know. What if I write something? The Dodo keeps no pens but steel pens; and those I always stick through the paper, and can turn to no other account.

What am I to do? Even if I could have the bandy-legged baby knocked up and brought here, I could offer him nothing but sherry, and that would be the death of him. He would never hold up his head again if he touched it. I can't go to bed, because I have conceived a mortal hatred for my bedroom; and I can't go away, because there is no train for my place of destination until morning. To burn the biscuits will be but a fleeting joy; still it is a temporary relief, and here they go on the fire! Shall I break the plate? First let me look at the back, and see who made it. COPELAND.

Copeland! Stop a moment. Was it yesterday I visited

Copeland's works, and saw them making plates? In the confusion of travelling about, it might be yesterday or it might be yesterday month; but I think it was yesterday. I appeal to the plate. The plate says, decidedly, yesterday. I find the plate, as I look at it, growing into a companion.

Don't you remember (says the plate) how you steamed away, yesterday morning, in the bright sun and the east wind, along the valley of the sparkling Trent? Don't you recollect how many kilns you flew past, looking like the bowls of gigantic tobacco-pipes, cut short off from the stem and turned upside down? And the fires—and the smoke—and the roads made with bits of crockery, as if all the plates and dishes in the civilised world had been Macadamised, expressly for the laming of all the horses? Of course I do!

And don't you remember (says the plate) how you alighted at Stoke—a picturesque heap of houses, kilns, smoke, wharfs, canals, and river, lying (as was most appropriate) in a basin —and how, after climbing up the sides of the basin to look at the prospect, you trundled down again at a walking-match pace, and straight proceeded to my father's, Copeland's, where the whole of my family, high and low, rich and poor, are turned out upon the world from our nursery and seminary, covering some fourteen acres of ground? And don't you remember what we spring from:—heaps of lumps of clay, partially prepared and cleaned in Devonshire and Dorsetshire, whence said clay principally comes—and hills of flint, without which we should want our ringing sound, and should never be musical? And as to the flint, don't you recollect that it is first burnt in kilns, and is then laid under the four iron feet of a demon slave, subject to violent stamping fits, who, when they come on, stamps away insanely with his four iron legs, and would crush all the flint in the Isle of Thanet to powder, without leaving off? And as to the clay, don't you recollect how it is put into mills or teazers, and is sliced, and dug, and cut at, by endless knives, clogged and sticky, but persistent—and is pressed out of that machine through a square trough, whose form it takes—and is cut off in square lumps and thrown into a vat, and there mixed with water, and beaten to a pulp by paddle-wheels—and is then run into a rough house, all rugged beams and ladders splashed with white,—superintended by Grindoff the Miller in his working clothes, all splashed with white,—where it passes through no end of machinery-moved sieves all splashed with white, arranged in an ascending scale of fineness (some so fine, that three hundred silk threads cross each other in a single square inch of their surface), and all in a violent state of ague with their teeth for ever chattering, and their bodies for ever shivering! And as to the flint again, isn't it mashed and mollified and troubled and soothed, exactly as rags are in a paper-mill, until it is reduced to a pap so fine that it contains no atom of "grit" perceptible to the nicest taste? And as to the flint and the clay together, are they not, after all this, mixed in the proportion of five of clay to one of flint, and isn't the compound—known as "slip"—run into oblong troughs, where its superfluous moisture may evaporate; and finally, isn't it slapped and banged and beaten and patted and kneaded and wedged and knocked about like butter, until it becomes a beautiful grey dough, ready for the potter's use?

In regard of the potter, popularly so called (says the plate), you don't mean to say you have forgotten that a workman called a Thrower is the man under whose hand this grey dough takes the shapes of the simpler household vessels as quickly as the eye can follow? You don't mean to say you cannot call him up before you, sitting, with his attendant woman, at his potter's wheel—a disc about the size of a dinner-plate, revolving on two drums slowly or quickly as he wills—who made you a complete breakfast-set for a bachelor, as a good-humoured little off-hand joke? You remember how he took up as much dough as he wanted, and, throwing it on his wheel, in a moment fashioned it into a teacup—caught up more clay and made a saucer—a larger dab and whirled it into a teapot—winked at a smaller dab and converted it into the lid of the teapot, accurately fitting by the measurement of his eye alone—coaxed a middle-sized dab for two seconds, broke it, turned it over at the rim, and made a milkpot—laughed, and turned out a slop-basin—coughed, and provided for the sugar? Neither, I think, are you oblivious of the newer mode of making various articles, but especially basins, according to which improvement a mould revolves instead of a disc? For you *must* remember (says the plate) how you saw the mould of a little basin spinning round and round, and how the workmen smoothed and pressed a handful of dough upon it, and how with an instrument called a profile (a piece of wood, representing the profile of a basin's foot) he cleverly scraped and carved the ring which makes the base of any such basin, and then took the basin off the lathe like a doughy skull-cap to be dried, and afterwards (in what is called a green state) to be put into a second lathe, there to be finished and burnished with a steel burnisher? And as to moulding in general (says the plate), it can't be necessary for me to remind you that all ornamental articles, and indeed all articles not quite circular, are made in moulds. For you must remember how you saw the vegetable dishes, for example, being made in moulds; and how the handles of teacups, and the spouts of teapots, and the feet of tureens, and so forth, are all made in little separate moulds, and are each stuck on to the body corporate, of which it is destined to form a part, with a stuff called "slag," as quickly as you can recollect it. Further, you learnt—you know you did—in the same visit, how the beautiful sculptures in the delicate new material called Parian, are all constructed in moulds; how, into that material, animal bones are ground up, because the phosphate of lime contained in bones makes it translucent; how everything is moulded, before going into the fire, one-fourth larger than it is intended to come out of the fire, because it shrinks in that proportion in the intense heat; how, when a figure shrinks unequally, it is spoiled—emerging from the furnace a mis-shapen birth; a

big head and a little body, or a little head and a big body,
or a Quasimodo with long arms and short legs, or a Miss
Biffin with neither legs nor arms worth mentioning.

And as to the Kilns, in which the firing takes place, and in
which some of the more precious articles are burnt repeatedly,
in various stages of their process towards completion,—as to
the Kilns (says the plate, warming with the recollection), if
you don't remember THEM with a horrible interest, what did
you ever go to Copeland's for? When you stood inside of
one of those inverted bowls of a Pre-Adamite tobacco-pipe,
looking up at the blue sky through the open top far off, as
you might have looked up from a well, sunk under the centre
of the pavement of the Pantheon at Rome, had you the least
idea where you were? And when you found yourself surrounded, in that dome-shaped cavern, by innumerable columns
of an unearthly order of architecture, supporting nothing,
and squeezed close together as if a Pre-Adamite Samson had
taken a vast Hall in his arms and crushed it into the smallest
possible space, had you the least idea what they were? No
(says the plate), of course not! And when you found that
each of those pillars was a pile of ingeniously made vessels
of coarse clay—called Saggers—looking, when separate, like
raised-pies for the table of the mighty Giant Blunderbore,
and now all full of various articles of pottery ranged in
them in baking order, the bottom of each vessel serving for
the cover of the one below, and the whole Kiln rapidly filling
with these, tier upon tier, until the last workman should
have barely room to crawl out, before the closing of the
jagged aperture in the wall and the kindling of the gradual
fire; did you not stand amazed to think that all the year
round these dread chambers are heating, white hot—and
cooling—and filling—and emptying—and being bricked up
—and broken open—humanly speaking, for ever and ever?
To be sure you did! And standing in one of those Kilns
nearly full, and seeing a free crow shoot across the aperture
a-top, and learning how the fire would wax hotter and hotter

by slow degrees, and would cool similarly through a space of from forty to sixty hours, did no remembrance of the days when human clay was burnt oppress you? Yes. I think so! I suspect that some fancy of a fiery haze and a shortening breath, and a growing heat, and a gasping prayer; and a figure in black interposing between you and the sky (as figures in black are very apt to do), and looking down, before it grew too hot to look and live, upon the Heretic in his edifying agony—I say I suspect (says the plate) that some such fancy was pretty strong upon you when you went out into the air, and blessed God for the bright spring day and the degenerate times!

After that, I needn't remind you what a relief it was to see the simplest process of ornamenting this "biscuit" (as it is called when baked) with brown circles and blue trees—converting it into the common crockery-ware that is exported to Africa, and used in cottages at home. For (says the plate) I am well persuaded that you bear in mind how those particular jugs and mugs were once more set upon a lathe and put in motion; and how a man blew the brown colour (having a strong natural affinity with the material in that condition) on them from a blowpipe as they twirled; and how his daughter, with a common brush, dropped blotches of blue upon them in the right places; and how, tilting the blotches upside down, she made them run into rude images of trees, and there an end.

And didn't you see (says the plate) planted upon my own brother that astounding blue willow, with knobbed and gnarled trunk, and foliage of blue ostrich feathers, which gives our family the title of "willow pattern"? And didn't you observe, transferred upon him at the same time, that blue bridge which spans nothing, growing out from the roots of the willow; and the three blue Chinese going over it into a blue temple, which has a fine crop of blue bushes sprouting out of the roof; and a blue boat sailing above them, the mast of which is burglariously sticking itself into the foundations of a blue villa, suspended sky-high, surmounted by a lump of blue rock, sky-higher, and a couple of billing blue birds, sky-highest—together with the rest of that amusing blue landscape, which has, in deference to our revered ancestors of the Cerulean Empire, and in defiance of every known law of perspective, adorned millions of our family ever since the days of platters? Didn't you inspect the copper-plate on which my pattern was deeply engraved? Didn't you perceive an impression of it taken in cobalt colour at a cylindrical press, upon a leaf of thin paper, streaming from a plunge-bath of soap and water? Wasn't the paper impression daintily spread, by a light-fingered damsel (you *know* you admired her!), over the surface of the plate, and the back of the paper rubbed prodigiously hard —with a long tight roll of flannel, tied up like a round of hung beef—without so much as ruffling the paper, wet as it was? Then (says the plate), was not the paper washed away with a sponge, and didn't there appear, set off upon the plate, *this* identical piece of Pre-Raphaelite blue distemper which you now behold? Not to be denied! I had seen all this—and more. I had been shown, at Copeland's, patterns of beautiful design, in faultless perspective, which are causing the ugly old willow to wither out of public favour; and which, being quite as cheap, insinuate good wholesome natural art into the humblest households. When Mr. and Mrs. Sprat have satisfied their material tastes by that equal division of fat and lean which has made their *ménage* immortal; and have, after the elegant tradition, "licked the platter clean," they can—thanks to modern artists in clay—feast their intellectual tastes upon excellent delineations of natural objects.

This reflection prompts me to transfer my attention from the blue plate to the forlorn but cheerfully painted vase on the sideboard. And surely (says the plate) you have not forgotten how the outlines of such groups of flowers as you see there, are printed, just as I was printed, and are afterwards shaded and filled in with metallic colours by women and girls ? As to the aristocracy of our order, made of the finer clay— porcelain peers and peeresses;—the slabs, and panels, and table-tops, and tazze; the endless nobility and gentry of dessert, breakfast, and tea services; the gemmed perfume bottles, and scarlet and gold salvers; you saw that they were painted by artists, with metallic colours laid on with camel-hair pencils, and afterwards burnt in.

And talking of burning in (says the plate), didn't you find that every subject, from the willow pattern to the landscape after Turner—having been framed upon clay or porcelain biscuit—has to be glazed ? Of course, you saw the glaze— composed of various vitreous materials—laid over every article; and of course you witnessed the close imprisonment of each piece in saggers upon the separate system rigidly enforced by means of fine-pointed earthenware stilts placed between the articles to prevent the slightest communication or contact. We had in my time—and I suppose it is the same now— fourteen hours' firing to fix the glaze and to make it "run" all over us equally, so as to put a good shiny and unscratchable surface upon us. Doubtless, you observed that one sort of glaze—called printing-body—is burnt into the better sort of ware *before* it is printed. Upon this you saw some of the finest steel engravings transferred, to be fixed by an after glazing—didn't you ? Why, of course you did !

Of course I did. I had seen and enjoyed everything that the plate recalled to me, and had beheld with admiration how the rotatory motion which keeps this ball of ours in its place in the great scheme, with all its busy mites upon it, was necessary throughout the process, and could only be dispensed with in the fire. So, listening to the plate's reminders, and musing upon them, I got through the evening after all, and went to bed. I made but one sleep of it—for which I have no doubt I am also indebted to the plate—and left the lonely Dodo in the morning, quite at peace with it, before the bandy-legged baby was up.

OUR HONOURABLE FRIEND

WE are delighted to find that he has got in! Our honourable friend is triumphantly returned to serve in the next Parliament. He is the honourable member for Verbosity—the best represented place in England.

Our honourable friend has issued an address of congratulation to the Electors, which is worthy of that noble constituency, and is a very pretty piece of composition. In electing him, he says, they have covered themselves with glory, and England has been true to herself. (In his preliminary address he had remarked, in a poetical quotation of great rarity, that nought could make us rue, if England to herself did prove but true.)

Our honourable friend delivers a prediction, in the same document, that the feeble minions of a faction will never hold up their heads any more; and that the finger of scorn will point at them in their dejected state, through countless ages of time. Further, that the hireling tools that would destroy the sacred bulwarks of our nationality are unworthy of the name of Englishman; and that so long as the sea shall roll around our ocean-girded isle, so long his motto shall be, No surrender. Certain dogged persons of low principles and no intellect, have disputed whether anybody knows who the minions are, or what the faction is, or which are the hireling tools and which the sacred bulwarks, or what it is that is never to be surrendered, and if not, why not? But, our honourable friend the member for Verbosity knows all about it.

Our honourable friend has sat in several parliaments, and given bushels of votes. He is a man of that profundity in the matter of vote-giving, that you never know what he means. When he seems to be voting pure white, he may be in reality voting jet black. When he says Yes, it is just as likely as not—or rather more so—that he means No. This is the statesmanship of our honourable friend. It is in this, that he differs from mere unparliamentary men. *You* may not know what he meant then, or what he means now; but, our honourable friend knows, and did from the first know, both what he meant then, and what he means now; and when he said he didn't mean it then, he did in fact say, that he means it now. And if you mean to say that you did not then, and do not now, know what he did mean then, or does mean now, our honourable friend will be glad to receive an explicit declaration from you whether you are prepared to destroy the sacred bulwarks of our nationality.

Our honourable friend, the member for Verbosity, has this great attribute, that he always means something, and always means the same thing. When he came down to that House and mournfully boasted in his place, as an individual member of the assembled Commons of this great and happy country, that he could lay his hand upon his heart, and solemnly declare that no consideration on earth should induce him, at any time or under any circumstances, to go as far north as Berwick-upon-Tweed; and when he nevertheless, next year, did go to Berwick-upon-Tweed, and even beyond it, to Edinburgh; he had one single meaning, one and indivisible. And God forbid (our honourable friend says) that he should waste another argument upon the man who professes that he cannot understand it! "I do NOT, gentlemen," said our honourable friend, with indignant emphasis and amid great cheering, on one such public occasion. "I do NOT, gentlemen,

THE MEMBER FOR VERBOSITY

I am free to confess, envy the feelings of that man whose mind is so constituted as that he can hold such language to me, and yet lay his head upon his pillow, claiming to be a native of that land,

> Whose march is o'er the mountain-wave,
> Whose home is on the deep!"

(Vehement cheering, and man expelled.)

When our honourable friend issued his preliminary address to the constituent body of Verbosity on the occasion of one particular glorious triumph, it was supposed by some of his enemies, that even he would be placed in a situation of difficulty by the following comparatively trifling conjunction of circumstances. The dozen noblemen and gentlemen whom our honourable friend supported, had " come in," expressly to do a certain thing. Now, four of the dozen said, at a certain place, that they didn't mean to do that thing, and had never meant to do it; another four of the dozen said, at another certain place, that they did mean to do that thing, and had always meant to do it; two of the remaining four said, at two other certain places, that they meant to do half of that thing (but differed about which half), and to do a variety of nameless wonders instead of the other half; and one of the remaining two declared that the thing itself was dead and buried, while the other as strenuously protested that it was alive and kicking. It was admitted that the parliamentary genius of our honourable friend would be quite able to reconcile such small discrepancies as these; but, there remained the additional difficulty that each of the twelve made entirely different statements at different places, and that all the twelve called everything visible and invisible, sacred and profane, to witness, that they were a perfectly impregnable phalanx of unanimity. This, it was apprehended, would be a stumbling-block to our honourable friend.

The difficulty came before our honourable friend, in this way. He went down to Verbosity to meet his free and independent constituents, and to render an account (as he informed them in the local papers) of the trust they had confided to his hands—that trust which it was one of the proudest privileges of an Englishman to possess—that trust which it was the proudest privilege of an Englishman to hold. It may be mentioned as a proof of the great general interest attaching to the contest, that a Lunatic whom nobody employed or knew, went down to Verbosity with several thousand pounds in gold, determined to give the whole away—which he actually did; and that all the publicans opened their houses for nothing. Likewise, several fighting men, and a patriotic group of burglars sportively armed with life-preservers, proceeded (in barouches and very drunk) to the scene of action at their own expense; these children of nature having conceived a warm attachment to our honourable friend, and intending, in their artless manner, to testify it by knocking the voters in the opposite interest on the head.

Our honourable friend being come into the presence of his constituents, and having professed with great suavity that he was delighted to see his good friend Tipkisson there, in his working-dress—his good friend Tipkisson being an inveterate saddler, who always opposes him, and for whom he has a mortal hatred—made them a brisk, ginger-beery sort of speech, in which he showed them how the dozen noblemen and gentlemen had (in exactly ten days from their coming in) exercised a surprisingly beneficial effect on the whole financial condition of Europe, had altered the state of the exports and imports for the current half-year, had prevented the drain of gold, had made all that matter right about the glut of the raw material, and had restored all sorts of balances with which the superseded noblemen and gentlemen had played the deuce—and all this, with wheat at so much a quarter, gold at so much an ounce, and the Bank of England discounting good bills at so much per cent.! He might be asked, he observed in a peroration of great power, what were his principles? His principles were what they always had been. His principles were written in the countenances of the lion and unicorn; were stamped indelibly upon the royal shield which those grand animals supported, and upon the free words of fire which that shield bore. His principles were, Britannia and her sea-king trident! His principles were, commercial prosperity co-existently with perfect and profound agricultural contentment; but short of this he would never stop. His principles were, these,—with the addition of his colours nailed to the mast, every man's heart in the right place, every man's eye open, every man's hand ready, every man's mind on the alert. His principles were these, concurrently with a general revision of something—speaking generally—and a possible readjustment of something else, not to be mentioned more particularly. His principles, to sum up all in a word, were, Hearths and Altars, Labour and Capital, Crown and Sceptre, Elephant and Castle. And now, if his good friend Tipkisson required any further explanation from him, he (our honourable friend) was there, willing and ready to give it.

Tipkisson, who all this time had stood conspicuous in the crowd, with his arms folded and his eyes intently fastened on our honourable friend: Tipkisson, who throughout our honourable friend's address had not relaxed a muscle of his visage, but had stood there, wholly unaffected by the torrent of eloquence: an object of contempt and scorn to mankind (by which we mean, of course, to the supporters of our honourable friend); Tipkisson now said that he was a plain man (Cries of "You are indeed!"), and that what he wanted to know was, what our honourable friend and the dozen noblemen and gentlemen were driving at?

Our honourable friend immediately replied, "At the illimitable perspective."

It was considered by the whole assembly that this happy statement of our honourable friend's political views ought, immediately, to have settled Tipkisson's business and covered him with confusion; but, that implacable person, regardless of the execrations that were heaped upon him from all sides (by which we mean, of course, from our honourable friend's side), persisted in retaining an unmoved countenance, and obstinately retorted that if our honourable friend meant that, he wished to know what *that* meant?

It was in repelling this most objectionable and indecent opposition, that our honourable friend displayed his highest qualifications for the representation of Verbosity. His warmest supporters present, and those who were best acquainted with his generalship, supposed that the moment was come when he would fall back upon the sacred bulwarks of our nationality. No such thing. He replied thus : " My good friend Tipkisson, gentlemen, wishes to know what I mean when he asks me what we are driving at, and when I candidly tell him, at the illimitable perspective, he wishes (if I understand him) to know what I mean?" " I do!" says Tipkisson, amid cries of " Shame " and " Down with him." " Gentlemen," says our honourable friend, " I will indulge my good friend Tipkisson, by telling him, both what I mean and what I don't mean. (Cheers and cries of " Give it him!") Be it known to him then, and to all whom it may concern, that I do mean altars, hearths, and homes, and that I don't mean mosques and Mohammedanism!" The effect of this home-thrust was terrific. Tipkisson (who is a Baptist) was hooted down and hustled out, and has ever since been regarded as a Turkish Renegade who contemplates an early pilgrimage to Mecca. Nor was he the only discomfited man. The charge, while it stuck to him, was magically transferred to our honourable friend's opponent, who was represented in an immense variety of placards as a firm believer in Mahomet; and the men of Verbosity were asked to choose between our honourable friend and the Bible, and our honourable friend's opponent and the Koran. They decided for our honourable friend, and rallied round the illimitable perspective.

It has been claimed for our honourable friend, with much appearance of reason, that he was the first to bend sacred matters to electioneering tactics. However this may be, the fine precedent was undoubtedly set in a Verbosity election: and it is certain that our honourable friend (who was a disciple of Brahma in his youth, and was a Buddhist when we had the honour of travelling with him a few years ago) always professes in public more anxiety than the whole Bench of Bishops, regarding the theological and doxological opinions of every man, woman, and child, in the United Kingdom.

As we began by saying that our honourable friend has got in again at this last election, and that we are delighted to find that he has got in, so we will conclude. Our honourable friend cannot come in for Verbosity too often. It is a good sign; it is a great example. It is to men like our honourable friend, and to contests like those from which he comes triumphant, that we are mainly indebted for that ready interest in politics, that fresh enthusiasm in the discharge of the duties of citizenship, that ardent desire to rush to the poll, at present so manifest throughout England. When the contest lies (as it sometimes does) between two such men as our honourable friend, it stimulates the finest emotions of our nature, and awakens the highest admiration of which our heads and hearts are capable.

It is not too much to predict that our honourable friend will be always at his post in the ensuing session. Whatever the question be, or whatever the form of its discussion; address to the crown, election petition, expenditure of the public money, extension of the public suffrage, education, crime; in the whole house, in committee of the whole house, in select committee; in every parliamentary discussion of every subject, everywhere: the Honourable Member for Verbosity will most certainly be found.

OUR SCHOOL

WE went to look at it, only this last Midsummer, and found that the Railway had cut it up root and branch. A great trunk-line had swallowed the playground, sliced away the schoolroom, and pared off the corner of the house: which, thus curtailed of its proportions, presented itself, in a green stage of stucco, profilewise towards the road, like a forlorn flat-iron without a handle, standing on end.

It seems as if our schools were doomed to be the sport of change. We have faint recollections of a Preparatory Day-School, which we have sought in vain, and which must have been pulled down to make a new street, ages ago. We have dim impressions, scarcely amounting to a belief, that it was over a dyer's shop. We know that you went up steps to it; that you frequently grazed your knees in doing so; that you generally got your leg over the scraper, in trying to scrape the mud off a very unsteady little shoe. The mistress of the Establishment holds no place in our memory; but, rampant on one eternal door-mat, in an eternal entry long and narrow, is a puffy pug-dog, with a personal animosity towards us, who triumphs over Time. The bark of that baleful Pug, a certain radiating way he had of snapping at our undefended legs, the ghastly grinning of his moist black muzzle and white teeth, and the insolence of his crisp tail curled like a pastoral crook, all live and flourish. From

236

an otherwise unaccountable association of him with a fiddle, we conclude that he was of French extraction, and his name *Fidèle*. He belonged to some female, chiefly inhabiting a back-parlour, whose life appears to us to have been consumed in sniffing, and in wearing a brown beaver bonnet. For her, he would sit up and balance cake upon his nose, and not eat it until twenty had been counted. To the best of our belief we were once called in to witness this performance; when, unable, even in his milder moments, to endure our presence, he instantly made at us, cake and all.

Why a something in mourning, called "Miss Frost," should still connect itself with our preparatory school, we are unable to say. We retain no impression of the beauty of Miss Frost—if she were beautiful; or of the mental fascinations of Miss Frost—if she were accomplished; yet her name and her black dress hold an enduring place in our remembrance. An equally impersonal boy, whose name has long since shaped itself unalterably into "Master Mawls," is not to be dislodged from our brain. Retaining no vindictive feeling towards Mawls—no feeling whatever, indeed—we infer that neither he nor we can have loved Miss Frost. Our first impression of Death and Burial is associated with this formless pair. We all three nestled awfully in a corner one wintry day, when the wind was blowing shrill, with Miss Frost's pinafore over our heads; and Miss Frost told us in a whisper about somebody being "screwed down." It is the only distinct recollection we preserve of these impalpable creatures, except a suspicion that the manners of Master Mawls were susceptible of much improvement. Generally speaking, we may observe that whenever we see a child intently occupied with its nose, to the exclusion of all other subjects of interest, our mind reverts, in a flash, to Master Mawls.

But, the School that was Our School before the Railroad came and overthrew it, was quite another sort of place. We were old enough to be put into Virgil when we went there, and to get Prizes for a variety of polishing on which the rust has long accumulated. It was a School of some celebrity in its neighbourhood—nobody could have said why —and we had the honour to attain and hold the eminent position of first boy. The master was supposed among us to know nothing, and one of the ushers was supposed to know everything. We are still inclined to think the first-named supposition perfectly correct.

We have a general idea that its subject had been in the leather trade, and had bought us—meaning Our School—of another proprietor who was immensely learned. Whether this belief had any real foundation, we are not likely ever to know now. The only branches of education with which he showed the least acquaintance, were, ruling and corporally punishing. He was always ruling ciphering-books with a bloated mahogany ruler, or smiting the palms of offenders with the same diabolical instrument, or viciously drawing a pair of pantaloons tight with one of his large hands, and caning the wearer with the other. We have no doubt whatever that this occupation was the principal solace of his existence.

A profound respect for money pervaded Our School, which was, of course, derived from its Chief. We remember an idiotic goggle-eyed boy, with a big head and half-crowns without end, who suddenly appeared as a parlour-boarder, and was rumoured to have come by sea from some mysterious part of the earth where his parents rolled in gold. He was usually called "Mr." by the Chief, and was said to feed in the parlour on steaks and gravy; likewise to drink currant wine. And he openly stated that if rolls and coffee were ever denied him at breakfast, he would write home to that unknown part of the globe from which he had come, and cause himself to be recalled to the regions of gold. He was put into no form or class, but learnt alone, as little as he liked—and he liked very little—and there was a belief among us that this was because he was too wealthy to be "taken down." His special treatment, and our vague association of him with the sea, and with storms, and sharks, and Coral Reefs occasioned the wildest legends to be circulated as his history. A tragedy in blank verse was written on the subject —if our memory does not deceive us, by the hand that now chronicles these recollections—in which his father figured as a Pirate, and was shot for a voluminous catalogue of atrocities: first imparting to his wife the secret of the cave in which his wealth was stored, and from which his only son's half-crowns now issued. Dumbledon (the boy's name) was represented as "yet unborn" when his brave father met his fate; and the despair and grief of Mrs. Dumbledon at that calamity was movingly shadowed forth as having weakened the parlour-boarder's mind. This production was received with great favour, and was twice performed with closed doors in the dining-room. But, it got wind, and was seized as libellous, and brought the unlucky poet into severe affliction. Some two years afterwards, all of a sudden one day, Dumbledon vanished. It was whispered that the Chief himself had taken him down to the Docks, and re-shipped him for the Spanish Main; but nothing certain was ever known about his disappearance. At this hour, we cannot thoroughly disconnect him from California.

Our School was rather famous for mysterious pupils. There was another—a heavy young man, with a large double-cased silver watch, and a fat knife the handle of which was a perfect tool-box—who unaccountably appeared one day at a special desk of his own, erected close to that of the Chief, with whom he held familiar converse. He lived in the parlour, and went out for his walks, and never took the least notice of us—even of us, the first boy—unless to give us a deprecatory kick, or grimly to take our hat off and throw it away, when he encountered us out of doors, which unpleasant ceremony he always performed as he passed—not even condescending to stop for the purpose. Some of us believed that the classical attainments of this phenomenon were terrific, but that his penmanship and arithmetic were defective, and he had come there to mend them; others, that he was going to set up a school, and had paid the Chief "twenty-five pound down," for leave to see Our School at work. The gloomier spirits even said that he was going to buy us; against which contingency, conspiracies were set on foot for a general defection and running away. However, he never did that. After staying for a quarter, during which period, though closely observed, he was never seen to do anything but make pens out of quills, write small hand in a secret portfolio, and punch the point of the sharpest blade in his knife into his desk all over it, he too disappeared, and his place knew him no more.

There was another boy, a fair, meek boy, with a delicate complexion and rich curling hair, who, we found out, or thought we found out (we have no idea now, and probably had none then, on what grounds, but it was confidentially revealed from mouth to mouth), was the son of a Viscount who had deserted his lovely mother. It was understood that if he had his rights, he would be worth twenty thousand a year. And that if his mother ever met his father, she would shoot him with a silver pistol, which she carried, always loaded to the muzzle, for that purpose. He was a very suggestive topic. So was a young Mulatto, who was always believed (though very amiable) to have a dagger about him somewhere. But, we think they were both outshone, upon the whole, by another boy who claimed to have been born on the twenty-ninth of February, and to have only one birthday in five years. We suspect this to have been a fiction—but he lived upon it all the time he was at Our School.

The principal currency of Our School was slate pencil. It had some inexplicable value, that was never ascertained, never reduced to a standard. To have a great hoard of it was somehow to be rich. We used to bestow it in charity, and confer it as a precious boon upon our chosen friends. When the holidays were coming, contributions were solicited for

240

ertain boys whose relatives were in India, and who were appealed for under the generic name of "Holiday-stoppers," —appropriate marks of remembrance that should enliven and cheer them in their homeless state. Personally, we always contributed these tokens of sympathy in the form of slate pencil, and always felt that it would be a comfort and a treasure to them.

Our School was remarkable for white mice. Red-polls, linnets, and even canaries, were kept in desks, drawers, hat-boxes, and other strange refuges for birds; but white mice were the favourite stock. The boys trained the mice, much better than the masters trained the boys. We recall one white mouse, who lived in the cover of a Latin dictionary, who ran up ladders, drew Roman chariots, shouldered muskets, turned wheels, and even made a very creditable appearance on the stage as the Dog of Montargis. He might have achieved greater things, but for having the misfortune to mistake his way in a triumphal procession to the Capitol, when he fell into a deep inkstand, and was dyed black and drowned. The mice were the occasion of some most ingenious engineering, in the construction of their houses and instruments of performance. The famous one belonged to a company of proprietors, some of whom have since made Rail-roads, Engines, and Telegraphs; the chairman has erected mills and bridges in New Zealand.

The usher at Our School, who was considered to know everything as opposed to the Chief, who was considered to know nothing, was a bony, gentle-faced, clerical-looking young man in rusty black. It was whispered that he was sweet upon one of Maxby's sisters (Maxby lived close by, and was a day pupil), and further that he "favoured Maxby." As we remember, he taught Italian to Maxby's sisters on half-holidays. He once went to the play with them, and wore a white waistcoat and a rose: which was considered among us equivalent to a declaration. We were of opinion on that occasion, that to the last moment he expected Maxby's father to ask him to dinner at five o'clock, and therefore neglected his own dinner at half-past one, and finally got none. We exaggerated in our imaginations the extent to which he punished Maxby's father's cold meat at supper ; and we agreed to believe that he was elevated with wine and water when he came home. But, we all liked him ; for he had a good knowledge of boys, and would have made it a much better school if he had had more power. He was writing master, mathematical master, English master, made out the bills, mended the pens, and did all sorts of things. He divided the little boys with the Latin master (they were smuggled through their rudimentary books, at odd times when there was nothing else to do), and he always called at parents' houses to inquire after sick boys, because he had gentlemanly manners. He was rather musical, and on some remote quarter-day had bought an old trombone ; but a bit of it was lost, and it made the most extraordinary sounds when he sometimes tried to play it of an evening. His holidays never began (on account of the bills) until long after ours ; but, in the summer vacations he used to take pedestrian excursions with a knap-sack ; and at Christmas time, he went to see his father at Chipping Norton, who we all said (on no authority) was a dairy-fed pork-butcher. Poor fellow ! He was very low all day on Maxby's sister's wedding-day, and afterwards was thought to favour Maxby more than ever, though he had been expected to spite him. He has been dead these twenty years. Poor fellow !

Our remembrance of Our School, presents the Latin master as a colourless doubled-up near-sighted man with a crutch, who was always cold, and always putting onions into his ears for deafness, and always disclosing ends of flannel under all his garments, and almost always applying a ball of pocket-handkerchief to some part of his face with a screwing action round and round. He was a very good scholar, and took great pains where he saw intelligence and a desire to learn : otherwise, perhaps not. Our memory presents him (unless teased into a passion) with as little energy as colour—as having been worried and tormented into monotonous feebleness—as having had the best part of his life ground out of him in a Mill of boys. We remember with terror how he fell asleep one sultry afternoon with the little smuggled class before him, and awoke not when the footstep of the Chief fell heavy on the floor; how the Chief aroused him, in the midst of a dread silence, and said, "Mr. Blinkins, are you ill, sir?" how he blushingly replied, "Sir, rather so;" how the Chief retorted with severity, "Mr. Blinkins, this is no place to be ill in" (which was very, very true), and walked back solemn as the ghost in Hamlet, until, catching a wandering eye, he caned that boy for inattention, and happily expressed his feelings towards the Latin master through the medium of a substitute.

There was a fat little dancing-master who used to come in a gig, and taught the more advanced among us hornpipes (as an accomplishment in great social demand in after life); and there was a brisk little French master who used to come in the sunniest weather, with a handleless umbrella, and to whom the Chief was always polite, because (as we believed), if the Chief offended him, he would instantly address the Chief in French, and for ever confound him before the boys with his inability to understand or reply.

There was besides, a serving man, whose name was Phil. Our retrospective glance presents Phil as a shipwrecked carpenter, cast away upon the desert island of a school, and carrying into practice an ingenious inkling of many trades. He mended whatever was broken, and made whatever was wanted. He was general glazier, among other things, and mended all the broken windows—at the prime cost (as was darkly rumoured among us) of ninepence, for every square charged three-and-six to parents. We had a high opinion of his mechanical genius, and generally held that the Chief "knew something bad of him," and on pain of divulgence enforced Phil to be his bondsman. We particularly remember that Phil had a sovereign contempt for learning: which engenders in us a respect for his sagacity, as it implies his accurate observation of the relative positions of the Chief and the ushers. He was an impenetrable man, who waited at table between whiles, and throughout "the half" kept the boxes in severe custody. He was morose, even to the Chief, and never smiled, except at breaking-up, when, in acknowledgment of the toast, "Success to Phil! Hooray!" he would slowly carve a grin out of his wooden face, where it would remain until we were all gone. Nevertheless, one time when we had the scarlet fever in the school, Phil nursed all the sick boys of his own accord, and was like a mother to them.

There was another school not far off, and of course Our School could have nothing to say to that school. It is mostly the way with schools, whether of boys or men. Well! the railway has swallowed up ours, and the locomotives now run smoothly over its ashes.

> So fades and languishes, grows dim and dies,
> All that this world is proud of,

—and is not proud of, too. It had little reason to be proud of Our School, and has done much better since in that way, and will do far better yet.

OUR VESTRY

We have the glorious privilege of being always in hot water if we like. We are a shareholder in a Great Parochial British Joint Stock Bank of Balderdash. We have a Vestry in our borough, and can vote for a vestryman—might even *be* a vestryman, mayhap, if we were inspired by a lofty and noble ambition. Which we are not.

Our Vestry is a deliberative assembly of the utmost dignity and importance. Like the Senate of ancient Rome, its awful gravity overpowers (or ought to overpower) barbarian visitors. It sits in the Capitol (we mean in the capital building erected for it), chiefly on Saturdays, and shakes the earth to its centre with the echoes of its thundering eloquence, in a Sunday paper.

To get into this Vestry in the eminent capacity of Vestryman, gigantic efforts are made, and Herculean exertions used. It is made manifest to the dullest capacity at every election, that if we reject Snozzle we are done for, and that if we fail to bring in Blunderbooze at the top of the poll, we are unworthy of the dearest rights of Britons. Flaming placards are rife on all the dead walls in the borough, public-houses hang out banners, hackney-cabs burst into full-grown flowers of type, and everybody is, or should be, in a paroxysm of anxiety.

At these momentous crises of the national fate, we are

much assisted in our deliberations by two eminent volunteers; one of whom subscribes himself A Fellow Parishioner, the other, A Rate-Payer. Who they are, or what they are, or where they are, nobody knows; but, whatever one asserts, the other contradicts. They are both voluminous writers, indicting more epistles than Lord Chesterfield in a single week; and the greater part of their feelings are too big for utterance in anything less than capital letters. They require the additional aid of whole rows of notes of admiration, like balloons, to point their generous indignation; and they sometimes communicate a crushing severity to stars. As thus:

MEN OF MOONEYMOUNT.

Is it, or is it not, a * * * to saddle the parish with a debt of £2,745 6s. 9d., yet claim to be a RIGID ECONOMIST?

Is it, or is it not, a * * * to state as a fact what is proved to be *both a moral and a* PHYSICAL IMPOSSIBILITY?

Is it, or is it not, a * * * to call £2,745 6s. 9d. nothing; and nothing, something?

Do you, or do you *not* want a * * * TO REPRESENT YOU IN THE VESTRY?

Your consideration of these questions is recommended to you by

A FELLOW PARISHIONER.

It was to this important public document that one of our first orators, MR. MAGG (of Little Winkling Street), adverted, when he opened the great debate of the fourteenth of November by saying, "Sir, I hold in my hand an anonymous slander" —and when the interruption, with which he was at that point assailed by the opposite faction, gave rise to that memorable discussion on a point of order which will ever be remembered with interest by constitutional assemblies. In the animated debate to which we refer, no fewer than thirty-seven gentlemen, many of them of great eminence, including MR. WIGSBY (of Chumbledon Square), were seen upon their legs at one time; and it was on the same great occasion that DOGGINSON—regarded in our Vestry as "a regular John Bull: " we believe, in consequence of his having always made up his mind on every subject without knowing anything about it—informed another gentleman of similar principles on the opposite side, that if he "cheek'd him," he would resort to the extreme measure of knocking his blessed head off.

This was a great occasion. But, our Vestry shines habitually. In asserting its own pre-eminence, for instance, it is very strong. On the least provocation, or on none, it will be clamorous to know whether it is to be "dictated to," or "trampled on," or "ridden over rough-shod." Its great watchword is Self-government. That is to say, supposing our Vestry to favour any little harmless disorder like Typhus Fever, and supposing the Government of the country to be, by any accident, in such ridiculous hands, as that any of its authorities should consider it a duty to object to Typhus Fever—obviously an unconstitutional objection—then, our Vestry cuts in with a terrible manifesto about Self-government, and claims its independent right to have as much Typhus Fever as pleases itself. Some absurd and dangerous persons have represented, on the other hand, that though our Vestry may be able to "beat the bounds" of its own parish, it may not be able to beat the bounds of its own diseases; which (say they) spread over the whole land, in an ever-expanding circle of waste, and misery, and death, and widowhood, and orphanage, and desolation. But, our Vestry makes short work of any such fellows as these.

It was our Vestry—pink of Vestries as it is—that in support of its favourite principle took the celebrated ground of denying the existence of the last pestilence that raged in England, when the pestilence was raging at the Vestry doors. Dogginson said it was plums; Mr. Wigsby (of Chumbledon Square) said it was oysters; Mr. Magg (of Little Winkling Street) said, amid great cheering, it was the newspapers. The noble indignation of our Vestry with that un-English institution the Board of Health, under those circumstances, yields one of the finest passages in its history. It wouldn't hear of rescue. Like Mr. Joseph Miller's Frenchman, it would be drowned and nobody should save it. Transported beyond grammar by its kindled ire, it spoke in unknown tongues, and vented unintelligible bellowings, more like an ancient oracle than the modern oracle it is admitted on all hands to be. Rare exigencies produce rare things; and even our Vestry, new hatched to the woful time, came forth a greater goose than ever.

But this, again, was a special occasion. Our Vestry, at more ordinary periods, demands its meed of praise.

Our Vestry is eminently parliamentary. Playing at Parliament is its favourite game. It is even regarded by some of its members as a chapel of ease to the House of Commons: a Little Go to be passed first. It has its strangers' gallery, and its reported debates (see the Sunday paper before mentioned), and our Vestrymen are in and out of order, and on and off their legs, and above all are transcendently quarrelsome, after the pattern of the real original.

Our Vestry being assembled, Mr. Magg never begs to trouble Mr. Wigsby with a simple inquiry. He knows better than that. Seeing the honourable gentleman, associated in their minds with Chumbledon Square, in his place, he wishes to ask that honourable gentleman what the intentions of himself, and those with whom he acts, may be, on the subject of the paving of the district known as Piggleum Buildings? Mr. Wigsby replies (with his eye on next Sunday's paper) that in reference to the question which has been put to him by the honourable gentleman opposite, he must take leave to say, that if that honourable gentleman had had the courtesy to give him notice of that question, he (Mr. Wigsby) would have consulted with his colleagues in reference to the advisability, in the present state of the discussions on the new paving-rate, of answering that question. But, as the honourable gentleman has NOT had the courtesy to give him notice

of that question (great cheering from the Wigsby interest),
he must decline to give the honourable gentleman the satisfaction he requires. Mr. Magg, instantly rising to retort, is
received with loud cries of " Spoke ! " from the Wigsby interest,
and with cheers from the Magg side of the house. Moreover,
five gentlemen rise to order, and one of them, in revenge for
being taken no notice of, petrifies the assembly by moving
that this Vestry do now adjourn ; but, is persuaded to with-
draw that awful proposal, in consideration of its tremendous
consequences if persevered in. Mr. Magg, for the purpose of
being heard, then begs to move, that you, sir, do now pass
to the order of the day ; and takes that opportunity of saying, that if an honourable gentleman whom he has in his
eye, and will not demean himself by more particularly naming
(oh, oh, and cheers), supposes that he is to be put down by
clamour, that honourable gentleman—however supported he
may be, through thick and thin, by a Fellow Parishioner,
with whom he is well acquainted (cheers and counter-cheers,
Mr. Magg being invariably backed by the Rate-Payer)—will
find himself mistaken. Upon this, twenty members of our
Vestry speak in succession concerning what the two great
men have meant, until it appears, after an hour and twenty
minutes, that neither of them meant anything. Then our
Vestry begins business.

We have said that, after the pattern of the real original,
our Vestry in playing at Parliament is transcendently quarrelsome. It enjoys a personal altercation above all things.
Perhaps the most redoubtable case of this kind we have ever
had—though we have had so many that it is difficult to
decide—was that on which the last extreme solemnities passed
between Mr. Tiddypot (of Gumption House) and Captain
Banger (of Wilderness Walk).

In an adjourned debate on the question whether water could
be regarded in the light of a necessary of life ; respecting which
there were great differences of opinion, and many shades of
sentiment ; Mr. Tiddypot, in a powerful burst of eloquence

against that hypothesis, frequently made use of the expression that such and such a rumour had "reached his ears." Captain Banger, following him, and holding that, for purposes of ablution and refreshment, a pint of water per diem was necessary for every adult of the lower classes, and half a pint for every child, cast ridicule upon his address in a sparkling speech, and concluded by saying that instead of those rumours having reached the ears of the honourable gentleman, he rather thought the honourable gentleman's ears must have reached the rumours, in consequence of their well-known length. Mr. Tiddypot immediately rose, looked the honourable and gallant gentleman full in the face, and left the Vestry.

The excitement, at this moment painfully intense, was heightened to an acute degree when Captain Banger rose, and also left the Vestry. After a few moments of profound silence—one of those breathless pauses never to be forgotten— Mr. Chib (of Tucket's Terrace, and the father of the Vestry) rose. He said that words and looks had passed in that assembly, replete with consequences which every feeling mind must deplore. Time pressed. The sword was drawn, and while he spoke the scabbard might be thrown away. He moved that those honourable gentlemen who had left the Vestry be recalled, and required to pledge themselves upon their honour that this affair should go no farther. The motion being by a general union of parties unanimously agreed to (for everybody wanted to have the belligerents there, instead of out of sight: which was no fun at all), Mr. Magg was deputed to recover Captain Banger, and Mr. Chib himself to go in search of Mr. Tiddypot. The Captain was found in a conspicuous position, surveying the passing omnibuses from the top step of the front-door immediately adjoining the beadle's box; Mr. Tiddypot made a desperate attempt at resistance, but was overpowered by Mr. Chib (a remarkably hale old gentleman of eighty-two), and brought back in safety.

Mr. Tiddypot and the Captain being restored to their places, and glaring on each other, were called upon by the chair to abandon all homicidal intentions, and give the Vestry an assurance that they did so. Mr. Tiddypot remained profoundly silent. The Captain likewise remained profoundly silent, saving that he was observed by those around him to fold his arms like Napoleon Buonaparte, and to snort in his breathing—actions but too expressive of gunpowder.

The most intense emotion now prevailed. Several members clustered in remonstrance round the Captain, and several round Mr. Tiddypot; but, both were obdurate. Mr. Chib then presented himself amid tremendous cheering, and said, that not to shrink from the discharge of his painful duty, he must now move that both honourable gentlemen be taken into custody by the beadle, and conveyed to the nearest police-office, there to be held to bail. The union of parties still continuing, the motion was seconded by Mr. Wigsby—on all usual occasions Mr. Chib's opponent—and rapturously carried with only one dissentient voice. This was Dogginson's, who said from his place "Let 'em fight it out with fistes;" but whose coarse remark was received as it merited.

The beadle now advanced along the floor of the Vestry, and beckoned with his cocked hat to both members. Every breath was suspended. To say that a pin might have been heard to fall, would be feebly to express the all-absorbing interest and silence. Suddenly, enthusiastic cheering broke out from every side of the Vestry. Captain Banger had risen —being, in fact, pulled up by a friend on either side, and poked up by a friend behind.

The Captain said, in a deep determined voice, that he had every respect for that Vestry and every respect for that chair; that he also respected the honourable gentleman of Gumpton House; but, that he respected his honour more. Hereupon the Captain sat down, leaving the whole Vestry much affected. Mr. Tiddypot instantly rose, and was received with the same encouragement. He likewise said—and the exquisite art of this orator communicated to the observation an air of freshness and novelty—that he too had every respect for that Vestry; that he too had every respect for that chair. That he too respected the honourable and gallant gentleman of Wilderness Walk; but, that he too respected his honour more. "Hows'ever," added the distinguished Vestryman, "if the honourable and gallant gentleman's honour is never more doubted and damaged than it is by me, he's all right." Captain Banger immediately started up again, and said that after those observations, involving as they did ample concession to his honour without compromising the honour of the honourable gentleman, he would be wanting in honour as well as in generosity, if he did not at once repudiate all intention of wounding the honour of the honourable gentleman, or saying anything dishonourable to his honourable feelings. These observations were repeatedly interrupted by bursts of cheers. Mr. Tiddypot retorted that he well knew the spirit of honour by which the honourable and gallant gentleman was so honourably animated, and that he accepted an honourable explanation, offered in a way that did him honour; but, he trusted that the Vestry would consider that his (Mr. Tiddypot's) honour had imperatively demanded of him that painful course which he had felt it due to his honour to adopt. The Captain and Mr. Tiddypot then touched their hats to one another across the Vestry, a great many times, and it is thought that these proceedings (reported to the extent of several columns in next Sunday's paper) will bring them in as churchwardens next year.

All this was strictly after the pattern of the real original, and so are the whole of our Vestry's proceedings. In all their debates, they are laudably imitative of the windy and wordy slang of the real original, and of nothing that is better in it. They have headstrong party animosities, without any reference to the merits of questions; they tack a surprising amount of debate to a very little business; they set more store by forms than they do by substances :—all very like the real original! It has been doubted in our borough, whether our Vestry is of any utility; but our own conclusion is, that it is of the use to the Borough that a diminishing mirror is to a painter, as enabling it to perceive in a small focus of absurdity all the surface defects of the real original.

OUR BORE

It is unnecessary to say that we keep a bore. Everybody does. But, the bore whom we have the pleasure and honour of enumerating among our particular friends, is such a generic bore, and has so many traits (as it appears to us) in common with the great bore family, that we are tempted to make him the subject of the present notes. May he be generally accepted!

Our bore is admitted on all hands to be a good-hearted man. He may put fifty people out of temper, but he keeps his own. He preserves a sickly solid smile upon his face, when other faces are ruffled by the perfection he has attained in his art, and has an equable voice which never travels out of one key or rises above one pitch. His manner is a manner of tranquil interest. None of his opinions are startling. Among his deepest-rooted convictions, it may be mentioned that he considers the air of England damp, and holds that our lively neighbours—he always calls the French our lively neighbours—have the advantage of us in that particular. Nevertheless he is unable to forget that John Bull is John Bull all the world over, and that England with all her faults is England still.

Our bore has travelled. He could not possibly be a complete bore without having travelled. He rarely speaks of his travels without introducing, sometimes on his own plan of construction, morsels of the language of the country—which he always translates. You cannot name to him any little remote town in France, Italy, Germany, or Switzerland but he knows it well; stayed there a fortnight under peculiar circumstances. And talking of that little place, perhaps you know a statue over an old fountain, up a little court, which is the second—no, the third—stay—yes, the third turning on the right, after you come out of the Post-house, going up the hill towards the market? You *don't* know that statue? Nor that fountain? You surprise him! They are not usually seen by travellers (most extraordinary, he has never yet met with a single traveller who knew them, except one German, the most intelligent man he ever met in his life!) but he thought that you would have been the man to find them out. And then he describes them, in a circumstantial lecture half an hour long, generally delivered behind a door which is constantly being opened from the other side; and implores you, if you ever revisit that place, now do go and look at that statue and fountain!

Our bore, in a similar manner, being in Italy, made a discovery of a dreadful picture, which has been the terror of a large portion of the civilized world ever since. We have seen the liveliest men paralysed by it, across a broad dining-table. He was lounging among the mountains, sir, basking in the mellow influences of the climate, when he came to *una piccola chiesa*—a little church—or perhaps it would be more correct to say *una piccolissima cappella*—the smallest chapel you can possibly imagine—and walked in. There was nobody inside but a *cieco*—a blind man—saying his prayers, and a *vecchio padre*—old friar—rattling a money-box. But, above the head of that friar, and immediately to the right of the altar as you enter—to the right of the altar? No. To the left of the altar as you enter—or say near the centre—there hung a painting (subject, Virgin and Child) so divine in its expression, so pure and yet so warm and rich in its tone, so fresh in its touch, at once so glowing in its colour and so statuesque in its repose, that our bore cried out in an ecstasy, "That's the finest picture in Italy!" And so it is, sir. There is no doubt of it. It is astonishing that that picture is so little known. Even the painter is uncertain. He afterwards took Blumb, of the Royal Academy (it is to be observed that our bore takes none but eminent people to see sights, and that none but eminent people take our bore), and you never saw a man so affected in your life as Blumb was. He cried like a child! And then our bore begins his description in detail —for all this is introductory—and strangles his hearers with the folds of the purple drapery.

By an equally fortunate conjunction of accidental circumstances, it happened that when our bore was in Switzerland, he discovered a Valley, of that superb character, that Chamouni is not to be mentioned in the same breath with it. This is how it was, sir. He was travelling on a mule—had been in the saddle some days—when, as he and the guide, Pierre Blanquo: whom you may know, perhaps?—our bore is sorry you don't, because he's the only guide deserving of the name—as he and Pierre were descending, towards evening, among those everlasting snows, to the little village of La Croix, our bore observed a mountain track turning off sharply to the right. At first he was uncertain whether it *was* a track at all, and in fact, he said to Pierre, " *Qu'est que c'est donc, mon ami?*—What is that, my friend?" " *Où, monsieur?* " said Pierre—"Where, sir?" "*Là!*—there!" said our bore. "*Monsieur, ce n'est rien de tout*—sir, it's nothing at all," said Pierre. "*Allons!*—Make haste. *Il va neiger*—it's going to snow!" But, our bore was not to be done in that way, and he firmly replied, "I wish to go in that direction—*je veux y aller*. I am bent upon it—*je suis déterminé. En avant!*— go ahead!" In consequence of which firmness on our bore's part, they proceeded, sir, during two hours of evening, and three of moonlight (they waited in a cavern till the moon was up), along the slenderest track, overhanging perpendicularly the most awful gulfs, until they arrived, by a winding descent, in a valley that possibly, and he may say probably, was never visited by any stranger before. What a valley! Mountains piled on mountains, avalanches stemmed by pine forests; waterfalls, châlets, mountain-torrents, wooden bridges, every conceivable picture of Swiss scenery! The whole village turned out to receive our bore. The peasant girls kissed him, the men shook hands with him, one old lady of benevolent appearance wept upon his breast. He was conducted, in a primitive triumph, to the little inn : where he was taken ill next morning, and lay for six weeks, attended by the amiable hostess (the same benevolent old lady who had wept over night) and her charming daughter, Fanchette. It is nothing to say that they were attentive to him ; they doted on him. They called him in their simple way, *l'Ange Anglais*—the English Angel. When our bore left the valley, there was not a dry eye in the place ; some of the people attended him for miles. He begs and entreats of you as a personal favour, that if you ever go to Switzerland again (you have mentioned that your last visit was your twenty-third), you will go to that valley, and see Swiss scenery for the first time. And if you want really to know the pastoral people of Switzerland, and to understand them, mention, in that valley, our bore's name!

Our bore has a crushing brother in the East, who, somehow or other, was admitted to smoke pipes with Mehemet Ali, and instantly became an authority on the whole range of Eastern matters, from Haroun Alraschid to the present Sultan. He is in the habit of expressing mysterious opinions on this wide range of subjects, but on questions of foreign policy more particularly, to our bore, in letters ; and our bore is continually sending bits of these letters to the newspapers (which they never insert), and carrying other bits about in his pocket-book. It is even whispered that he has been seen at the Foreign Office, receiving great consideration from the messengers, and having his card promptly borne into the sanctuary of the temple. The havoc committed in society by this Eastern brother is beyond belief. Our bore is always ready with him. We have known our bore to fall upon an intelligent young sojourner in the wilderness, in the first sentence of a narrative, and beat all confidence out of him with one blow of his brother. He became omniscient, as to foreign policy, in the smoking of those pipes with Mehemet Ali. The balance of power in Europe, the machinations of the Jesuits, the gentle and humanising influence of Austria, the position and prospects of that hero of the noble soul who is worshipped by happy France, are all easy reading to our bore's brother. And our bore is so provokingly self-denying about him! "I don't pretend to more than a very general knowledge of these subjects myself," says he, after enervating the intellects of several strong men, "but these are my brother's opinions, and I believe he is known to be well-informed."

The commonest incidents and places would appear to have been made special, expressly for our bore. Ask him whether he ever chanced to walk, between seven and eight in the morning, down St. James's Street, London, and he will tell you, never in his life but once. But, it's curious that that once was in eighteen thirty; and that as our bore was walking down the street you have just mentioned, at the hour you have just mentioned—half-past seven—or twenty minutes to eight. No! Let him be correct!—exactly a quarter before eight by the palace clock—he met a fresh-coloured, grey-haired, good-humoured looking gentleman, with a brown umbrella, who, as he passed him, touched his hat and said, "Fine morning, sir, fine morning!"—William the Fourth!

Ask our bore whether he has seen Mr. Barry's new Houses of Parliament, and he will reply that he has not yet inspected them minutely, but, that you remind him that it was his singular fortune to be the last man to see the old Houses of Parliament before the fire broke out. It happened in this way. Poor John Spine, the celebrated novelist, had taken him over to South Lambeth to read to him the last few chapters of what was certainly his best book—as our bore told him at the time, adding, "Now, my dear John, touch it, and you'll spoil it!"—and our bore was going back to the club by way of Millbank and Parliament Street, when he stopped to think of Canning, and look at the Houses of Parliament. Now, you know far more of the philosophy of Mind than our bore does, and are much better able to explain to him than he is to explain to you why or wherefore, at that particular time, the thought of fire should come into his head. But, it did. It did. He thought, What a national calamity if an edifice connected with so many associations should be consumed by fire! At that time there was not a single soul in the street but himself. All was quiet, dark, and solitary. After contemplating the building for a minute —or, say a minute and a half, not more—our bore proceeded on his way, mechanically repeating, What a national calamity if such an edifice, connected with such associations, should be destroyed by—— A man coming towards him in a violent state of agitation completed the sentence, with the exclamation, Fire! Our bore looked round, and the whole structure was in a blaze.

In harmony and union with these experiences, our bore never went anywhere in a steamboat but he made either the best or the worst voyage ever known on that station. Either he overheard the captain say to himself, with his hands clasped, "We are all lost!" or the captain openly declared to him that he had never made such a run before, and never should be able to do it again. Our bore was in that express train on that railway, when they made (unknown to the passengers) the experiment of going at the rate of a hundred miles an hour. Our bore remarked on that occasion to the other people in the carriage, "This is too fast, but sit still!" He was at the Norwich musical festival when the extraordinary echo for which science has been wholly unable to account, was heard for the first and last time. He and the bishop heard it at the same moment, and caught each other's eye. He was present at that illumination of St. Peter's, of which the Pope is known to have remarked, as he looked at it out of his window in the Vatican, "*O Cielo! Questa cosa non sara fatta, mai ancora, come questa*—O Heaven! this thing will never be done again, like this!" He has seen every lion he ever saw, under some remarkably propitious circumstances. He knows there is no fancy in it, because in every case the showman mentioned the fact at the time, and congratulated him upon it.

At one period of his life, our bore had an illness. It was an illness of a dangerous character for society at large. Innocently remark that you are very well, or that somebody else is very well; and our bore, with a preface that one never knows what a blessing health is until one has lost it, is reminded of that illness, and drags you through the whole of its symptoms, progress, and treatment. Innocently remark that you are not well, or that somebody else is not well, and the same inevitable result ensues. You will learn how our bore felt a tightness about here, sir, for which he couldn't account, accompanied with a constant sensation as if he were being stabbed—or, rather, jobbed—that expresses it more correctly—jobbed—with a blunt knife. Well, sir! This went on, until sparks began to flit before his eyes, water-wheels to turn round in his head, and hammers to beat incessantly thump, thump, thump, all down his back—along the whole of the spinal vertebræ. Our bore, when his sensations had come to this, thought it a duty he owed to himself to take advice, and he said, Now, whom shall I consult? He naturally thought of Callow, at that time one of the most eminent physicians in London, and he went to Callow. Callow said, "Liver!" and prescribed rhubarb and calomel, low diet, and moderate exercise. Our bore went on with this treatment, getting worse every day, until he lost confidence in Callow, and went to Moon, whom half the town was then mad about. Moon was interested in the case; to do him justice he was very much interested in the case; and he said, "Kidneys!" He altered the whole treatment, sir—

gave strong acids, cupped, and blistered. This went on, our bore still getting worse every day, until he openly told Moon it would be a satisfaction to him if he would have a consultation with Clatter. The moment Clatter saw our bore, he said, "Accumulation of fat about the heart!" Snugglewood, who was called in with him, differed, and said, "Brain!" But, what they all agreed upon was, to lay our bore upon his back, to shave his head, to leech him, to administer enormous quantities of medicine, and to keep him low; so that he was reduced to a mere shadow, you wouldn't have known him, and nobody considered it possible that he could ever recover. This was his condition, sir, when he heard of Jilkins—at that period in a very small practice, and living in the upper part of a house in Great Portland Street; but still, you understand, with a rising reputation among the few people to whom he was known. Being in that condition in which a drowning man catches at a straw, our bore sent for Jilkins. Jilkins came. Our bore liked his eye, and said, "Mr. Jilkins, I have a presentiment that you will do me good." Jilkins's reply was characteristic of the man. It was, "Sir, I mean to do you good." This confirmed our bore's opinion of his eye, and they went into the case together—went completely into it. Jilkins then got up, walked across the room, came back, and sat down. His words were these. "You have been humbugged. This is a case of indigestion, occasioned by deficiency of power in the Stomach. Take a mutton chop in half-an-hour, with a glass of the finest old sherry that can be got for money. Take two mutton chops to-morrow, and two glasses of the finest old sherry. Next day, I'll come again." In a week our bore was on his legs, and Jilkins's success dates from that period!

Our bore is great in secret information. He happens to know many things that nobody else knows. He can generally tell you where the split is in the Ministry; he knows a deal about the Queen; and has little anecdotes to relate of the royal nursery. He gives you the judge's private opinion of Sludge the murderer, and his thoughts when he tried him. He happens to know what such a man got by such a transaction, and it was fifteen thousand five hundred pounds, and his income is twelve thousand a year. Our bore is also great in mystery. He believes, with an exasperating appearance of profound meaning, that you saw Parkins last Sunday?—Yes, you did.—Did he say anything particular?—No, nothing particular.—Our bore is surprised at that.—Why?—Nothing. Only he understood that Parkins had come to tell you something.—What about?—Well! our bore is not at liberty to mention what about. But, he believes you will hear that from Parkins himself, soon, and he hopes it may not surprise you as it did him. Perhaps, however, you never heard about Parkins's wife's sister?—No.—Ah! says our bore, that explains it!

Our bore is also great in argument. He infinitely enjoys a long humdrum, drowsy interchange of words of dispute about nothing. He considers that it strengthens the mind, consequently, he "don't see that," very often. Or, he would be glad to know what you mean by that. Or, he doubts that. Or, he has always understood exactly the reverse of that. Or, he can't admit that. Or, he begs to deny that. Or, surely you don't mean that. And so on. He once advised us; offered us a piece of advice, after the fact, totally impracticable and wholly impossible of acceptance, because it supposed the fact, then eternally disposed of, to be yet in abeyance. It was a dozen years ago, and to this hour our bore benevolently wishes, in a mild voice, on certain regular occasions, that we had thought better of his opinion.

The instinct with which our bore finds out another bore, and closes with him, is amazing. We have seen him pick his man out of fifty men, in a couple of minutes. They love to go (which they do naturally) into a slow argument on a previously exhausted subject, and to contradict each other, and to wear the hearers out, without impairing their own perennial freshness as bores. It improves the good understanding between them, and they get together afterwards, and bore each other amicably. Whenever we see our bore behind a door with another bore, we know that when he comes forth, he will praise the other bore as one of the most intelligent men he ever met. And this bringing us to the close of what we had to say about our bore, we are anxious to have it understood that he never bestowed this praise on us.

A MONUMENT OF FRENCH FOLLY

It was profoundly observed by a witty member of the Court of Common Council, in Council assembled in the City of London, in the year of our Lord one thousand eight hundred and fifty, that the French are a frog-eating people, who wear wooden shoes.

We are credibly informed, in reference to the nation whom this choice spirit so happily disposed of, that the caricatures and stage representations which were current in England some half a century ago, exactly depict their present condition. For example, we understand that every Frenchman, without exception, wears a pigtail and curl-papers. That he is extremely sallow, thin, long-faced, and lantern-jawed. That the calves of his legs are invariably undeveloped; that his legs fail at the knees, and that his shoulders are always higher than his ears. We are likewise assured that he rarely tastes any food but soup maigre, and an onion; that he always says, "By Gar! Aha! Vat you tell me, sare?" at the end of every sentence he utters; and that the true generic name of his race is the Mounseers, or the Parly-voos. If he be not a dancing-master, or a barber, he must be a cook; since no other trades but those three are congenial to the tastes of the people, or permitted by the Institutions of the country. He is a slave, of course. The ladies of France (who are also slaves) invariably have their heads tied up in Belcher handkerchiefs, wear long earrings, carry tambourines, and beguile the weariness of their yoke by singing in head voices through their noses—principally to barrel-organs.

It may be generally summed up, of this inferior people, that they have no idea of anything.

Of a great Institution like Smithfield, they are unable to form the least conception. A Beast Market in the heart of Paris would be regarded an impossible nuisance. Nor have they any notion of slaughter-houses in the midst of a city. One of these benighted frog-eaters would scarcely understand your meaning, if you told him of the existence of such a British bulwark.

It is agreeable, and perhaps pardonable, to indulge in a little self-complacency when our right to it is thoroughly established. At the present time, to be rendered memorable by a final attack on that good old market which is the (rotten) apple of the Corporation's eye, let us compare ourselves, to our national delight and pride as to these two subjects of slaughter-house and beast-market, with the outlandish foreigner.

The blessings of Smithfield are too well understood to need recapitulation; all who run (away from mad bulls and pursuing oxen) may read. Any market-day they may be beheld in glorious action. Possibly the merits of our slaughter-houses are not yet quite so generally appreciated.

Slaughter-houses, in the large towns of England, are always (with the exception of one or two enterprising towns) most numerous in the most densely crowded places, where there is the least circulation of air. They are often underground, in cellars; they are sometimes in close back yards; sometimes (as in Spitalfields) in the very shops where the meat is sold. Occasionally, under good private management, they are ventilated and clean. For the most part, they are unventilated and dirty; and, to the reeking walls, putrid fat and other offensive animal matter clings with a tenacious hold. The busiest slaughter-houses in London are in the neighbourhood of Smithfield, in Newgate Market, in White-chapel, in Newport Market, in Leadenhall Market, in Clare Market. All these places are surrounded by houses of a poor description, swarming with inhabitants. Some of them are close to the worst burial-grounds in London. When the slaughter-house is below the ground, it is a common practice to throw the sheep down areas, neck and crop—which is exciting, but not at all cruel. When it is on the level surface, it is often extremely difficult of approach. Then, the beasts have to be worried, and goaded, and pronged, and tail-twisted, for a long time before they can be got in —which is entirely owing to their natural obstinacy. When it is not difficult of approach, but is in a foul condition, what they see and scent makes them still more reluctant to enter—which is their natural obstinacy again. When they do get in at last, after no trouble and suffering to speak of (for, there is nothing in the previous journey into the heart of London, the night's endurance in Smithfield, the struggle out again, among the crowded multitude, the coaches, carts, waggons, omnibuses, gigs, chaises, phaetons, cabs, trucks, dogs, boys, whoopings, roarings, and ten thousand other distractions), they are represented to be in a most unfit state to be killed, according to microscopic examinations made of their fevered blood by one of the most distinguished physiologists in the world, PROFESSOR OWEN—but that's humbug. When they *are* killed, at last, their reeking carcases are hung in impure air, to become, as the same Professor will explain to you, less nutritious and more unwholesome—but he is only an *un*common counsellor, so don't mind *him*. In half a quarter of a mile's length of Whitechapel, at one time, there shall be six hundred newly slaughtered oxen hanging up, and seven hundred sheep —but, the more the merrier—proof of prosperity. Hard by Snow Hill and Warwick Lane, you shall see the little children, inured to sights of brutality from their birth, trotting along the alleys, mingled with troops of horribly busy pigs, up to their ankles in blood—but it makes the young rascals hardy.

THE JOLLY OLD ENGLISH ROAST BEEF

Into the imperfect sewers of this overgrown city, you shall have the immense mass of corruption, engendered by these practices, lazily thrown out of sight, to rise, in poisonous gases, into your house at night, when your sleeping children will most readily absorb them, and to find its languid way, at last, into the river that you drink—but, the French are a frog-eating people who wear wooden shoes, and it's O the roast beef of England, my boy, the jolly old English roast beef.

It is quite a mistake—a new-fangled notion altogether—to suppose that there is any natural antagonism between putrefaction and health. They know better than that, in the Common Council. You may talk about Nature, in her wisdom, always warning man through his sense of smell, when he draws near to something dangerous; but, that won't go down in the City. Nature very often don't mean anything. Mrs. Quickly says that prunes are ill for a green wound; but whosoever says that putrid animal substances are ill for a green wound, or for robust vigour, or for anything or for anybody, is a humanity-monger and a humbug. Britons never, never, never, &c., therefore. And prosperity to cattle-driving, cattle-slaughtering, bone-crushing, blood-boiling, trotter-scraping, tripe-dressing, paunch-cleaning, gut-spinning, hide-preparing, tallow-melting, and other salubrious proceedings, in the midst of hospitals, churchyards, workhouses, schools, infirmaries, refuges, dwellings, provision-shops, nurseries, sick-beds, every stage and baiting-place in the journey from birth to death!

These *un*common counsellors, your Professor Owens and fellows, will contend that to tolerate these things in a civilised city, is to reduce it to a worse condition than BRUCE found to prevail in ABYSSINIA. For there (say they) the jackals and wild dogs came at night to devour the offal; whereas, here there are no such natural scavengers, and quite as savage customs. Further, they will demonstrate that nothing in Nature is intended to be wasted, and that besides the

267

waste which such abuses occasion in the articles of health and life—main sources of the riches of any community—they lead to a prodigious waste of changing matters, which might, with proper preparation, and under scientific direction, be safely applied to the increase of the fertility of the land. Thus (they argue) does Nature ever avenge infractions of her beneficent laws, and so surely as Man is determined to warp any of her blessings into curses, shall they become curses, and shall he suffer heavily. But, this is cant. Just as it is cant of the worst description to say to the London Corporation, "How can you exhibit to the people so plain a spectacle of dishonest equivocation, as to claim the right of holding a market in the midst of the great city, for one of your vested privileges, when you know that when your last market holding charter was granted to you by King Charles the First, Smithfield stood IN THE SUBURBS OF LONDON, and is in that very charter so described in those five words?"—which is certainly true, but has nothing to do with the question.

Now to the comparison, in these particulars of civilisation, between the capital of England, and the capital of that frog-eating and wooden-shoe wearing country, which the illustrious Common Councilman so sarcastically settled.

In Paris, there is no Cattle Market. Cows and calves are sold within the city, but, the Cattle Markets are at Poissy, about thirteen miles off, on a line of railway; and at Sceaux, about five miles off. The Poissy market is held every Thursday; the Sceaux market, every Monday. In Paris, there are no slaughter-houses, in our acceptation of the term. There are five public Abattoirs—within the walls, though in the suburbs—and in these all the slaughtering for the city must be performed. They are managed by a Syndicat or Guild of Butchers, who confer with the Minister of the Interior on all matters affecting the trade, and who are consulted when any new regulations are contemplated for its government. They are, likewise, under the vigilant superintendence of the police. Every butcher must be licensed : which proves him at once to be a slave, for we don't license butchers in England—we only license apothecaries, attorneys, post-masters, publicans, hawkers, retailers of tobacco, snuff, pepper, and vinegar—and one or two other little trades, not worth mentioning. Every arrangement in connexion with the slaughtering and sale of meat, is matter of strict police regulation. (Slavery again, though we certainly have a general sort of Police Act here.)

But, in order that the reader may understand what a monument of folly these frog-eaters have raised in their abattoirs and cattle-markets, and may compare it with what common counselling has done for us all these years, and would still do but for the innovating spirit of the times, here follows a short account of a recent visit to these places :

It was as sharp a February morning as you would desire to feel at your fingers' ends when I turned out—tumbling over a chiffonier with his little basket and rake, who was picking up the bits of coloured paper that had been swept out, over-night, from a Bon-Bon shop—to take the Butchers' Train to Poissy. A cold, dim light just touched the high roofs of the Tuileries which have seen such changes, such distracted crowds, such riot and bloodshed ; and they looked as calm, and as old, all covered with white frost, as the very Pyramids. There was not light enough, yet, to strike upon the towers of Notre Dame across the water ; but I thought of the dark pavement of the old Cathedral as just beginning to be streaked with grey ; and of the lamps in the " House of God," the Hospital close to it, burning low and being quenched ; and of the keeper of the Morgue going about with a fading lantern, busy in the arrangement of his terrible waxwork for another sunny day.

The sun was up, and shining merrily when the butchers and I, announcing our departure with an engine shriek to sleepy Paris, rattled away for the Cattle Market. Across

the country, over the Seine, among a forest of scrubby trees
—the hoar frost lying cold in shady places, and glittering
in the light—and here we are at Poissy! Out leap the
butchers, who have been chattering all the way like madmen,
and off they straggle for the Cattle Market (still chattering,
of course, incessantly), in hats and caps of all shapes, in coats
and blouses, in calf-skins, cow-skins, horse-skins, furs, shaggy
mantles, hairy coats, sacking, baize, oil-skin, anything you
please that will keep a man and a butcher warm, upon a
frosty morning.

Many a French town have I seen, between this spot of
ground and Strasburg or Marseilles, that might sit for your
picture, little Poissy! Barring the details of your old
church, I know you well, albeit we make acquaintance, now,
for the first time. I know your narrow, straggling, winding
streets, with a kennel in the midst, and lamps slung across. I
know your picturesque street-corners, winding up-hill Heaven
knows why or where! I know your tradesmen's inscriptions,
in letters not quite fat enough; your barbers' brazen basins
dangling over little shops; your Cafés and Estaminets, with
cloudy bottles of stale syrup in the windows, and pictures
of crossed billiard cues outside. I know this identical grey
horse with his tail rolled up in a knot like the "back hair"
of an untidy woman, who won't be shod, and who makes
himself heraldic by clattering across the street on his hind-
legs, while twenty voices shriek and growl at him as a
Brigand, an accursed Robber, and an everlastingly-doomed Pig.
I know your sparkling town-fountain, too, my Poissy, and am
glad to see it near a cattle-market, gushing so freshly, under
the auspices of a gallant little sublimated Frenchman wrought
in metal, perched upon the top. Through all the land of
France I know this unswept room at The Glory, with its
peculiar smell of beans and coffee, where the butchers crowd
about the stove, drinking the thinnest of wine from the
smallest of tumblers; where the thickest of coffee-cups
mingle with the longest of loaves, and the weakest of lump

sugar; where Madame at the counter easily acknowledges the homage of all entering and departing butchers; where the billiard-table is covered up in the midst like a great bird-cage—but the bird may sing by-and-by!

A bell! The Calf Market! Polite departure of butchers. Hasty payment and departure on the part of amateur Visitor. Madame reproaches Ma'amselle for too fine a susceptibility in reference to the devotion of a Butcher in a bear-skin. Monsieur, the landlord of The Glory, counts a double handful of sous, without an unobliterated inscription, or an undamaged crowned head, among them.

There is little noise without, abundant space, and no confusion. The open area devoted to the market is divided into three portions: the Calf Market, the Cattle Market, the Sheep Market. Calves at eight, cattle at ten, sheep at mid-day. All is very clean.

The Calf Market is a raised platform of stone, some three or four feet high, open on all sides, with a lofty overspreading roof, supported on stone columns, which give it the appearance of a sort of vineyard from Northern Italy. Here, on the raised pavement, lie innumerable calves, all bound hind-legs and fore-legs together, and all trembling violently—perhaps with cold, perhaps with fear, perhaps with pain; for, this mode of tying, which seems to be an absolute superstition with the peasantry, can hardly fail to cause great suffering. Here, they lie, patiently in rows, among the straw, with their stolid faces and inexpressive eyes, superintended by men and women, boys and girls; here they are inspected by our friends, the butchers, bargained for, and bought. Plenty of time; plenty of room; plenty of good humour. "Monsieur François in the bear-skin, how do you do, my friend? You come from Paris by the train? The fresh air does you good. If you are in want of three or four fine calves this market morning, my angel, I, Madame Doche, shall be happy to deal with you. Behold these calves, Monsieur François! Great Heaven, you are doubtful!

Well, sir, walk round and look about you. If you find better
for the money, buy them. If not, come to me!" Monsieur
François goes his way leisurely, and keeps a wary eye upon
the stock. No other butcher jostles Monsieur François;
Monsieur François jostles no other butcher. Nobody is
flustered and aggravated. Nobody is savage. In the midst
of the country blue frocks and red handkerchiefs, and the
butchers' coats, shaggy, furry, and hairy : of calf-skin, cow-skin,
horse-skin, and bear-skin : towers a cocked hat and a blue cloak.
Slavery! For *our* Police wear great-coats and glazed hats.

But now the bartering is over, and the calves are sold.
"Ho! Gregoire, Antoine, Jean, Louis! Bring up the carts,
my children! Quick, brave infants! Hola! Hi!"

The carts, well littered with straw, are backed up to the
edge of the raised pavement, and various hot infants carry
calves upon their heads, and dextrously pitch them in, while
other hot infants, standing in the carts, arrange the calves,
and pack them carefully in straw. Here is a promising
young calf, not sold, whom Madame Doche unbinds. Pardon
me, Madame Doche, but I fear this mode of tying the four
legs of a quadruped together, though strictly à la mode, is
not quite right. You observe, Madame Doche, that the cord
leaves deep indentations in the skin, and that the animal is
so cramped at first as not to know, or even remotely suspect
that he *is* unbound, until you are so obliging as to kick him,
in your delicate little way, and pull his tail like a bell-rope.
Then, he staggers to his knees, not being able to stand, and
stumbles about like a drunken calf, or the horse at Franconi's,
whom you may have seen, Madame Doche, who is supposed
to have been mortally wounded in battle. But, what is this
rubbing against me, as I apostrophise Madame Doche? It is
another heated infant with a calf upon his head. "Pardon,
Monsieur, but will you have the politeness to allow me to
pass?" "Ah, sir, willingly. I am vexed to obstruct the
way." On he staggers, calf and all, and makes no allusion
whatever either to my eyes or limbs.

Now, the carts are all full. More straw, my Antoine, to shake over these top rows; then, off we will clatter, rumble, jolt, and rattle, a long row of us, out of the first town-gate, and out at the second town-gate, and past the empty sentry-box, and the little thin square bandbox of a guardhouse, where nobody seems to live: and away for Paris, by the paved road, lying, a straight, straight line, in the long, long avenue of trees. We can neither choose our road, nor our pace, for that is all prescribed to us. The public convenience demands that our carts should get to Paris by such a route, and no other (Napoleon had leisure to find that out, while he had a little war with the world upon his hands), and woe betide us if we infringe orders.

Droves of oxen stand in the Cattle Market, tied to iron bars fixed into posts of granite. Other droves advance slowly down the long avenue, past the second town-gate, and the first town-gate, and the sentry-box, and the bandbox, thawing the morning with their smoky breath as they come along. Plenty of room; plenty of time. Neither man nor beast is driven out of his wits by coaches, carts, waggons, omnibuses, gigs, chaises, phaetons, cabs, trucks, boys, whoop-ings, roarings, and multitudes. No tail-twisting is necessary —no iron pronging is necessary. There are no iron prongs here. The market for cattle is held as quietly as the market for calves. In due time, off the cattle go to Paris; the drovers can no more choose their road, nor their time, nor the numbers they shall drive, than they can choose their hour for dying in the course of nature.

Sheep next. The sheep-pens are up here, past the Branch Bank of Paris established for the convenience of the butchers, and behind the two pretty fountains they are making in the Market. My name is Bull: yet I think I should like to see as good twin fountains—not to say in Smithfield, but in England anywhere. Plenty of room; plenty of time. And here are sheep-dogs, sensible as ever, but with a certain French air about them—not without a suspicion of dominoes

273

—with a kind of flavour of moustache and beard—demonstrative dogs, shaggy and loose where an English dog would be tight and close—not so troubled with business calculations as our English drovers' dogs, who have always got their sheep upon their minds, and think about their work, even resting, as you may see by their faces; but, dashing, showy, rather unreliable dogs: who might worry me instead of their legitimate charges if they saw occasion—and might see it somewhat suddenly.

The market for sheep passes off like the other two; and away they go, by *their* allotted road to Paris. My way being the Railway, I make the best of it at twenty miles an hour; whirling through the now high-lighted landscape; thinking that the inexperienced green buds will be wishing, before long, they had not been tempted to come out so soon; and wondering who lives in this or that château, all window and lattice, and what the family may have for breakfast this sharp morning.

After the Market comes the Abattoir. What abattoir shall I visit first? Montmartre is the largest. So I will go there.

The abattoirs are all within the walls of Paris, with an eye to the receipt of the octroi duty; but, they stand in open places in the suburbs, removed from the press and bustle of the city. They are managed by the Syndicat or Guild of Butchers, under the inspection of the Police. Certain smaller items of the revenue derived from them are in part retained by the Guild for the payment of their expenses, and in part devoted by it to charitable purposes in connexion with the trade. They cost six hundred and eighty thousand pounds; and they return to the city of Paris an interest on that outlay, amounting to nearly six and a-half per cent.

Here, in a sufficiently dismantled space is the Abattoir of Montmartre, covering nearly nine acres of ground, surrounded by a high wall, and looking from the outside like a cavalry barrack. At the iron gates is a small functionary in a large cocked hat. " Monsieur desires to see the abattoir? Most certainly." State being inconvenient in private transactions, and Monsieur being already aware of the cocked hat, the functionary puts it into a little official bureau which it almost fills, and accompanies me in the modest attire—as to his head—of ordinary life.

Many of the animals from Poissy have come here. On the arrival of each drove, it was turned into yonder ample space, where each butcher who had bought, selected his own purchases. Some, we see now, in these long perspectives of stalls with a high overhanging roof of wood and open tiles rising above the walls. While they rest here, before being slaughtered, they are required to be fed and watered, and the stalls must be kept clean. A stated amount of fodder must always be ready in the loft above; and the supervision is of the strictest kind. The same regulations apply to sheep and calves; for which, portions of these perspectives are strongly railed off. All the buildings are of the strongest and most solid description.

After traversing these lairs, through which, besides the upper provision for ventilation just mentioned, there may be a thorough current of air from opposite windows in the side walls, and from doors at either end, we traverse the broad, paved, court-yard until we come to the slaughter-houses. They are all exactly alike, and adjoin each other, to the number of eight or nine together, in blocks of solid building. Let us walk into the first.

It is firmly built and paved with stone. It is well lighted, thoroughly aired, and lavishly provided with fresh water. It has two doors opposite each other; the first, the door by which I entered from the main yard; the second, which is opposite, opening on another smaller yard, where the sheep and calves are killed on benches. The pavement of that yard, I see, slopes downward to a gutter, for its being more easily cleansed. The slaughter-house is fifteen feet high, sixteen feet and a-half wide, and thirty-three feet long. It is fitted with a powerful windlass, by which one man at the handle can bring the head of an ox down to the ground to receive the blow from the pole-axe that is to fell him—with the means of raising the carcass and keeping it suspended during the after-operation of dressing—and with hooks on which carcasses can hang, when completely prepared, without touching the walls. Upon the pavement of this first stone chamber, lies an ox scarcely dead. If I except the blood draining from him, into a little stone well in a corner of the pavement, the place is free from offence as the Place de la Concorde. It is infinitely purer and cleaner, I know, my friend the functionary, than the Cathedral of Notre Dame. Ha, ha! Monsieur is pleasant, but, truly, there is reason, too, in what he says.

I look into another of these slaughter-houses. "Pray enter," says a gentleman in bloody boots. "This is a calf I have killed this morning. Having a little time upon my hands, I have cut and punctured this lace pattern in the coats of his stomach. It is pretty enough. I did it to divert myself." —"It is beautiful, Monsieur, the slaughterer!" He tells me I have the gentility to say so.

I look into rows of slaughter-houses. In many, retail dealers, who have come here for the purpose, are making bargains for meat. There is killing enough, certainly, to satiate an unused eye; and there are steaming carcasses enough, to suggest the expediency of a fowl and salad for dinner; but, everywhere, there is an orderly, clean, well-systematised routine of work in progress—horrible work at the best, if you please; but, so much the greater reason why it should be made the best of. I don't know (I think I have observed, my name is Bull) that a Parisian of the lowest order is particularly delicate, or that his nature is remarkable for an infinitesimal infusion of ferocity; but, I do know, my potent, grave, and common counselling Signors, that he is forced, when at this work, to submit himself to a thoroughly good system, and to make an Englishman very heartily ashamed of you.

CLEANLINESS AND ORDER

Here, within the walls of the same abattoir, in other roomy and commodious buildings, are a place for converting the fat into tallow and packing it for market—a place for cleansing and scalding calves' heads and sheep's feet—a place for preparing tripe—stables and coach-houses for the butchers—innumerable conveniences, aiding in the diminution of offensiveness to its lowest possible point, and the raising of cleanliness and supervision to their highest. Hence, all the meat that goes out of the gate is sent away in clean covered carts. And if every trade connected with the slaughtering of animals were obliged by law to be carried on in the same place, I doubt, my friend, now reinstated in the cocked hat (whose civility these two francs imperfectly acknowledge, but appear munificently to repay), whether there could be better regulations than those which are carried out at the Abattoir of Montmartre. Adieu, my friend, for I am away to the other side of Paris, to the Abattoir of Grenelle! And there I find exactly the same thing on a smaller scale, with the addition of a magnificent Artesian well, and a different sort of conductor, in the person of a neat little woman with neat little eyes, and a neat little voice, who picks her neat little way among the bullocks in a very neat little pair of shoes and stockings.

Such is the Monument of French Folly which a foreigneering people have erected, in a national hatred and antipathy for common counselling wisdom. That wisdom, assembled in the City of London, having distinctly refused, after a debate of three days long, and by a majority of nearly seven to one, to associate itself with any Metropolitan Cattle-Market unless it be held in the midst of the City, it follows that we shall lose the inestimable advantages of common counselling protection, and be thrown, for a market, on our own wretched resources. In all human probability we shall thus come, at last, to erect a monument of folly very like this French monument. If that be done, the consequences are obvious.

A MONUMENT OF FRENCH FOLLY

The leather trade will be ruined, by the introduction of American timber, to be manufactured into shoes for the fallen English; the Lord Mayor will be required, by the popular voice, to live entirely on frogs; and both these changes will (how, is not at present quite clear, but certainly somehow or other) fall on that unhappy landed interest which is always being killed, yet is always found to be alive—and kicking.

THE LAMPLIGHTER

"IF you talk of Murphy and Francis Moore, gentlemen," said the lamplighter who was in the chair, "I mean to say that neither of 'em ever had any more to do with the stars than Tom Grig had."

"And what had *he* to do with 'em?" asked the lamplighter who officiated as vice.

"Nothing at all," replied the other; "just exactly nothing at all."

"Do you mean to say you don't believe in Murphy, then?" demanded the lamplighter who had opened the discussion.

"I mean to say I believe in Tom Grig," replied the chairman. "Whether I believe in Murphy, or not, is a matter between me and my conscience; and whether Murphy believes in himself, or not, is a matter between him and his conscience. Gentlemen, I drink your healths."

The lamplighter who did the company this honour, was seated in the chimney-corner of a certain tavern, which has been, time out of mind, the Lamplighters' House of Call. He sat in the midst of a circle of lamplighters, and was the cacique, or chief of the tribe.

If any of our readers have had the good fortune to behold a lamplighter's funeral, they will not be surprised to learn that lamplighters are a strange and primitive people; that they rigidly adhere to old ceremonies and customs which have been handed down among them from father to son since the first public lamp was lighted out of doors; that they intermarry, and betroth their children in infancy; that they enter into no plots or conspiracies (for who ever heard of a traitorous lamplighter?); that they commit no crimes against the laws of their country (there being no instance of a murderous or burglarious lamplighter); that they are, in short, notwithstanding their apparently volatile and restless character, a highly moral and reflective people: having among themselves as many traditional observances as the Jews, and being, as a body, if not as old as the hills, at least as old as the streets. It is an article of their creed that the first faint glimmering of true civilization shone in the first street-light maintained at the public expense. They trace their existence and high position in the public esteem, in a direct line to the heathen mythology; and hold that the history of Prometheus himself is but a pleasant fable, whereof the true hero is a lamplighter.

"Gentlemen," said the lamplighter in the chair, "I drink your healths."

"And perhaps, Sir," said the vice, holding up his glass, and rising a little way off his seat and sitting down again, in token that he recognised and returned the compliment, "perhaps you will add to that condescension by telling us who Tom Grig was, and how he came to be connected in your mind with Francis Moore, Physician."

"Hear, hear, hear!" cried the lamplighters generally.

"Tom Grig, gentlemen," said the chairman, "was one of us; and it happened to him, as it don't often happen to a public character in our line, that he had his what-you-may-call-it cast."

"His head?" said the vice.

"No," replied the chairman, "not his head."

"His face, perhaps?" said the vice. "No, not his face." "His legs?" "No, not his legs." Nor yet his arms, nor his hands, nor his feet, nor his chest, all of which were severally suggested.

"His nativity, perhaps?"

"That's it," said the chairman, awakening from his thoughtful attitude at the suggestion. "His nativity. That's what Tom had cast, gentlemen."

"In plaster?" asked the vice.

"I don't rightly know how it's done," returned the chairman. "But I suppose it was."

And there he stopped as if that were all he had to say; whereupon there arose a murmur among the company, which at length resolved itself into a request, conveyed through the vice, that he would go on. This being exactly what the chairman wanted, he mused for a little time, performed that agreeable ceremony which is popularly termed wetting one's whistle, and went on thus:

"Tom Grig, gentlemen, was, as I have said, one of us; and I may go further, and say he was an ornament to us, and such a one as only the good old times of oil and cotton could have produced. Tom's family, gentlemen, were all lamplighters."

"Not the ladies, I hope?" asked the vice.

"They had talent enough for it, Sir," rejoined the chairman, "and would have been, but for the prejudices of society. Let women have their rights, Sir, and the females of Tom's family would have been every one of 'em in office. But that emancipation hasn't come yet, and hadn't then, and consequently they confined themselves to the bosoms of their families, cooked the dinners, mended the clothes, minded the children, comforted their husbands, and attended to the house-keeping generally. It's a hard thing upon the women, gentlemen, that they are limited to such a sphere of action as this; very hard.

"I happen to know all about Tom, gentlemen, from the circumstance of his uncle by his mother's side, having been my particular friend. His (that's Tom's uncle's) fate was a melancholy one. Gas was the death of him. When it was first talked of, he laughed. He wasn't angry; he laughed at the credulity of human nature. 'They might as well talk,' he says, 'of laying on an everlasting succession of glow-worms;' and then he laughed again, partly at his joke, and partly at poor humanity.

"In course of time, however, the thing got ground, the experiment was made, and they lighted up Pall Mall. Tom's uncle went to see it. I've heard that he fell off his ladder fourteen times that night, from weakness, and that he would certainly have gone on falling till he killed himself, if his last tumble hadn't been into a wheelbarrow which was going his way, and humanely took him home. 'I foresee in this,' says Tom's uncle faintly, and taking to his bed as he spoke —'I foresee in this,' he says, 'the breaking up of our profession. There's no more going the rounds to trim by daylight, no more dribbling down of the oil on the hats and bonnets of ladies and gentlemen when one feels in spirits. Any low fellow can light a gas-lamp. And it's all up.' In this state of mind, he petitioned the government for—I want a word again, gentlemen—what do you call that which they give to people when it's found out, at last, that they've never been of any use, and have been paid too much for doing nothing?"

"Compensation?" suggested the vice.

"That's it," said the chairman. "Compensation. They didn't give it him, though, and then he got very fond of his country all at once, and went about saying that gas was a death-blow to his native land, and that it was a plot of the radicals to ruin the country and destroy the oil and cotton trade for ever, and that the whales would go and kill themselves privately, out of sheer spite and vexation at not being caught. At last he got right-down cracked; called his tobacco-pipe a gas-pipe; thought his tears were lamp-oil; and went on with all manner of nonsense of that sort, till one night he hung himself on a lamp-iron in Saint Martin's Lane, and there was an end of *him*.

A STRANGE OLD GENTLEMAN

"Tom loved him, gentlemen, but he survived it. He shed a tear over his grave, got very drunk, spoke a funeral oration that night in the watch-house, and was fined five shillings for it, in the morning. Some men are none the worse for this sort of thing. Tom was one of 'em. He went that very afternoon on a new beat: as clear in his head, and as free from fever as Father Mathew himself.

"Tom's new beat, gentlemen, was—I can't exactly say where, for that he'd never tell; but I know it was in a quiet part of town, where there were some queer old houses. I have always had it in my head that it must have been somewhere near Canonbury Tower in Islington, but that's a matter of opinion. Wherever it was, he went upon it, with a bran-new ladder, a white hat, a brown holland jacket and trousers, a blue neck-kerchief, and a sprig of full-blown double wall-flower in his button-hole. Tom was always genteel in his appearance, and I have heard from the best judges, that if he had left his ladder at home that afternoon, you might have took him for a lord.

"He was always merry, was Tom, and such a singer, that if there was any encouragement for native talent, he'd have been at the opera. He was on his ladder, lighting his first lamp, and singing to himself in a manner more easily to be conceived than described, when he hears the clock strike five, and suddenly sees an old gentleman with a telescope in his hand, throw up a window and look at him very hard.

"Tom didn't know what could be passing in this old gentleman's mind. He thought it likely enough that he might be saying within himself, 'Here's a new lamplighter—a good-looking young fellow—shall I stand something to drink?' Thinking this possible, he keeps quite still, pretending to be very particular about the wick, and looks at the old gentleman sideways, seeming to take no notice of him.

"Gentlemen, he was one of the strangest and most mysterious-looking files that ever Tom clapped his eyes on. He was dressed all slovenly and untidy, in a great gown of

a kind of bed-furniture pattern, with a cap of the same on his head; and a long old flapped waistcoat; with no braces, no strings, very few buttons—in short, with hardly any of those artificial contrivances that hold society together. Tom knew by these signs, and by his not being shaved, and by his not being over-clean, and by a sort of wisdom not quite awake, in his face, that he was a scientific old gentleman. He often told me that if he could have conceived the possibility of the whole Royal Society being boiled down into one man, he should have said the old gentleman's body was that Body.

"The old gentleman claps the telescope to his eye, looks all round, sees nobody else in sight, stares at Tom again, and cries out very loud :

"'Hal-loa!'

"'Halloa, Sir,' says Tom from the ladder; 'and halloa again, if you come to that.'

"'Here's an extraordinary fulfilment,' says the old gentleman, 'of a prediction of the planets.'

"'Is there?' says Tom. 'I'm very glad to hear it.'

"'Young man,' says the old gentleman, 'you don't know me.'

"'Sir,' says Tom, 'I have not that honour; but I shall be happy to drink your health, notwithstanding.'

"'I read,' cries the old gentleman, without taking any notice of this politeness on Tom's part—'I read what's going to happen, in the stars.'

"Tom thanked him for the information, and begged to know if anything particular was going to happen in the stars, in the course of a week or so; but the old gentleman, correcting him, explained that he read in the stars what was going to happen on dry land, and that he was acquainted with all the celestial bodies.

"'I hope they're all well, Sir,' says Tom,—'everybody.'

"'Hush!' cries the old gentleman. 'I have consulted the book of Fate with rare and wonderful success. I am versed in the great sciences of astrology and astronomy. In my house here, I have every description of apparatus for observing the course and motion of the planets. Six months ago, I derived from this source, the knowledge that precisely as the clock struck five this afternoon a stranger would present himself—the destined husband of my young and lovely niece —in reality of illustrious and high descent, but whose birth would be enveloped in uncertainty and mystery. Don't tell me yours isn't,' says the old gentleman, who was in such a hurry to speak that he couldn't get the words out fast enough, ' for I know better.'

" Gentlemen, Tom was so astonished when he heard him say this, that he could hardly keep his footing on the ladder, and found it necessary to hold on by the lamp-post. There *was* a mystery about his birth. His mother had always admitted it. Tom had never known who was his father, and some people had gone so far as to say that even *she* was in doubt.

" While he was in this state of amazement, the old gentleman leaves the window, bursts out of the house-door, shakes the ladder, and Tom, like a ripe pumpkin, comes sliding down into his arms.

"' Let me embrace you,' he says, folding his arms about him, and nearly lighting up his old bed-furniture gown at Tom's link. ' You're a man of noble aspect. Everything combines to prove the accuracy of my observations. You have had mysterious promptings within you,' he says; ' I know you have had whisperings of greatness, eh?' he says.

"' I think I have,' says Tom—Tom was one of those who can persuade themselves to anything they like—' I've often thought I wasn't the small beer I was taken for.'

"' You were right,' cries the old gentleman, hugging him again. ' Come in. My niece awaits us.'

"' Is the young lady tolerable good-looking, Sir?' says Tom, hanging fire rather, as he thought of her playing the piano, and knowing French, and being up to all manner of accomplishments.

"'She's beautiful!' cries the old gentleman, who was in such a terrible bustle that he was all in a perspiration. 'She has a graceful carriage, an exquisite shape, a sweet voice, a countenance beaming with animation and expression; and the eye,' he says, rubbing his hands, 'of a startled fawn.'

"Tom supposed this might mean, what was called among his circle of acquaintance, 'a game eye;' and, with a view to this defect, inquired whether the young lady had any cash.

"'She has five thousand pounds,' cries the old gentleman. 'But what of that? what of that? A word in your ear. I'm in search of the philosopher's stone. I have very nearly found it—not quite. It turns everything to gold; that's its property.'

"Tom naturally thought it must have a deal of property; and said that when the old gentleman did get it, he hoped he'd be careful to keep it in the family.

"'Certainly,' he says, 'of course. Five thousand pounds! What's five thousand pounds to us? What's five million?' he says. 'What's five thousand million? Money will be nothing to us. We shall never be able to spend it fast enough.'

"'We'll try what we can do, Sir,' says Tom.

"'We will,' says the old gentleman. 'Your name?'

"'Grig,' says Tom.

"The old gentleman embraced him again, very tight; and without speaking another word, dragged him into the house in such an excited manner, that it was as much as Tom could do to take his link and ladder with him, and put them down in the passage.

"Gentlemen, if Tom hadn't been always remarkable for his love of truth, I think you would still have believed him when he said that all this was like a dream. There is no better way for a man to find out whether he is really asleep or awake, than calling for something to eat. If he's in a dream, gentlemen, he'll find something wanting in the flavour, depend upon it.

THE FAVOURITE OF THE PLANETS

"Tom explained his doubts to the old gentleman, and said that if there was any cold meat in the house, it would ease his mind very much to test himself at once. The old gentleman ordered up a venison pie, a small ham, and a bottle of very old Madeira. At the first mouthful of pie and the first glass of wine, Tom smacks his lips and cries out, 'I'm awake—wide awake;' and to prove that he was so, gentlemen, he made an end of 'em both.

"When Tom had finished his meal (which he never spoke of afterwards without tears in his eyes), the old gentleman hugs him again, and says, 'Noble stranger! let us visit my young and lovely niece.' Tom, who was a little elevated with the wine, replies, 'The noble stranger is agreeable!' At which words the old gentleman took him by the hand, and led him to the parlour; crying as he opened the door, 'Here is Mr. Grig, the favourite of the planets!'

"I will not attempt a description of female beauty, gentlemen, for every one of us has a model of his own that suits his own taste best. In this parlour that I'm speaking of, there were two young ladies; and if every gentleman present, will imagine two models of his own in their places, and will be kind enough to polish 'em up to the very highest pitch of perfection, he will then have a faint conception of their uncommon radiance.

"Besides these two young ladies, there was their waiting-woman, that under any other circumstances Tom would have looked upon as a Venus; and besides her, there was a tall, thin, dismal-faced young gentleman, half man and half boy, dressed in a childish suit of clothes very much too short in the legs and arms; and looking, according to Tom's comparison, like one of the wax juveniles from a tailor's door, grown up and run to seed. Now, this youngster stamped his foot upon the ground and looked very fierce at Tom, and Tom looked fierce at him—for to tell the truth, gentlemen, Tom more than half suspected that when they entered the room he was kissing one of the young ladies; and for anything

Tom knew, you observe, it might be *his* young lady—which was not pleasant.

"'Sir,' says Tom, 'before we proceed any further, will you have the goodness to inform me who this young Salamander'—Tom called him that for aggravation, you perceive, gentlemen—'who this young Salamander may be?'

"'That, Mr. Grig,' says the old gentleman, 'is my little boy. He was christened Galileo Isaac Newton Flamstead. Don't mind him. He's a mere child.'

"'And a very fine child too,' says Tom—still aggravating, you'll observe—'of his age, and as good as fine, I have no doubt. How do you do, my man?' with which kind and patronising expressions, Tom reached up to pat him on the head, and quoted two lines about little boys, from Doctor Watts's Hymns, which he had learnt at a Sunday School.

"It was very easy to see, gentlemen, by this youngster's frowning and by the waiting-maid's tossing her head and turning up her nose, and by the young ladies turning their backs and talking together at the other end of the room, that nobody but the old gentleman took very kindly to the noble stranger. Indeed, Tom plainly heard the waiting-woman say of her master, that so far from being able to read the stars as he pretended, she didn't believe he knew his letters in 'em, or at best that he had got further than words in one syllable; but Tom, not minding this (for he was in spirits after the Madeira), looks with an agreeable air towards the young ladies, and, kissing his hand to both, says to the old gentleman, 'Which is which?'

"'This,' says the old gentleman, leading out the handsomest, if one of 'em could possibly be said to be handsomer than the other—'this is my niece, Miss Fanny Barker.'

"'If you'll permit me, Miss,' says Tom, 'being a noble stranger and a favourite of the planets, I will conduct myself as such.' With these words, he kisses the young lady in a very affable way, turns to the old gentleman, slaps him on the back, and says, 'When's it to come off, my buck?'

"The young lady coloured so deep, and her lip trembled so much, gentlemen, that Tom really thought she was going to cry. But she kept her feelings down, and turning to the old gentleman, says, 'Dear uncle, though you have the absolute disposal of my hand and fortune, and though you mean well in disposing of 'em thus, I ask you whether you don't think this is a mistake? Don't you think, dear uncle,' she says, 'that the stars must be in error? Is it not possible that the comet may have put 'em out?'

"'The stars,' says the old gentleman, 'couldn't make a mistake if they tried. Emma,' he says to the other young lady.

"'Yes, papa,' says she.

"'The same day that makes your cousin Mrs. Grig will unite you to the gifted Mooney. No remonstrance—no tears. Now, Mr. Grig, let me conduct you to that hallowed ground, that philosophical retreat, where my friend and partner, the gifted Mooney of whom I have just now spoken, is even now pursuing those discoveries which shall enrich us with the precious metal, and make us masters of the world. Come, Mr. Grig,' he says.

"'With all my heart, Sir,' replies Tom; 'and luck to the gifted Mooney, say I—not so much on his account as for our worthy selves!' With this sentiment, Tom kissed his hand to the ladies again, and followed him out; having the gratification to perceive, as he looked back, that they were all hanging on by the arms and legs of Galileo Isaac Newton Flamstead, to prevent him from following the noble stranger, and tearing him to pieces.

"Gentlemen, Tom's father-in-law that was to be, took him by the hand, and having lighted a little lamp, led him across a paved court-yard at the back of the house, into a very large, dark, gloomy room: filled with all manner of bottles, globes, books, telescopes, crocodiles, alligators, and other scientific instruments of every kind. In the centre of this room was a stove or furnace, with what Tom called a pot, but which in my opinion was a crucible, in full boil. In one corner was a sort of ladder leading through the roof; and up this ladder the old gentleman pointed, as he said in a whisper:

"'The observatory. Mr. Mooney is even now watching for the precise time at which we are to come into all the riches of the earth. It will be necessary for he and I, alone in that silent place, to cast your nativity before the hour arrives. Put the day and minute of your birth on this piece of paper, and leave the rest to me.'

"'You don't mean to say,' says Tom, doing as he was told and giving him back the paper, 'that I'm to wait here long, do you? It's a precious dismal place."

"'Hush!" says the old gentleman. 'It's hallowed ground. Farewell!'

"'Stop a minute,' says Tom. 'What a hurry you're in! What's in that large bottle yonder?'

"'It's a child with three heads,' says the old gentleman; 'and everything else in proportion.'

"'Why don't you throw him away?' says Tom. 'What do you keep such unpleasant things here for?'

"'Throw him away!' cries the old gentleman. 'We use him constantly in astrology. He's a charm.'

"'I shouldn't have thought it,' says Tom, 'from his appearance. *Must* you go, I say?'

"The old gentleman makes him no answer, but climbs up the ladder in a greater bustle than ever. Tom looked after his legs till there was nothing of him left, and then sat down to wait; feeling (so he used to say) as comfortable as if he was going to be made a freemason, and they were heating the pokers.

"Tom waited so long, gentlemen, that he began to think it must be getting on for midnight at least, and felt more dismal and lonely than ever he had done in all his life. He tried every means of whiling away the time, but it never had seemed to move so slow. First, he took a nearer view of the child with three heads, and thought what a comfort it must have been to his parents. Then he looked up a long telescope which was pointed out of the window, but saw nothing particular, in consequence of the stopper being on at the other end. Then he came to a skeleton in a glass case, labelled, 'Skeleton of a Gentleman—prepared by Mr. Mooney,'—which made him hope that Mr. Mooney might not be in the habit of preparing gentlemen that way without their own consent. A hundred times, at least, he looked into the pot where they were boiling the philosopher's stone down to the proper consistency, and wondered whether it was nearly done. 'When it is,' thinks Tom, 'I'll send out for six-penn'orth of sprats, and turn 'em into gold fish for a first experiment.' Besides which, he made up his mind, gentlemen, to have a country-house and a park; and to plant a bit of it with a double row of gas-lamps a mile long, and go out every night with a French-polished mahogany ladder, and two servants in livery behind him, to light 'em for his own pleasure.

"At length and at last, the old gentleman's legs appeared upon the steps leading through the roof, and he came slowly down: bringing along with him, the gifted Mooney. This Mooney, gentlemen, was even more scientific in appearance than his friend; and had, as Tom often declared upon his word and honour, the dirtiest face we can possibly know of, in this imperfect state of existence.

"Gentlemen, you are all aware that if a scientific man isn't absent in his mind, he's of no good at all. Mr. Mooney was so absent, that when the old gentleman said to him, 'Shake hands with Mr. Grig,' he put out his leg. 'Here's a mind, Mr. Grig!' cries the old gentleman in a rapture. 'Here's philosophy! Here's rumination! Don't disturb him,' he says, 'for this is amazing!'

"Tom had no wish to disturb him, having nothing particular to say; but he was so uncommonly amazing, that the old gentleman got impatient, and determined to give him an electric shock to bring him to—'for you must know, Mr. Grig,' he says, 'that we always keep a strongly charged battery, ready for that purpose.' These means being resorted to, gentlemen, the gifted Mooney revived with a loud roar, and he no sooner came to himself than both he and the old gentleman looked at Tom with compassion, and shed tears abundantly.

"'My dear friend,' says the old gentleman to the Gifted, 'prepare him.'

"'I say,' cries Tom, falling back, 'none of that, you know. No preparing by Mr. Mooney if you please.'

"'Alas!' replies the old gentleman, 'you don't understand us. My friend, inform him of his fate.—I can't.'

"The Gifted mustered up his voice, after many efforts, and informed Tom that his nativity had been carefully cast, and he would expire at exactly thirty-five minutes, twenty-seven seconds, and five-sixths of a second past nine o'clock, a.m., on that day two months.

"Gentlemen, I leave you to judge what were Tom's feelings at this announcement, on the eve of matrimony and endless riches. 'I think,' he says in a trembling voice, 'there must be a mistake in the working of that sum. Will you do me the favour to cast it up again?'—'There is no mistake,' replies the old gentleman, 'it is confirmed by Francis Moore, Physician. Here is the prediction for to-morrow two months.' And he showed him the page, where sure enough were these words—'The decease of a great person may be looked for, about this time.'

"'Which,' says the old gentleman, 'is clearly you, Mr. Grig.'

"'Too clearly,' cries Tom, sinking into a chair, and giving one hand to the old gentleman, and one to the Gifted. 'The orb of day has set on Thomas Grig for ever!'

"At this affecting remark, the Gifted shed tears again, and the other two mingled their tears with his, in a kind—if I may use the expression—of Mooney and Co.'s entire. But the old gentleman recovering first, observed that this was only a reason for hastening the marriage, in order that Tom's distinguished race might be transmitted to posterity; and requesting the Gifted to console Mr. Grig during his temporary absence, he withdrew to settle the preliminaries with his niece immediately.

"And now, gentlemen, a very extraordinary and remarkable occurrence took place; for as Tom sat in a melancholy way in one chair, and the Gifted sat in a melancholy way in another, a couple of doors were thrown violently open, the two young ladies rushed in, and one knelt down in a loving attitude at Tom's feet, and the other at the Gifted's. So far, perhaps, as Tom was concerned—as he used to say— you will say there was nothing strange in this: but you will be of a different opinion when you understand that Tom's young lady was kneeling to the Gifted, and the Gifted's young lady was kneeling to Tom.

"'Halloa! stop a minute!' cries Tom; 'here's a mistake. I need condoling with by sympathising woman, under my afflicting circumstances; but we're out in the figure. Change partners, Mooney.'

"'Monster!' cries Tom's young lady, clinging to the Gifted.

"'Miss!' says Tom. 'Is *that* your manners?'

"'I abjure thee!' cries Tom's young lady. 'I renounce thee. I never will be thine. Thou,' she says to the Gifted, 'art the object of my first and all-engrossing passion. Wrapt in thy sublime visions, thou hast not perceived my love; but, driven to despair, I now shake off the woman and avow it. Oh, cruel, cruel man!' With which reproach she laid her head upon the Gifted's breast, and put her arms about him in the tenderest manner possible, gentlemen.

"'And I,' says the other young lady, in a sort of ecstasy, that made Tom start—'I hereby abjure my chosen husband too. Hear me, Goblin!'—this was to the Gifted—'Hear me! I hold thee in the deepest detestation. The maddening interview of this one night has filled my soul with love—but not for thee. It is for thee, for thee, young man,' she cries to Tom. 'As Monk Lewis finely observes, Thomas, Thomas, I am thine, Thomas, Thomas, thou art mine : thine for ever, mine for ever!' with which words, she became very tender likewise.

"Tom and the Gifted, gentlemen, as you may believe, looked at each other in a very awkward manner, and with thoughts not at all complimentary to the two young ladies. As to the Gifted, I have heard Tom say often, that he was certain he was in a fit, and had it inwardly.

"'Speak to me! Oh, speak to me!' cries Tom's young lady to the Gifted.

"'I don't want to speak to anybody,' he says, finding his voice at last, and trying to push her away. 'I think I had better go. I'm—I'm frightened,' he says, looking about as if he had lost something.

"'Not one look of love!' she cries. 'Hear me while I declare——'

"'I don't know how to look a look of love,' he says, all in a maze. 'Don't declare anything. I don't want to hear anybody.'

"'That's right!' cries the old gentleman (who it seems had been listening). 'That's right! Don't hear her. Emma shall marry you to-morrow, my friend, whether she likes it or not, and *she* shall marry Mr. Grig.'

"Gentlemen, these words were no sooner out of his mouth than Galileo Isaac Newton Flamstead (who it seems had been listening too) darts in, and spinning round and round, like a young giant's top, cries, 'Let her. Let her. I'm fierce; I'm furious. I give her leave. I'll never marry anybody after this—never. It isn't safe. She is the falsest of the false,' he cries, tearing his hair and gnashing his teeth; 'and I'll live and die a bachelor!'

"'The little boy,' observed the Gifted gravely, 'albeit of tender years, has spoken wisdom. I have been led to the contemplation of woman-kind, and will not adventure on the troubled waters of matrimony.'

A DREADFUL CRASH

"'What!' says the old gentleman, 'not marry my daughter! Won't you, Mooney? Not if I make her? Won't you? Won't you?'

"'No,' says Mooney, 'I won't. And if anybody asks me any more, I'll run away, and never come back again.'

"'Mr. Grig,' says the old gentleman, 'the stars must be obeyed. You have not changed your mind because of a little girlish folly—eh, Mr. Grig?'

"Tom, gentlemen, had had his eyes about him, and was pretty sure that all this was a device and trick of the waiting-maid, to put him off his inclination. He had seen her hiding and skipping about the two doors, and had observed that a very little whispering from her pacified the Salamander directly. 'So,' thinks Tom, 'this is a plot—but it won't fit.'

"'Eh, Mr. Grig?' says the old gentleman.

"'Why, Sir,' says Tom, pointing to the crucible, 'if the soup's nearly ready——'

"'Another hour beholds the consummation of our labours,' returned the old gentleman.

"'Very good,' says Tom, with a mournful air. 'It's only for two months, but I may as well be the richest man in the world even for that time. I'm not particular, I'll take her, Sir. I'll take her.'

"The old gentleman was in a rapture to find Tom still in the same mind, and drawing the young lady towards him by little and little, was joining their hands by main force, when all of a sudden, gentlemen, the crucible blows up, with a great crash; everybody screams; the room is filled with smoke; and Tom, not knowing what may happen next, throws himself into a Fancy attitude, and says, 'Come on, if you're a man!' without addressing himself to anybody in particular.

"'The labours of fifteen years!' says the old gentleman, clasping his hands and looking down upon the Gifted, who was saving the pieces, 'are destroyed in an instant!'—And I am told, gentlemen, by-the-bye, that this same philosopher's stone would have been discovered a hundred times at least, to speak within bounds, if it wasn't for the one unfortunate circumstance that the apparatus always blows up, when it's on the very point of succeeding.

"Tom turns pale when he hears the old gentleman expressing himself to this unpleasant effect, and stammers out that if it's quite agreeable to all parties, he would like to know exactly what has happened, and what change has really taken place in the prospects of that company.

"'We have failed for the present, Mr. Grig,' says the old gentleman, wiping his forehead. 'And I regret it the more, because I have in fact invested my niece's five thousand pounds in this glorious speculation. But don't be cast down,' he says, anxiously—'in another fifteen years, Mr. Grig——'

"'Oh!' cries Tom, letting the young lady's hand fall. 'Were the stars very positive about this union, Sir?'

"'They were,' says the old gentleman.

"'I'm sorry to hear it,' Tom makes answer, 'for it's no go, Sir.'

"'No what!' cries the old gentleman.

"'Go, Sir,' says Tom, fiercely. 'I forbid the banns.' And with these words—which are the very words he used—he sat himself down in a chair, and, laying his head upon the table, thought with a secret grief of what was to come to pass on that day two months.

"Tom always said, gentlemen, that that waiting-maid was the artfullest minx he had ever seen; and he left it in writing in this country when he went to colonize abroad, that he was certain in his own mind she and the Salamander had blown up the philosopher's stone on purpose, and to cut him out of his property. I believe Tom was in the right, gentlemen; but whether or no, she comes forward at this point, and says, 'May I speak, Sir?' and the old gentleman answering, 'Yes, you may,' she goes on to say that 'the stars are no doubt quite right in every respect, but Tom is not the man.' And she says, 'Don't you remember, Sir, that when the clock struck five this afternoon, you gave Master Galileo a rap on the head with your telescope, and told him to get out of the way?' 'Yes, I do,' says the old gentleman. 'Then,' says the waiting-maid, 'I say he's the man, and the prophecy is fulfilled.' The old gentleman staggers at this, as if somebody had hit him a blow on the chest, and cries, 'He! why he's a boy!' Upon that, gentlemen, the Salamander cries out that he'll be twenty-one next Lady-day; and complains that his father has always been so busy with the sun round which the earth revolves, that he has never taken any notice of the son that revolves round him; and that he hasn't had a new suit of clothes since he was fourteen; and that he wasn't even taken out of nankeen frocks and trousers till he was quite unpleasant in 'em; and touches on a good many more family matters to the same purpose. To make short of a long story, gentlemen, they all talk together, and cry together, and remind the old gentleman that as to the noble family, his own grandfather would have been lord mayor if he hadn't died at a dinner the year before; and they show him by all kinds of arguments that if the cousins are married, the prediction comes true every way. At last, the old gentleman being quite convinced, gives in; and joins their hands; and leaves his daughter to marry anybody she likes; and they are all well pleased; and the Gifted as well as any of them.

"In the middle of this little family party, gentlemen, sits Tom all the while, as miserable as you like. But, when every-thing else is arranged, the old gentleman's daughter says, that their strange conduct was a little device of the waiting-maid's to disgust the lovers he had chosen for 'em, and will he forgive her? and if he will, perhaps he might even find her a husband—and when she says that, she looks uncommon hard at Tom. Then the waiting-maid says that, oh dear! she couldn't abear Mr. Grig should think she wanted him to marry her; and that she had even gone so far as to refuse the last lamplighter, who was now a literary character (having set up as a bill-sticker); and that she hoped Mr. Grig would not suppose she was on her last legs by any means, for the baker was very strong in his attentions at that moment, and as to the butcher, he was frantic. And I don't know how much more she might have said, gentlemen (for, as you know, this kind of young women are rare ones to talk), if the old gentleman hadn't cut in suddenly, and asked Tom if he'd have her, with ten pounds to recompense him for his loss of time and disappointment, and as a kind of bribe to keep the story secret.

"'It don't much matter, Sir,' says Tom, 'I ain't long for this world. Eight weeks of marriage, especially with this young woman, might reconcile me to my fate. I think,' he says, 'I could go off easy after that.' With which he embraces her with a very dismal face, and groans in a way that might move a heart of stone—even of philosopher's stone.

"' Egad,' says the old gentleman, 'that reminds me—this bustle put it out of my head—there was a figure wrong. He'll live to a green old age—eighty-seven at least!'

"' How much, Sir?' cries Tom.

"'Eighty-seven!' says the old gentleman.

"Without another word, Tom flings himself on the old gentleman's neck; throws up his hat; cuts a caper; defies the waiting-maid; and refers her to the butcher.

"'You won't marry her!' says the old gentleman, angrily.

"'And live after it!' says Tom. 'I'd sooner marry a mermaid with a small-tooth comb and looking-glass.'

"'Then take the consequences,' says the other.

"With those words—I beg your kind attention here, gentlemen, for it's worth your notice—the old gentleman wetted the forefinger of his right hand in some of the liquor from the crucible that was spilt on the floor, and drew a small triangle on Tom's forehead. The room swam before his eyes, and he found himself in the watch-house."

"Found himself *where?*" cried the vice, on behalf of the company generally.

"In the watch-house," said the chairman. "It was late

at night, and he found himself in the very watch-house from which he had been let out that morning."

"Did he go home?" asked the vice.

"The watch-house people rather objected to that," said the chairman; "so he stopped there that night, and went before the magistrate in the morning. 'Why, you're here again, are you?' says the magistrate, adding insult to injury; 'we'll trouble you for five shillings more, if you can conveniently spare the money.' Tom told him he had been enchanted, but it was of no use. He told the contractors the same, but they wouldn't believe him. It was very hard upon him, gentlemen, as he often said, for was it likely he'd go and invent such a tale? They shook their heads and told him he'd say anything but his prayers—as indeed he would; there's no doubt about that. It was the only imputation on his moral character that ever *I* heard of."

TO BE READ AT DUSK

ONE, two, three, four, five. There were five of them.

Five couriers, sitting on a bench outside the convent on the summit of the Great St. Bernard in Switzerland, looking at the remote heights, stained by the setting sun as if a mighty quantity of red wine had been broached upon the mountain top, and had not yet had time to sink into the snow.

This is not my simile. It was made for the occasion by the stoutest courier, who was a German. None of the others took any more notice of it than they took of me, sitting on another bench on the other side of the convent door, smoking my cigar, like them, and—also like them—looking at the reddened snow, and at the lonely shed hard by, where the bodies of belated travellers, dug out of it, slowly wither away, knowing no corruption in that cold region.

The wine upon the mountain top soaked in as we looked; the mountain became white; the sky, a very dark blue; the wind rose; and the air turned piercing cold. The five couriers buttoned their rough coats. There being no safer man to imitate in all such proceedings than a courier, I buttoned mine.

The mountain in the sunset had stopped the five couriers in a conversation. It is a sublime sight, likely to stop conversation. The mountain being now out of the sunset, they resumed. Not that I had heard any part of their previous discourse; for indeed, I had not then broken away from the American gentleman, in the travellers' parlour of the convent, who, sitting with his face to the fire, had undertaken to realise to me the whole progress of events which had led to the accumulation by the Honourable Ananias Dodger of one of the largest acquisitions of dollars ever made in our country.

"My God!" said the Swiss courier, speaking in French, which I do not hold (as some authors appear to do) to be such an all-sufficient excuse for a naughty word, that I have only to write it in that language to make it innocent; "if you talk of ghosts——"

"But I *don't* talk of ghosts," said the German.

"Of what then?" asked the Swiss.

"If I knew of what then," said the German, "I should probably know a great deal more."

It was a good answer, I thought, and it made me curious. So, I moved my position to that corner of my bench which was nearest to them, and leaning my back against the convent wall, heard perfectly, without appearing to attend.

"Thunder and lightning!" said the German, warming, "when a certain man is coming to see you, unexpectedly; and, without his own knowledge, sends some invisible messenger, to put the idea of him into your head all day, what do you call that? When you walk along a crowded street—at Frankfort, Milan, London, Paris—and think that a passing stranger is like your friend Heinrich, and then that another passing stranger is like your friend Heinrich, and so begin to have a strange foreknowledge that presently you'll meet your friend Heinrich—which you do, though you believed him at Trieste—what do you call *that?*"

"It's not uncommon, either," murmured the Swiss and the other three.

"Uncommon!" said the German. "It's as common as cherries in the Black Forest. It's as common as maccaroni at

Naples. And Naples reminds me! When the old Marchesa Senzanima shrieks at a card-party on the Chiaja—as I heard and saw her, for it happened in a Bavarian family of mine, and I was overlooking the service that evening—I say, when the old Marchesa starts up at the card-table, white through her rouge, and cries, 'My sister in Spain is dead! I felt her cold touch on my back!'—and when that sister *is* dead at the moment—what do you call that?"

"Or when the blood of San Gennaro liquefies at the request of the clergy—as all the world knows that it does regularly once a-year, in my native city," said the Neapolitan courier after a pause, with a comical look, "what do you call that?"

"*That!*" cried the German. "Well, I think I know a name for that."

"Miracle?" said the Neapolitan, with the same sly face.

The German merely smoked and laughed; and they all smoked and laughed.

"Bah!" said the German, presently. "I speak of things that really do happen. When I want to see the conjurer, I pay to see a professed one, and have my money's worth. Very strange things do happen without ghosts. Ghosts! Giovanni Baptista, tell your story of the English bride. There's no ghost in that, but something full as strange. Will any man tell me what?"

As there was a silence among them, I glanced around. He whom I took to be Baptista was lighting a fresh cigar. He presently went on to speak. He was a Genoese, as I judged.

"The story of the English bride?" said he. "Basta! one ought not to call so slight a thing a story. Well, it's all one. But it's true. Observe me well, gentlemen, it's true. That which glitters is not always gold; but what I am going to tell, is true."

He repeated this more than once.

Ten years ago, I took my credentials to an English gentleman at Long's Hotel, in Bond Street, London, who was about to travel—it might be for one year, it might be for two. He approved of them; likewise of me. He was pleased to make inquiry. The testimony that he received was favourable. He engaged me by the six months, and my entertainment was generous.

He was young, handsome, very happy. He was enamoured of a fair young English lady, with a sufficient fortune, and they were going to be married. It was the wedding-trip, in short, that we were going to take. For three months' rest in the hot weather (it was early summer then) he had hired an old place on the Riviera, at an easy distance from my city, Genoa, on the road to Nice. Did I know that place? Yes; I told him I knew it well. It was an old palace with great gardens. It was a little bare, and it was a little dark and gloomy, being close surrounded by trees; but it was spacious, ancient, grand, and on the seashore. He said it had been so described to him exactly, and he was well pleased that I knew it. For its being a little bare of furniture, all such places were. For its being a little gloomy, he had hired it principally for the gardens, and he and my mistress would pass the summer weather in their shade.

"So all goes well, Baptista?" said he.

"Indubitably, signore; very well."

We had a travelling chariot for our journey, newly built for us, and in all respects complete. All we had was complete; we wanted for nothing. The marriage took place. They were happy. *I* was happy, seeing all so bright, being so well situated, going to my own city, teaching my language in the rumble to the maid, la bella Carolina, whose heart was gay with laughter: who was young and rosy.

The time flew. But I observed—listen to this, I pray! (and here the courier dropped his voice)—I observed my mistress sometimes brooding in a manner very strange; in a frightened manner; in an unhappy manner; with a cloudy, uncertain alarm upon her. I think that I began to notice this

308

when I was walking up hills by the carriage side, and master had gone on in front. At any rate, I remember that it impressed itself upon my mind one evening in the South of France, when she called to me to call master back; and when he came back, and walked for a long way, talking encouragingly and affectionately to her, with his hand upon the open window, and hers in it. Now and then, he laughed in a merry way, as if he were bantering her out of something. By-and-by, she laughed, and then all went well again.

It was curious. I asked la bella Carolina, the pretty little one, Was mistress unwell?—No.—Out of spirits?—No.—Fearful of bad roads, or brigands?—No. And what made it more mysterious was, the pretty little one would not look at me in giving answer, but *would* look at the view.

But, one day she told me the secret.

"If you must know," said Carolina, "I find, from what I have overheard, that mistress is haunted."

"How haunted?'

"By a dream."

"What dream?"

"By a dream of a face. For three nights before her marriage, she saw· a face in a dream—always the same face, and only One.'

"A terrible face?"

"No. The face of a dark, remarkable-looking man, in black, with black hair and a grey moustache—a handsome man except for a reserved and secret air. Not a face she ever saw, or at all like a face she ever saw. Doing nothing in the dream but looking at her fixedly, out of darkness."

"Does the dream come back?"

"Never. The recollection of it is all her trouble."

"And why does it trouble her?"

Carolina shook her head.

"That's master's question," said la bella. "She don't know. She wonders why, herself. But I heard her tell him, only last night, that if she was to find a picture of that face in our Italian house (which she is afraid she will) she did not know how she could ever bear it."

Upon my word I was fearful after this (said the Genoese courier) of our coming to the old palazzo, lest some such ill-starred picture should happen to be there. I knew there were many there; and, as we got nearer and nearer to the place, I wished the whole gallery in the crater of Vesuvius. To mend the matter, it was a stormy dismal evening when we, at last, approached that part of the Riviera. It thundered; and the thunder of my city and its environs, rolling among the high hills, is very loud. The lizards ran in and out of the chinks in the broken stone wall of the garden, as if they were frightened; the frogs bubbled and croaked their loudest; the sea-wind moaned, and the wet trees dripped; and the lightning—body of San Lorenzo, how it lightened!

We all know what an old palace in or near Genoa is— how time and the sea air have blotted it—how the drapery painted on the outer walls has peeled off in great flakes of plaster—how the lower windows are darkened with rusty bars of iron—how the courtyard is overgrown with grass— how the outer buildings are dilapidated—how the whole pile seems devoted to ruin. Our palazzo was one of the true kind. It had been shut up close for months. Months?—years!—it had an earthy smell, like a tomb. The scent of the orange trees on the broad back terrace, and of the lemons ripening on the wall, and of some shrubs that grew around a broken fountain, had got into the house somehow, and had never been able to get out again. There was, in every room, an aged smell, grown faint with confinement. It pined in all the cupboards and drawers. In the little rooms of communication between great rooms, it was stifling. If you turned a picture —to come back to the pictures—there it still was, clinging to the wall behind the frame, like a sort of bat.

The lattice-blinds were close shut, all over the house. There were two ugly, grey old women in the house, to take care of it; one of them with a spindle, who stood winding and mumbling in the doorway, and who would as soon have let in the devil as the air. Master, mistress, la bella Carolina, and I, went all through the palazzo. I went first, though I have named myself last, opening the windows and the lattice-blinds, and shaking down on myself splashes of rain, and scraps of mortar, and now and then a dozing mosquito, or a monstrous, fat, blotchy, Genoese spider.

When I had let the evening light into a room, master, mistress, and la bella Carolina, entered. Then, we looked round at all the pictures, and I went forward again into another room. Mistress secretly had great fear of meeting with the likeness of that face—we all had; but there was no such thing. The Madonna and Bambino, San Francisco, San Sebastiano, Venus, Santa Caterina, Angels, Brigands, Friars, Temples at Sunset, Battles, White Horses, Forests, Apostles, Doges, all my old acquaintances many times repeated?—yes. Dark, handsome man in black, reserved and secret, with black hair and grey moustache, looking fixedly at mistress out of darkness?—no.

At last we got through all the rooms and all the pictures, and came out into the gardens. They were pretty well kept, being rented by a gardener, and were large and shady. In one place there was a rustic theatre, open to the sky; the stage a green slope; the coulisses, three entrances upon a side, sweet-smelling leafy screens. Mistress moved her bright eyes, even there, as if she looked to see the face come in upon the scene; but all was well.

"Now, Clara," master said, in a low voice, "you see that it is nothing? You are happy."

Mistress was much encouraged. She soon accustomed herself to that grim palazzo, and would sing, and play the harp, and copy the old pictures, and stroll with master under the green trees and vines all day. She was beautiful. He was happy. He would laugh and say to me, mounting his horse for his morning ride before the heat:

"All goes well, Baptista!"

"Yes, signore, thank God, very well."

We kept no company. I took la bella to the Duomo and Annunciata, to the Café, to the Opera, to the village Festa, to the Public Garden, to the Day Theatre, to the Marionetti. The pretty little one was charmed with all she saw. She learnt Italian—heavens! miraculously! Was mistress quite forgetful of that dream? I asked Carolina sometimes. Nearly, said la bella—almost. It was wearing out.

One day master received a letter, and called me.

"Baptista!"

"Signore!"

"A gentleman who is presented to me will dine here to-day. He is called the Signor Dellombra. Let me dine like a prince."

It was an odd name. I did not know that name. But, there had been many noblemen and gentlemen pursued by Austria on political suspicions, lately, and some names had changed. Perhaps this was one. Altro! Dellombra was as good a name to me as another.

When the Signor Dellombra came to dinner (said the Genoese courier in the low voice, into which he had subsided once before), I showed him into the reception-room, the great sala of the old palazzo. Master received him with cordiality, and presented him to mistress. As she rose, her face changed, she gave a cry, and fell upon the marble floor.

Then, I turned my head to the Signor Dellombra, and saw that he was dressed in black, and had a reserved and secret air, and was a dark, remarkable-looking man, with black hair and a grey moustache.

Master raised mistress in his arms, and carried her to her own room, where I sent la bella Carolina straight. La bella told me afterwards that mistress was nearly terrified to death, and that she wandered in her mind about her dream, all night.

Master was vexed and anxious—almost angry, and yet full of solicitude. The Signor Dellombra was a courtly gentleman, and spoke with great respect and sympathy of mistress's being so ill. The African wind had been blowing for some days (they had told him at his hotel of the Maltese Cross), and he knew that it was often hurtful. He hoped the beautiful lady would recover soon. He begged permission to retire, and to renew his visit when he should have the happiness of hearing that she was better. Master would not allow of this, and they dined alone.

He withdrew early. Next day he called at the gate, on horseback, to inquire for mistress. He did so two or three times in that week.

What I observed myself, and what la bella Carolina told me, united to explain to me that master had now set his mind on curing mistress of her fanciful terror. He was all kindness, but he was sensible and firm. He reasoned with her, that to encourage such fancies was to invite melancholy, if not madness. That it rested with herself to be herself. That if she once resisted her strange weakness, so successfully as to receive the Signor Dellombra as an English lady would receive any other guest, it was for ever conquered. To make an end, the signore came again, and mistress received him without marked distress (though with constraint and apprehension still), and the evening passed serenely. Master was so delighted with this change, and so anxious to confirm it, that the Signor Dellombra became a constant guest. He was accomplished in pictures, books, and music; and his society, in any grim palazzo, would have been welcome.

I used to notice, many times, that mistress was not quite recovered. She would cast down her eyes and droop her head, before the Signor Dellombra, or would look at him with a terrified and fascinated glance, as if his presence had some evil influence or power upon her. Turning from her to him, I used to see him in the shaded gardens, or the large half-lighted sala, looking, as I might say, " fixedly upon her out of darkness." But, truly, I had not forgotten la bella Carolina's words describing the face in the dream.

After his second visit I heard master say:

"Now, see, my dear Clara, it's over! Dellombra has come and gone, and your apprehension is broken like glass."

"Will he—will he ever come again?" asked mistress.

"Again? Why, surely, over and over again! Are you cold?" (she shivered).

"No, dear—but—he terrifies me: are you sure that he need come again?"

"The surer for the question, Clara!" replied master, cheerfully.

But, he was very hopeful of her complete recovery now, and grew more and more so every day. She was beautiful. He was happy.

"All goes well, Baptista?" he would say to me again.

"Yes, signore, thank God; very well."

We were all (said the Genoese courier, constraining himself to speak a little louder), we were all at Rome for the Carnival. I had been out, all day, with a Sicilian, a friend of mine, and a courier, who was there with an English family. As I returned at night to our hotel, I met the little Carolina, who never stirred from home alone, running distractedly along the Corso.

"Carolina! What's the matter?"

"O Baptista! O, for the Lord's sake! where is my mistress?"

"Mistress, Carolina?"

"Gone since morning—told me, when master went out on his day's journey, not to call her, for she was tired with not resting in the night (having been in pain), and would lie in bed until the evening; then get up refreshed. She is gone! —she is gone! Master has come back, broken down the door, and she is gone! My beautiful, my good, my innocent mistress!"

The pretty little one so cried, and raved, and tore herself that I could not have held her, but for her swooning on my arm as if she had been shot. Master came up—in manner, face, or voice, no more the master that I knew, than I was he. He took me (I laid the little one upon her bed in the hotel, and left her with the chamber-women), in a carriage, furiously through the darkness, across the desolate Campagna. When it was day, and we stopped at a miserable post-house, all the horses had been hired twelve hours ago, and sent away in different directions. Mark me! by the Signor Dellombra, who had passed there in a carriage, with a frightened English lady crouching in one corner.

I never heard (said the Genoese courier, drawing a long breath) that she was ever traced beyond that spot. All I know is, that she vanished into infamous oblivion, with the dreaded face beside her that she had seen in her dream.

"What do you call *that?*" said the German courier, triumphantly. "Ghosts! There are no ghosts *there!* What do you call this, that I am going to tell you? Ghosts! There are no ghosts *here!*"

I took an engagement once (pursued the German courier) with an English gentleman, elderly and a bachelor, to travel through my country, my Fatherland. He was a merchant who traded with my country and knew the language, but who had never been there since he was a boy—as I judge, some sixty years before.

His name was James, and he had a twin-brother John, also a bachelor. Between these brothers there was a great affection. They were in business together, at Goodman's Fields, but they did not live together. Mr. James dwelt in Poland Street, turning out of Oxford Street, London; Mr. John resided by Epping Forest.

Mr. James and I were to start for Germany in about a week. The exact day depended on business. Mr. John came to Poland Street (where I was staying in the house), to pass that week with Mr. James. But, he said to his brother on the second day, "I don't feel very well, James. There's not much the matter with me; but I think I am a little gouty. I'll go home and put myself under the care of my old house-keeper, who understands my ways. If I get quite better, I'll come back and see you before you go. If I don't feel well enough to resume my visit where I leave it off, why *you* will come and see *me* before you go." Mr. James, of course, said he would, and they shook hands—both hands, as they always did—and Mr. John ordered out his old-fashioned chariot and rumbled home.

It was on the second night after that—that is to say, the fourth in the week—when I was awoke out of my sound sleep by Mr. James coming into my bedroom in his flannel-gown, with a lighted candle. He sat upon the side of my bed, and looking at me, said:

"Wilhelm, I have reason to think I have got some strange illness upon me."

I then perceived that there was a very unusual expression in his face.

"Wilhelm," said he, "I am not afraid or ashamed to tell you what I might be afraid or ashamed to tell another man. You come from a sensible country, where mysterious things are inquired into and are not settled to have been weighed and measured—or to have been unweighable and unmeasurable—or in either case to have been completely disposed of, for all time—ever so many years ago. I have just now seen the phantom of my brother."

I confess (said the German courier) that it gave me a little tingling of the blood to hear it.

"I have just now seen," Mr. James repeated, looking full at me, that I might see how collected he was, "the phantom of my brother John. I was sitting up in bed, unable to sleep, when it came into my room, in a white dress, and regarding me earnestly, passed up to the end of the room, glanced at some papers on my writing-desk, turned, and, still looking earnestly at me as it passed the bed, went out at the door. Now, I am not in the least mad, and am not in the least disposed to invest that phantom with any external existence out of myself. I think it is a warning to me that I am ill ; and I think I had better be bled."

I got out of bed directly (said the German courier) and began to get on my clothes, begging him not to be alarmed, and telling him that I would go myself to the doctor. I was just ready, when we heard a loud knocking and ringing at the street door. My room being an attic at the back, and Mr. James's being the second-floor room in the front, we went down to his room, and put up the window, to see what was the matter.

"Is that Mr. James?" said a man below, falling back to the opposite side of the way to look up.

"It is," said Mr. James, "and you are my brother's man, Robert."

"Yes, Sir. I am sorry to say, Sir, that Mr. John is ill. He is very bad, Sir. It is even feared that he may be lying at the point of death. He wants to see you, Sir. I have a chaise here. Pray come to him. Pray lose no time."

Mr. James and I looked at one another. "Wilhelm," said he, "this is strange. I wish you to come with me!" I helped him to dress, partly there and partly in the chaise ; and no grass grew under the horses' iron shoes between Poland Street and the Forest.

Now, mind! (said the German courier) I went with Mr. James into his brother's room, and I saw and heard myself what follows.

His brother lay upon his bed, at the upper end of a long bed-chamber. His old housekeeper was there, and others were there : I think three others were there, if not four, and they had been with him since early in the afternoon. He was in white, like the figure—necessarily so, because he had his night-dress on. He looked like the figure—necessarily so, because he looked earnestly at his brother when he saw him come into the room.

But, when his brother reached the bed-side, he slowly

317

raised himself in bed, and looking full upon him, said these words:

"JAMES, YOU HAVE SEEN ME BEFORE, TO-NIGHT—AND YOU KNOW IT!"

And so died!

I waited, when the German courier ceased, to hear something said of this strange story. The silence was unbroken. I looked round, and the five couriers were gone: so noiselessly that the ghostly mountain might have absorbed them into its eternal snows. By this time, I was by no means in a mood to sit alone in that awful scene, with the chill air coming solemnly upon me—or, if I may tell the truth, to sit alone anywhere. So I went back into the convent-parlour, and, finding the American gentleman still disposed to relate the biography of the Honourable Ananias Dodger, heard it all out.

SUNDAY UNDER
THREE HEADS

DEDICATION

TO THE RIGHT REVEREND THE BISHOP OF LONDON

My Lord,

You were among the first, some years ago, to expatiate on the vicious addiction of the lower classes of society to Sunday excursions; and were thus instrumental in calling forth occasional demonstrations of those extreme opinions on the subject, which are very generally received with derision, if not with contempt.

Your elevated station, my Lord, affords you countless opportunities of increasing the comforts and pleasures of the humbler classes of society—not by the expenditure of the smallest portion of your princely income, but by merely sanctioning with the influence of your example, their harmless pastimes, and innocent recreations.

That your Lordship would ever have contemplated Sunday recreations with so much horror, if you had been at all acquainted with the wants and necessities of the people who indulged in them, I cannot imagine possible. That a Prelate of your elevated rank has the faintest conception of the

DEDICATION

extent of those wants, and the nature of those necessities, I do not believe.

For these reasons, I venture to address this little Pamphlet to your Lordship's consideration. I am quite conscious that the outlines I have drawn, afford but a very imperfect description of the feelings they are intended to illustrate; but I claim for them one merit—their truth and freedom from exaggeration. I may have fallen short of the mark, but I have never overshot it : and while I have pointed out what appears to me, to be injustice on the part of others, I hope I have carefully abstained from committing it myself.

I am,

My Lord,

Your Lordship's most obedient,

Humble Servant,

TIMOTHY SPARKS.

June, 1836.

I

THERE are few things from which I derive greater pleasure, than walking through some of the principal streets of London on a fine Sunday, in summer, and watching the cheerful faces of the lively groups with which they are thronged. There is something, to my eyes at least, exceedingly pleasing in the general desire evinced by the humbler classes of society, to appear neat and clean on this their only holiday. There are many grave old persons, I know, who shake their heads with an air of profound wisdom, and tell you that poor people dress too well now-a-days; that when they were children, folks knew their stations in life better; that you may depend upon it, no good will come of this sort of thing in the end, —and so forth: but I fancy I can discern in the fine bonnet of the working-man's wife, or the feather-bedizened hat of his child, no inconsiderable evidence of good feeling on the part of the man himself, and an affectionate desire to expend the few shillings he can spare from his week's wages, in improving the appearance and adding to the happiness of those who are nearest and dearest to him. This may be a very heinous and unbecoming degree of vanity, perhaps, and the money might possibly be applied to better uses; it must not be forgotten, however, that it might very easily be devoted to worse: and if two or three faces can be rendered happy and contented, by a trifling improvement of outward appearance, I cannot help thinking that the object is very cheaply purchased, even at the expense of a smart gown, or a gaudy riband. There is a great deal of very unnecessary cant about the over-dressing of the common people. There is not a manufacturer or tradesman in existence, who would not employ a man who takes a reasonable degree of pride in the appearance of himself and those about him, in preference to a sullen, slovenly fellow, who works doggedly on, regardless of his own clothing and that of his wife and children, and seeming to take pleasure or pride in nothing.

The pampered aristocrat, whose life is one continued round of licentious pleasures and sensual gratifications; or the gloomy enthusiast, who detests the cheerful amusements he can never enjoy, and envies the healthy feelings he can never know, and who would put down the one and suppress the other, until he made the minds of his fellow-beings as besotted and distorted as his own;—neither of these men can by possibility form an adequate notion of what Sunday really is to those whose lives are spent in sedentary or laborious occupations, and who are accustomed to look forward to it through their whole existence, as their only day of rest from toil, and innocent enjoyment.

The sun that rises over the quiet streets of London on a bright Sunday morning, shines till his setting, on gay and happy faces. Here and there, so early as six o'clock, a young man and woman in their best attire, may be seen hurrying along on their way to the house of some acquaintance, who is included in their scheme of pleasure for the day; from whence, after stopping to take "a bit of breakfast," they sally forth, accompanied by several old people, and a whole crowd of young ones, bearing large hand-baskets full of provisions, and Belcher handkerchiefs done up in bundles, with the neck of a bottle sticking out at the top, and closely-packed apples bulging out at the sides,—and away they hurry along the streets leading to the steam-packet wharfs, which are already plentifully sprinkled with parties bound for the same destination. Their good humour and delight know no bounds —for it is a delightful morning, all blue over head, and nothing like a cloud in the whole sky; and even the air of the river at London Bridge is something to them, shut up as they have been, all the week, in close streets and heated rooms. There are dozens of steamers to all sorts of places—Gravesend, Greenwich, and Richmond; and such numbers of people, that when you have once sat down on the deck, it is all but a moral impossibility to get up again—to say nothing of walking about, which is entirely out of the question. Away they go, joking and laughing, and eating and drinking, and admiring everything they see, and pleased with everything they hear, to climb Windmill Hill, and catch a glimpse of the rich corn-fields and beautiful orchards of Kent; or to stroll among the fine old trees of Greenwich Park, and survey the wonders of Shooter's Hill and Lady James's Folly; or to glide past the beautiful meadows of Twickenham and Richmond, and to gaze with a delight which only people like them can know, on every lovely object in the fair prospect around. Boat follows boat, and coach succeeds coach, for the next three hours; but all are filled, and all with the same kind of people—neat and clean, cheerful and contented.

They reach their places of destination, and the taverns are crowded; but there is no drunkenness or brawling, for the class of men who commit the enormity of making Sunday excursions, take their families with them: and this in itself would be a check upon them, even if they were inclined to dissipation, which they really are not. Boisterous their mirth may be, for they have all the excitement of feeling that fresh air and green fields can impart to the dwellers in crowded cities, but it is innocent and harmless. The glass is circulated, and the joke goes round; but the one is free from excess, and the other from offence; and nothing but good humour and hilarity prevail.

In streets like Holborn and Tottenham Court Road, which form the central market of a large neighbourhood, inhabited by a vast number of mechanics and poor people, a few shops are open at an early hour of the morning; and a very poor man, with a thin and sickly woman by his side, may be seen with their little basket in hand, purchasing the scanty quantity of necessaries they can afford, which the time at which the man receives his wages, or his having a good deal of work to do, or the woman's having been out charing till a late hour, prevented their procuring over-night. The coffee-shops too, at which clerks and young men employed in counting-houses can procure their breakfasts, are also open. This class comprises, in a place like London, an enormous number of people, whose limited means prevent their engaging for their lodgings any other apartment than a bedroom, and who have consequently no alternative but to take their breakfasts at a coffee-shop, or go without it altogether. All these places, however, are quickly closed; and by the time the church bells begin to ring, all appearance of traffic has ceased. And then, what are the signs of immorality that meet the eye? Churches are well filled, and Dissenters' chapels are crowded to suffocation. There is no preaching to empty benches, while the drunken and dissolute populace run riot in the streets.

Here is a fashionable church, where the service commences at a late hour, for the accommodation of such members of the congregation—and they are not a few—as may happen to have lingered at the Opera far into the morning of the Sabbath; an excellent contrivance for poising the balance between God and Mammon, and illustrating the ease with which a man's duties to both, may be accommodated and adjusted. How the carriages rattle up, and deposit their richly-dressed burdens beneath the lofty portico! The powdered footmen glide along the aisle, place the richly-bound prayer-books on the pew desks, slam the doors, and hurry away, leaving the fashionable members of the congregation to inspect each other through their glasses, and to dazzle and glitter in the eyes of the few shabby people in the free seats. The organ peals forth, the hired singers commence a short hymn, and the congregation condescendingly rise, stare about them, and converse in whispers. The clergyman enters the reading-desk,—a young man of noble family and elegant demeanour, notorious at Cambridge for his knowledge of horse-flesh and dancers, and celebrated at Eton for his hopeless stupidity. The service commences. Mark the soft voice in which he reads, and the impressive manner in which he applies his white hand, studded with brilliants, to his perfumed hair. Observe the graceful emphasis with which he offers up the prayers for the King, the Royal Family, and all the Nobility; and the nonchalance with which he hurries over the more uncomfortable portions of the service, the seventh commandment for instance, with a studied regard for the taste and feeling of his auditors, only to be equalled by that displayed by the sleek divine who succeeds him, who murmurs, in a voice kept down by rich feeding, most comfortable doctrines for exactly twelve minutes, and then arrives at the anxiously expected " Now to God," which is the signal for the dismissal of the congregation. The organ is again heard; those who have been asleep wake up, and those who have kept awake, smile and seem greatly relieved; bows and congratulations are exchanged, the livery servants are all bustle and commotion, bang go the steps, up jump the footmen, and off rattle the carriages: the inmates discoursing on the dresses of the congregation, and congratulating themselves on having set so excellent an example to the community in general, and Sunday-pleasurers in particular.

Enter a less orthodox place of religious worship, and observe the contrast. A small close chapel with a white-washed wall, and plain deal pews and pulpit, contains a closely-packed congregation, as different in dress, as they are opposed in manner, to that we have just quitted. The hymn is sung—not by paid singers, but by the whole assembly at the loudest pitch of their voices, unaccompanied by any musical instrument, the words being given out, two lines at a time, by the clerk. There is something in the sonorous quavering of the harsh voices, in the lank and hollow faces of the men, and the sour solemnity of the women, which bespeaks this a stronghold of intolerant zeal and ignorant enthusiasm. The preacher enters the pulpit. He is a coarse, hard-faced man of forbidding aspect, clad in rusty black, and bearing in his hand a small plain Bible from which he selects some passage for his text, while the hymn is concluding. The congregation fall upon their knees, and are hushed into profound stillness as he delivers an extempore prayer, in which he calls upon the Sacred Founder of the Christian faith to bless his ministry, in terms of disgusting and impious familiarity not to be described. He begins his oration in a drawling tone, and his hearers listen with silent attention. He grows warmer as he proceeds with his subject, and his gesticulation becomes proportionately violent. He clenches his fists, beats the book upon the desk before him, and swings his arms wildly about his head. The congregation murmur their acquiescence in his doctrines: and a short groan, occasionally bears testimony to the moving nature of his eloquence. Encouraged by these symptoms of approval, and working himself up to a pitch of enthusiasm amounting almost to frenzy, he denounces sabbath-breakers with the direst vengeance of offended Heaven. He stretches his body half out of the pulpit, thrusts forth his arms with frantic gestures, and blasphemously calls upon The Deity to visit with eternal torments, those who turn aside from the word, as interpreted and preached by—himself. A low moaning is heard, the women rock their bodies to and fro, and wring their hands; the preacher's fervour increases, the perspiration starts upon his brow, his face is flushed, and he clenches his hands convulsively, as he draws a hideous and appalling picture of the horrors preparing for the wicked in a future state. A great excitement is visible among his hearers, a scream is heard, and some young girl falls senseless on the floor. There is a momentary rustle, but it is only for a moment—all eyes are turned towards the preacher. He pauses, passes his handkerchief across his face, and looks complacently round. His voice resumes its natural tone, as with mock humility he offers up a thanksgiving for having been successful in his efforts, and having been permitted to rescue one sinner from the path of evil. He sinks back into his seat, exhausted with the violence of his ravings; the girl is removed, a hymn is sung, a petition for some measure for securing the better observance of the Sabbath, which has been prepared by the good man, is read; and his worshipping admirers struggle who shall be the first to sign it.

But the morning service has concluded, and the streets are again crowded with people. Long rows of cleanly-dressed charity children, preceded by a portly beadle and a withered schoolmaster, are returning to their welcome dinner; and it is evident, from the number of men with beer-trays who are running from house to house, that no inconsiderable portion of the population are about to take theirs at this early hour. The bakers' shops in the humbler suburbs especially, are filled with men, women, and children, each anxiously waiting for the Sunday dinner. Look at the group of children who surround that working man who has just emerged from the baker's shop at the corner of the street, with the reeking dish, in which a diminutive joint of mutton simmers above a vast heap of half-browned potatoes. How the young rogues clap their hands, and dance round their father, for very joy at the prospect of the feast: and how anxiously the youngest and chubbiest of the lot, lingers on tiptoe by his side, trying to get a peep into the interior of the dish. They turn up the street, and the chubby-faced boy trots on as fast as his little legs will carry him, to herald the approach of the dinner to " Mother " who is standing with a baby in her arms on the doorstep, and who seems almost as pleased with the whole scene as the children themselves; whereupon "baby" not precisely understanding the importance of the business in hand, but clearly perceiving that it is something unusually lively, kicks and crows most lustily, to the unspeakable delight of all the children and both the parents: and the dinner is borne into the house amidst a shouting of small voices, and jumping of fat legs, which would fill Sir Andrew Agnew with astonishment; as well it might, seeing that Baronets, generally speaking, eat pretty comfortable dinners all the week through, and cannot be expected to understand what people feel, who only have a meat dinner on one day out of every seven.

The bakings being all duly consigned to their respective owners, and the beer-man having gone his rounds, the church bells ring for afternoon service, the shops are again closed, and the streets are more than ever thronged with people; some who have not been to church in the morning, going to it now; others who have been to church, going out for a walk; and others—let us admit the full measure of their guilt—going for a walk, who have not been to church at all. I am afraid the smart servant of all work, who has been loitering at the corner of the square for the last ten minutes, is one of the latter class.. She is evidently waiting for somebody, and though she may have made up her mind to go to church with him one of these mornings, I don't think they have any such intention on this particular afternoon. Here he is, at last. The white trousers, blue coat, and yellow waistcoat—and more especially that cock of the hat—indicate, as surely as inanimate objects can, that Chalk Farm and not the parish church, is their destination. The girl colours up, and puts out her hand with a very awkward affectation of indifference. He gives it a gallant squeeze, and away they walk, arm in arm, the girl just looking back towards her "place" with an air of conscious self-importance, and nodding to her fellow-servant who has gone up to the two-pair-of-stairs window, to take a full view of " Mary's young man," which being communicated to William, he takes off his hat to the fellow-servant : a proceeding which affords unmitigated satisfaction to all parties, and impels the fellow-servant to inform Miss Emily confidentially, in the course of the evening, " that the young man as Mary keeps company with, is one of the most genteelest young men as ever she see."

The two young people who have just crossed the road, and are following this happy couple down the street, are a fair specimen of another class of Sunday-pleasurers.   There is a dapper smartness, struggling through very limited means, about the young man, which induces one to set him down at once as a junior clerk to a tradesman or attorney.   The girl no one could possibly mistake.   You may tell a young woman in the employment of a large dress-maker, at any time, by a certain neatness of cheap finery and humble following of fashion, which pervade her whole attire; but unfortunately there are other tokens not to be misunderstood —the pale face with its hectic bloom, the slight distortion of form which no artifice of dress can wholly conceal, the unhealthy stoop, and the short cough—the effects of hard work and close application to a sedentary employment, upon a tender frame.   They turn towards the fields.   The girl's countenance brightens, and an unwonted glow rises in her face.   They are going to Hampstead or Highgate, to spend their holiday afternoon in some place where they can see the sky, the fields, and trees, and breathe for an hour or two the pure air, which so seldom plays upon that poor girl's form, or exhilarates her spirits.

I would to God, that the iron-hearted man who would deprive such people as these of their only pleasures, could feel the sinking of heart and soul, the wasting exhaustion of mind and body, the utter prostration of present strength and future hope, attendant upon that incessant toil which lasts from day to day, and from month to month; that toil which is too often protracted until the silence of midnight, and resumed with the first stir of morning. How marvellously would his ardent zeal for other men's souls, diminish after a short probation, and how enlightened and comprehensive would his views of the real object and meaning of the institution of the Sabbath become!

The afternoon is far advanced—the parks and public drives are crowded. Carriages, gigs, phaetons, stanhopes, and vehicles of every description, glide smoothly on. The promenades are filled with loungers on foot, and the road is thronged with loungers on horseback. Persons of every class are crowded together, here, in one dense mass. The plebeian, who takes his pleasure on no day but Sunday, jostles the patrician, who takes his, from year's end to year's end. You look in vain for any outward signs of profligacy or debauchery. You see nothing before you but a vast number of people, the denizens of a large and crowded city, in the needful and rational enjoyment of air and exercise.

It grows dusk. The roads leading from the different places of suburban resort, are crowded with people on their return home, and the sound of merry voices rings through the gradually darkening fields. The evening is hot and sultry. The rich man throws open the sashes of his spacious dining-room, and quaffs his iced wine in splendid luxury. The poor man, who has no room to take his meals in, but the close apartment to which he and his family have been confined throughout the week, sits in the tea-garden of some famous tavern, and drinks his beer in content and comfort. The fields and roads are gradually deserted, the crowd once more pour into the streets, and disperse to their several homes; and by midnight all is silent and quiet, save where a few stragglers linger beneath the window of some great man's house, to listen to the strains of music from within: or stop to gaze upon the splendid carriages which are waiting to convey the guests from the dinner-party of an Earl.

There is a darker side to this picture, on which, so far from its being any part of my purpose to conceal it, I wish to lay particular stress. In some parts of London, and in many of the manufacturing towns of England, drunkenness and profligacy in their most disgusting forms, exhibit in the open streets on Sunday, a sad and a degrading spectacle. We need go no farther than St. Giles's, or Drury Lane, for sights and scenes of a most repulsive nature. Women with scarcely the articles of apparel which common decency requires, with forms bloated by disease, and faces rendered hideous by habitual drunkenness—men reeling and staggering along—children in rags and filth—whole streets of squalid and miserable appearance, whose inhabitants are lounging in the public road, fighting, screaming, and swearing—these are the common objects which present themselves in, these are the well-known characteristics of, that portion of London to which I have just referred.

And why is it, that all well-disposed persons are shocked, and public decency scandalised, by such exhibitions?

These people are poor—that is notorious. It may be said that they spend in liquor, money with which they might purchase necessaries, and there is no denying the fact; but let it be remembered that even if they applied every farthing of their earnings in the best possible way, they would still be very—very poor. Their dwellings are necessarily uncomfortable, and to a certain degree unhealthy. Cleanliness might do much, but they are too crowded together, the streets are too narrow, and the rooms too small, to admit of their ever being rendered desirable habitations. They work very hard all the week. We know that the effect of prolonged and arduous labour, is to produce, when a period of rest does arrive, a sensation of lassitude which it requires the application of some stimulus to overcome. What stimulus have they? Sunday comes, and with it a cessation of labour. How are they to employ the day, or what inducement have they to employ it, in recruiting their stock of health? They see little parties, on pleasure excursions, passing through the streets; but they cannot imitate their example, for they have not the means. They may walk, to be sure, but it is exactly the inducement to walk that they require. If every one of these men knew, that by taking the trouble to walk two or three miles he would be enabled to share in a good game of cricket, or some athletic sport, I very much question whether any of them would remain at home.

But you hold out no inducement, you offer no relief from listlessness, you provide nothing to amuse his mind, you afford him no means of exercising his body. Unwashed and unshaven, he saunters moodily about, weary and dejected. In lieu of the wholesome stimulus he might derive from nature, you drive him to the pernicious excitement to be gained from art. He flies to the gin-shop as his only resource; and when, reduced to a worse level than the lowest brute in the scale of creation, he lies wallowing in the kennel, your saintly lawgivers lift up their hands to heaven, and exclaim for a law which shall convert the day intended for rest and cheerfulness, into one of universal gloom, bigotry, and persecution.

II

THE provisions of the bill introduced into the House of Commons by Sir Andrew Agnew, and thrown out by that House on the motion for the second reading, on the 18th of May in the present year, by a majority of 32, may very fairly be taken as a test of the length to which the fanatics, of which the honourable Baronet is the distinguished leader, are prepared to go. No test can be fairer; because while on the one hand this measure may be supposed to exhibit all that improvement which mature reflection and long delibera-tion may have suggested, so on the other it may very reasonably be inferred, that if it be quite as severe in its provisions, and to the full as partial in its operation, as those which have preceded it and experienced a similar fate, the disease under which the honourable Baronet and his friends labour, is perfectly hopeless, and beyond the reach of cure.

The proposed enactments of the bill are briefly these :— All work is prohibited on the Lord's day, under heavy penalties, increasing with every repetition of the offence. There are penalties for keeping shops open—penalties for drunkenness—penalties for keeping open houses of entertain-ment—penalties for being present at any public meeting or assembly—penalties for letting carriages, and penalties for hiring them—penalties for travelling in steam-boats, and

SUNDAY UNDER THREE HEADS

penalties for taking passengers—penalties on vessels com-
mencing their voyage on Sunday—penalties on the owners
of cattle who suffer them to be driven on the Lord's day—
penalties on constables who refuse to act, and penalties for
resisting them when they do. In addition to these trifles,
the constables are invested with arbitrary, vexatious, and
most extensive powers; and all this in a bill which sets out
with a hypocritical and canting declaration that " nothing is
more acceptable to God than the *true and sincere* worship of
Him according to His holy will, and that it is the bounden
duty of Parliament to promote the observance of the Lord's
day, by protecting every class of society against being required
to sacrifice their comfort, health, religious privileges, and
conscience, for the convenience, enjoyment, or supposed
advantage of any other class on the Lord's day "! The idea
of making a man truly moral through the ministry of
constables, and sincerely religious under the influence of
penalties, is worthy of the mind which could form such a
mass of monstrous absurdity as this bill is composed of.

The House of Commons threw the measure out certainly,
and by so doing retrieved the disgrace—so far as it could be
retrieved—of placing among the printed papers of Parliament,
such an egregious specimen of legislative folly; but there
was a degree of delicacy and forbearance about the debate
that took place, which I cannot help thinking as unnecessary
and uncalled for, as it is unusual in Parliamentary discussions.
If it had been the first time of Sir Andrew Agnew's attempting to palm such a measure upon the country, we might
well understand, and duly appreciate, the delicate and com-
passionate feeling due to the supposed weakness and imbecility
of the man, which prevented his proposition being exposed
in its true colours, and induced this Hon. Member to bear
testimony to his excellent motives, and that Noble Lord to
regret that he could not—although he had tried to do so—
adopt any portion of the bill. But when these attempts
have been repeated, again and again; when Sir Andrew Agnew

has renewed them session after session, and when it has
become palpably evident to the whole House that

> His impudence of proof in every trial,
> Kens no polite, and heeds no plain denial—

it really becomes high time to speak of him and his legislation, as they appear to deserve, without that gloss of politeness, which is all very well in an ordinary case, but rather
out of place when the liberties and comforts of a whole
people are at stake.

In the first place, it is by no means the worst characteristic
of this bill, that it is a bill of blunders : it is, from beginning
to end, a piece of deliberate cruelty, and crafty injustice.
If the rich composed the whole population of this country,
not a single comfort of one single man would be affected by
it. It is directed exclusively, and without the exception of
a solitary instance, against the amusements and recreations
of the poor. This was the bait held out by the Hon. Baronet
to a body of men, who cannot be supposed to have any very
strong sympathies in common with the poor, because they
cannot understand their sufferings or their struggles. This
is the bait, which will in time prevail, unless public attention
is awakened, and public feeling exerted, to prevent it.

Take the very first clause, the provision that no man shall
be allowed to work on Sunday—"That no person, upon the
Lord's day, shall do, or hire, or employ any person to do any
manner of labour, or any work of his or her ordinary calling."
What class of persons does this affect? The rich man? No.
Menial servants, both male and female, are specially exempted
from the operation of the bill. "Menial servants" are among
the poor people. The bill has no regard for them. The
Baronet's dinner must be cooked on Sunday, the Bishop's
horses must be groomed, and the Peer's carriage must be
driven. So the menial servants are put utterly beyond the
pale of grace ;—unless indeed, they are to go to heaven
through the sanctity of their masters, and possibly they
might think even that, rather an uncertain passport.

There is a penalty for keeping open, houses of entertainment. Now, suppose the bill had passed, and that half-a-dozen adventurous licensed victuallers, relying upon the excitement of public feeling on the subject, and the consequent difficulty of conviction (this is by no means an improbable supposition), had determined to keep their houses and gardens open, through the whole Sunday afternoon, in defiance of the law. Every act of hiring or working, every act of buying or selling, or delivering, or causing anything to be bought or sold, is specifically made a separate offence—mark the effect. A party, a man and his wife and children, enter a tea-garden, and the informer stations himself in the next box, from whence he can see and hear everything that passes. "Waiter !" says the father. "Yes, Sir." "Pint of the best ale !" "Yes, Sir." Away runs the waiter to the bar, and gets the ale from the landlord. Out comes the informer's note-book—penalty on the father for hiring, on the waiter for delivering, and on the landlord for selling, on the Lord's day. But it does not stop here. The waiter delivers the ale, and darts off, little suspecting the penalties in store for him. "Hollo," cries the father, "waiter !" "Yes, Sir." "Just get this little boy a biscuit, will you ?" "Yes, Sir." Off runs the waiter again, and down goes another case of hiring, another case of delivering, and another case of selling ; and so it would go on *ad infinitum*, the sum and substance of the matter being, that every time a man or woman cried "Waiter !" on Sunday, he or she would be fined not less than forty shillings, nor more than a hundred ; and every time a waiter replied, "Yes, Sir," he and his master would be fined in the same amount : with the addition of a new sort of window duty on the landlord, to wit, a tax of twenty shillings an hour for every hour beyond the first one, during which he should have his shutters down on the Sabbath.

With one exception, there are perhaps no clauses in the whole bill, so strongly illustrative of its partial operation, and the intention of its framer, as those which relate to travelling on Sunday. Penalties of ten, twenty, and thirty pounds, are mercilessly imposed upon coach proprietors who shall run their coaches on the Sabbath; one, two, and ten pounds upon those who hire, or let to hire, horses and carriages upon the Lord's day, but not one syllable about those who have no necessity to hire, because they have carriages and horses of their own; not one word of a penalty on liveried coachmen and footmen. The whole of the saintly venom is directed against the hired cabriolet, the humble fly, or the rumbling hackney-coach, which enables a man of the poorer class to escape for a few hours from the smoke and dirt, in the midst of which he has been confined throughout the week: while the escutcheoned carriage and the dashing cab, may whirl their wealthy owners to Sunday feasts and private oratorios, setting constables, informers, and penalties, at defiance. Again, in the description of the places of public resort which it is rendered criminal to attend on Sunday, there are no words comprising a very fashionable promenade. Public discussions, public debates, public lectures and speeches, are cautiously guarded against; for it is by their means that the people become enlightened enough to deride the last efforts of bigotry and superstition. There is a stringent provision for punishing the poor man who spends an hour in a news-room, but there is nothing to prevent the rich one from lounging away the day in the Zoological Gardens.

There is, in four words, a mock proviso, which affects to forbid travelling "with any animal" on the Lord's day. This, however, is revoked, as relates to the rich man, by a subsequent provision. We have then a penalty of not less than fifty, nor more than one hundred pounds, upon any person participating in the control, or having the command of any vessel which shall commence her voyage on the Lord's day, should the wind prove favourable. The next time this bill is brought forward (which will no doubt be at an early period of the next session of Parliament) perhaps it will be better to amend this clause by declaring, that from and after

the passing of the act, it shall be deemed unlawful for the
wind to blow at all upon the Sabbath. It would remove a
great deal of temptation from the owners and captains of
vessels.

The reader is now in possession of the principal enacting
clauses of Sir Andrew Agnew's bill, with the exception of
one, for preventing the killing or taking of "*fish, or other
wild animals*," and the ordinary provisions which are inserted
for form's sake in all acts of Parliament. I now beg his
attention to the clauses of exemption.

They are two in number. The first exempts menial servants
from any rest, and all poor men from any recreation : outlaws
a milkman after nine o'clock in the morning, and makes
eating-houses lawful for only two hours in the afternoon ;
permits a medical man to use his carriage on Sunday, and
declares that a clergyman may either use his own, or hire
one.

The second is artful, cunning, and designing; shielding the
rich man from the possibility of being entrapped, and affecting at the same time, to have a tender and scrupulous regard,
for the interests of the whole community. It declares, " that
nothing in this act contained, shall extend to works of piety,
charity, or necessity."

What is meant by the word "necessity" in this clause ?
Simply this—that the rich man shall be at liberty to make
use of all the splendid luxuries he has collected around him,
on any day in the week, because habit and custom have
rendered them "necessary" to his easy existence; but that
the poor man who saves his money to provide some little
pleasure for himself and family at lengthened intervals, shall
not be permitted to enjoy it. It is not "necessary" to him :
---Heaven knows, he very often goes long enough without it.
This is the plain English of the clause. The carriage and
pair of horses, the coachman, the footman, the helper, and
the groom, are "necessary" on Sundays, as on other days, to
the bishop and the nobleman ; but the hackney-coach, the

hired gig, or the taxed cart, cannot possibly be "necessary" to the working-man on Sunday, for he has it not at other times. The sumptuous dinner and the rich wines, are "necessaries" to a great man in his own mansion: but the pint of beer and the plate of meat, degrade the national character in an eating-house.

Such is the bill for promoting the true and sincere worship of God according to his Holy Will, and for protecting every class of society against being required to sacrifice their health and comfort on the Sabbath. Instances in which its operation would be as unjust, as it would be absurd, might be multiplied to an endless amount; but it is sufficient to place its leading provisions before the reader. In doing so, I have purposely abstained from drawing upon the imagination for possible cases; the provisions to which I have referred, stand in so many words upon the bill as printed by order of the House of Commons; and they can neither be disowned, nor explained away.

Let us suppose such a bill as this, to have actually passed both branches of the legislature; to have received the royal assent; and to have come into operation. Imagine its effect in a great city like London.

Sunday comes, and brings with it a day of general gloom and austerity. The man who has been toiling hard all the week, has been looking towards the Sabbath, not as to a day of rest from labour, and healthy recreation, but as one of grievous tyranny and grinding oppression. The day which his Maker intended as a blessing, man has converted into a curse. Instead of being hailed by him as his period of relaxation, he finds it remarkable only as depriving him of every comfort and enjoyment. He has many children about him, all sent into the world at an early age, to struggle for a livelihood; one is kept in a warehouse all day, with an interval of rest too short to enable him to reach home, another walks four or five miles to his employment at the docks, a third earns a few shillings weekly, as an errand boy, or office messenger; and the employment of the man himself, detains him at some distance from his home from morning till night. Sunday is the only day on which they could all meet together, and enjoy a homely meal in social comfort; and now they sit down to a cold and cheerless dinner: the pious guardians of the man's salvation having, in their regard for the welfare of his precious soul, shut up the bakers' shops. The fire blazes high in the kitchen chimney of these well-fed hypocrites, and the rich steams of the savoury dinner scent the air. What care they to be told that this class of men have neither a place to cook in—nor means to bear the expense, if they had?

Look into your churches—diminished congregations, and scanty attendance. People have grown sullen and obstinate, and are becoming disgusted with the faith which condemns them to such a day as this, once in every seven. And as you cannot make people religious by Act of Parliament, or force them to church by constables, they display their feeling by staying away.

Turn into the streets, and mark the rigid gloom that reigns over everything around. The roads are empty, the fields are deserted, the houses of entertainment are closed. Groups of filthy and discontented-looking men, are idling about at the street corners, or sleeping in the sun; but there are no decently-dressed people of the poorer class, passing to and fro. Where should they walk to? It would take them an hour, at least, to get into the fields, and when they reached them, they could procure neither bite nor sup, without the informer and the penalty. Now and then, a carriage rolls smoothly on, or a well-mounted horseman, followed by a liveried attendant, canters by; but with these exceptions, all is as melancholy and quiet as if a pestilence had fallen on the city.

Bend your steps through the narrow and thickly-inhabited streets, and observe the sallow faces of the men and women who are lounging at the doors, or lolling from the windows. Regard well the closeness of these crowded rooms, and the noisome exhalations that rise from the drains and kennels; and then laud the triumph of religion and morality, which condemns people to drag their lives out in such stews as these, and makes it criminal for them to eat or drink in the fresh air, or under the clear sky. Here and there, from some half-opened window, the loud shout of drunken revelry strikes upon the ear, and the noise of oaths and quarrelling—the effect of the close and heated atmosphere—is heard on all sides. See how the men all rush to join the crowd that are making their way down the street, and how loud the execrations of the mob become as they draw nearer. They have assembled round a little knot of constables, who have seized the stock-in-trade, heinously exposed on Sunday, of some miserable walking-stick seller, who follows clamouring for his property. The dispute grows warmer and fiercer, until at last some of the more furious among the crowd, rush forward to restore the goods to their owner. A general conflict takes place; the sticks of the constables are exercised in all directions; fresh assistance is procured; and half a dozen of the assailants are conveyed to the station-house, struggling, bleeding, and cursing. The case is taken to the police-office on the following morning; and after a frightful amount of perjury on both sides, the men are sent to prison for resisting the officers, their families to the workhouse to keep them from starving: and there they both remain for a month afterwards, glorious trophies of the sanctified enforcement of the Christian Sabbath. Add to such scenes as these, the profligacy, idleness, drunkenness, and vice, that will be committed to an extent which no man can foresee, on Monday, as an atonement for the restraint of the preceding day; and you have a very faint and imperfect picture of the religious effects of this Sunday legislation, supposing it could ever be forced upon the people.

But let those who advocate the cause of fanaticism, reflect well upon the probable issue of their endeavours. They may by perseverance, succeed with Parliament. Let them ponder on the probability of succeeding with the people. You may deny the concession of a political question for a time, and a nation will bear it patiently. Strike home to the comforts of every man's fireside—tamper with every man's freedom and liberty—and one month, one week, may rouse a feeling abroad, which a king would gladly yield his crown to quell, and a peer would resign his coronet to allay.

It is the custom to affect a deference for the motives of those who advocate these measures, and a respect for the feelings by which they are actuated. They do not deserve it. If they legislate in ignorance, they are criminal and dishonest; if they do so with their eyes open, they commit wilful injustice; in either case, they bring religion into contempt. But they do NOT legislate in ignorance. Public prints, and public men, have pointed out to them again and again, the consequences of their proceedings. If they persist in thrusting themselves forward, let those consequences rest upon their own heads, and let them be content to stand upon their own merits.

It may be asked, what motives can actuate a man who has so little regard for the comfort of his fellow-beings, so little respect for their wants and necessities, and so distorted a notion of the beneficence of his Creator. I reply, an envious, heartless, ill-conditioned dislike to seeing those whom fortune has placed below him, cheerful and happy—an intolerant confidence in his own high worthiness before God, and a lofty impression of the demerits of others—pride, selfish pride, as inconsistent with the spirit of Christianity itself, as opposed to the example of its Founder upon earth.

To these may be added another class of men—the stern and gloomy enthusiasts, who would make earth a hell, and religion a torment: men who, having wasted the earlier part of their lives in dissipation and depravity, find themselves when scarcely past its meridian, steeped to the neck in vice, and shunned like a loathsome disease. Abandoned by the world, having nothing to fall back upon, nothing to remember

344

but time mis-spent, and energies misdirected, they turn their eyes and not their thoughts to Heaven, and delude themselves into the impious belief, that in denouncing the lightness of heart of which they cannot partake, and the rational pleasures from which they never derived enjoyment, they are more than remedying the sins of their old career, and—like the founders of monasteries and builders of churches, in ruder days—establishing a good set claim upon their Maker.

III

THE supporters of Sabbath Bills, and more especially the extreme class of Dissenters, lay great stress upon the declarations occasionally made by criminals from the condemned cell or the scaffold, that to Sabbath-breaking they attribute their first deviation from the path of rectitude ; and they point to these statements, as an incontestable proof of the evil consequences which await a departure from that strict and rigid observance of the Sabbath, which they uphold. I cannot help thinking that in this, as in almost every other respect connected with the subject, there is a considerable degree of cant, and a very great deal of wilful blindness. If a man be viciously disposed—and with very few exceptions, not a man dies by the executioner's hands, who has not been in one way or other a most abandoned and profligate character for many years—if a man be viciously disposed, there is no doubt that he will turn his Sunday to bad account, that he will take advantage of it, to dissipate with other bad characters as vile as himself; and that in this way, he may trace his first yielding to temptation, possibly his first commission of crime, to an infringement of the Sabbath. But this would be an argument against any holiday at all. If his holiday had been Wednesday instead of Sunday, and he had devoted it to the same improper uses, it would have been productive of the same results. It is too much to judge

346

of the character of a whole people, by the confessions of the very worst members of society. It is not fair, to cry down things which are harmless in themselves, because evil-disposed men may turn them to bad account. Who ever thought of deprecating the teaching poor people to write, because some porter in a warehouse had committed forgery? Or into what man's head did it ever enter, to prevent the crowding of churches, because it afforded a temptation for the picking of pockets?

When the Book of Sports, for allowing the peasantry of England to divert themselves with certain games in the open air, on Sundays, after evening service, was published by Charles the First, it is needless to say the English people were comparatively rude and uncivilised. And yet it is extraordinary to how few excesses it gave rise, even in that day, when men's minds were not enlightened, or their passions moderated, by the influence of education and refinement. That some excesses were committed through its means, in the remoter parts of the country, and that it was discontinued in those places, in consequence, cannot be denied: but generally speaking, there is no proof whatever on record, of its having had any tendency to increase crime, or to lower the character of the people.

The Puritans of that time, were as much opposed to harmless recreations and healthful amusements as those of the present day, and it is amusing to observe that each in their generation, advance precisely the same description of arguments. In the British Museum, there is a curious pamphlet got up by the Agnews of Charles's time, entitled " A Divine Tragedie lately acted, or a Collection of sundry memorable examples of God's Judgements upon Sabbath Breakers, and other like Libertines in their unlawful Sports, happening within the realme of England, in the compass only of two yeares last past, since the Booke (of Sports) was published, worthy to be knowne and considered of all men, especially such who are guilty of the sinne, or archpatrons

thereof." This amusing document, contains some fifty or
sixty veritable accounts of balls of fire that fell into churchyards and upset the sporters, and sporters that quarrelled and
upset one another, and so forth: and among them is one
anecdote containing an example of a rather different kind,
which I cannot resist the temptation of quoting, as strongly
illustrative of the fact, that this blinking of the question has
not even the recommendation of novelty.

"A woman about Northampton, the same day that she
heard the booke for sports read, went immediately, and
having 3. pence in her purse, hired a fellow to goe to the
next towne to fetch a Minstrell, who coming, she with others
fell a dauncing, which continued within night; at which time
shee was got with child, which at the birth shee murthering,
was detected and apprehended, and being convented before
the justice, shee confessed it, and withal told the occasion of
it, saying it was her falling to sport on the Sabbath, upon
the reading of the Booke, so as for this treble sinfull act, her
presumptuous profaning of the Sabbath, w^h. brought her
adultory and that murther. Shee was according to the Law
both of God and man, put to death. Much sinne and misery
followeth upon Sabbath-breaking."

It is needless to say, that if the young lady near Northampton had "fallen to sport" of such a dangerous description,
on any other day but Sunday, the first result would probably
have been the same: it never having been distinctly shown
that Sunday is more favourable to the propagation of the
human race than any other day in the week. The second
result—the murder of the child—does not speak very highly
for the amiability of her natural disposition; and the whole
story, supposing it to have had any foundation at all, is
about as much chargeable upon the Book of Sports, as upon
the Book of Kings. Such "sports" have taken place in Dissenting Chapels before now; but religion has never been
blamed in consequence; nor has it been proposed to shut up
the chapels on that account.

A VILLAGE CHURCH

The question, then, very fairly arises, whether we have any reason to suppose that allowing games in the open air on Sundays, or even providing the means of amusement for the humbler classes of society on that day, would be hurtful and injurious to the character and morals of the people.

I was travelling in the west of England a summer or two back, and was induced by the beauty of the scenery, and the seclusion of the spot, to remain for the night in a small village, distant about seventy miles from London. The next morning was Sunday; and I walked out, towards the church. Groups of people—the whole population of the little hamlet apparently—were hastening in the same direction. Cheerful and good-humoured congratulations were heard on all sides, as neighbours overtook each other, and walked on in company. Occasionally I passed an aged couple, whose married daughter and her husband were loitering by the side of the old people, accommodating their rate of walking to their feeble pace, while a little knot of children hurried on before; stout young labourers in clean round frocks; and buxom girls with healthy, laughing faces, were plentifully sprinkled about in couples, and the whole scene was one of quiet and tranquil content-ment, irresistibly captivating. The morning was bright and pleasant, the hedges were green and blooming, and a thousand delicious scents were wafted on the air, from the wild flowers which blossomed on either side of the footpath. The little church was one of those venerable simple buildings which abound in the English counties; half overgrown with moss and ivy, and standing in the centre of a little plot of ground, which, but for the green mounds with which it was studded, might have passed for a lovely meadow. I fancied that the old clanking bell which was now summoning the congregation together, would seem less terrible when it rung out the knell of a departed soul, than I had ever deemed possible before—that the sound would tell only of a welcome to calmness and rest, amidst the most peaceful and tranquil scene in nature.

I followed into the church—a low-roofed building with

small arched windows, through which the sun's rays streamed upon a plain tablet on the opposite wall, which had once recorded names, now as undistinguishable on its worn surface, as were the bones beneath, from the dust into which they had resolved. The impressive service of the Church of England was spoken—not merely *read*—by a grey-headed minister, and the responses delivered by his auditors, with an air of sincere devotion as far removed from affectation or display, as from coldness or indifference. The psalms were accompanied by a few instrumental performers, who were stationed in a small gallery extending across the church at the lower end, over the door: and the voices were led by the clerk, who, it was evident, derived no slight pride and gratification from this portion of the service. The discourse was plain, unpretending, and well adapted to the comprehension of the hearers. At the conclusion of the service, the villagers waited in the churchyard, to salute the clergyman as he passed; and two or three, I observed, stepped aside, as if communicating some little difficulty, and asking his advice. This, to guess from the homely bows, and other rustic expressions of gratitude, the old gentleman readily conceded. He seemed intimately acquainted with the circumstances of all his parishioners; for I heard him inquire after one man's youngest child, another man's wife, and so forth; and that he was fond of his joke, I discovered from overhearing him ask a stout, fresh-coloured young fellow, with a very pretty bashful-looking girl on his arm, "when those banns were to be put up?"—an inquiry which made the young fellow more fresh-coloured, and the girl more bashful, and which, strange to say, caused a great many other girls who were standing round, to colour up also, and look anywhere but in the faces of their male companions.

As I approached this spot in the evening about half an hour before sunset, I was surprised to hear the hum of voices, and occasionally a shout of merriment from the meadow beyond the churchyard; which I found, when I reached the stile, to be occasioned by 'a very animated game of cricket, in which the boys and young men of the place were engaged, while the females and old people were scattered about: some seated on the grass watching the progress of the game, and others sauntering about in groups of two or three, gathering little nosegays of wild roses and hedge flowers. I could not but take notice of one old man in particular, with a bright-eyed grand-daughter by his side, who was giving a sunburnt young fellow some instructions in the game, which he received with an air of profound deference, but with an occasional glance at the girl, which induced me to think that his attention was rather distracted from the old gentleman's narration of the fruits of his experience. When it was his turn at the wicket, too, there was a glance towards the pair every now and then, which the old grandfather very complacently con-sidered as an appeal to his judgment of a particular hit, but which a certain blush in the girl's face, and a downcast look of the bright eye, led me to believe was intended for somebody else than the old man,—and understood by somebody else, too, or I am much mistaken.

I was in the very height of the pleasure which the contem-plation of this scene afforded me, when I saw the old clergy-man making his way towards us. I trembled for an angry interruption to the sport, and was almost on the point of crying out, to warn the cricketers of his approach; he was so close upon me, however, that I could do nothing but remain still, and anticipate the reproof that was preparing. What was my agreeable surprise to see the old gentleman standing at the stile, with his hands in his pockets, surveying the whole scene with evident satisfaction! And how dull I must have been, not to have known till my friend the grandfather (who, by-the-bye, said he had been a wonderful cricketer in his time) told me, that it was the clergyman himself who had established the whole thing: that it was his field they played in; and that it was he who had purchased stumps, bats, ball, and all!

SUNDAY UNDER THREE HEADS

It is such scenes as this, I would see near London, on a Sunday evening. It is such men as this, who would do more in one year to make people properly religious, cheerful, and contented, than all the legislation of a century could ever accomplish.

It will be said—it has been very often—that it would be matter of perfect impossibility to make amusements and exercises succeed in large towns, which may be very well adapted to a country population. Here, again, we are called upon to yield to bare assertions on matters of belief and opinion, as if they were established and undoubted facts. That there is a wide difference between the two cases, no one will be prepared to dispute; that the difference is such as to prevent the application of the same principle to both, no reasonable man, I think, will be disposed to maintain. The great majority of the people who make holiday on Sunday now, are industrious, orderly, and well-behaved persons. It is not unreasonable to suppose that they would be no more inclined to an abuse of pleasures provided for them, than they are to an abuse of the pleasures they provide for themselves; and if any people, for want of something better to do, resort to criminal practices on the Sabbath as at present observed, no better remedy for the evil can be imagined, than giving them the opportunity of doing something which will amuse them, and hurt nobody else.

The propriety of opening the British Museum to respectable people on Sunday, has lately been the subject of some discussion. I think it would puzzle the most austere of the Sunday legislators to assign any valid reason for opposing so sensible a proposition. The Museum contains rich specimens from all the vast museums and repositories of Nature, and rare and curious fragments of the mighty works of art, in bygone ages : all calculated to awaken contemplation and inquiry, and to tend to the enlightenment and improvement of the people. But attendants would be necessary, and a few men would be employed upon the Sabbath. They certainly would; but how many? Why, if the British Museum, and the National Gallery, and the Gallery of Practical Science, and every other exhibition in London, from which knowledge is to be derived and information gained, were to be thrown open on a Sunday afternoon, not fifty people would be required to preside over the whole: and it would take treble the number to enforce a Sabbath bill in any three populous parishes.

I should like to see some large field, or open piece of ground, in every outskirt of London, exhibiting each Sunday evening on a larger scale, the scene of the little country meadow. I should like to see the time arrive, when a man's attendance to his religious duties might be left to that religious feeling which most men possess in a greater or less degree, but which was never forced into the breast of any man by menace or restraint. I should like to see the time when Sunday might be looked forward to, as a recognised day of relaxation and enjoyment, and when every man might feel, what few men do now, that religion is not incompatible with rational pleasure and needful recreation.

How different a picture would the streets and public places then present! The museums, and repositories of scientific and useful inventions, would be crowded with ingenious mechanics and industrious artisans, all anxious for information, and all unable to procure it at any other time. The spacious saloons would be swarming with practical men: humble in appearance, but destined, perhaps, to become the greatest inventors and philosophers of their age. The labourers who now lounge away the day in idleness and intoxication, would be seen hurrying along, with cheerful faces and clean attire, not to the close and smoky atmosphere of the public-house, but to the fresh and airy fields. Fancy the pleasant scene. Throngs of people, pouring out from the lanes and alleys of the metropolis, to various places of common resort at some short distance from the town, to join in the refreshing sports and exercises of the day—the children gambolling in crowds upon the grass, the mothers looking on, and enjoying themselves the little game they seem only to direct; other parties strolling along some pleasant walks, or reposing in the shade of the stately trees; others again intent upon their different amusements. Nothing should be heard on all sides, but the sharp stroke of the bat as it sent the ball skimming along the ground, the clear ring of the quoit, as it struck upon the iron peg: the noisy murmur of many voices, and the loud shout of mirth and delight, which would awaken the echoes far and wide, till the fields rung with it. The day would pass away, in a series of enjoyments which would awaken no painful reflections when night arrived; for they would be calculated to bring with them, only health and contentment. The young would lose that dread of religion, which the sour austerity of its professors too often inculcates in youthful bosoms; and the old would find less difficulty in persuading them to respect its observances. The drunken and dissipated, deprived of any excuse for their misconduct, would no longer excite pity but disgust. Above all, the more ignorant and humble class of men, who now partake of many of the bitters of life, and taste but few of its sweets, would naturally feel attachment and respect for that code of morality, which, regarding the many hardships of their station, strove to alleviate its rigours, and endeavoured to soften its asperity.

This is what Sunday might be made, and what it might be made without impiety or profanation. The wise and beneficent Creator who places men upon earth, requires that they shall perform the duties of that station of life to which they are called, and He can never intend that the more a man strives to discharge those duties, the more he shall be debarred from happiness and enjoyment. Let those who have six days in the week for all the world's pleasures, appropriate the seventh to fasting and gloom, either for their own sins or those of other people, if they like to bewail them; but let those who employ their six days in a worthier manner, devote their seventh to a different purpose. Let divines set the example of true morality : preach it to their flocks in the morning, and dismiss them to enjoy true rest in the afternoon ; and let them select for their text, and let Sunday legislators take for their motto, the words which fell from the lips of that Master, whose precepts they misconstrue, and whose lessons they pervert—" The Sabbath was made for man, and not man to serve the Sabbath."

This book, designed by
William B. Taylor
is a production of
Edito-Service S.A., Geneva

Printed in Switzerland